Outback Summer

Robert Coenraads

Coenraads GEMS Publishing

First Published in Australia in 2025
by Coenraads GEMS Publishing, Sydney
www.robertcoenraads.com.au

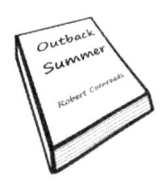

Outback Summer by Robert Raymond
Coenraads, 270 pp. 85,000 words, 6 x 9 in.
(152.4 x 228.6 mm), Garamond 11.5 pt,
line spacing 1.1, B&W on cream paper.
Cover design, cover photo and illustrations
by Robert Raymond Coenraads

A catalogue record for this
book is available from the
National Library of Australia

ISBN 978-1-923330-00-9

Copyright © Robert R Coenraads 2025
This book is copyright, apart for the purposes of study, teaching,
research, criticism or review, or as otherwise permitted under the
Australian Copyright Act 1968—no part may be reproduced by
any means without prior permission from the author.

Outback Summer is available to enjoy in various formats
ISBN 978-1-923330-00-9 Paperback (this book)
ISBN 978-1-923330-01-6 Hardcover
ISBN 978-1-923330-02-3 Large print
ISBN 978-1-923330-03-0 E-book
ISBN 978-1-923330-04-7 Audiobook

DEDICATION

For my loved ones, so that they can know me better

ACKNOWLEDGMENTS

After living and working in the Outback awhile, it gets under your skin—its iron-red landscape co-mingling with the iron of your own blood.

You can feel its call—even from within the dark asphalt city canyons you still feel its call: The dry and cracked grey floodplain soil, spongy and powdery underfoot—the raw sun upon your back, filling you with warmth and energy, burning you until you melt beneath its presence—the tranquil shade-dappled water of the serpentine river beckoning you into its refreshing, yet sometimes-treacherous, embrace.

Those who cast off the prejudiced blinkers of ignorance lay themselves open to the profound spirituality of this relationship.

And the outback town, full of the trajectories of people's storylines jostling about—coming together, crossing briefly, moving apart—full of life, energy and emotions—lives driven by mateship, yet full of opposites; love, laughter, ambition and hope; versus the vices of desire, prejudice, anger and jealousy.

This story takes place on Ngemba (Ngiyampaa)-Baakandji-Kurnu Country—the Darling River Floodplains, the Mulga Lands, and the Cobar Peneplain bioregions within the Bourke Shire, New South Wales.

As author, I wish to acknowledge the Traditional Custodians of these lands and pay my respects to their Elders, past present and future

CONTENTS

DEDICATION iii

ACKNOWLEDGMENTS v

CONTENTS vi

MAPS viii

ILLUSTRATIONS viii

CHAPTER 1.   DARK RIDER 1

CHAPTER 2.   COUSIN RENÉ 8

CHAPTER 3.   THE DRILLERS 15

CHAPTER 4.   FIRST DAY ON THE JOB 25

CHAPTER 5.   SUZIE, THE DRILLER'S DAUGHTER 43

CHAPTER 6.   ROD'S DISAPPOINTMENT 50

CHAPTER 7.   THE ROYAL, MICK'S PUB 55

CHAPTER 8.   THE CARRIERS' ARMS, CHIEF'S PUB 64

CHAPTER 9.   THE OXFORD, PADDY'S PUB 73

CHAPTER 10. TROUBLED WATERS 85

CHAPTER 11. BETH, PETE'S SISTER 92

CHAPTER 12. CARLA 100

CHAPTER 13. THE SWIMMING LESSON 105

CHAPTER 14. THE KILLING ROOM CHALLENGE 114

CHAPTER 15. ROD MUST CHOOSE 122

CHAPTER 16. CARLA'S BROTHER, JOEY 132

CHAPTER 17. THE COUPON 140

CHAPTER 18. THE ELYSIAN 149

CHAPTER 19. ROD PLUMBS ROCK BOTTOM.. 156

CHAPTER 20. NIGHT IN WONDERLAND.. 164

CHAPTER 21. POLYGONUM BILLABONG 173

CHAPTER 22. FAREWELL TO BOURKE 181

CHAPTER 23. SECOND SUMMER 187

CHAPTER 24. BOURKE STILL OUT OF REACH 195

CHAPTER 25. TOORALE HOMESTEAD 205

CHAPTER 26. THE RESCUE 212

CHAPTER 27. CHIEF STANDS TALL 219

CHAPTER 28. DAY OUT WITH CARLA 227

CHAPTER 29. A NEW BEGINNING 240

CHAPTER 30. FUTURE TOGETHER 248

EPILOGUE 251

PLAY LIST 256

GLOSSARY 258

MAPS

MURRAY-DARLING INLAND WATERWAY x

BOURKE SHIRE MAP xi

BOURKE TOWN MAP xii

ILLUSTRATIONS

THE MITCHELL 2

WELCOME 9

SPIDER 16

SUZIE 18

RENE SHELLEKENS 26

DOWLING TANK 29

RICKY AND DAN 31

BRAVING THE HIGH BOARD 33

THE DIVING LESSON 35

HOTELS OF BOURKE 38

THE OXLEY CLUB 40

THE DREAM 42

ROD AND SUZI, DOWLING TANK 48

MICK TALLON 61

CHIEF AND HIS MATES 67

PADDY AND HIS MATES 80

PETE 93

BETH 94

THE PARTY	109
MEATWORKS	117
THE RACE	127
RIVER SWING	137
CARLA	141
ED SYMMONDS	147
BUG EYE VIEW	151
ROTUNDA, CENTRAL PARK	159
WONDERLAND CINEMA	169
NIGHT IN WONDERLAND	171
FAREWELL	184
SYDNEY HARBOUR	186
PARTY GIRLS	191
MICHAEL LEU	193
ROD CONWAY	194
DIVING FOR BOTTLES	201
CHARLIE BOWMAN SPIRIT OF TOORALE	217
NORTH BOURKE BRIDGE	223
MT TALOWLA	229
TOORALE BALLROOM	231
INVASION DAY	237
ELDORADO	245
CELESTIAL CAMP	249
MORRALL'S PIES AND RICE'S CORDIALS	253

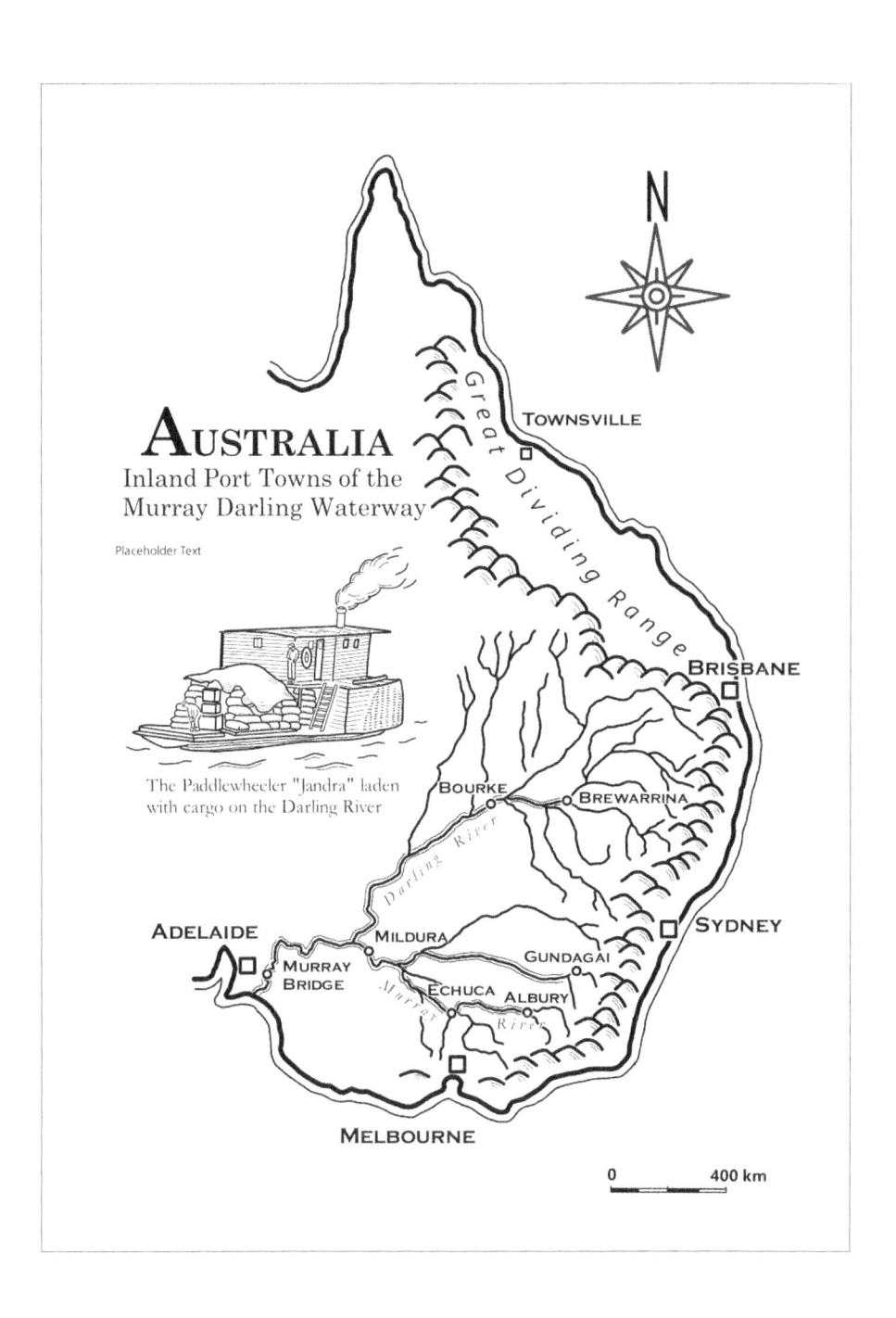

Australia
Inland Port Towns of the
Murray Darling Waterway

Placeholder Text

The Paddlewheeler "Jandra" laden with cargo on the Darling River

TOWNSVILLE

BRISBANE

BOURKE BREWARRINA

Darling River

ADELAIDE MILDURA SYDNEY

MURRAY BRIDGE GUNDAGAI

Murray River ECHUCA ALBURY

MELBOURNE

Great Dividing Range

0   400 km

BOURKE SHIRE

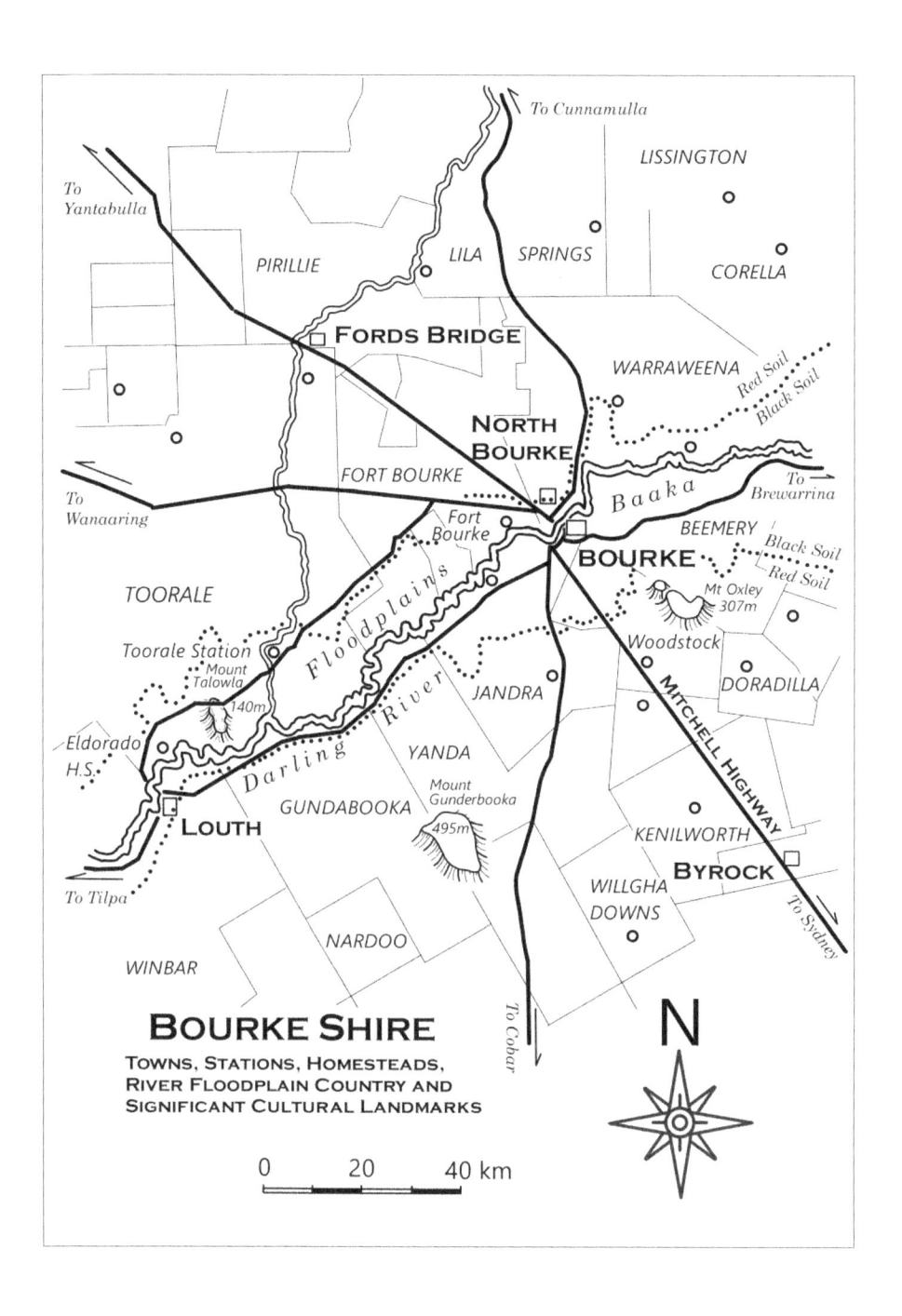

Towns, Stations, Homesteads, River Floodplain Country and Significant Cultural Landmarks

BOURKE TOWNSHIP
STREET PLAN AND ATTRACTIONS

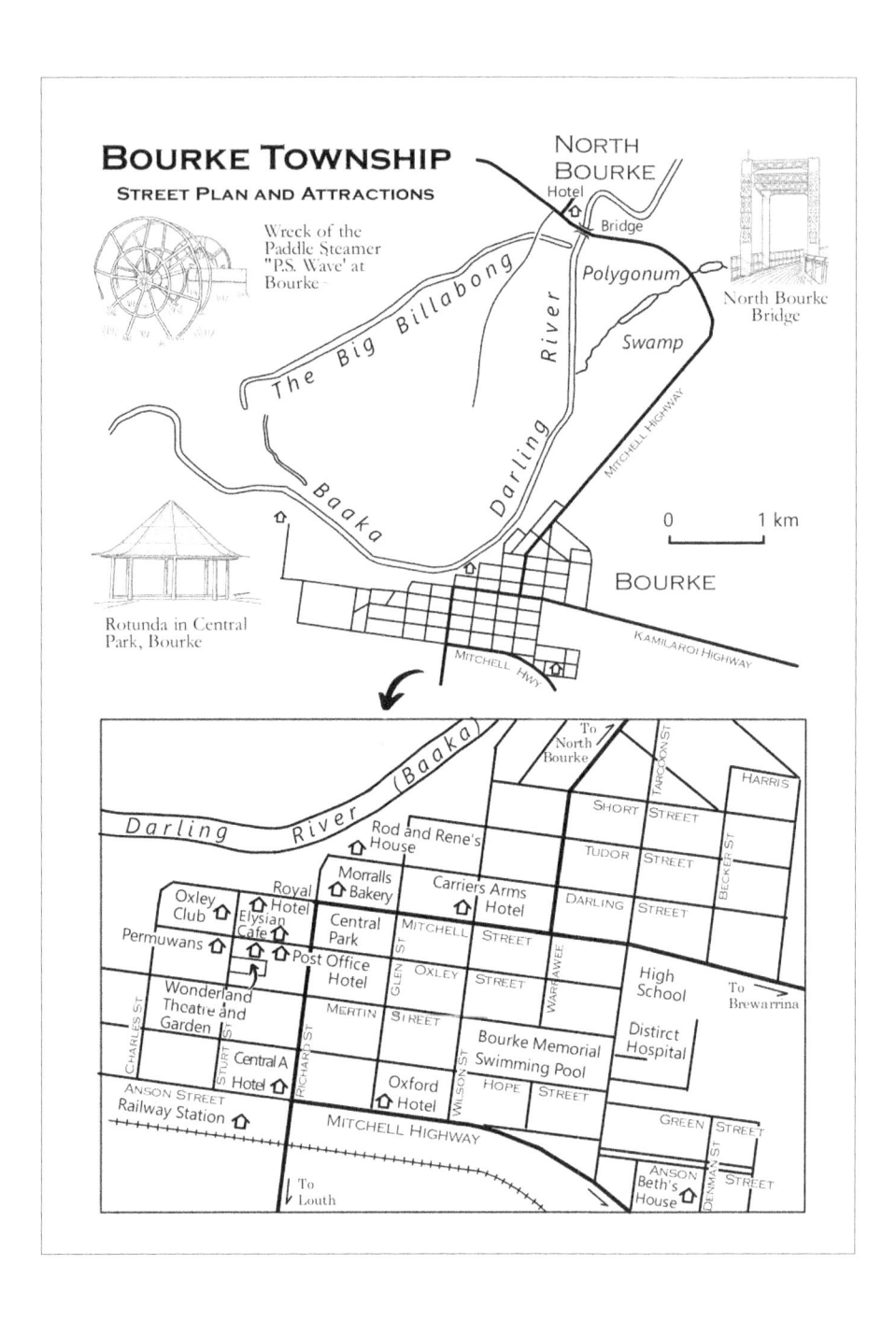

Wreck of the Paddle Steamer "P.S. Wave" at Bourke

The Big Billabong

Baaka

Darling River

NORTH BOURKE
Hotel
Bridge
Polygonum Swamp
North Bourke Bridge

MITCHELL HIGHWAY

0   1 km

BOURKE

KAMILAROI HIGHWAY

MITCHELL HWY

Rotunda in Central Park, Bourke

Darling River (Baaka)

To North Bourke

TARCOON ST
HARRIS
SHORT STREET
TUDOR STREET
BECKER ST
DARLING STREET

Rod and Rene's House
Morralls Bakery
Carriers Arms Hotel
Oxley Club
Royal Hotel
Elysian Cafe
Central Park
MITCHELL STREET
Permuwans
Post Office Hotel
GLEN ST
OXLEY STREET
WARREGO
High School
To Brewarrina
Wonderland Theatre and Garden
MERTIN STREET
CHARLES ST
Central A Hotel
SURT ST
RICHARD ST
Bourke Memorial Swimming Pool
District Hospital
ANSON STREET
Railway Station
Oxford Hotel
WILSON ST
HOPE STREET
MITCHELL HIGHWAY
GREEN STREET
ANSON STREET
DENMAN ST
Beth's House
To Louth

xii

CHAPTER 1. DARK RIDER

THE MITCHELL HIGHWAY from Nyngan to Bourke is just so straight—about 200 kilometres of dead flat straight, designed with a ruler and the stroke of a pen to lay open the great Australian interior to conquest from the east. On the Mitchell, even at dangerously high speeds, travellers feel as if they are standing still—an optical illusion that has cost many dearly over the years.

Rod Conway eased back on the throttle of his Kawasaki Mach III. He sat poised astride the eve of an outback summer that would leave his life changed forever.

He'd let her rip for a bit along the empty outback highway[1]—something he could never do in the crowded city—craving the raw thrust of the bike's 60 horsepower 500cc triple cylinder motor and thrill of its exhilarating top speed. But the weather out here was just too damn hot. He knew the middle piston of that model was notoriously prone to jam in its cylinder, seizing the motor. Rod shuddered, easing further the throttle as he imagined a 200-kilometre-per-hour rear-wheel lock up, throwing the bike into a violent tailspin and smearing him all over the road. Besides, the smell of road kill littering the edges of the highway served a powerful warning—a stray kangaroo, or a galah in the face, at that speed spelt certain death.

The day had been heating steadily, like the inside of a pressure cooker, since mid-morning.

---

[1]. Theme music, see Play List

ROBERT R. COENRAADS

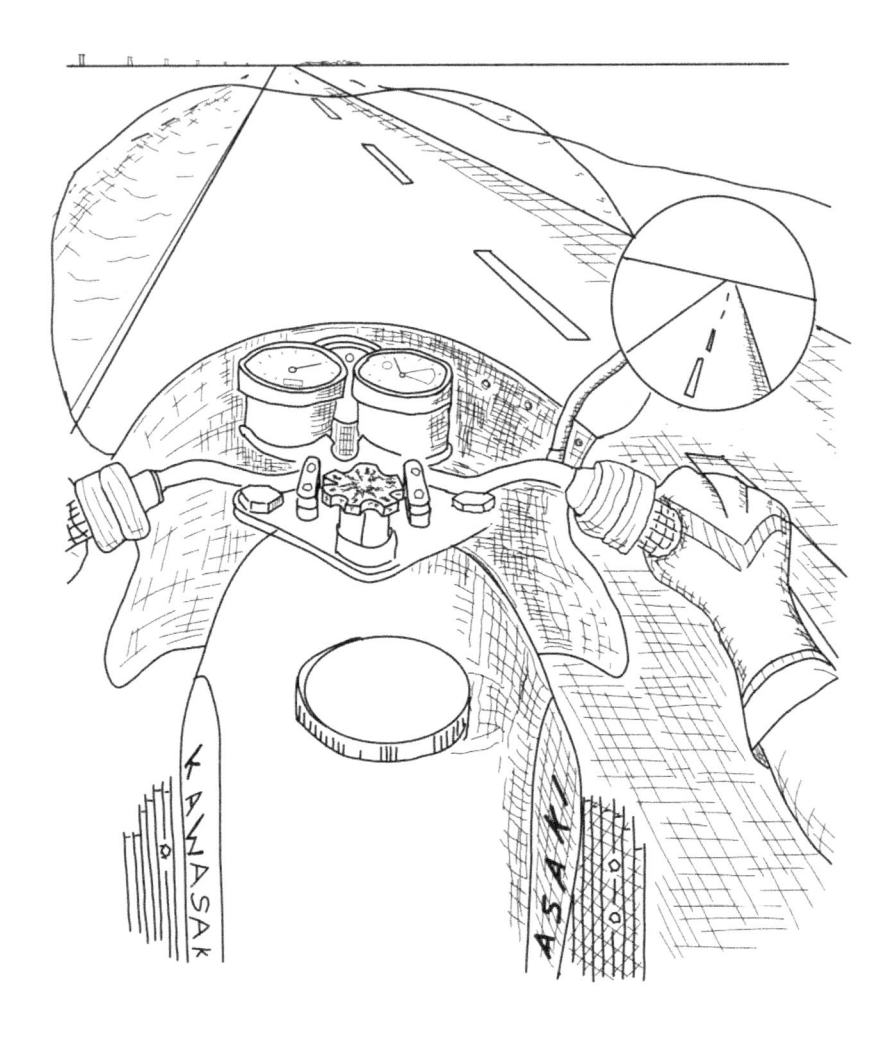

"THE MITCHELL"

Robert Coenraads
2023

Despite the wind, Rod was boiling in his dark leathers and feeling sleepy. Even the tar of the road seemed to melt upward into a shimmering afternoon heat haze. He sped on, hypnotized by the mirage.

Suddenly, the sharp blast of an air horn and, out of nowhere, a black and chrome motorcycle blurred past, its matching leather-clad rider tucked in low behind a sweeping faring. As the bike overtook, its anonymous rider turned, lifting the tinted visor of his full-face helmet, to glare at Rod. He cut in hard, forcing Rod to brake sharply. The rider jabbed the air angrily with his middle finger, before turning forward, gunning his bike into the distance.

'Damn, what in the hell was I doing, drifting around the road like that?' Rod's mind snapped into the moment, his face colouring at his stupid mistake. 'He'd be doing the ton at least.' Rod wondered if the rider, fast diminishing into the horizon, might also be heading to Bourke, still a couple of hours northwest. He didn't look like the kind of bloke you'd want to tangle with.

The monotonous countryside sped past, grey-blue salt bush and gidgee scrub stretching like a drab blanket from horizon to horizon, and in the hours of spare boredom, Rod began to reflect on his journey into the unknown and on his 20-year-long life in general. He'd never been this far inland before, in fact he'd barely been anywhere outside of the capitals, Melbourne and Sydney, where he grew up. He was excited, looking forward to adventure.

Rod crossed the Great Dividing Range yesterday, greeting dawn at Katoomba, pushing north-westwards, via Dubbo, towards the great Australian Outback. He'd overnighted in a ten-dollar hotel along the way, picking up a pie and chips for dinner from the milk bar next door. He ate alone on the wooden veranda overlooking the main street, sitting on a sagging velour couch, hidden in the evening shadows, as the rhythmic music of endless celebrations, pulsed from the pub below. The comforts and support of home seemed so distant now. Later he'd walked to the telephone box by the post office, letting parents know he was okay, entertaining them with safe snippets about his journey thus far until his last twenty cents clanked into the coin box. Saying official good byes, he let the conversation drift on past the warning beeps until they were cut off.

Rod had passed second-year geology at Macquarie University, getting the letter in the mail just last week—flying colours all subjects. He was proud of that, and he'd worked damn hard for it too, but it had come at a cost. Before now he'd barely had his nose out of his text books, his family home, or the humdrum existence of daily life on Sydney's leafy North Shore, a routine broken only by occasional wild revelry at some student party or another. Topical news events of the day; the Whitlam reforms and unprecedented sacking of an Australian Prime Minister, Ronald Ryan's hanging, the Vietnam Draft, or even the murder of Beatle John Lennon; drifted like vague shadows through the empty space between Rod Conway's ears, more-or-less unnoticed. Apart from studies and the usual hormone-fuelled turmoil of adolescence, there wasn't much going on inside his head—his mind a blank page waiting for life's experiences to imprint. Besides, there were more important things for a young bloke journeying into manhood to think about—like girls for one thing, and motorbikes for another. Proud as he was of his achievements, the journey, the space and freedom out here, were forcing him to rethink outside the square; so much yet to do, so much to see and explore.

Rod was heading west to meet his cousin René Schellekens, geologist with a mining company exploring the Bourke district, who'd organized summer vacation work on the Doradilla Tin Project. Rod wondered what it would be like, being a field hand for René, his mind drifting back to his uncle's house in suburban Melbourne, its ample backyard always a surprise of in-season, well-tended vegetable beds and shady fruit trees, the place of carefree family visits where he'd grown up, playing cowboys or soldiers with his brother and cousins, dressing up in Uncle John's WWII Dutch uniforms, helmet and gas mask. They were the children of Europeans, self-reliant immigrants arriving in waves upon Australian shores in the aftermath of the war; all young, bright-eyed and eager to forge a new life amongst the boundless opportunities of a growing nation barely 200 years old. The eldest child, René, should've been leader, but he was quieter, studious, keeping to himself. His bedroom shelves were crammed full of rocks and minerals, plaster of Paris dinosaurs—even a pet blue-tongue lizard, 'Oswald', coiled and embalmed in a preserves jar after he died. Rod remembered how he'd slip into the room's museum-like solitude to read the specimen labels, finely-penned in India ink, and their matching catalogue entries; mineral name, chemical formula, locality, physical properties; all in neatly-ruled exercise books. Rod hadn't seen much of him in recent years; not since René graduated and left home to travel the length and breadth of Australia in search of precious ores, nor since Rod's father moved the family to Sydney; following his company's head office there. Rod looked forward to meeting his cousin again, hoping he hadn't changed over the intervening years.

Rod's mind idled over what he'd read about Bourke in an encyclopaedia before leaving:

The town, named after the then colonial governor Sir Richard Bourke, was surveyed in 1869, starting life as a garrison, Fort Bourke, set up to deal with the region's troublesome indigenous inhabitants.

How exciting it sounded, as he imagined the soldiers with their gold-buttoned red jackets, black hats and rifles, firing down from their log-walled stockade upon the bloodthirsty natives threatening the settlement with their spear-throwing savagery. Life would have been hard for the first colonialists in those days. Growing up, he'd watched his fair share of cowboy and Indian movies and wondered if the Aborigines would've been like that. He knew from the NSW Gallery's colonial art collection, visited on one school excursion or another, that they were coal black, naked apart from skeletal ochre line work painted on their bodies, and they didn't wear furs or feathers like the red Indians, but he'd never seen any movies about them on the telly. Rod wondered if they scalped their hapless victims like the Apaches did.

He pondered other interesting stuff he'd recently learned about his destination.

Bourke, an inland port town, situated on the Darling River—part of the spidery network of inland waterways that opened up the Australian interior to trade and commerce during the late 1800's. The Murray-Darling system with some 6,700 km of navigable waterways, carried fleets of paddle steamers laden with cargo from the Murray Mouth near Adelaide as far upstream as the Queensland border.

Rod's mind began wandering again in the heat as he tried to imagine what Bourke looked like, picturing riverboat captains, bulging cargo nets and bustling plank wharves piled high with goods of all sorts...

By the 1880's Bourke had grown to host a Cobb & Co. Coach terminus, several paddle boat companies running the Murray-Darling River trade, and an Afghan overland camel transport hub.

... Paddle-wheelers and horse-drawn stage coaches; ambushes and highway robberies; gun-toting sheriffs in pursuit of outlaw bushrangers... Rod imagined it just like the Wild West would be.

He shut his eyes for a few seconds, savouring the dancing images, the relief from the burning highway glare, relaxing...

Suddenly, in an adrenalin jolt, he snapped them open again, his heart pounding.

"Damn…" He'd lost focus again, drifting across the bitumen towards the red earth table drain. "That was way too close."

Desperate for sleep, Rod pulled to the side of the road, steering his bike towards the railway line running parallel to the bitumen beyond the trees. He searched for a spot, anywhere to lie down in the shade. Damn ants, they were under every bush, and flies swarmed into his eyes and nose the moment he pulled off his helmet. He'd leave it on, he decided, with the visor down; besides it made a comfortable pillow. Collapsing onto the clearest spot of red earth amongst the sprawling pademelon vines, he drifted off, figuring it would take the ants, or whatever else came along, more that the few minutes sleep he needed to find their way through his leathers.

Startling to the sound of a goods train clanking along the track, Rod bolted upright wondering how long he'd slept. Not too long, he calculated, glancing at the sun, still high in the afternoon sky. He leapt onto his bike, deciding to race the goods train into Bourke. This railway was important to the region's development too, he remembered;

By 1885 the Great Western Railway Line reached Bourke making the town far more accessible, but ultimately spelling the end for the earlier coach, river and camel services…

Two hours later, Rod swept around the final bend where the highway snaked its way across the railway level crossing, past the looming abattoirs—an ugly complex of grey tin buildings—and along the final straight into town. Greeted by the first buildings of town, he scanned the signs;

'Welcome to Bourke', 'Lions Club', 'Rotary Club', 'Speed limit 60 kph'; 'Town Population 2,530.'

Rod slowed his bike and pulled over onto the dusty verge by the population sign, relieved to be at his long journey's end, tired and thirsty from the dry heat.

'Here at last! My outback home for the summer,' he thought, gratefully wondering at what adventures the town would bring. Glancing up at the bold numbers on the sign above his head, he reflected, 'Well, I suppose that makes me number 2,531?' Reaching into his jacket pocket, he pulled out the crumpled mud map of the town René had sent him.

Rod hung a right at the Central Australian Hotel, its shady balconies festooned with patrons enjoying a leisurely afternoon, their iron horses angle-parked around the perimeter. A black motorbike on the footpath caught his eye—the same one that passed him a few hours back!

CHAPTER 2. COUSIN RENÉ

ROD HEADED along Richard Street, through the centre of town, towards Darling Street by the river, where his cousin's company was renting a house to serve as office and accommodation.

Pulling into the driveway at number seven, Rod lifted off his full-face helmet, pushing back his long curly hair. At the sound of his bike, his cousin emerged from the backyard to greet him, wearing stubbies and a green short-sleeve work shirt. Tall and lean, his deeply-tanned arms and legs were more muscular than Rod remembered, and he sported a thick black beard; René had become a real mining man[2].

"Long time no see, René!" Rod said, trying to figure how many years it must have been. "A beard like that doesn't just grow overnight."

René's beard creased into a broad open smile as he extended a powerful hand.

"Hi Rod, how was the trip up? Hot enough for you? It's been over forty since lunchtime," he said, wiping away the sweat running from under the brim of his battered leather hat. "Bring your bike round the back. Park it in the shade beside the shed, and then we'll head inside for a cold drink."

René led the way through the side gate and Rod followed, pushing his bike past a yellow Land Rover ute parked in the driveway. It was bristling with winches and other work gear. René stopped to unpeg his field clothes, hanging like stiff cardboard from the wires of the Hills Hoist*.

"Would y' look at that! I only hung those out ten minutes ago," he noted incredulously.

---

*See Glossary of Australian Slang, Idiomatic Expressions and other Iconic Terms used in Outback Summer

OUTBACK SUMMER

"WELCOME"

Robert Coenraads
2024

"What's that mound over there?' Rod asked, intrigued by the low earthen bank snaking its way through the back yards of the houses. "I thought you were on the river?"

"That is the famous Darling River, Rod. Come take a look." René led the way, pushing underneath the loose wire strands of the back fence, climbing up amongst the tufts of dry grass onto the hard grey clay bank which fell away on its far side into a deep bare channel. "The paddle steamers once came by here on their way to Bree. They'd pull in at the Port of Bourke on the river bend just over there," René pointed with a stick fallen from one of the shady river gums lining the bank, "and they'd tie up at the Sturt Street wharves to unload and load their cargo. Those old wharves have long since rotted away."

Rod eyed off the sluggish strand of muddy brown water lying in its bare dirt channel, trying to picture how it might have looked back then. He wondered how the river could've carried any kind of boat, let alone the cargo-laden paddle wheelers of old.

"What happened to the river?" Rod had always felt comfortable asking René question after question when he was younger; as if his cousin were some kind of talking encyclopaedia. René always had the answer; he'd always done his homework. Rod relaxed, slipping straight back into this easy relationship with his cousin as if no time at all had passed

"It died I guess," René answered philosophically. "Once grazing, and farming, took off in the district the Darling began to silt up, dry out bit by bit, season after season. Eventually it became too shallow for the boats. Nowadays, most of the water is diverted for irrigation. The big cotton farms just out of town suck up a hell of a lot of water. Some years, the river stops running completely."

"What's the earth dam for then? Why's it higher than the rest of the ground?"

"It's called a levee. The old river still frightens a lot of people. She can rise fast when it rains a lot, believe you me. Over the decades, the townsfolk built the levee right around Bourke to protect it from the floodwaters." René climbed down off the levee and walked through the yard to the back door, still sweating from his afternoon's labour.

"Come in out of the hot sun, Rod. Can I get you a cold beer? It must've been a long day?"

The question took Rod by surprise. He'd never been offered a beer by René before, or anyone in his family for that matter. He couldn't remember René ever drinking. Rod's mates were all into beer—well one year they weren't and the next moment everybody was into it like some kind of teenage rite of passage. He couldn't see the use himself. Perhaps because what he'd seen it do to his schoolmates. One mate in particular degenerated at every party, his long-time girlfriend desperately dragging his pathetic slug-like body toward the toilet for him to throw up. She was usually too late, mopping up after him. It was inevitable she'd leave him in the end, which only made matters worse, completing his downward spiral into a miserable, snivelling sad-sack. Alcohol ruled his life after that and he'd just sit crying quietly by himself in the corner. Nobody could help him after he hit rock bottom, and eventually everyone gave up trying. Rod sometimes wondered what became of 'Freddie the Failure' when they all went their separate ways after school finished.

René headed into the small linoleum-tiled kitchen, grabbing a cold bottle out of the fridge. He flipped off its cap with a bottle opener hanging on a nail in the wall, in a smooth single-action movement that only comes with years of practice, and raised the bottle to his lips.

"Ahhh……. that sure hits the spot! Now, how about that cold beer, Rod?" René repeated the offer.

"Er… No thanks. I'll be fine René". His gaze swept over the classic fibro-design house. Faded floral-print curtains hung over the windows of the large lounge room, fighting a losing battle against the fierce heat of the westerly afternoon sun, and over in one corner sat a forest of what must have been several dozen potted plastic palms. There were no other ornaments, only a Mortein fly-spray pump, sitting prominently on the sideboard, speaking of other battles. The place was small compared to his parent's house in Sydney; kind of plain and ordinary, but it had a welcoming feel, functional and no fuss. It was his new home now—his Bourke home.

"Well, there's some orange juice or soft drink in the fridge, grab a glass and help yourself. Then go bring in your swag. Your bedroom's the one at the end of the lounge room, right next to the bathroom." René sat down on the comfortable couch facing the windows and took another deep swig from his longneck.

"After you've settled in, Rod, would you mind helping me take some rubbish down to the tip in the Landy? It's only five minutes away and I can show you round Bourke at the same time."

Rod was impressed by the picturesque town with its neat little houses and well-maintained gardens, his interest heightened by the sounds of watery play, laughter, and flashes of colourful bikinis as René cruised by Bourke Olympic Pool on Mertin Street. Rod made a mental note of the street name; he'd definitely get back there later. They continued past the modern district hospital and high school, and then back along Oxley Street, past Central Park with its well-watered flower beds, cross paths and pretty rotunda. The main block of Oxley Street was lined with old-fashioned glass-fronted shops, while an impressive colonial courthouse stood on the corner, its tall roofed watch tower overlooking the greenery of Central Park.

"It's one of my favourites; colonial Spanish style with an inner courtyard." René said, slowing the car so Rod could take a closer look. "You'll be coming down the main street a lot; it's only three minutes' walk from home." He drove on a little further. "There's the grand old Post Office Hotel, and, look, on the right, the Elysian Café, decked out with art deco booth seats. I reckon you'll like their milkshakes, Rod. Chocolate, if I remember right;" René added with a broad smile, "big steel cup and plenty of ice cream. See for yourself how popular it is."

Rod observed the throng of youth spilling from the fly strip curtain covering the café door; their laughter drifting in through the open car window, sun-bleached blonde hair and leggy tanned skin, caught his attention. He made another important mental note.

At the end of the shopping precinct René turned down a street on the left.

"There's the open-air cinema," he pointed, "Mrs Randall's Wonderland Picture Garden. Not much to look at from the outside, but nothing beats a movie on deck chairs under the stars on a fine night. We'll give it a try one evening, Rod. It's open all through summer."

'Wow' Rod breathed, catching sight of more golden skin and free flowing hair—beautiful ebony this time. Sometimes he amazed even himself at the acuity of his peripheral vision. On the opposite corner, a girl in faded jean cut-offs and t-shirt manoeuvred her pushbike out of the supermarket carpark onto the footpath[3]. The bike had high chopper handlebars and an ample basket in front laden with bread and groceries. 'This town's looking better all the time,' Rod had to admit to himself.

Presently they passed beyond the town centre and after a few blocks Rod noticed the houses looking more and more run down, tired and old, with broken window panes, sad sagging fences and leaning gateposts, their gardens unkempt and overgrown. Here and there, further along, the rusted shells of burnt-out cars lay strewn about in drunken disorder, surrounded by smashed beer-bottle glass.

"What's happened here, René? It looks like a bombshell hit the place!" Rod asked, surprised by the stark contrast of these streets?

"This is where the other side of town lives." René answered, speaking in a matter-of-fact tone. "Nobody ever comes through these parts, except to dump their rubbish."

"What other side?"

"The original inhabitants of our country, Rod."

"What? you mean the Aborigines?" Rod's interest was suddenly piqued. He remembered what he had learnt about the Australian Aboriginals in high-school history classes, about Captain Cook discovering them, jet black and naked, spears raised in angry defiance, when he rowed ashore in Botany Bay.

"It's a sad story really. They were treated worse than the convicts, hunted by the English soldiers for sport. The early settlers nearly shot or poisoned their primitive race out of existence, but somehow they survived. They never fully recovered though."

"I didn't think there were any more of them left, René? I've never seen one before. Are there many?"

"You'll never see any around your North Shore, Rod. The townsfolk don't talk much about what happens down here. Just look at the place!" René explained, glancing across at his cousin.

With a thousand questions forming in his mind, Rod wasn't sure what to ask René first, so fell silent for the rest of the drive to the tip and back. René's comments, played about in his mind like a red rag to a bull. He was thirsting to know more about these mysterious people, why they all lived in the one part of town, why they were dangerous, and what had happened to their houses and cars. He craned his neck, looking around, to see if he could spot anyone, but the streets were deserted that scorching Saturday afternoon. Rod knew that, somehow, despite what René said, he'd find out more about this part of town.

Later, René prepared dinner. While they were sitting at the dining room table enjoying their steak, potatoes and vegetables, he explained his plans.

"Tomorrow I'm going out to the project area to see the drillers, so you can come out for a look around and meet them. I've got some field hands ready to start next week. You'll be working in the bush with them."

"What are they like?"

"Local lads, in their last year of high school, or maybe a bit older—they were keen for the work. The abattoir is only other place around town, and that's hit-and-miss. Nobody ever knows what's happening there from day to day. Otherwise, you've got to go out of town to the stations for work. I reckon they'll be smart enough for the job and put in the effort."

Rod listened intently, so René, noting his cousin's interest, counted them off. "There's the fire chief's grandson Mark, and the two schoolmates Ricky and Dan. Dan's brother's got a bit of a reputation for trouble around town, but Dan's OK. I think you'll get on well with them all, no problems. Anyway, Rod, it's been a long day for you," René concluded. "Why don't you get some rest now and tomorrow I'll show you over the old mine."

"You're the boss, René! See you in the morning then," Rod replied, despite a queue of questions a hundred long, but there'd be plenty of time for all that later; René knew everything there was to know about everything.

Later, as Rod lay in his small bedroom on the point of sleep, his thoughts drifted back on where he had come to in his life, miles from home, on the eve of his first field geology job. A warm familiar sensation enveloped him. He'd long felt a deep connection with the Earth, her interior workings and complex outer shell of life. René started all that too, back when Rod was in primary school, presenting him with a treasure box brimming with lustrous crystal and mineral specimens, plus Herbert Zim's illustrated Golden Guide detailing their chemical and physical properties. Rod could visualize each in its place on his cabinet shelves at home; smoky quartz, black tourmaline, green beryl, purple amethyst and red garnet, plus all of the important ores of iron, copper, lead and zinc.

He was glad to be in Bourke and what a bonus having his own cousin as boss!

CHAPTER 3. THE DRILLERS

NEXT MORNING, René pulled up the Land Rover in front of a large truck-mounted drilling rig. Its colourful blue-painted derrick, raised like a huge Christmas tree over the flat landscape, was positioned over a drill hole. As the vehicle stopped, two men in work gear and white helmets downed tools and walked over.

"John, this is Rod Conway." René spoke to the older and larger of the two. "He'll be starting on the grid next week."

John pulled off his work gloves, greeting Rod with a big bear-paw of a handshake.

"G'day, Rod. Welcome to Doradilla. This is my offsider Bill, but everybody calls him Spider."

"G'day, John, nice to meet you. Where'd the name Spider come from then?" Rod couldn't help but ask.

"He's light, nimble and quick." John answered. "He'll climb anywhere, up and over the drill rig like a spider if ever there's a problem. He'll fix 'em all too and keep my old girl running like clockwork. Best damn offsider I've ever had."

Spider stood proudly beside John, basking in the compliment.

"Do you guys live here on site?" Rod asked, looking at the caravan parked next to a stand of shady trees about fifty metres away. It had a green canvas awning, fold out chairs and barbeque hot plate set up in front.

"Yeah," John replied. "It's a comfy set up, nice and quiet out here. We don't have to drive anywhere, except into town to pick up supplies once a week. I like it out bush."

ROBERT R. COENRAADS

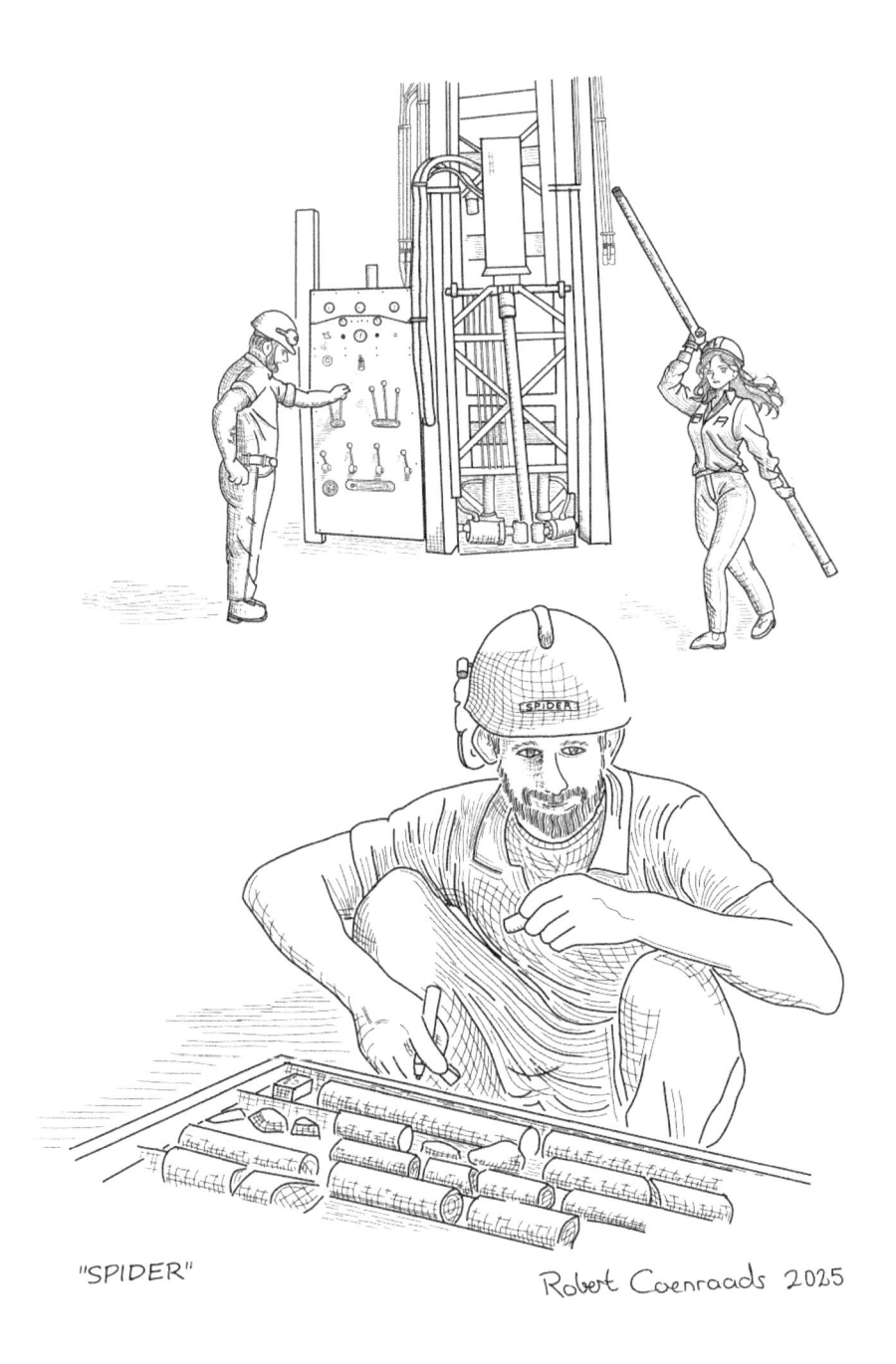

"SPIDER"

"Fridays we drive into Byrock for a bit of a change," Spider added, "dinner and drinks at the pub."

"We might not be able to do much work or drinkin' next week. The weather's comin' down from Queensland and the Bureau's predicting heavy rain." John cautioned. "Although y' wouldn't believe it lookin' at the clear skies today."

Rod noticed a tall slim girl in grease-stained jeans and a chequered work shirt coming out of the caravan. Her blonde hair was tied back in a ponytail and she was wearing leather gloves and a helmet, same as the others. Must be John's daughter, he figured judging by her age, about the same as his. A blue cattle dog leapt out of the doorway closely on her heels.

"Suzie," John turned, calling out to her, "could you bring the other Stillson? We'll pull out of the hole this arvo and change the bit ready for Monday morning." John walked towards the neat rows of galvanized core trays stacked up next to the drill rig. "René, come take a look at this morning's core. We got some promising traces of pyrite."

Spider turned to leave as Suzie approached, on her way to the drill rig. Rod wanted an excuse to talk to her, but couldn't come up with anything of interest to say to either as much as he tried.

"That's the biggest monkey wrench I've ever seen. It must be over a metre long!" he exclaimed in a lame attempt to make conversation as she walked past carrying the long tool over to the drilling rig. He watched her briefly before dropping his eyes to his shoes. He didn't want to stare. Crikey, she's pretty, he couldn't help but think. Rod pushed the thought from his mind, trying not to acknowledge it; he wasn't too comfortable around girls, particularly good-looking ones. Acknowledging his desire turned the game into a challenge into which he was thrust like an involuntary conscript; a war in which the girl was the target, the outpost on the hill to be captured. Conversation became like a battle then, each sentence, a volley of shots back and forth, each side parrying for victory; advance followed by tactical retreat. Memories of his high school days flooded back; most days were a battle there, starting every morning the moment, he walked in the front gate where Sally and Alice would be lying in wait to ambush him.

"It's called a forty-eight-inch Stillson, mate," Spider corrected, his braying voice cutting into Rod's thoughts. "There's only one monkey around here." He'd sensed Rod's inexperience and Rod sensed an attack.

"Suzie," Spider called, "come over here for a sec, an' show the Stillson to the new field hand."

ROBERT R. COENRAADS

"SUZIE"

Robert Coenraads
2024

She turned and started walking back from the rig.

"Yeah," Suzie gave a snort of a laugh, looking at Spider and then over at Rod. "I'll bet ya he's never seen one of these before where he's from." She seemed to know what Spider had in mind, reading his thoughts and body language, using that easy mental telepathic ability that comes from working closely with somebody, day after day, on a heavy, dangerous job where every move has to be the correct one. Suzie held out the Stillson waiting for Spider's next move. Rod couldn't figure it out; it looked rehearsed, like a trick they'd played before.

Spider took the tool from Suzie and passed it to Rod, tossing it to him, ever so lightly, gently, but just enough so Rod would have to bear its full heft in his hand. It was obvious Spider knew what would happen next.

The 11-kilogram pipe wrench slipped through Rod's outstretched fingers, its unexpected weight thudding heavily to the ground, narrowly missing his foot.

"Not wearin' your steel caps today, mate? They're regulation around here y' know." Spider said, deftly picking up the pipe wrench and handing it back to Suzie. Then, having put the new boy in his place, Spider sauntered off towards the drill rig.

Rod had hardly said more than a few words, been challenged, and had failed the initiation test humiliatingly. He recognized that fact painfully, made even worse as it had happened in front of Suzie. Rod chose to ignore the challenge—what else could he do?

"Hey, that's one heavy wrench," he commented lamely to Suzie.

"Yeah, they do take a bit of getting used to." Suzie answered mercifully. "We use a pair of them, y' know," she went on, explaining, "to break the connections between the drill rods. It's hard work pulling up a few hundred metres of drill string to get at the diamond bit on the end. Currently we're sitting at 120 metres and we're gonna pull all that up today. We're the fastest team in the district, y' know."

"That's really amazing." Rod still felt rather foolish, but quickly tried to think of some more questions he could ask Suzie before she went away. "How often do y' have to change bits?"

"Depends on the type of ground we're in. My dad's one of the best drillers about," she added proudly, "so we don't change them as often as most. It takes a lot of experience to learn how to feel the rocks—to listen to what they are telling you—things like how much pressure to put on the drill bit; or how fast to drive ahead. If you don't get it right, you'll burn out the bit in a few metres. And they're not cheap y' know. My dad's been teaching me all of that since I was little." Suzie paused for a moment, studying Rod's reaction, her eyes scanning his face, checking to see if he was really interested in what she was saying. Satisfied, she continued. "Hard ground, volcanic rock like we're in now, wears 'em out quicker y' see, but in softer ground, sedimentary rocks, like sandstone and shale, the bits last a lot longer."

Rod found himself attracted to Suzie's talk of drilling into the earth; of rocks and geology. He ventured another glance at her body, lean and well-shaped from hard physical outdoor activity, firm beneath her tight-fitting work clothes. "What are you studying?" He asked.

"Next year I'm planning on doing vet science. I love animals." She looked down at the handsome blue kelpie waiting patiently by her side, ruffling the fur of her neck fondly. "Red goes everywhere with me, y' know."

"You should do geology!" Rod shot back, nervously stumbling a bit over his words, but trying to choose them carefully. "You'd be really good at it 'cause you already know half the stuff. I'm studying it at Macquarie Uni. It isn't too bad a school y' know."

Suzie looked at Rod, recognising that he was paying her a compliment. Her freckled nose crinkled into a smile. "You never know! That's what I reckon my dad'd like me to do. Now that high school's done, I'm looking forward to life on campus; freedom, independence and whole bunch of new friends..."

"C'mon let's get a move on Suzie, and get this job done." Spider called out impatiently from the rig, his words slicing deep into their conversation. He'd noted, with a hint of irritation, she was still speaking to the new boy. "I don't wanna be here all bloody afternoon, y' know!"

"See ya, Rod." Suzie smiled, slung the heavy Stillson easily over one shoulder and turned towards the rig.

"Come on Rod," René called from the Land Rover. "We've got to head home. I'll show you the rest of the place in the morning."

Later that afternoon Rod walked downtown to pick up the groceries René ordered from the supermarket. René said they'd take it in turns to cook tea and tonight was his go. At first it seemed a really big deal, but René showed him how it was done, making it seem so easy—first get the spuds on the boil for about 15 minutes, throw in some chopped carrots and beans, then start the lamb chops and sausages frying—timing it all to be ready at the same time. White-sliced bread and butter on a side plate always made up for any shortages.

Rod was coming along the footpath distractedly reflecting on how at home his mother did all the cooking, each night, every meal. He hadn't given it a thought before—he and his brother called in from backyard play, 6:00pm sharp without fail when dad came home from the office, and they'd all sit down to a steaming hot meal.

Rod looked up when suddenly, in front of him, a bicycle, the girl on the bike from yesterday afternoon, was heading straight for him, her basket laden with groceries. He hadn't been paying attention and she'd expected him to move out of the way. As she corrected to avoid him, Rod stepped aside, both in the same direction. Damn, he thought as they collided, groceries spilling forward over the pavement, one out of two chances, and I got it wrong as usual!

"Ohh...Sorry....I'm so sorry." Rod exclaimed, catching the bike's handlebars in time, holding them firmly to stop both bike and rider from toppling hard onto the concrete. "I'm such an idiot for not watching where I was going." Rod looked briefly at her face, noting how beautiful it looked close up, before turning away, surveying the scene around them; a loaf of bread, celery, lettuce, and carrots; oranges and apples rolling like marbles in every direction. Crikey! A carton of eggs too, upside down on the pavement—he prayed none of those had broken. Then, adding to his shame, he felt a familiar warmth surge into his cheeks; it was unstoppable. His face reddened as he took in the carnage, watching her get off her bike; she was the very last person he wanted to bump into this way. "Let me help you pick up all of your stuff," he stammered.

"No, really, it's my fault. I shouldn't be riding on the footpath." She gave the slightest of smiles, apologetic, before turning away, bending down to gather her scattered goods. Rod helped, hoping for a quick and merciful end, lost for further words.

Then, while thinking that things couldn't possibly get any worse, Rod heard the growl of a motorcycle engine and looked up. It was Dark Rider cruising the main drag. He'd slowed to a crawl, his anonymous tinted visor swivelled towards them, surveying the disaster scene. The girl looked up at him at the same time, raising her hand in a brief salute, before turning her attention to repacking her basket.

He must be a local, Rod realised, as Dark Rider continued to stare; now focusing directly on him, burning into him. Rod could sense the wordless hostility as the local checked out the newcomer. Did Dark Rider recognise him from the highway? Rod wondered. What was going on?

"I'm really sorry about that," Rod called to the girl with the ebony hair one last time as she straddled her overloaded bike. She turned, giving him another Mona Lisa smile, then rode away. Damn, I didn't even ask her name—I couldn't have, not like this, he thought, standing there like a circus clown, his face still flushed and hot. He could never seem to stop it happening—he was better at colour change than a chameleon—even if nothing embarrassing was happening, with the slightest thought about what his face might do, he could make it turn deep crimson.

Rod's thoughts turned again to Sally and Alice waiting for him at the school gates. He'd had a bubble-gum crush on Alice for nearly four years, dreamt endlessly of kissing her[4], but all that time too embarrassed to say a word to her.

Never in his life had he talked to girls—no sister, no girl cousins and on top of all that, his parents had imprisoned him in a private all-boys grammar for all of his primary years. A fine, expensive school it was too, but he shuddered at the memory of its unusual social norms. Thank goodness they moved to Sydney as he probably would have ended up trapped in that boys' school till he was seventeen.

The co-ed high school took a bit of adjusting. When Sally found out about his crush on Alice they'd lie in wait to ambush Rod. The school gates were the best place; everyone came through that way between about 8:30 and 9:00am. There were other longer ways into the school; Rod knew them all, but, if they didn't get him at the front gates, there was always morning recess or lunch.

"Hey look Alice. Look who's coming along now. Good morning Rod, how are you today?" Sally did all the talking. Alice never said much, always looking away or down at her feet. Rod couldn't remember making eye contact with her once during the entire four-year ordeal.

"Hello Sally, Alice." Rod would reply hoping it would be enough, or just say nothing, slipping as quickly as he could through the gates, diving for cover from the barrage of words.

"Hey Rod, you do like Alice don't you? Aren't you going to stop and have a little talk to her? Look at that, Alice, he really does like you, he's blushing. Aww...c'mon Rod don't go away, stay here with us. Don't you think he should stay, Alice?"

Suffering in that way, he must've exercised his blushing muscles at least once or twice a day for most of his high school career and, in the end, he only spoke to Alice once, just before she left.

It was a chance meeting in the science labs after class; none of his friends were about and neither was her shadow, Sally. After four years, day after day of schoolboy hope and yearning, it had to be right now, or never again. He steeled himself for the confrontation.

"I really like you, Alice… I suppose one of your friends must have told you that," he muttered, avoiding eye contact, his face glowing, ears burning. "I have for a long time, you know."

"Well, why haven't you ever said anything to me?" She replied. "You're always mucking around with your show-off mates. I always thought you must've been like that too."

"No, it's not like that…" he stammered, recoiling in shock at her reaction, chancing a quick glance at her face, but not long enough to read it properly. He thought she looked disappointed. Rod had nothing to lose now, but the right words still wouldn't come.

"I could never say anything, not with Sally always there. I'm no good with words, at talking. I tried to show you. I told everyone else hoping you'd find out" he managed to blurt out, eyes fixed on the floor. "I even carved your name in the wet concrete when they fixed the footpath outside your house."

"Well, it's way too late for us to talk now. My parents are moving to the country and they're gonna put me in a new school[5]. I'm sorry Rod…"

What a pathetic clown he'd been. Rod suffered through his entire being every time that painful memory flooded back, hammering him to a quivering pulp. He could turn himself crimson, even alone in his own room, just thinking about it. So, he escaped, burying himself in his schoolwork, excelling at the challenge; it gave him satisfaction as he rose through the ranks becoming the best in his class, and life was far less complicated that way.

His blushing skills, honed to a fine art over the years, were as still as keen as ever; Rod reflected, And today again! Was this a problem he'd have to live with forever?

"Y'd better watch your back, mate!" A voice cut in.

"Huh?" Rod realised he'd been standing on the footpath, daydreaming, a brown paper bag full of groceries tucked under each arm. How long had he been there? He looked around at the old man next to him. "What was that?"

"That bloke on the motorbike, mate; Y' don't wanna get on the wrong side of him," the wizened old man finished before turning to continue his slow perambulation beneath the shady awnings of Bourke's main street.

CHAPTER 4. FIRST DAY ON THE JOB

IT WAS STILL DARK when Rod stepped out into the early morning coolness, pulling the front door of the house closed after him. René fired up the Land Rover and they crawled out of town through Bourke's quiet streets, the pale-yellow headlight beams searching the road ahead. Mark waited for them a few blocks down from the Royal Hotel by the front gate of his house. His barrel-chested frame sat on a metal Esky box containing his lunch and drinks for the day. Further along, Ricky waited on the corner opposite the shadowy art-deco outline of the Central Australian Hotel. Finally, they picked up Dan standing by the 'Welcome to Bourke' sign, next to his Esky. Everyone chattered excitedly in anticipation of their first day on the job as the Landy motored out of town, south-eastwards along the long straight of the Mitchell Highway into the middle of nowhere.

By the time they neared the Doradilla turnoff thirty minutes later, the red dawn had begun and all were silent, mesmerised by the drone of the Landy's engine and the early hour. Rod sleepily watched the ball of red growing out of the eastern horizon, slowly bleeding orange light into the outback sky.

"It's going to be another hot one," René predicted, breaking the quiet. "I can feel it already. At lunchtime I'll take you to the dam for a swim."

First up, René took them to the old Doradilla Copper Mine. Its weathered wooden head frame and pulleys silhouetted in the early morning sunlight, towered over an open timbered shaft. Piles of broken rock and ore lay strewn over the ground, along with rusty boilers and other abandoned relics from a bygone era.

"RENE SCHELLEKENS"

Robert Coenraads
2024

"Ancient volcanoes pumped mineral-rich fluids into the rocks all around here. The main vein runs along a deep fracture right under our feet." René explained, showing them pieces of heavy greenish ore. "The old timers mined this stuff a half century ago."

Rod knelt down and dropped a pebble into the shaft, watching it disappear into the blackness. He counted, listening for the plop as it hit the water below.

"One…two…three…four…five seconds…Bingo! That's about 125 metres to the water table!"

"And that's about as far as they could go down, Rod." René continued. "The old timers could only mine the top part of the lode; cursing the water when it seeped in through the walls, flooding their deeper tunnels. We're angling our drill holes below their old workings to see how far the rich-ore goes on down. There's a bonanza of copper, zinc and tin down there, plus quite a bit of iron too. That's why you and the boys will be running magnetic surveys in a grid pattern over the whole area. Your job is to detect these minerals and follow where the rich vein heads underground."

"Right on!!!" Rod could feel the excitement rising. He'd gone into geology because of René and now he'd be working alongside his cousin, putting into practice all he'd learnt at university. "Where do we start, René?"

"It's not going to be all fun and games," René warned. "First, you've got to survey in the grid by chain and compass. You'll use axes and slash hooks to cut kilometres of straight lines through the scrub; it's tough, backbreaking work, but don't worry, I'll show you how it's done."

The others, who hadn't seemed so interested in René's explanations, focused as they were shown their task. They keenly understood the meaning of a challenge.

"Hey Mark," Dan yelled exuberantly, "reckon you'll be able to keep up with Rick and me choppin' down all them mulga trees?"

"Yeah, no worries, mate," barrel-chested Mark boomed back. "Just don't find y'rselves standin' around in my dust, that's all."

"Hey," Dan turned his lanky frame to face Rod, studying him critically. "How do y' reckon a university fella from the big city's goin' to handle this kind of work?"

"Yeah, do y' think y 're up to it?" Dan's shadow, Ricky, echoed.

"We'll just have to see then," Rod laughed. He could sense it, the competitive tension simmering in the challenge, underlying their every word and action. Although he'd stood back and said nothing, carefully distancing himself from their conversational thrust and parry, he knew this would involve him as well, especially as an outsider. He, even more so, would be expected to rise to the challenge, proving himself by working harder and faster than them. He would need to earn their respect, gain their loyalty.

"There's a big iced water bottle in the back of the Land Rover," René's instructions broke Rod's thoughts. "Have a drink before we start and keep your hats on," he cautioned the boys while he had their attention. "Drink plenty throughout the day, but don't guzzle it all at once or it'll cramp your stomach. No doubt it'll go over forty again today by lunchtime. We'll be working six till two then back home before three, so you'll miss the worst of it."

René turned towards Rod. "The sun's your worst enemy out here, the lads already know that. If you want to spend your whole life outdoors you've got to take care of yourself. You'll always be working with field teams, so make their task fun and lead from the front. You'll get the job done that way."

René taught them more tricks of the trade that day, and throughout their first week. In the fierce heat beneath the burning outback sun, they learned how to hold a slash hook, wielding it to lay open the bush with broad sweeping strokes; how to hone their tool to razor-sharpness on the oil stone; and how to survey a grid and lay pegs in a straight line using a chain and sighting compass. It was basic, straightforward work, yet intensely physical—the hardest challenge Rod had ever faced, yet he soaked up every second of it like an eager sponge. Under its repetitive routine the team bonded into a cohesive unit as the days wore on, developing that sense of mateship that only grows through challenging circumstances.

They ate their lunch beneath the mulga shade at Dowling Tank, the property's principal dam located by the airstrip. It was barely more than a muddy hole in the red dirt enclosed by earthen banks, but, every day without fail, its brown waters welcomed them in their cool embrace. Nobody wasted a second; stripping down and plunging in; chasing, shouting, splashing about on a flotilla of truck inner-tubes borrowed from the drillers. And after their refreshing lunchtime rest, it was never too hard to put in another few hours of work before two o'clock knock-off.

OUTBACK SUMMER

"DOWLING TANK"

Robert Coenraads
2024

"The boys said they were heading to the pool after work. Are you coming René?" Rod asked as he raced to his bedroom to grab his cozzies, the fly-screen door of the house banging closed after him.

"No thanks," René said reaching into the fridge for a cold tinnie. He snapped back the ring pull drinking in its first cool hiss. "I'll just sit awhile and relax. I've got a bit of paper work to get through." He pointed to a dog-eared manila folder on the dining room table, crammed with receipts and invoices. "Off you go then. Have fun with your new mates and try not to get too sunburnt."

Rod gave René the thumbs up. Stuffing an oversized beach towel into a bag, he grabbed some coins, threw on his helmet, and made the ride to the Bourke Memorial Pool in two minutes flat.

He admired his bike as he carefully parked it near the cyclone wire fence of the pool complex. They'd come a long way together he reflected, remembering what it looked like when he first got it off his mate's older brother, a motorcycle mechanic. It came into the workshop as an abandoned wreck and sat there for years. Nobody bothered with it and eventually they gave it to him. Rod smiled, recalling his enthusiasm. He spent hours on it, stripping it to its frame and working on its powerful 500cc two-stroke motor. He'd restored the petrol tank to its original 1969 colours—white with a dark blue racing stripe—and lovingly buffed every piece of cast aluminium on the motor until it shone as brightly as chrome. Lightweight at only 174 kg, it was highly over-powered for its size; a finicky machine requiring careful riding, lest it live up to its nickname, 'The Widow Maker'.

It was still only three in the afternoon when Rod arrived at the pool; Bourke's relentless midsummer sun still high on its westerly trajectory across the cloudless outback sky. The temperature must've been well over a hundred in the shade and probably still climbing. Greeted by the aroma of hot meat pies and salty deep-fried chips, and the raucous shouts of kids in their swimmers, noisily ordering takeaways from the kiosk, Rod paid the entrance fee with the sixty cents in his board shorts pocket. Once out from under the shade of the buildings, he pulled off his shirt and shoes, feeling the sun's fierce sting on his back and shoulders and the soles of his feet burning as he gingerly crossed the yellow concrete path. He stepped quickly, glad to reach the grass.

The Bourke Olympic Pool sparkled in the mid-afternoon light like an outback oasis, surrounded by a mirage of soft, well-watered, manicured lawn. It was a dream-come-true after the day's hot, heavy work.

OUTBACK SUMMER

"RICKY AND DAN"
Robert Coenraads 2025

Rod picked an empty part of the deep end and, in one running bound, cleared the edge of the pool in a smooth dive, plunging deep into its welcoming aqua waters. He hung motionless in the blue void for a few moments, letting the coolness wash over him in waves, sucking away the heat and tiredness of the day's toil from his body. Rod opened his eyes; he could see ringlets of bright sunlight dancing on the bottom and, above, the kicking feet and legs of the people splashing about on the surface. Relaxing completely, he pulled himself slowly along the blue-tiled pool bottom, eventually surfacing at the opposite wall.

"Whoa man, that's great!" He breathed deeply, flicking back his wet hair, and looked up, only to find his workmates Dan and Ricky looking back down at him. He smiled; those two were a real pair, rarely apart. Rick stood shorter, stockier, blue-eyed, his frizzy ball of blonde hair silhouetted in the sunlight; Dan was leaner, taller, his dripping hair, straight and dark brown, matching his upturned, mischievous eyes. Without all their work clobber, clad just in board shorts, they looked much younger, although it was obvious Ricky had been out in the sun all day, his pale chest stamped with a distinct burnt vee rising into a red neck and face; Dan's complexion was darker, his tan more even.

"Hey Rod. Nice looking bike you've got there, mate." Dan spoke first. "It's a 500 cc isn't it? I'll bet y' she's nearly as fast as my brother's. He's got a black Kawa 650 with matching faring—a real beauty. He rides it around town all the time. Haven't y' seen it yet?"

Decent blokes the both of them, Rod reflected. Beneath all their puff and bravado, they were good work mates, keen as mustard. They'd worked hard today, and were eager to learn too, always asking about this rock or that, or telling him stories about growing up in in the outback, as they toiled away the hours, slashing their ruler-straight grid through the mulga; so many stories it was hard to believe they were only sixteen and still at school. Rod couldn't help but wonder about Dan's brother's bike; surely it couldn't be the same one? No, he couldn't be Dark Rider; that would be too much of a coincidence.

"Is he here today, Dan?"

"Nah…he never comes to the pool; says it's just a place for kids. Right now, he'd still be at work."

"How'd ya learn to hold your breath like that, Rod?" Ricky piped up.

"Dad's been teachin' me since I was a kid. It's all about relaxing and moving really slowly so y' don't burn up all your energy. I can go a lot further than that!"

OUTBACK SUMMER

"BRAVING THE
HIGH BOARD"

Robert Coenraads
2024

"How far you reckon you can go underwater then?" Ricky interrogated.

"Dunno Rick, I reckon maybe the length of the pool if I put my mind to it. Y' gotta become at one with the water, y' know." Rod started to explain, then stopped. He could see from their faces that his new friends had lost interest and were anxious to re-join their mates.

"We're doin' some diving off the high board with Paddy an' the others. Do y' wanna come over and see?"

Rod walked with them to the boards at the end of the swimming pool. He watched as they took turns to bomb, jump or dive off, mostly choosing the low board but sometimes daring to use the high one, while a group of bikini-clad girls looked on, laughing at their antics. As they lounged about in a group on the towel-strewn grass, Rod couldn't help but notice that fresh-skinned leanness and perfection of body that only teenage girls can possess. One of the blokes stood apart from the rabble, a tall lean guy of fair complexion with reddish hair. Dan and Ricky had mentioned his name was Paddy, one of the notorious O'Sullivan clan, an Irish family with a reputation around the district for fighting; he was the unspoken leader of the group. Rod noted how everyone moved out of his way, how he never seemed to wait in line behind the others. He was doing some impressive trick dives off the high board, much to the delight of the girls. Rod had never done high diving, but it looked fun. Lining up in the queue, he tried a few dives, even a somersault or two off the low board and, before long, convinced himself it shouldn't be too difficult to have a go at the high board.

Rod took his turn in the queue of dripping bodies, climbing the ladder onto the top platform and was surprised to see how much further away the water looked from up there. Perhaps if he'd been alone, he would have retreated to the low board for more practice, but he could sense all eyes upon him and so there was no backing down, no way out of it! No point in hesitating in front of the girls, he figured as he positioned himself nervously on the edge of the high board.

He'd planned a single forward roll and so, without further ado, attempted to execute it. Spinning uncontrollably through the air, his body tensed and, after what seemed like forever, he smacked down hard on the water's surface right on the flat of his back.

It was a horrible slapping sound, so loud that he was sure everyone around the pool must have heard, and the pain was something to be imagined. His head spun. Rod sank into the water letting it envelop him, exhaling and sinking to the bottom as the searing, stinging pain slowly ebbed.

OUTBACK SUMMER

"THE DIVING LESSON"   Robert Coenraads
                                            2024

35

He lay there a while relaxing, regaining himself until he realized he'd better surface before somebody thought to jump in and rescue him. Feeling foolish, he swam sheepishly to the side of the pool, trying to recover composure.

"You've got a lot of guts to try that one, mate. It must've hurt." It was Paddy, the tall Irish bloke. He stood, hands on hips, his bright blue eyes looking down at Rod from the edge of the pool. "How'd y' get it in your head to try a roll like that on y'r first time on the high board?" He asked.

"I've been watching you all afternoon, trying to learn how it's done." Rod answered climbing out of the pool, glancing ruefully at his cherry-red back. "You made it look too easy, I just had t' give it a go!"

"Up there you've gotta imagine you're on top of the world ready to fly, but you've gotta relax, mate. Let your body take control and switch off your brain. Once you clear the board, tuck yourself into a tight ball, head down. Wait until you finish the roll, your body will tell you when it's time to come out of it and complete the dive." Paddy instructed. "One roll's straightforward; two's a bit harder. Anyway, come over here mate, an' I'll show y' how it's done."

Later that evening, Rod stood in the small kitchen preparing the evening meal as was his custom now, every second night. Already the routine felt comfortable and second nature. Earlier he'd been by the store again for something he'd forgotten, his sixth sense telling exactly the right moment to go. This time, as the girl with the ebony hair rode by on the footpath, he stood aside, straight and proud like a matador, performing a deep bow, majestically sweeping his arm to the side for her to pass. She'd smiled a beautiful wide smile; Rod now smiling himself as he remembered it.

"René," Rod called, poking his head out of the kitchen door, "have you noticed how everybody talks funny out here in the country?"

"Well, they obviously think you sound different too—maybe like a silver-spooned city boy with a plum up his bum," René laughed, looking up from his bookwork. "Mister professor-head! Didn't I hear them calling you that today?"

"Yeah right," Rod laughed. "But I've already started workin' on it! Y' know, mate 'cause I don't wanna stand out like a sore thumb round here."

"That's the way! No problems…Go get 'em, mate," René joined, beard shaking heartily. "Ease up a bit and just go with the flow, Rod."

Returning to the stove, Rod's thoughts drifted back to high school, the English teacher strutting out front like a fighting cock in his garish plumage and elegant cravat reciting poetry or acting out Shakespeare. Everyone thought he was a bit gay. Nobody cared about the amazing precision language offered; dictionaries too heavy to carry, crammed with every word ever invented for economy of speech, elegance and perfect diction. Back then Rod collected as many as his brain could handle, assimilating them into his lexicon, honing his parlance, parrying with his teachers. He excelled at their application, pinnacling at university until, one day, reddening still at its memory, his epiphany came during an erudite failure of a class presentation. Never again would he portentously strive for a uniqueness nobody else understood, vowing only to use common phrases all would know. But he was already sunk; drowning in a sea of words leaking though holes, too many to patch, in an old wooden tub. He'd always be 'Mr Professor Head.'

After dinner Rod stepped out into the evening's coolness to explore the town. He'd stretch his legs a little, walk off his meal and seek solace for an active mind before going to bed. His walks had become nightly habit as he worked his way systematically around Bourke's grid of streets.

That evening he strolled around Central Park and the blocks closest to the town centre, encountering a number of ornate buildings standing like beacons in the relative darkness of Bourke's quiet streets. This must be where the action happens, Rod guessed, judging by the dull thud of music within and rows of work utes angle-parked out front. Like a moth to a candle, Rod was drawn as he passed, peering into their windows; curious to discover what lay within. But it was getting late and he was wasted after an emotional day; Rod decided he'd venture back another night for a better look.

By the time Rod returned home, René was finishing his bookwork on the dining room table, stapling together the ordered piles of receipts he'd listed in his expenses' ledger. He put them all back into the manilla envelope as Rod came in the front door.

"I can't believe the number of hotels for a place this size, René," Rod exclaimed to his cousin. "There's got to be at least one on every corner. Lively places too, by the look of it! How many are there?"

"Yeah, right, there's no shortage of entertainment establishments in Bourke. How else are the locals going to have a good time?

HOTELS OF

"THE OXFORD"

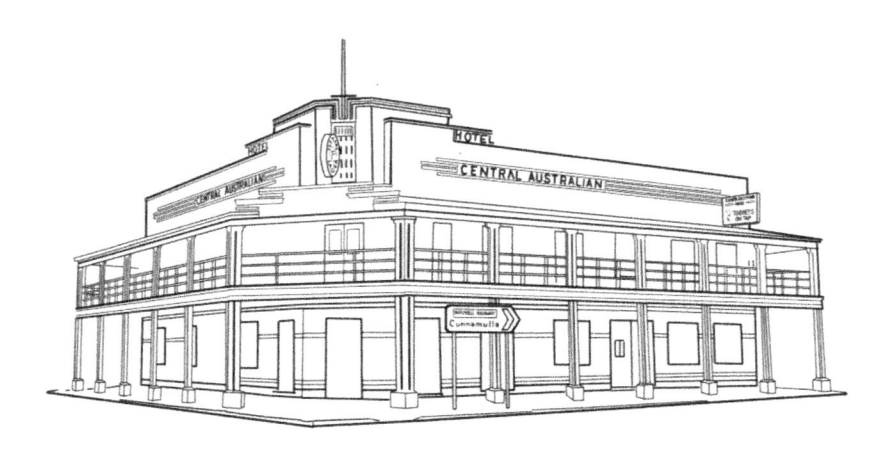

"THE CENTRAL AUSTRALIAN"

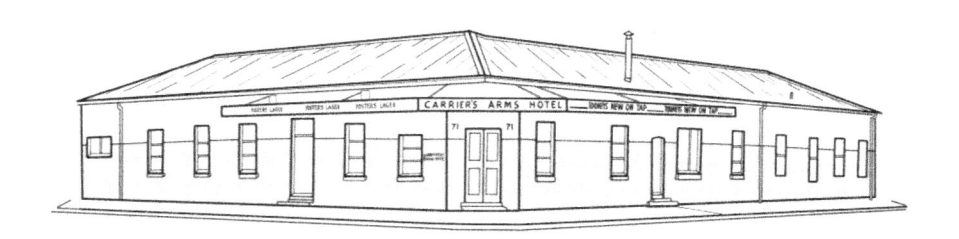

"THE CARRIER'S ARMS"

BOURKE

"THE RIVERVIEW"

"THE POST OFFICE HOTEL"

"THE ROYAL"

Robert Coenraads
2024

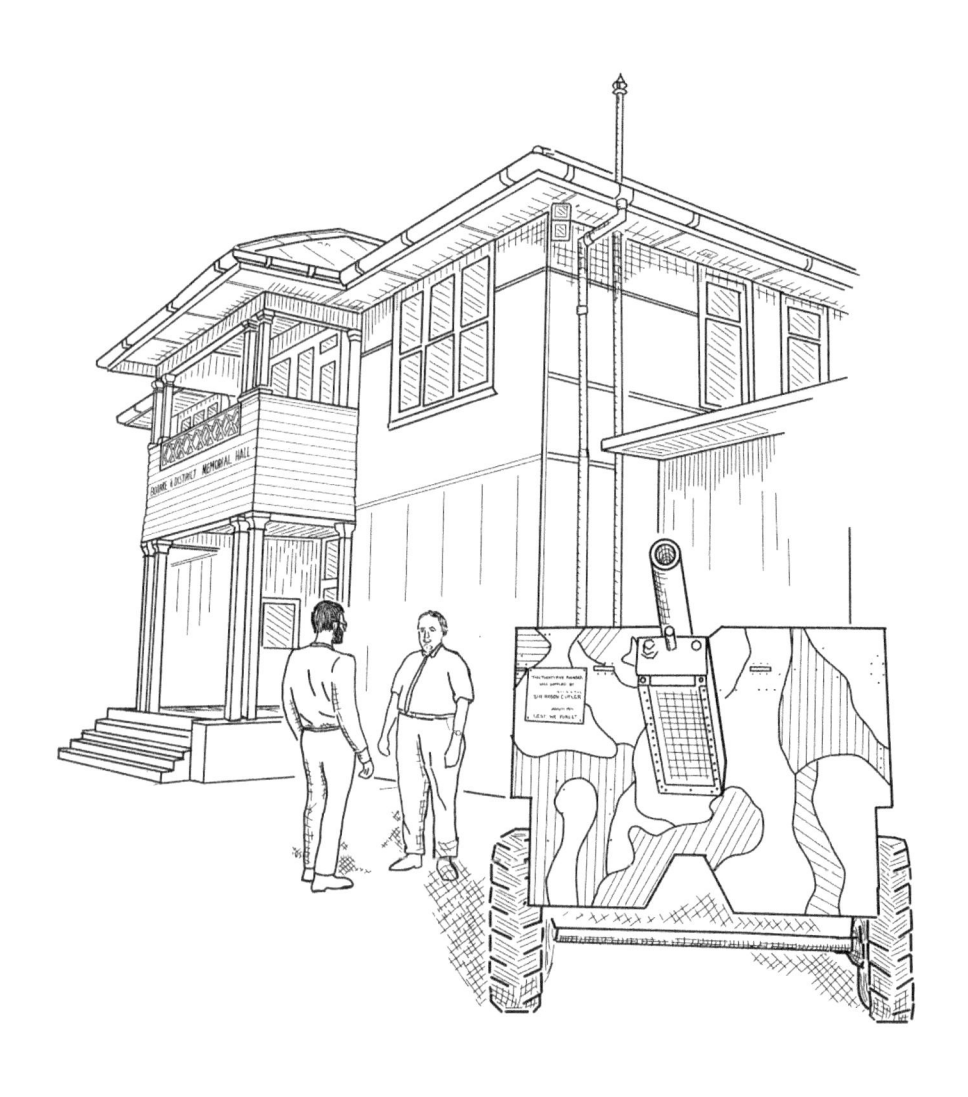

"THE OXLEY CLUB"

I've gotten to know most." René laughed, counting them off on his fingers. "There's the Oxford on the highway, the Royal down by the old port, the Post Office Hotel in the main street, the Central Australian by the railway station, the Carriers' and the Federal along Mitchell Street, and the North Bourke Hotel—a total of seven!"

"Oh… And that's not all," René added after a moment's thought. "There's entertainment at the Bowling Club, the Golf Club, and the RSL."

"There's no shortage of spare time around here, ay? So, I guess I'll have plenty of opportunity to check them all out," Rod said, imagining girls, music, dancing and rooms cram packed with gaming tables and coloured lights.

"The clubs are fine, but some of the others are no-go zones." René cautioned, picking up on his cousin's plans. "There's a few to avoid hanging around, like the Carriers' Arms. Even I won't go in there."

"Don't worry René, I reckon if I'm careful I should be okay."

René's caution intrigued him. He wanted to find out more, but it was late; recalling their 4:30 am start was not too many hours away. The mystery of forbidden places fascinated him; provoking an urge to explore them—like the part of town where the Aboriginals live, on the way to the tip. He wondered about what stories these places held.

"Remember, I've done Judo for years," he added, noting René's concern at his last remark: "even captained the last campus tournament!"

"THE DREAM" 2024
Robert Coenraads

CHAPTER 5. SUZIE, THE DRILLER'S DAUGHTER

ROD HEARD the rain start Friday evening. He lay in bed drifting off to sleep to its hypnotic rhythm as it pelted down on the tin roof and kept up, non-stop, throughout the hot night. In his broken slumber, disturbed by the loud drumming, a passing parade of disquieting images he couldn't quite recall came and went. He saw the muddy river behind the house swelling into an angry torrent, overtopping its levee, and spilling into the streets of the sleeping town. He imagined it beneath his room, seeping up through the cracks in the floorboards, lapping at the base of his bed.

Waking next morning, he felt the slightest tinge of disappointment to find everything in his room quite dry. The rain didn't let up all weekend, but the levee held firm.

"We've got problems out at site we need to sort out," René announced Sunday afternoon. "I was talking to John on the radio today and he couldn't get into town to pick up supplies yesterday morning. His truck and Land Rover are bogged. We'll have to try to get there Monday morning, even though the red soil will be like quicksand. I've had to put the boys off 'till at least Tuesday or Wednesday"

"If John's got both his vehicles bogged, how're we gonna manage to do that?"

René shrugged. "They're running low on supplies, so we've got to try. We've got a winch and all the other gear on-board the Land Rover to do the job. I'll show you how it works before we go out."

By next morning the rain had stopped leaving the dawn sky clear and cool as they drove southeast along the Mitchell towards Doradilla Station. During the first 30 minutes of easy-going bitumen, Rod's hopes built that the track might've dried overnight but, as soon as they turned off the tar and crossed the railway tracks, Rod saw great muddy pools stretching across the red dirt and knew there'd be trouble. René stopped for Rod to get out and lock the front hubs into four-wheel drive before they dropped into the first puddle. René kept up speed, just enough to prevent the vehicle bogging, but not so much that they would slide off the track into the trees.

"And this is the best part of the track," René said, fighting with the steering wheel as the Land Rover fishtailed precariously from side to side. At length they came to an open bowl-shaped depression near the airstrip, which resembled an inland sea rather than the usual red desert. René pushed on, judging the best way through, trying to figure out where the track headed beneath the expanse of muddy water, but eventually, about half way across, the vehicle sank up to its running boards in the thick sticky mud.

"We'll have to winch our way out of this one," René announced. "Life's one big learning experience, Rod—I've done it before, and now it's your turn. By the time you've finished, you'll be able to get yourself out of anywhere like a pro." He had already shown Rod how to use the hand operated winch—how to attach the cable to the front bumper bar and the other end around a sturdy tree ahead of the vehicle.

"What are we going to tie the cable to? It's not gonna reach the trees." Rod asked worriedly.

"Use the spare wheel as an anchor point. Tie the cable around the wheel and bury it. It'll take the weight of the vehicle. There's a shovel on the back."

Rod opened the passenger door and hesitated as he looked down at the sea of roiled red mud cut by water filled furrows splayed apart by the vehicle's wheels, all just inches below the running board. There was nothing solid for him to stand on within easy distance.

René looked at his concerned face, laughing. "The first step's the one you never get used to, Rod; it's always the worst. Don't worry about it. In five minutes, you'll be so muddy you won't care less. Go for it, Rod," he laughed. "Jump in!"

Rod took a last look at his new work boots he'd so lovingly spit-polished before leaving Sydney, and stepped out—immediately sinking to his knees in the ooze. Cold water soaked into his socks and sucking mud pulled on his boots with every step as he made his way round back of the Land Rover and then towards a small hillock out in front of the vehicle. He dropped onto his knees and began working the soft ground.

About fifteen minutes later Rod had a hole deep enough to bury the spare wheel and the cable stretched between it and the front bumper bar. René gave him the thumbs up from inside the cab.

"Whoa… How's that!" Rod exclaimed, working the winch handle back and forth, rewarded for his efforts as the vehicle slowly crept forward, gaining about twenty metres.

By the time Rod had dug the spare wheel into the ground several more times and lifted it back onto the Land Rover, he was caked from head to toe with thick wet mud—only two blinking eyeballs and his broad smile shining through the red mask. René looked out of the window, laughing at the sight of him—but they were finally free!

"Great work, Rod, you've got us through the mire. And I've gotta say, it's the worst bogging I've ever been in. Now, jump in and let's get these supplies to John and his crew."

"Righto then! Let's go." Rod felt ten-foot tall, his heart swollen with pride at René's words. He'd gotten them out of their 'worst bogging ever.' Life sure was different out here compared with back home, far more physical, intimate, earthy, and he loved every minute of it.

About ten minutes later they were at the drill site by which time the mud caking his skin and clothes had begun to dry. John, Spider and Suzie came over from the drill rig where they were working on the water pump. Rod noticed how grubby they all looked. René had mentioned the water in the dam had gone over their pumps in the storm, so they obviously weren't taking showers or washing clothes.

"You're a life-saver René. We've just about run out of everything," John announced. "I hope the streak of bad luck's broken now," he laughed. "I told you, y' should've never called this one 'hole thirteen'!"

"Don't thank me," René replied. "Rod did all the hard work. Just take a look at him." René pointed as Rod came around the Land Rover, his white teeth shining with pride. He felt the mask of mud crackle on his face as he smiled.

"Good t' see you're puttin' him to some good use anyway," Spider commented wryly.

René, John and Spider picked up the boxes of drilling supplies while Suzie grabbed the fresh groceries and headed for the caravan, Red Dog barking and turning excited circles behind her.

"Let me give you a hand with those, Suzie," Rod said, lifting another cardboard box out of the back of the Land Rover and following her over to the caravan. "I'll pass 'em to you and you can put them inside. It's best that

I don't get too close to anything clean." Rod stood at the flyscreen door of the caravan holding the next box. He watched Suzie as she bent down to pack the supplies into the cupboards under the bench. She came back to the door.

"What happened to you anyway?" Suzie asked, studying his face as she took the next box out of his hands.

"It's a great technique, y' know," Rod started. "I'm glad René knew about it, otherwise we'd still be stuck out there, right now," he added modestly before explaining how the spare wheel saved them. "It still took us most of the day to get here."

"Well," Suzie exclaimed as he finished, "I reckon we owe you one! You're a bit of a hero for managing to get here, then!" She said smiling.

Rod looked at her. He liked the idea of being Suzie's hero and could feel himself start to redden at the thought. He smiled back at her confidently, happy for the mud coating his cheeks. "Thanks!" he replied, looking down at his shoes.

"Take a jump into the dam before heading back. It'll get all the mud off," she continued. "I go there for a swim each day to cool off."

"Do y' have the time now? That is, after we get this gear packed away. What's the best way over all this wet ground?" Rod asked hopefully. "Maybe your dad, René and Spider would like to come along?"

"Spiders hate water," She laughed, "and they're about to have a beer anyway. I don't think there's much doin' this arvo, but I'll ask my dad if I can go."

Rod marched down the red earthen bank and into the dam, still wearing his clothes, boots and hat, laughing as he went. As he submerged, a great muddy red stain spread around him in the still brown water. Suzie stripped off her work gear, down to a red bikini, and leapt over the top of Rod in an arching dive. Red Dog barked excitedly from the shore as she swam with powerful strokes towards the middle of the dam. "C'mon Rod," she called. "I'll race ya to the other side."

"Not much chance of that. I'm nearly drowning here," Rod spluttered, his wet clothes and heavy boots dragging him under. "Just a sec, wait up a bit."

Struggling onto the slippery bank, he threw his boots, socks and shirt into a sodden pile before plunging back into to water in hot pursuit. As he swam, Rod felt the water glide past his skin; a thin sun-heated layer on top and frigid beneath.

Suzie was too quick, and with the head start had easily beat him. She was sitting on an inner tube on the sloping bank, her feet dangling in the water, by the time he reached the other side. Rod came up and sat next to her. It had been a hot, hard day and he felt clean, fresh and relaxed now.

"What a place, Suzie! Great idea of yours to come here!" He studied her wet, sun-streaked hair, noting the tiny water droplets glistening like jewels in the sunlight on the smooth, brown skin of her shoulders. Red Dog had come bounding around the edge of the dam. He snuggled against her side and rested his wet muzzle in her lap.

"It's really beautiful here at this time of day, Rod," she answered. The sun was beginning to yield its power to the coming night. Shadows had started to lengthen and the late afternoon light glowed a beautiful golden yellow in the treetops.

"If you sit here for a while, really still," she continued, "sometimes you see kangaroos and emus, or maybe a bunch of wild pigs coming down to the dam for a drink. I just love it here, y' know."

"Can you imagine how great it'd be to live out here, Suzie? Out here on the land." Rod chose his words carefully, following her thoughts, to build up an image in her mind. "Imagine a fine wooden homestead with a big wood stove to cook on in the kitchen, and a big wide verandah[6]. Y' could sit there with Red in the afternoons overlooking the dam. Just over there, perhaps." He pointed to a taller stand of handsome-looking trees just back from the water's edge. "What do you reckon?"

"Yeah, I can imagine that." she replied dreamily, moving a little closer to Rod. "It'd be much nicer than a box in the suburbs, I reckon. Maybe one day, Y' never know."

"Imagine a pot roast slow-cooking in the old cast iron stove," Rod continued, drinking in the late afternoon's beauty, Suzie so close now he could feel the heat of her body, "the smell of wood smoke blending with the aroma of the meal, wafting down to the water's edge as you're sitting by the dam drying off after your swim. Just like now!" He began to get caught up in his own story, imagining himself building that small homestead for her, working the land; how it would be, just him and Suzie living there together.

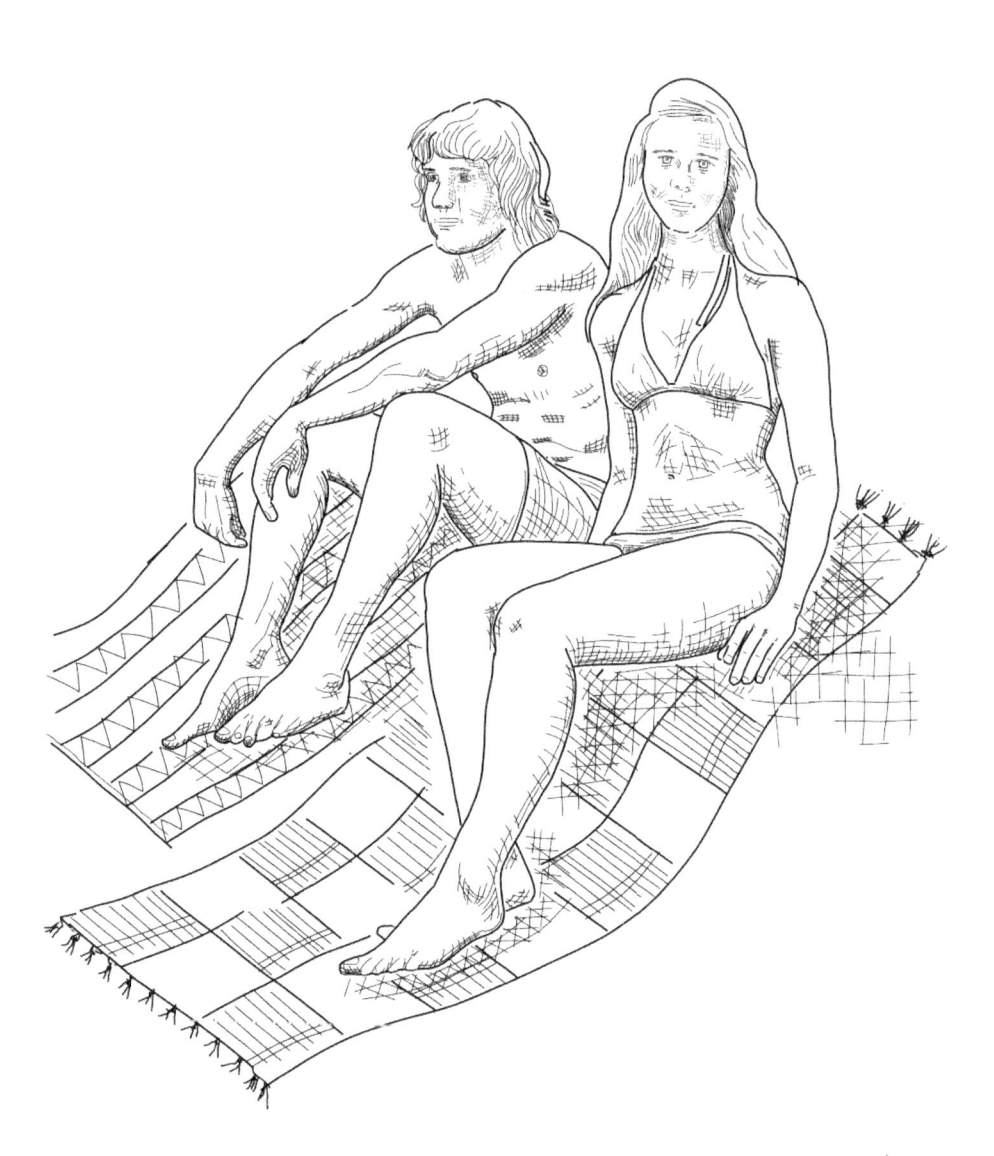

"ROD & SUZIE
DOWLING TANK"

Robert Coenraads
2024

"Hey Rod, I reckon I could handle a piece of that roast and veggies with all the trimmings right about now!"

Suzie's comment broke into his idyllic musings, and then he remembered…

"I'm sorry for going on like that, Suzie. You must be pretty hungry by now?"

"I reckon I really haven't had too much time to think about it, until you brought it up just now," she laughed. "We keep a stock of extra flour just in case, so we've been making a lot of dampers lately. But you're right, now that you mention it, I guess we've all been looking forward to a good square meal of meat and veggies with all the trimmings…"

The sound of an engine broke into the silence of Rod's dream world, as the roof of the yellow Land Rover came into view over the far wall of the dam. A bunch of pink galahs, startled by the noise, lifted off in a screeching cloud from the water's edge. René stopped the Land Rover on top of the dam wall and leant out of the window.

"C'mon Rod," he called, "We've got to get moving and see if we can get back over the airstrip before dark, and let these guys get on with their tea. It'll be their first decent feed in a few days."

Rod jumped to his feet, "C'mon then Suzie, race y' back to the other side?" He shouted as he dove in.

"Y' know what, Suzie?" Rod ventured later on, just before climbing into the passenger seat of the Land Rover, and while she was the only one in earshot. "It was great being your 'hero for the day'." He chose the same words she used earlier, deciding to speak his feelings—carefully searching for that middle road hidden between the easy road of saying nothing, which he knew would always lead to a dead end, and the hard rocky road littered with broken, clumsy, eager words which also invariably led nowhere. Rod couldn't be sure what she was thinking but, in the fading afternoon light, he imagined he saw her cheeks colour ever so slightly. She looked down for a moment, then back up at his face.

"Yeah, it was a great day, especially now we're not going hungry," she laughed, waving as René started to drive off.

CHAPTER 6. ROD'S DISAPPOINTMENT

BY WEDNESDAY the ground at Doradilla had dried and their daily routine had returned pretty-much back to normal, although working in the forty-degree afternoon temperatures and near-one hundred percent humidity was sticky and unpleasant. Rod's lunch-time swim in the dam and long afternoons at the Bourke pool had become daily highlights but, much to his disappointment, he wasn't bumping into Suzie and the drilling team; barely even catching sight of them as they drove past the rig each day coming and going from site. John and René held their planning meetings during the day while Rod and his team worked, cutting and laying the grid. Although the two teams were vital halves of an integrated whole, with John's drill hole locations being dependent on René's geologic interpretations; the two teams' different daily duties meant that they just never met.

"The driller's got a daughter, maaaate…I hear she's pretty." Dan started on the theme one lunchtime.

"Real pretty, she is." Ricky replied. "I seen her on the drill rig the other day. Her dad would really wanna keep her locked up nice and safe out here rather than let 'er loose in town."

"Yeah, she's absolutely gorgeous," Rod reminisced. He'd learnt how to play the boys' game now, take part in the light easy-going banter between good mates, permeating their daily lives. It could be pretty rough at times but he was used to the language now; equal to the best of it, and could give back as quickly as it came.

"An' she comes here for a swim every arvo after we've gone home—in a red bikini—an' she jumps into the water—right about there, where you're standin', Rick." Rod added point after point as they came into his head. "Really fast swimmer she is too. I reckon she could nearly beat me in a race."

"How d' you know all that, Conway?" Dan challenged. "I bet ya makin' it all up."

"Yeah, bullshit, ya lyin' mongrel!" Ricky chimed in, his blue eyes mischievous.

"Nah mate! It's all fair dinkum. I was swimmin' here with her the other day," Rod paused a moment for effect, studying their disbelieving faces. "Y' can go an' ask René if y' don't believe me," he added confidently.

"René," Rod ventured to ask his cousin during dinner that evening, "Do y' think I could go out and stay with the drillers this weekend? Perhaps watch them work and pick up few things. Suzie told me they usually work right through and I'm really interested in learning more about drilling."

Rod knew he'd have no trouble with the hard work and he'd certainly learn a lot. As a greenhorn, they'd give him a hell of a rough time out there, especially Spider. He knew that for sure, but figured it'd be worth it if he got to spend more time with Suzie.

"It doesn't look too hard, and I'd pick it up quickly. What do you think, René?" he continued enthusiastically.

"No, it's not too difficult, Rod, just plenty of hard yakka and heavy lifting. I reckon you'd fit right in out there." René replied, considering the possibility. "I'd drop you and your swag off at their camp after work on Friday afternoon, plus bit of extra food to tide you over the weekend—but I'd have to speak to John about it all first..."

René's answer faded into garble as Rod defocused, already imagining how his weekend would be—three whole afternoons alone with Suzie at the dam, getting to know her better. He could just picture the look on Ricky and Dan's disbelieving faces, peering through the dusty back glass of the Landy, as René drove off, leaving him there with Suzie on Friday arvo. He could hardly wait!

But René hadn't come down in the last shower. Suspecting there might be a bit more to his cousin's sudden enthusiasm for drilling than met the eye, he decided now was the best time to break the news he'd heard at the driller's camp earlier that day.

"By the way, Rod, speaking of John, he told me Suzie's heading back to Adelaide on the weekend." René added the fact, throwing it into the conversation as offhandedly as he could. "She's going to spend a bit of time with her mum in Adelaide before uni starts in March."

Rod's daydreaming's faded, his mind snapping to attention.

"She wanted to say goodbye to you, Rod…"

Disappointment swept over him in sickening waves as René's words sank in. The fun of learning about drilling seemed pointless now without Suzie. He stood pokerfaced, hoping René wouldn't notice the turmoil churning in his heart. He pictured his and Suzie's lives; straight lines being drawn on a blank page, starting in opposite corners, coming together for the briefest of moments through a strange coincidence of events, intersecting momentarily, then moving apart, diverging on their predestined trajectories. He felt pathetic, utterly powerless to change or control the course of his own life or anyone else's for that matter. His duties and commitments, his studies, his job, his responsibilities to his parents and everyone else, sat upon him like a massive lead weight. He could feel it crushing the free spirit within him.

"Tomorrow, before they start drilling, I'll bring you over to the rig," René continued, "so you can have a few minutes to say goodbye while I chat with John."

"Yeah, thanks," he tried to straighten his shoulders, lifting his head to look at René. "I'm going to bed now. See you in the morning then."

The following morning, Rod's spirits had sunk to their lowest ebb as René steered the Landy toward the bright blue rig being readied for the new day. He was worn out. Like a scratched record, he'd played the same line over and over, tossing and turning, sweating in his twisted bedsheets, dreaming fitfully; it hadn't been one of his best nights.

Rod felt uneasy having to say goodbye. What would he say anyway? Suzie could've been an ideal match if things had been different. He sensed she liked him, he knew it, but there's no way those subtle feelings for him could compete with her grand wide-open plans for the future; with the excitement that lay ahead for her as a young attractive woman. How could she even think to change course, let alone contemplate a life together with him for any more than that brief nostalgic moment, as they imagined building a simple homestead together, by the dam in the tranquillity of the Australian outback? He knew she'd sensed his feelings for her, but, being two years younger, she would never realise the painful sting he keenly felt of their not-quite being-in-the-right-place-at-the-right-time-of-their-lives. Their paths were, at the present moment, on different courses.

"See ya Rod. Thanks for dropping by to say goodbye. I reckon you'll have a great summer and I hope it all goes well with your studies next year."

"Yeah, likewise Suzie."

"I wish I could hang around for a couple more swims but I've got heaps to do, getting ready for my first year at uni," she added flippantly.

Rod could sense it now; not really a coolness but a distancing, even though they were alone, standing close, face to face. Suzie wasn't concerned in the slightest that life's random circumstance was about to carry them apart. Rod knew he was, for her, just a brief passing scene, one of the countless many to come, in the passing adventure of her rich, young life. Suzie was a tantalising dream just outside of his reach.

My God, she's so beautiful, I just wanna curl up and die, his heart cried, tearing at his chest as he felt her feelings for him withdraw, turning instead towards a big, bright future looming ahead; Rod could feel it, feel himself fading into her history—a snippet of pleasant memory along her life's path; but that was too painful to accept. His quiet suffering reached agonising heights as he realised, he would never take her in his arms—perhaps that day at the dam, for a fleeting moment, the time might have been right, or perhaps if chance allowed her to stay just one more weekend—but not now. She was turning to face her own exciting future. Should he blurt it out now, just how much he loved her? —stammer out those blabbering, grovelling, begging words. He knew how useless that would be. No, he'd hold his dignity, resist the urge to throw himself upon his knees before her, and they would part as friends, with unspoilt memory of their short but beautiful experience—of their fleeting moment in time together.

"Yeah, likewise, Suzie. I reckon you'll really enjoy starting uni next year," He said studying her pretty face for the last time.

Suzie's spirit was free, unbridled; which is what attracted him so much to her. Poised on the brink of discovery, the excitement of her whole life lay ahead—university, the other students she'd meet who would fall in love with her, and the endless potential of her future beyond. Rod had tasted that life already and knew how Suzie felt now, soaring into the heavens; yesterday's gone and tomorrow 's come—nothing to hold her back[7].

Sure, he'd been her 'hero for a day', but that's all it ever was, one day in Suzie's life, and that day had passed. It was now time to say goodbye, and the only thing left was to face that fact.

"Thanks, and good luck in your studies too, Rod."

"See ya later then, Suzie."

CHAPTER 7. THE ROYAL, MICK'S PUB

AS ROD'S physically-demanding mornings rolled into an endless summer of late afternoons at the pool, his memories of Suzie gradually lost their painful edge. He never spoke of her with his mates– at first because it hurt too much, then, one day, because he plain forgot. The gang was his family now—everything he needed—as if he'd lived in Bourke all his life. His university, Sydney home, even his parents, seemed like someone else's vague memory, as distant as the kilometres lying between them; exorcised from his mind as their presence only reminded him of his commitments come start of term in March next year. The burning intensity and clarity of the present moment was all that mattered now[8]. He was one of a close circle. In it were his workmates, the girls, and of course Paddy, who'd taken him under his wing as protégé, teaching him about life in and out of the pool—their friendship growing stronger from that first failed back flop. He was now adept on the high board, experimenting with forward rolls, back somersaults and handstands—so many his chlorine-washed eyes and ears ached by afternoon's end.

"Hey Rod, what's the beach like?" Donna asked.

Rod wondered why the girls in the gang found him so interesting. There were about four of them, two or three at any one time, coming after school to swim, jump on the trampoline or laze about on the pool lawn mixing with the blokes, before heading home for tea. The girls on campus rarely said a word, passing right on by, preoccupied with their studies. Come to think of it, he was probably just the same.

But here, lying in the shade on a cool, damp towel, he felt comfortable, in an easy, natural way, chatting or mucking about. Perhaps it was because he was an 'out-of-towner', someone different from the rest. They'd often ask him about life beyond Bourke.

"There's miles of golden, sun-drenched sands to lie on, Donna, the roar of white foaming breakers, framed by a horizon of ultramarine ocean of a shade one hundred times intenser than Bourke pool's deep-end." Rod answered, with that hint of embellishment reserved especially for Donna.

"Don't be so garrulous Rod, and, by the way, that's 'more intense' not 'intenser'," Donna corrected, staring at him through thick glasses set on a serious face.

She often wore that face, always more grown up than the others and René would laugh when Rod imitated her, always coming up with a big-word—something new and expressive to try out on all willing to put up with her. His own long, expressive gushing and invented-on-the-spot words seemed only to incite Donna into further conversational parrying.

"Don't be so pugnacious about it, Donna. You're just too fastidious, and actually I think you're probably a hypochondriac."

"Well, now you're just being obnoxious, Rod."

"So, what are the big downtown department stores like?" Trish cut in. "I've gotta get to Sydney soon."

"They're every girl's dream," Rod waltzed, "gleaming chrome and smoked glass complexes stretching skyward, their multi-levels connected by escalators and walkways, and each level lined with shops stretching further than the eye can see, their shelves overflowing with every imaginable item for sale. There's usually a Hoyts, food courts and way more."

"Dubbo's about as far as I've ever got," Beth put in resignedly, "but I wanna go to Luna Park one day."

Beth was a real beauty, her rich bronze skin and matching hair which cascaded in waves down the small of her back, lightening into a sun-bleached blonde at the tips—her lithe suntanned body offset by a pale aqua bikini. Rod could barely keep his gaze from her as she lay on the grass, mucking about with the others. Trish was shorter with dark curly hair, deeply tanned and likewise gorgeous. She wore a one-piece or, some days, a brief black bikini—and on bikini days, she'd never be talked into going off the high board. Donna had a thinner boyish figure, Anne-of-Green-Gables hair and pale freckled skin that wouldn't take a tan no matter how hard she worked on it.

Countrifying his North Shore diction became second nature with his mates, but with the girls he never gave it a thought, rambling on as he pleased. Smilingly, he wondered how he'd go upon his return to the city, before the thought vanished into irrelevance.

"But, nothing in the big smoke beats what you've got in Bourke," Rod qualified his descriptions. "Crowded shopping centres and city streets were never my cup of tea. Working here in the outback is the best y' know. You've got the wide-open desert, horizon-to-horizon sky, well-watered parks and gardens and, of course, the pool. And out here you've got all the time in the world to enjoy it."

Rod wasn't sure the Western Plains girls grasped the wholesome balance of their easy-going country existence that he appreciated as an outsider, especially those who'd never seen the world that lay beyond Bourke's levees. He'd weave his own questions about their lives, families and school into gaps in the conversation.

As the lazy afternoons wore on and, with their curiosity sated, Rod settled even more—eventually no longer an outsider, just another one of the gang. That sense of belonging was so strong; the feeling of being part of a real group, a gang of close friends, always ready to laugh, joke around and have fun. He'd reached the pinnacle of existence.

One of the prettiest was the girl with the ebony hair, the one with the bike. He'd only see her sometimes, late afternoons, as he headed home or to the supermarket. She was never at the pool, although he'd casually searched the complex on several occasions. Nowadays he'd wave as they passed, and she'd smile back, but there was never occasion for a chat. Her name remained a quest he wondered if he'd ever solve. Rod contemplated timing his supermarket visit with hers, so she'd still be inside shopping, and he'd meet her by chance in the aisles. But then what could he say?

'Hi, it's just me, the clumsy bloke who spilled your groceries all over the footpath the other day. No, I promise I won't do it again!' he'd laugh. 'By the way, my name's Rod in case you've got the slightest bit of interest in knowing it. What's your name, if you don't mind me asking? Well, I'd better not take up too much of your time. Perhaps I might bump into you again? No…No, I don't mean that literally," he might laugh again at his own lame joke, hoping she'd join in. "Goodbye then…' No way, Rod shuddered, the very thought of such a pathetic encounter weakening his knees to the point of collapse.

"None of the girls we know ride a bike. They all walk to the pool," Ricky and Dan answered when Rod asked, as offhandedly as he could, one day, if they knew of any girls who had bikes. He knew the slightest mention of girls could bring on a chorus of comment if he didn't tread carefully. He knew them well enough by now and could imagine what they would say:

"Who've you got a crush on now? Maaaate? What d' y' reckon Rick?"

"Dunno who it could be mate. Whatever happened to that driller's daughter you was braggin' all about the other day?"

"Yeah, we've not heard another word about her lately, have we mate? I reckon that one's finished!"

"Short and pimply for you next time, I reckon mate. Safest bet 'cause she's never gonna run out on ya for something better. That's because nothing better's ever gonna want her." Rick would laugh raucously.

"Hang on a minute, I reckon Donna-four-eyes would be a good mate for him!" Dan would join in heartily. "He could spend all his money on her, shopping down in Sydney. Didn't y' see her eyes light up when Rod was tellin' his stories about the 'big smoke'? Maaaate."

"Yeah, very true, Dan, C'mon mate, let's go tell Paddy and the rest of the gang all about this news."

No way! He'd never let himself end up on the pointy end of such an interchange; memories flooding back of torment suffered at his high school's front gates. He swore to keep anything along those lines strictly confidential, vowing to preserve his reputation with the gang at all costs.

That night, Rod decided to enter one of the town's pubs he'd been checking out on his evening walks, choosing first the Royal on Mitchell Street. René told him it was Port of Bourke's original hotel; a welcoming hearth where weary paddle-wheeler captains and travellers could stop over on their long journeys up and down the Darling. The Royal was a broad colonial building set back one block from the river, its big bustling bar taking up the entire ground floor with ample accommodation located conveniently upstairs, the rooms opening onto a broad, wooden verandah overlooking the street.

As he pushed through the main doors of the hotel, the sound of a thousand separate conversations greeted him, reverberating in his ears, while a thick blue haze of cigarette smoke hung heavily in the air stinging his eyes. Rod made his way past the crowded tables and up to the bar.

"Do you make milkshakes?" Rod asked casually, leaning across the counter.

"Nah mate," the barman replied looking a little strangely at Rod, noting his youth and inexperience. "No dairy products allowed on the premises."

"Do y' have anything to eat then?" Rod tried again.

"Just some bags of Nobby's Nuts, mate," the barman answered. "Do y' want any? Would y' like a beer, perhaps?"

"Er…no thanks mate," Rod replied. His mind wandered back to an end-of-school party—one of the many coming-of-age celebrations that seemed to blur into one fuzzy memory. The one he'd thrown at his house stood out above the rest. Freddie the Failure was wasted as usual, he remembered, reflecting again on the downfall of his mate, face down on the front lawn amongst the scattered pizza boxes and beer bottles. Vic and Pete nearly stacked their cars that evening too, racing in the new subdivision. He remembered how they'd wandered back into the party weak-kneed and ashen-faced. He could have lost a whole bunch of mates that evening if things had gone differently, and it was all because of the stupid drink. They'd brought along cartons of it to the party. He'd refused to touch it then, so why start now?

"Why don't you sell different stuff here? I'm sure the people would buy it."

"Can't do it mate. We've only got the liquor licence." The barman replied, fast losing interest in this peculiar character. He had other people coming in, waiting to be served, so, when the stranger didn't reply, he walked off. Rod stood there for a few moments longer, looking around the haze-filled room, wondering what he was going to do next. Feeling awkwardly out of place, he made ready to go back outside into the fresh air. Weird place, he reflected; grandest building in town, all light and promise from outside, but nothing useful inside!

"G'day maate! Where're y' from?" Rod heard a voice rise above the general din. Looking around he saw a lean, work-hardened middle-aged man with a shock of reddish hair sitting by himself at a small round table near the window.

He walked between the crowded tables towards the man. "I'm Rod Conway from Sydney."

"G'day Rod," the man said welcomingly, indicating the vacant stool. "I'm Mick. Mick Tallon, cook for the shearers 'n' drovers, workin' out of Toorale Station, these days.

"Toorale?" Rod echoed.

"Yeah, it's out on the Paka Tank-Tilpa Road." Mick spoke slowly with a strong Australian accent. It was so strong in fact, Rod had to listen carefully to catch what he said.

"Henry Lawson even worked there, out at the woolshed, back when old Charlie Bowman was a boy. The station was about 850,000 acres back then, running about 54,000 head of sheep."

As the evening wore on, Mick told stories of life on Toorale Station, firing Rod's imaginings—yarns of lonely campfires and starry desert nights; of long rides in the saddle with the stockmen, and of his mate, Charlie Bowman, the oldest stockman at close on a century in age. Mick's stories were of blood, sweat and tears; of hot hard work on the land; of red dust, blue skies, and blazing yellow sun. Rod had no idea whether Toorale was near or far, but it certainly sounded like a place he'd want to live and work.

Rod had a taste of that life now, holding up his own end of the tale. With weeks of field work at Doradilla under his belt, he'd begun to understand that same deep sense of connectedness to the land Mick that felt; and spoke of his own land and the secrets beneath its flat red surface—how he explored with modern science and technology, slowly discovering those secrets; listening to the quiet whisperings of the ancient landscape with his instruments.

The two of them sat together in another world, completely disconnected from the noisy smoky environment of the Royal Hotel, yet bonded together in mutual deep understanding. Without any further words, they understood each other perfectly. When Rod looked at the landscape, he sensed more than just the two dimensions of the endless red gidgee plains. He could peer into the third dimension, into the rocks hundreds of metres down and the mineral treasures held within; secrets the old miners knew about. And yet there was still more he could see—a fourth dimension. Once upon a time volcanoes existed here, the same ones that spewed mineral riches from Earth's depths ages ago, and had long since eroded flat; and Bourke once stood on the distant shores of a vast inland ocean; a shallow sea that teemed with giant reptilian life.

Mick's timescale was shorter than Rod's but he connected directly with the soul of Australia's colonial past—beyond his mate Charlie's century it was only a hundred years back to the times of British settlement. He spoke of hard work, valour and conquest—domination of untamed land and suppression of the elements by man's will. Rod realised that it was the iron will of people like Mick, the embodiment of those early struggles, that built this country, making Australia the great place that it is today.

OUTBACK SUMMER

"MICK TALLON"

Robert Coenraads
2024

At the end of the evening Mick told Rod that tomorrow he was heading back out to the Station for the rest of the summer.

"If ever y' get the chance y' can come out and stop with me an Charlie for a while at 'Toorale', Rod," he told him. "We'll have some good tucker and good yarn then, ay?

Rod made sure that he took careful note of that name on a handy beer coaster, just in case.

"Thanks mate," Rod shook Mick's calloused hand, holding it firmly, perhaps, a little longer than normal. "Y' just never know when the chance for a visit might pop up some day."

Later that evening, before turning in for the night, as he stepped out of the shower, reaching for his towel, Rod caught sight of himself in the full-length, wood-framed mirror on the bathroom wall. Light and shadows from the ceiling bulb playing on his body caused him to stop for a moment. His shoulders seemed broader and his arms thicker and stronger than he remembered and he noticed the chiselled lines of his back spreading out of his lean torso; how they rippled beneath his skin as he moved. It's got to be all the tough physical work I've been putting in each day, he concluded, as he couldn't recall noticing that effect before. Rod realized his body was changing, evolving, adapting to a life of toil upon the land. He lifted his arm and casually flexed a bicep, watching it swell into a hard ball, well-defined beneath his thin skin. He reflected on how adeptly the human body responded to demands placed upon it, and on how his chosen career of geology, combined beautifully the rigours of keen scientific investigation with the hard physical demands of field work. He was glad he'd chosen to study that discipline or, perhaps, how it seemed to have chosen him.

He was darker too than he remembered ever having been before. He'd gone lobster on day one, peeled, and then turned brown in summer's annual rite of passage. It's the long afternoons at the pool, Rod decided, looking at the pencil-sharp outline of his board shorts—the deep golden tan coloured skin of his back in stark contrast with the creamy white skin below. Rod moved closer to the mirror, carefully studying his face. He ran his fingers over the bronze skin of his cheeks—it was now about the same colour as his sun-bleached brown hair, so dark in fact that his blue eyes and white teeth seemed to shine strangely. He thought about the girls at the pool. They were all that colour too—a glorious golden brown—all except poor Donna that is, Rod remembered, his lips curling into a mischievous smile, always complaining about the heat and the sun. Tomorrow, he'd ask her what was up with her 'melanin' levels.

Rod enjoyed the feel of his freshly-showered skin, stroking his face gently, as he imagined how Beth's skin would feel the same way. The other day he'd brushed against her leg at the pool, remembering the electric moment, how it felt—firm and silky, like a downy peach. Rod imagined gently kissing her now, his emotions heightening as their smooth skins pressed together in deep embrace.

"Shave the bum-fluff off your face and grow yourself a proper geologist's beard," René challenged the other day. However, such a chore could wait for a future time. Right now, a bristly beard didn't quite fit into his sensual contemplations.

CHAPTER 8. THE CARRIERS' ARMS, CHIEF'S PUB

A NIGHT OR SO LATER, Rod found himself passing the Carriers' Arms Hotel on Mitchell Street. He'd been past it several times on his nightly walks but hadn't been inside. It was one René expressly told him not to visit— 'the worst of the bunch,' he'd said.

It was smallish and plain, a single-story, blue-and-white-painted building. An awning reaching out from the tin roof, stretched over the footpath. Although, the Carriers' wasn't much to look at from the outside, it was steeped in local lore. René liked to share the town's history with his cousin at any opportunity.

"When the overland route replaced the riverboats on the Murray-Darling, the Carriers' Arms became the staging point for Cobb & Co Transport Company in Bourke; the resting point for wagons and stage coaches on their journey north-westwards to Brewarrina."

René said the poet, Henry Lawson[9], frequented the Carriers'—sent Back o' Bourke by his editor to 'dry out' during the drought of '91 and '92. He stayed in the shack across the road from the pub. Nowadays the derelict shack had a distinct lean to it. "Riddled with termites," René said, "so they'll pull her down one of these days; a real pity to lose that bit of history..." Mick knew of Lawson too, so that bloke must've got around[9].

Lawson hated Bourke, a dry dusty hellhole, to quote his own poetry;

"*...there was nothing beautiful in Ninety-one and Ninety-two... Save grit and generosity of hearts that broke and healed again—The hottest drought that ever blazed could never parch the hearts of men ...*" (Bourke by Henry Lawson)

But, like many, he loved the undying mateship of its hard-working, hard-fighting, hard-drinking folk declaring the place to be 'mateship country'. Lawson said, 'if you know Bourke, you know Australia.'

Despite his best intentions to follow his cousin's sage words, Rod was curious, deciding then he would go inside and check out Lawson's pub—for sure he felt nervous, but it would just be a quick visit!

Rod pushed through the main doors into the blue-haze-filled, dimly-lit interior of the Carriers' Arms, his ears greeted by the familiar buzz of conversation. He just wanted to have a quick look around so thought to buy a drink and sit quietly for about five minutes. The place was not that full, a barman and perhaps a dozen people dotting a few bar stools and chairs arranged around several round wooden tables, the scene dimly lit by the yellowish glow from wrought-iron lamps on the wall. He could feel the inquiring gaze of the patrons following him as he walked to the bar, paid for his lemon squash and sat down at one of the stools with a good view of the room. At a table towards the middle of the room, he noticed an elderly gentleman, the dark weathered skin of his face offset by his white beard and hair. It was hard to say exactly how old he was, but he had such a masterful bearing. Was it the shape of his shoulders, or the way he sat, or perhaps the fact that he was doing the talking as the other two younger men listened?

"Hey son, come over here and join us." Was the old man talking to him? Rod looked around. Had he been carelessly staring at them?

Rod picked up his glass and walked over to the table. "Er... hello," he nodded.

Sit down over here awhile, son." The old man motioned towards a vacant chair. "Would you like a beer?"

"Er...no thank you." Rod replied, not quite sure what to say. "I already have a drink." He placed his nearly-full glass of squash on the table and took a seat.

The two younger men smiled. "Where y' from," one of them asked. The old man, whom they called 'Chief' listened quietly as they went through the familiar question and answer session.

At length Chief spoke. "So as a geologist y' must know a fair bit about the land." He was mildly testing him, exploring just how much he knew, Rod could sense it.

"Yeah," Rod replied, carefully measuring out his words, responding to Chief's test. "Every day our understanding grows as we walk it; learn more about it; explore it. We're looking deeper than anybody else who's ever been there before." He was beginning to realize how differently the people out here felt about the land; how much more a part of their lives it was compared to the city folk. In the big smoke, land didn't seem to mean anything much more than a place to build your house. In fact, he'd really never thought much about it before—the land was all covered over by buildings, asphalt, concrete or well-manicured grass; imprisoned beneath all of that, but out here the land was so free; untamed.

"Our people once roamed over all of these parts," the Chief reminisced. "Way before the town was here, following the Darling and the Warrego rivers, north and south, east and west with the seasons." Chief spoke like he had been there since the beginning, while the other two men, Sammy and Eddie, listened intently, nodding in agreement every now and then.

Chief, Sammy and Eddie must be descended from the original inhabitants of this area, Rod realized, excited by the prospect of talking to them, of hearing their stories. They weren't coal black like he imagined, perhaps only a little darker than any of Bourke's other sun-bronzed inhabitants, although it was difficult to say for sure in the dimly lit interior of the Carriers' Arms, and their plain working clothes were no different to his or anyone else's.

What were you thinking, Rod? He chastised himself, perhaps a little disappointed by the normality of everything about them. Did you really think they'd still be running around stark naked and carrying spears?' His mind drifted to the colonial paintings in the art gallery. How stupid, Rod reflected, that he could have even imagined they should be any different to anyone else.

"The river was our lifeline flowing through the billabong and swamp country of the floodplain," the Chief continued, carrying Rod's mind from the present back into a magic story world, painting pictures with his eloquent words, bringing his tales to life. "The river brought us fish and water, renewing our land season after season." Rod sensed Chief's deep love and respect for the land, as he waxed more poetic. Powerful scenes of these earlier times played in Rod's mind as he quietly listened. There was something spiritual about the way Chief looked at the land through his forefather's eyes. Rod sorely wished he could go back and experience those times past.

"Every summer the water snake awoke with the rains," the Chief continued. "It rose out of its channel and covered the river country, spreading out for miles and miles. The serpent became one with the land. It sang for the billabong birds and the eagles, and they would come. Our Baaka river called life forth from the dry parched earth."

OUTBACK SUMMER

"CHIEF AND HIS MATES"

Robert Coenraads
2025

It began to dawn upon Rod that the Chief's River serpent was part of a web-work of green highways crisscrossing the land, access ways for the ancient peoples travelling through Australia's dry, parched interior lands; superhighways full of water and lined with abundant life.

"Look at it now," one of the men spat bitterly, breaking Chief's spell, "a brown and sick old snake, trapped and slowly dying in its white man's cage. She's mostly dry nowadays, so y'd better enjoy it while she lasts, Rod."

Rod wished Sammy hadn't spoken; he had broken into the delicate crystal sphere of his dreamy imaginings, filling his mind with a filthy image; the one of the stinking brown snake lying dead and broken, buzzing with blowflies, alongside the Mitchell highway by the Doradilla turnoff. Rod knew exactly where it was, right where René slowed up to take the turn, and every morning he would have to wind his window up. He imagined the asphalt highway, the white man's black snake, running straight as an arrow, bare and hot and lined with road kill; dead straight for 200 kilometres, cutting an indecent swathe right through the ancient landscape. Rod understood where Sammy was coming from—his feelings of bitterness. The settlers had come, damming and draining the river, ruining their sacred land. They stripped it bare, ploughing it up, in their quest to conquer it.

"I've told y' before, Sammy," the Chief countered. "The river's not dead. D' y' think the levee can really hold her back if she sets her mind to it. She nearly got out the other day. She's just playin' with us a bit; givin' us a little bit of rope. Just enough t' hang ourselves. A hundred years is nothin' to her. You just wait and make damn sure y' live long enough t' see it happen."

Chief took a longer view, knowing in his heart nature could never be tamed—Rod could see that. He sat back quietly listening to the Chief's stories; he was captivated by the Chief's wisdom, as he too understood the power of time—four thousand, six hundred million years of it to forge today's Earth; time enough to crush a mighty ocean and push its twisted buckled sea floor kilometres into the air; turning sea into mountains, and mountains back into sea; time after time again.

But just then, the warm hypnotic ebb and flow of the evening was smashed completely. Sammy looked up, a look of sheer panic on his face as a large woman with curly black hair pushed her way through the doors of Carriers', wild eyes searching the room, her face matching the colour of her vivid red dress, flushed with anger.

"Where's that filthy mongrel dog?" She yelled. "If I get my hands on him, I'll kill 'im." Rod had never seen a woman look that angry before.

Sammy seemed to slump lower in his chair as if trying to make himself invisible, his face white as a sheet, and a look of sheer terror in his eyes.

As the woman caught sight of him, he leapt out of his chair like a scared rabbit, heading straight for the kitchen, making for the back door.

"I thought I'd find y' in here, y' good for nothin' bastard." She picked up an empty glass from the counter and threw it after him. The glass sailed past Rod's head, closer than comfort, smashing on the floor behind Sammy as he bolted through the kitchen. "Get y'rself home y' useless drunken bastard," she screamed, charging back out of the main doors of the Carriers', her ferocious shape blurring past the outside windows as she tore around the corner to try and head him off.

Rod was in shock but, looking around the room, he could see that nobody else seemed to have even raised an eyebrow over the incident. He looked back at Chief and Eddie, eyes wide in disbelief.

"Not to worry, mate, same thing happens every payday without fail," Eddie chuckled knowingly. "Makes a man glad he's single! That way you can do as y' please." Behind them, the barman resignedly swept the broken glass into a dustpan.

It was late by then and, after all of that commotion, Rod decided that it was time to head home. "Do y' come here often, Chief? I really want t' hear more about the river and the land. If y' don't mind, I mean?"

"You're welcome here anytime, son." The old Chief studied Rod thoughtfully.

"The Chief's here most afternoons till closing time," Eddie added. "I usually pick him up and bring 'im home again."

That evening Rod told René where he'd been; he wasn't one for keeping secrets from his cousin and, besides, he was too excited not to, figuring that what was done was done.

"Old Chief and his mates are just great, René, and they're harmless really," he enthused, carefully editing out the details of Sammy's angry wife and his own close call with the flying beer glass. "You've gotta come along too one day and hear some of their stories."

"I'm glad your evening went well," René concluded resignedly. "I suppose if you're sitting down listening to an old man's tales and only drinking lemon squash, nothing should go too badly wrong. I'm happy to leave it up to you, Rod, but just don't go expecting too much out of them down there at the Carriers' Arms."

After that first night, Rod often retuned to the Carriers' Arms, sometimes just for a few minutes, sometimes longer, and even once with his cousin, who'd joined him, perhaps, more out of curiosity to see what his young charge was getting up to, than anything else. Without fail, Rod would always find the Chief sitting at his table, either by himself or with Eddie, Sammy or a few others. Chief would greet him with a big smile and they would talk about the land, the river country and its seasonal cycles. Rod listened eagerly to all the Chief had to say, stories that set his imagination on fire.

From time to time, Rod shared stories of his own discoveries—what hidden secrets science was revealing bit by bit, unlocking the secret mineral riches of the Doradilla line of lode.

"I'm really starting to get a feeling about that connection you're talking about Chief. I can feel it sometimes when I'm out there working each day."

"It's not that hard to find, Rod. I can see you're trying, but ya just have to be open to it and it'll come to you naturally."

Although Chief listened to all he had to say with interest, Rod realized that Chief and his people's relationship with the land went far deeper than his own, it was more intimate. They had a primordial bond that someone, like him, from the city could never achieve unless he chose to get out. He'd been insulated from it all this time because of the way he lived—all day, all night, always locked inside one building or another, or perhaps on a road between the two, never realising there could be something deeper and more powerful. These people were the land and the land owned these people; they were one. Rod was sure that Mick, the drover's cook, would understand their deep connection.

Yes, Rod felt a wave of gratitude surge over him at Chief's sage words of encouragement. He felt sure that just by being here, living and working on this country, it was growing inside him too—his own connection was wakening from a lifelong dormancy, becoming more alive day by day.

Rod wondered how it would be to have Chief for a father—a wellspring of sacred knowledge lost to the modern world. During those evenings at the Carriers', Rod felt like a son, privileged to gain a lifetime's knowledge. Drinking in Chief's words, his desire burned to become one of the nomadic folks; a tracker living each day, moment by moment, reading the land. Rod's imagination transported him to those early times, naked and brown, hunting and gathering beneath the burning desert sun. He walked proudly alongside

Chief, learning about different berries and seeds—how to crush and grind the seed into flour using nardoo stones, heavy flat rocks secretly stashed at various campsites around the countryside; how to store the ingredients and prepare them according to age-old traditions, baking nutritious bread cakes to sustain them on their long marches. He'd be one of a lean efficient hunting pack, each member instinctively performing a particular role, perfectly coordinated like fingers on a hand. They'd track prey, sometimes for days, wearing it down to the point where they could take it as it lay prostrate on the ground. They'd trap emus and kangaroos, goannas and snakes, roasting them to perfection over hot coals till the steaming flesh came away from the bones, juicy and succulent. They'd travel in the cool of the night, navigating by the stars; using song-lines—roadmaps set to word and song, memorised over a lifetime and handed down through the generations—to guide them from waterhole to waterhole through vast tracts of featureless countryside, from boundary to boundary of their land, and beyond; living endless daily rhythms and seasonal cycles. He'd look forward to his favourite part of the day, setting camp under the river gums, relaxing in late afternoon shade, making a fire out of what lay around, sticks and bark and grass. When the river was up and times were good, they'd camp in one place a while, building huts and shelters around the edge of a billabong. There, they could feast for weeks, trapping cod in complex stone channels and shallow pools, fishing them out with a barbed spear.

"That takes a lot o' practice, y' know." Chief told Rod. "Y' gotta throw the spear back in closer than y' think 'cause the water plays tricks on you. There's nothin' better than a fresh fish done on the hot coals, Rod," Chief reminisced. "Morning's the best time 'cause the air is so still. You can hear all the sounds of the bush, an' the surface of the water's so smooth y' can tell where the fish are by their bubbles."

"One day I'll take you out there, son, just you an' me. We'll go out into the river country an' I'll show ya first hand," the Chief promised Rod with conviction, usually towards the end of most evenings. "I got my tools hidden 'round some of the swamps and billabongs. I know exactly where all of 'em are."

"What about this Sunday, Chief? Perhaps, we could go out then? It's my day off," Rod asked as he was about to head home for the evening, eager to try out some of the many new things he'd learnt about. "I could borrow the Landy and pick you up at sunrise? We could go out for the morning; to the spot you were telling me about -y' know, that waterhole out towards North Bourke?" He concluded enthusiastically.

"Maybe son, perhaps one day," Chief replied, his eyes staring dreamily into space. He'd do that sometimes Rod noticed, as if he were in his own world, beyond the time and space of the present moment. As if he were back out in the river country, no longer just sitting at a table in the Carriers' Arms, beer in his hand.

And so Rod's delightful meetings at the Carriers' washed over him, evening after evening—and he looked forward to them more and more as his feelings for the fatherly Chief grew stronger. No matter if he popped in earlier or later, they'd always be there talking.

Eddie mentioned that Chief lived near him in west Bourke as they almost always went home together, Rod recalled. Didn't he say it was in one of the last houses heading out of town towards the Weir? He hadn't visited that neck of the woods yet, but it shouldn't be too hard to find at all, Rod thought, reflecting again on how nice it was to live in a small town. "Yes!" he exclaimed on his walk home. "It'll work." I'll ask René for the Landy and call in on the Chief this weekend.

CHAPTER 9. THE OXFORD, PADDY'S PUB

"G'DAY MATE. How're ya going?" Rod called enthusiastically, pulling himself out of the water as Paddy O'Sullivan sauntered over to join the group on the grass by the diving boards. Rod could always count on the rest of the gang being there when he arrived at about half past three, while it was often Paddy's custom to show up a little after him.

"Y'r gettin' pretty bloody good at those double somersaults now," Paddy replied, looking at his student proudly.

"Thanks only to you, mate!" Rod appreciated Paddy's ongoing instruction and his almost-spiritual approach to mastery of the high board—and with all that constant practicing, smacking into the water, time after time, until his eardrums and sinuses ached, he was pleased to hear Paddy call him a pretty good diver.

"Dan, come here," Paddy instructed. "Here's a dollar. Go get us a drink, would ya mate? Pineapple for me and what'll it be for you Rod? And grab one for yourself while you're at it."

"Rice's cola, thanks mate," Rod replied, sitting down on his towel next to Paddy. They'd become closer over the past few weeks, but there was something deeper to Paddy, something darker, that Rod couldn't quite put his finger on; something simmering just below the surface, some smouldering anger or pent-up frustration. It never affected his relationship with Paddy, though Rick and Dan seemed almost scared of him, a kind of reverential fear. No one else in the group crossed swords with him either. In that way Paddy naturally assumed leadership of the gang.

Later, as they chatted by the turnstiles about to head home after yet-one-more lazy summer's afternoon at the pool, cool-skinned in the mellow reddening sunlight, sodden towels rolled around wet swimmers, Paddy drew Rod aside.

"Hey Rod, do y' reckon y'd like t' come meet some of my mates? Perhaps, we could get together for a bit of a yarn and a drink."

"Yeah, let's go down the main street to the Elysian and have a milkshake, or perhaps Morrall's for a pie? What about tomorrow arvo?" Rod replied without thinking too much about what Paddy was saying. "Do ya wanna bring the girls along?"

"The Elysian! Girls! A milk-bloody-shake!" Paddy replied incredulously narrowing his eyes at Rod. "Don't you go to the pub with your mates? A bloke like you from the city?" Paddy paused, waiting now for him to answer, to explain himself.

Rod sensed he'd said something wrong. Paddy was challenging him, staring at him. He paused a moment before replying.

"Sure I go to the pub, mate. Just last night I was at the Carriers' Arms. I go there all the time." Rod returned Paddy's stare, standing his ground.

"The Carriers Arms!" A surprised look came across Paddy's face. "What're y' doing going in there? That's a black pub," he said incredulously. "Didn't they throw you out?"

A black pub! That's ridiculous! How could there be such things as 'black' or 'white' pubs in modern society? Rod rolled the concept around in his mind. The Chief's an Aboriginal Elder, Eddie and Sammy are Aborigines too, and all the others drinking there, were fairly dark skinned. He'd never entertained the thought, but could it be that he was the only white bloke in there? After another pause, he answered Paddy.

"Nah mate, I keep a low profile. But I try not to stay too late as it can get a little rough," he paused, then added with a hint of embellishment. "The chairs and tables have to be bolted down in there, y' know and I reckon they'd bolt down the glasses too if they could, to stop them from flyin' around the place." It was a boldfaced lie, Rod knew it, and in the back of his mind he also knew he was betraying Chief and everyone else who went there—propagating a myth, the fear that everyone seemed to have of the place. Even René had never been in there until the other week. Rod softened his tone.

"I meet with Chief and his friends there. There's never any trouble with them. Chief's a great bloke and he's got so many stories about how life used to be, life before Bourke became a town."

Paddy was quiet for a bit. "Do y' go anywhere else then?" His tone had changed.

"Sure, sometimes I'll go to the Royal, the Post Office, the Central Australian, the Federal, the North Bourke Hotel, the RSL and the Bowling Club." Rod rattled off as many names as he could remember from the list of the town's hotels and clubs.

"What about the Oxford, mate? That's my watering hole?" Paddy asked.

Watering hole? Rod reflected, realising he hadn't given the concept much thought. He thought again about the Carriers' Arms knowing he could lay a sure bet he'd find the Chief there tonight. I guess people are creatures of habit, they won't go somewhere else, so it makes sense. He'd forgotten to mention the Oxford in his list. Rod paused briefly to carefully consider his answer.

"No, I haven't been to the Oxford yet."

"Right then Rod, I'll buy you a drink there tonight and introduce you to m' mates." Paddy announced before sauntering off.

"Righto mate," Rod agreed, recoiling somewhat at the thought of having drinks bought for him. He'd only recently become old enough to go to the pub, but that milestone too, he'd allowed to discreetly pass uncelebrated in his life. Some of his mates went to the Greengate in the elegant North Shore suburb of Killara to celebrate their coming of age—sculling from a yard glass before a cheering fan club, proving their manhood by seeing how much amber fluid they could chug down before collapsing into lifeless piles on the floor. He'd seen what it was like at parties; how stupid everyone acted, especially Freddie, throwing up everywhere. So, he'd pulled back, hiding in his studies, never bothering with hotels—that is until he came to Bourke.

"So, you're gonna leave us out tonight, are ya mate?" Dan said, spokesman for the small huddle backgrounding in on the conversation. "Paddy's never asked us t' go meet his mates, and now he's askin' you," Dan added with a hint of envy in his voice. He looked disappointed.

"Don't worry about it mate, next year it'll be our turn too," Ricky said expectantly. "Y' know they wouldn't let us in anyway Dan, even if Paddy did ask us. My dad took me for a look at his pub once. He's gonna take me there for my eighteenth."

"Yeah, don't worry about it. I gotta go to this thing tonight, but you guys have everything you need right here at the pool, out in the fresh air and sunshine." Rod answered Dan and Ricky, looking around at the others who'd come over now that Paddy was gone.

"You've got the water, the high boards, shady trees to lie under and the girls t' talk to. What more do you need?" Rod continued, trying to justify himself while they were still listening. "If y' go to the Elysian, they've got food and drink, and it doesn't stink of smoke an' beer in there. You can't buy anything but a beer in the pub. Beer's a waste of money and it's dearer than anything from the kiosk."

"But I just heard y' say you've been to all the pubs?" Dan answered testily. "So why are ya telling us not to go to them now?"

"Well, y' can bloody-well think what you like then," Rod replied, disappointed with himself for his earlier bravado and the fact that they weren't getting his drift. Somehow, he'd touched a raw nerve; Dan was taking it completely the wrong way.

"Anyway, who'd wanna go see a bunch of old blokes sitting round on bar stools in a smoke filled room drinkin' beer and tellin' a bunch of stories when y' could be here?"

"So y're just gonna leave us out then?" Dan finished.

"Look, all I'm trying to say is that I wouldn't be in such a hurry to go to the pub."

"Well, tell us what're they like then?" Ricky piped up eager for more details. "Which one do you reckon is the best? Have you gotten into any fights yet?"

"They're all the same," Rod replied, exasperated, realising they would never get it, no matter what he said. They just didn't have the experience.

"As for the fights, they're always gonna be there if you want 'em. It's up to you I suppose," he concluded.

Rod pushed through the turnstile gate and made his way down Mertin Street, the last of the sun's afternoon rays filtering through the green treetops. The great day he'd been having had lost its edge since Paddy caused Rick and Dan to start on him. What in the hell had he done wrong? Was it because he'd made light of an important ritual in their lives, criticized the symbolic beacon of their impending manhood? Rod imagined a shining lighthouse, standing proud at the entrance to a harbour, its beams drawing all the small boats, like moths, into the calm of its waters—their final destination. But just how safe was this haven really? The last thing he wanted was problems with his gang, and just when he thought it couldn't get any worse, he looked up to a menacing sound, the now-familiar rumble of a motorcycle engine. It was Dark Rider cruising slowly toward him along Mertin Street. The black visored helmet swivelled, fixing on him, as the bike slowly passed. Rod shrunk under the glare of piercing hatred, turning away from the malice emanating from those unknown eyes masked by the smoked visor. Glancing back, he wondered what was going to happen as the motorcycle slowed, pulling off the road onto the gravel near the pool entrance. Dark Rider beckoned with a leather clad arm and Dan ran out from the crowd still gathered by the turnstile. He leapt deftly onto the back of the bike. Dark Rider gunned the machine and, in a spectacular spray of gravel, sped away.

"Damn," Rod swore, Dark Rider's gotta be Dan's elder brother, and now he knows I'm hanging out with them at the pool. He's gonna ask Dan about it for sure.

Later that evening, Rod sat at the dining room table with René who was busy with the day's bookwork. "What's this all about 'black' hotels? Today at the pool, they were telling me the Carriers' Arms is a blacks-only pub."

René looked up from his work. "You're not going to find anything in the law books about that. There's no such thing as a black pub, or a white one for that matter," he paused for a moment, considering his next sentence, "but most of the time it just works out like that anyway."

"What do you mean, 'works out' that way? No one's ever stopped me from going into the Carriers'. You came there with me yourself. There weren't any 'Aboriginals Only' signs."

"Look Rod," René continued. "If the Aboriginals end up quarrelling drunk in the pub every pay-day, then that pub's going to get a reputation for being trouble. People out for a quiet drink won't want to go there; they'll get scared and they'll start going somewhere else. You know for yourself that it can get rough in the Carriers'. People worry about the blacks causing trouble, starting fights, so in most pubs they won't make them feel welcome. They'll call the police and toss them out at the first hint of trouble, and that's just the way it is," René explained. "There's no law about it, but it turns out like that anyway; you always end up with black pubs and white pubs."

"Did you notice how the tables are bolted to the floor in the Carriers Arms, René?" Rod ventured, deciding to repeat what he'd told Paddy, to weigh it into the conversation—testing René's reaction to that strange fact.

"That's so they can't throw them around, Rod, and that's why nobody in their right mind ever goes to the Carriers." René studied Rod's face resignedly, forehead creased with worry. "I know that you like talking to the

Chief, and I know you won't get into too much trouble with him about, but I really want you to promise me again you'll take care in there." René concluded emphatically. "The chance of an accident or a fight in a place like that is way higher than elsewhere else in town."

"No, you're right." Rod answered, wishing he hadn't brought up the chairs and tables story. René was normally sparse with cautionary words, reserving his sage advice for only the most critical of situations, so Rod accepted his concern, wondering again how the Carriers' and its patrons could have come to gain such a terrible reputation. "I promise I'll be very careful."

That evening after dinner Rod headed off. He wished he was going to the Carriers, but instead cut through Central Park, taking the short walk along Glen Street towards the Oxford Hotel. He approached the illuminated Toohey's sign, visible at a distance glowing like a beacon atop the low-set verandahed building. He felt a rising nervous anticipation, wondering how he would fit into Paddy's group dynamic and its established protocols, keenly aware that being bought a drink meant he would no longer be free to do as he pleased. He would become bound by the rules of well-established custom with which he had very little experience.

Rod pushed through the front doors of the pub into the noisy, smoke-filled room; into the typical scene he, by-now, expected, despite never having been in there before. He spotted Paddy with five of his mates settling down at a table by the bar and, figuring that they had just arrived a few minutes earlier, he headed over.

"G'day Paddy. How are y' going mate?" Rod called over the din, nervous about meeting Paddy in this environment. He'd much prefer the open space and informal setting of the pool.

"G'day Rod." Paddy turned, hand extended, smiling. "Glad y' could make it mate. This is Bald Pig and Little Pig." He introduced the two stocky blokes next to him.

Rod shook their hands, studying their faces and noting the appropriateness of their nicknames. Judging by their identical puffy pink skin, dribbling upturned snouts and beady eyes, they had to be brothers. He wisely refrained from a momentary urge to ask the obvious question; whether there was a middle pig in the family.

"And this is Blue and Oyster. Brad hasn't shown up yet." Paddy concluded the formalities.

As expected, Blue was the one with bright red hair and beard, his crest reminding Rod of a rooster in heat. As for the full-lipped Oyster, Rod was sure that his story would come out in the fullness of the evening.

"What beer are y' drinkin, Rod?" Paddy asked, getting up to buy the first round.

"Anything 'll do mate," Rod replied instinctively, giving the safest answer possible. He had little idea of what brand of beer was what. Tooheys seemed to be advertised everywhere, but with State rivalries, regional preferences, and strong town allegiances, to hazard an incorrect guess could have been a complete disaster. In fact, he really didn't want to have a beer at all, he didn't even like the taste, but it was one of those uncomfortable situations, or at least uncomfortable for him, where he felt there was no way out; no way to say 'no'.

Of course he could have always said, 'no thanks mate, I'll pass,' without too much difficulty, but somehow, he felt compelled to say 'yes', compelled to accept Paddy's offer of good will and friendship. To not do so would be a slight on Paddy and his group of friends, an offence, a rejection of their hospitality, and, as such, he would become an outcast.

Rod sensed how the evening would play out. Two hundred years of Australian custom, tradition and mateship was involved in the drinking rite he was now a part; a ritual of rounds that could last as long as the number of people in the group, twice that number, or even three times or more, and would likely go on all the way to 10:00 pm closing time.

He hadn't noticed it before in his one-on-one meetings with the Chief or Mick, but now, in here with these 'tough young guys' he sensed how the power of the group dynamic worked. If he went along with it, he'd be lured in by a convivial atmosphere of interesting yarns and tales, bravado and bluff; his resolve weakened by alcohol; and led into a sticky web, against which any struggle would be futile. Rod felt that subtle something in Paddy's character again; it was stronger in this environment, different to how he was at the pool. Was it real what he sensed, Rod asked himself, or was it just him? Perhaps was it because he was being compelled to perform in a certain prescribed ritual in here, sitting in this strange commercial environment, without the freedom to swim, dive or walk about. Rod wasn't sure, but something in the Oxford was putting him on edge; nowhere near as relaxed as he was at the pool.

"PADDY AND HIS MATES"

Robert Coenraads
2024

"Thanks mate." Rod smiled, taking the schooner from Red's outstretched hand and raising it in salute. "Thanks for inviting me here to meet y'r mates, Paddy."

He sipped gingerly at the frothy pale-amber liquid, grimacing inwardly at its bitter aftertaste. It'd have to be nearly as bad as chilled cat's piss! he reflected. 'What's the big deal about it anyway?'

Rod made himself relax, leaning back in his chair at the fringe of the group, letting the ebb and flow of the evening wash over him. After a while he began to feel more comfortable, sitting back listening to stories, enjoying how Paddy and his mates, obviously well-versed in the age-old art of storytelling, took turns in telling them; casting out a few choice facts, baiting them with a snippet of gossip, reeling back the listeners with just the right amount intrigue and suspense, until finally hooking them with the punch line. His mind began to wander. Chief, Eddie and Sammy would be doing the same thing over at the Carriers right now, telling their stories.

A while later, Rod looked down at his glass which was still nearly full, with another one lined up next to it that somebody else had bought, and it gradually dawned upon him that he didn't want to spend his evening, spend his whole life for that matter, sitting down listening to drinking tales or telling stories about what he was going to do with his life if he weren't just so damn busy listening to stories at the pub. This could end up going on all night, each and every night at any of a dozen pubs and clubs around town, he realised—if the publicans had their way. Crikey, thank goodness for 10 pm closing time, he reflected idly, thinking about that rule of law; the only saving grace for those who needed it. What if I had a family to get home to, or what if I couldn't afford to drink away my pay? Once you were in the routine, there was no way to break from your circle of drinking mates, to break the grip of the great Aussie tradition, without losing face—without losing your mates?

But just then his resolve strengthened; something changed his mind. He began to see everything clearly from a higher perspective, like sitting on a mountain top looking down upon all of the people leading their routine lives in the village below. No, he didn't even want to hang around till 10 pm.

"You've finally made it, mate—better late than never!" Paddy's voice rose above the rest, silencing the drone of conversation around him, cutting into Rod's deliberations.

A black-haired leather-clad figure pushed through the pub door, helmet under his arm. He'd spotted Paddy and was moving towards the table. His dark face scanned the room, eyes locking briefly on Rod, registering his presence, before searching on.

Rod blinked in surprise, recognising him immediately as Dark Rider. A jolt of adrenalin hit him in the chest: Things couldn't get too much worse—Dan's elder brother was one of Paddy's mates.

"Brad, this is Rod, the new boy in town. He's one of the pool gang now."

"Yeah, Dan's told me all about him." Dark Rider spoke softly, his measured and calm words barely hiding his menace.

"Er…. Hello…" Rod instinctively fumbled out his right hand, then, realising that Brad wasn't going to acknowledge him, pulled it back awkwardly. He lowered his eyes to the floor, face beginning to redden, hoping the others hadn't noticed.

Brad turned away to greet the others, joining the circle of mates. He took a stool on the opposite side of the table: His dark eyes still fixed on Rod.

"Rod's become quite a hit with the girls," Paddy continued, holding the floor, playing the ringleader. "They've all taken quite a fancy to him—especially Donna. She won't stop talking to him. 'Hard Rod' we're gonna have to call him now, I reckon."

"Tell us more then, mate, one of the pig brothers snorted. Their eyes glistened excitedly, upturned snouts almost dribbling with expectation. "When's it gonna happen with four-eyes then?" the other asked.

"Come on then mate," Blue weighed in, "don't hold back on us now."

Rod remained silent, still looking down, desperately wishing the questioning would cease. Paddy was no help, egging on the conversation, making him the centre of attention.

"Beth's the one I want," Oyster leered open-mouthed. "What a bombshell. Have y' checked her out lately … Maaaate!" Really grown up she has. Y' couldn't have missed seeing her at the pool, ay Rod? What d' y' reckon about her, maaate?"

Rod reddened, still looking down. He couldn't deny his feelings for Beth, imagining her at the pool, bronze-skinned, lying on the grass in her aqua bikini—the truth was he couldn't take his eyes of her when she was around. Three glasses of beer now stood on the table in front of him.

"Fresh from high school, maaate!" Bald Pig grunted rhythmically, rocking back and forth on his bar stool. He looked across at his little brother. "Better than fighting over them tired old sluts under North Bourke Bridge, ay mate?"

"Yeah, too right Baldy."

All the while Rod could feel Brad's penetrating dark silence; he'd said barely a word since arriving, just sat there. He'd reached rock bottom, the situation spiralling completely out of his control.

"Righto, we'll leave Rod with the four-eyed shag-on-a-rock. Oyster, you can have bombshell Beth, I'll get stuck into Trish, an' you two Pigs can fight over the old tart under the bridge," Blue summarised, his red crest seeming to swell with excitement. "Trisha's become a real spunk an I reckon she'd be a goer too."

Oyster's rubbery lips quivered excitedly as he puckered them in anticipation, while the Pig brothers slapped each other on the back, snorting with laughter, tickled pink to be part of Blue's story.

Blue continued, mercifully drawing the conversation away from Rod. "They weren't much t' look at when we were in school. Do ya remember how we used to follow them home and tease them on the way?"

Rod seized the moment. Most of the others were down to about their last quarter glass-full, and the conversation had swung around to their antics at high school. He got up from his stool.

"It's my shout. What'll it be this round, boys?" He carefully noted each of their orders, which was easy because they were all, without fail, "a schooner of Tooheys, thanks mate," and headed to the bar. He placed the order, added a lemon squash, which he tossed down on the spot to wash away the evening's beery aftertaste, paid the barman, and returned with the tray of drinks to the table, just as Blue was setting the scene for the next story—the one about how Oyster got his nickname.

Rod politely took his leave. "Nice t' meet all you blokes." He stood up. "I promised to help René get a few things ready, and then we've got a four o'clock start in the morning." Rod figured the only rival to the great Australian drinking tradition was the nation's solid work ethic. No matter what, each and every one of these blokes would front up to work without fail—either in a fit state or otherwise—and when it came to the crunch, would never let down a mate. They would all understand. He had to go do his duty.

"Nah! You don't have t' go yet, do ya mate? Y' gotta finish your drinks first," Bald pig grunted.

"We've still gotta hear if Donna's gonna get the real hard rod," Little Pig added.

Rod smiled lamely, ignoring the request. He turned to Paddy. "And thanks again for the invite, mate..."

"Hey Paddy, why don't y' get the new bloke out pig shooting with us," Brad cut in darkly. "Or what do y' reckon I show him the Killing Room?" It was the most Rod heard him say all evening.

"The Killing Room challenge," the pig brothers squealed in unison. "Yeah, take him to the Killing Room, Brad. What day do y' wanna do it, mate?"

Paddy and his friends nodded knowingly, as Rod turned and left the Oxford without a further word.

He hurried towards home, hunched over, hands thrust deeply into his pockets, glancing back at the pub once or twice, straining at anything sounding like a motor. 'Bloody evening couldn't have gone worse,' he reflected.

"Damn it! Bloody Paddy and his bloody mates," he swore. Now Brad knows my name and everything else about me. "Why does he hate me so much and what have I ever done to him?

"And that's all I bloody well need," he murmured. "Is that a man, or a pig, with a gun over there[10]?" No way I'm going hunting with those hoons; they'll probably end up shooting each other in the head—and what's all this about a bloody killing room?

He wondered how much of this would get back to the gang.

CHAPTER 10. TROUBLED WATERS

ROD SWUNG the long-handled slash hook deftly from side to side under the broad outback sky feeling the heat of the sun through the back of his shirt. He could fell a gidgee bush taller than himself in two powerful strokes—striking first from the left, down at an angle, the sharp blade biting into the base of the trunk below the branches; then back from the right. If he got the position just right, the two cuts would meet in a shallow vee and the shrub would fall under its own weight leaving a low stump. Kicking the fallen branches aside he'd deftly move on to the next.

He could feel himself becoming stronger, more skilled as the summer days and weeks wore on; his muscles bigger, harder, rippling beneath his shirt as he moved. He was sure this was the way human beings were meant to live, outdoors, doing hard physical work the body could thrive on, not sitting still all day in a dark office. Dan's lanky frame drew up behind him, bringing the sledgehammer, while Ricky followed faithfully behind pulling the long white tape through the path they'd just carved though the bush, then big barrel-chested Mark would follow up, carrying a heavy bundle of pegs. Rod measured each one out a further 50 metres from the previous, numbering its white-painted top before driving it into the red ground with the sledgehammer. Once he'd planted two pegs on either side of the baseline, the rest of them could be lined up perfectly by eye in lines that would run dead straight for kilometres, just as the Nazca had done to construct their gigantic glyphs on the Peruvian high plains a millennium and a half earlier. He was impatient for the results of the geological interpretation—it wouldn't be long now before they knew what precious ores lay hidden beneath the grid of tracks they were building—the treasure they were searching for.

Rod enjoyed laying the baseline, precisely oriented to 235 degrees magnetic, running parallel to the upturned rock beds on Doradilla, using the old brass lensatic sighting compass. Its numbered dial floated in an aqua fluid that reminded him of the Olympic pool; of the cool water he so looked forward to at the end of each day—that cherished split second of total embrace by its healing and restorative power.

Despite the tough conditions the team had pulled together well, but today they seemed unsettled. Rod couldn't put his finger on why—perhaps it was the unusually-oppressive heat. They'd just about finished for the day and were waiting for René to pick them up in the Land Rover. Rick was lying under a gidgee bush, hat over his face, living up to his well-earned nickname of 'Ricky-Rest-Time'. He'd just slaked his thirst, guzzling from his water bottle, rivulets running down the front of his t-shirt; Mark stood, hands on hips in an aggressive posture, facing Dan who sat on the ground sharpening his slash hook on the oil stone, coils of blue smoke rising from his cigarette. The tension between the two of them had been building all day, heating to boiling point. Mark had been teasing Dan; goading him to breaking point. Earlier, Ricky had tried to defend his best mate, but Rod hadn't been paying too much attention, absorbed in his notes, minding his own business. It was something about Aboriginal blood in Dan's family line, and now Mark was barking angrily at Dan. Rod's ears pricked up at the authoritative tone.

"Put out y'r bloody smoke, mate. Do y' want t' start a bloody fire? The bush will just take off in this heat." Mark ordered, his broad chest puffed out angrily, while Dan sat there lankily, head down, saying nothing.

"C'mon Mark, lay off Dan," Rod finally interjected, "and Dan, you stop getting worked up. He's just a being a big loudmouth. But it wouldn't be such a bad idea if you gave up your smoking, especially on a stinkin' hot day like today. You could start a fire out here, y' know." He hadn't said anything until now, but he wasn't keen on the tension and he didn't like smoking on site. But he realized he'd made a big mistake the moment he'd finished the last sentence.

Mark took it as support. "C'mon, mate y' heard what Rod said. Put the fag out, or I'll put it out for you."

When Dan didn't reply, didn't move a single muscle, Mark bent down, plucked the cigarette from his mouth, and butted it out, stabbing it against

Dan's chest through the open vee in his work shirt. "Do as y're bloody told, mate."

In one explosive movement, Dan was on his feet, face contorted in a mixture of surprise, pain and anger, savage intent in his eye. It was a face that could kill. Grabbing his slash hook, he swivelled his lanky body, swinging the implement viciously, without a second's hesitation. He sliced the air in a broad arc. The curved razor-sharp blade passed inches from Mark's throat, cutting a fine neat line across the front of his work shirt. At that very instant Mark had leant back, just in time, with no more than a mere split second to spare. The slash hook flew from Dan's hand, its blade biting deeply into a nearby tree. He threw himself to the ground, broken, sobbing.

Rod couldn't believe it, the scene playing through his brain in slow-motion like some old movie. Mark stood frozen in shock, his face white and expressionless; everybody was silent, speechless for what seemed like minutes, except for Ricky-Rest-Time who was still asleep under the tree, oblivious to it all. It was one of those moments, an instant in time, capable of shattering the lives of everyone involved, destroying them irreversibly and irreparably, which, by the grace of the gods, today was to pass unwritten in history's records—a story never to be told on the front page of the Bourke's Western Herald.

An eon passed in silence, each in their own world. How could it have reached this point, Rod wondered? René wasn't there so he was in charge. Should he have stopped it? But how, when he didn't even see it coming? Finally, he stated the obvious.

"Bloody hell, Mark! He nearly cut your bloody head off. You knew y' had that coming to you, didn't you mate!"

"You're gonna pay for that," Mark said, still ashen, looking down at his chest through the gaping slice across the front of his work shirt, assuring himself that he was really okay, that there was no cut, no blood.

"You try anything mate and you'll have to deal with the two of us," Ricky declared, defiant. He was alert now, on his feet, face flushed with anger. "Just nick off and leave him alone."

Afterwards at the pool, when he'd calmed down a bit, Dan opened up to Rod. Ricky stood alongside listening, always on the ready to support his mate.

"Mark's a real bastard, y' know, and he can't talk either, he's got coloured blood in him." Dan began. "His grandfather was a black tracker; he lived out in the bush at Byrock back in those days."

"Yeah, he won't ever admit it though, just because he's got blue eyes and he doesn't look like one." Ricky explained. "But we know the truth."

"Well, y' should've never lost your temper anyway. Why don't y' just forget about it. You're lucky y' didn't kill him. You'd be in jail right now instead of enjoying yourself here at the pool," Rod said, trying to change tack.

"My brother Brad's also part Aboriginal, y' know," Dan continued matter-of-factly.

"So what? Who cares who's got what blood in them?" Rod asked without thinking too much about it. He'd forgotten about the trip to the rubbish tip with René on his first day, but Dan's comments piqued his interest. He wondered why they were making such a fuss about all of this? His curiosity led him to ask on, despite his better judgement.

"Yeah, I've seen your brother about. He doesn't look any different to you or anyone else. So, what's the big deal?"

"Bein' a half breed's tough 'cause y' don't fit in anywhere, mate. You're not one of the full bloods and the whites won't have ya either. It was really hard for him at school but it toughened him up and made him the bloke he is today. My brother's got everything he wants now. He's got a good job and a nice bike," Dan concluded.

"Well, why'd he bother saying anything about it?" Rod's parents were both from Holland but he couldn't recall anyone ever making a big deal about it, even when he'd mentioned it at high school. Though, he reflected, he wouldn't have wanted to be a Wog back then either.

"Everybody's parents have to come from somewhere y' know," he suggested lamely. He couldn't think of what else to say.

"Don't matter, mate," Dan answered. "Everyone knows who y' are around here, all about your parents, grandparents, aunts and uncles, and nothing's going t' change that."

"What a load of B.S., mate!" Rod muttered, the conversation becoming way too complicated for his liking. Why should your parents matter so much to who you are or where you're going in life? He was stuck for clear words. "Everybody's nobody, mate. You start off as nothing and then y' have to study and work to become what you really wanna be."

"It doesn't work that way around here, mate. Bourke's a small town."

"Yeah right." Rod chose to leave it right there. What was Dan then? Was he part Aboriginal too? Or were several fathers and mothers coming into the picture now? He wasn't getting what Dan was telling him but could see he wasn't going to convince him otherwise. He wanted to change topic now.

"I'm heading down the main street this arvo 'cause I heard the girls talking about going to the Elysian for a milkshake. Do you and Ricky wanna come along?"

Later that afternoon they gathered at the Elysian Café, taking up an entire two tables and a booth with laughter and frivolity. Giant servings of hot chips lay in steaming heaps on a newspaper tray in the middle of each table, surrounded by a fence of rippled steel milkshake cups. Rod relaxed, his own heavy cup moist and cool in his hand, happy to be part of such a carefree scene; the same one, he imagined, being played out in every Australian country town. He loved the feeling of belonging.

Out of the café's wide fronted glass windows, a colour, a familiar movement caught his eye; the girl with the ebony hair riding her pushbike along the opposite footpath, heading towards the supermarket. He wondered idly if she might stop—perhaps attracted by all the noise and laughter emanating from within—she might come inside—but she didn't.

"Hey Rod, Dan told us that you're gonna go see Brad's killin' room," one of the girls in the booth tittered, sucking at the froth on her chocolate milkshake with a red-and-white-striped paper straw. "I wouldn't wanna do it."

"Neither would I," another added, "but I guess you've gotta do what you've gotta do. Don't ya?"

"Rod'll do it. Won't you Rod?" Donna piped up, adjusting the overly-large glasses resting on her pert upturned nose, looking disparagingly at her friends. "Nothing would ever scare him."

"Killing room?" Rod jerked, memories of his evening at the Oxford flooding back. "You've gotta be kidding. Why would I wanna go there?" Wherever 'there' was anyway, he wondered, knowing he'd look dumb if he asked. Bloody hell, it didn't take long for that news to spread itself around town!

"What?" Dan was incredulous, coming over from the other table with Rick in tow. "You're not gonna go then, mate? My brother's not gonna be happy when I tell him that."

"Yeah, he won't be pleased at all y' know," Ricky added. "Ya really gotta go, mate."

"Leave him alone you two," Beth piped up, the other girls looking around at her, surprised by her conviction. "Why should he go? Why does everybody in this town have to do whatever Brad or Paddy says anyway?"

"And they wanted me to go pig shooting too. No way José," Rod took Beth's cue, pushing forth into unchartered territory, taking the lead, giving more detail. He knew he had to justify himself after what Dan and Rick had said, on the defensive now, fearing he'd be branded a coward otherwise.

"Have you seen those two Pig brothers? I reckon it'd be like hunting down your own cousins. Y' wouldn't wanna get 'em mixed up, would you!" he laughed lamely at his own joke, realising he'd gone too far; but there was no way to take back those words now. Thankfully, the girls laughed a little too. Bald Pig and Little Pig obviously had a reputation around town, but he wondered how long it would take for his gaffe to make its way back to them.

Later that evening, over dinner, Rod filled René in about the slash hook incident.

"I don't think they're ever going to talk to each other again, René, and they're cousins and all. The atmosphere in the Landy on the way home was pretty tense."

"That's what Australian mateship is all about Rod. They'll probably settle it in a great big punch up one day, get the whole thing out of their system, and go back to being the best of mates again; thick as thieves and playing a joke on some other unsuspecting mate. Mateship's a pretty hard bond to break and, when it comes to the crunch, they'll always be there for one another in a time of real need. "But you've got to let it go Rod. Your job is to make sure that they don't hurt each other too badly in the process."

"But what are we going to do about it?" Rod pressed, fully expecting René to support Dan and help him reprimand Mark over his abusive behaviour.

"Dan shouldn't have reacted like that under any circumstances, no matter what Mark did to him. It's a hard lesson for both of them," René explained after some consideration. "Employees can't behave as they please on the job! But there's nothing much left to do about it now. You know they're all going to have to go, don't you?"

"Oh, no," Rod gasped involuntarily. He had grown to like Dan and his sidekick Rick, despite what they'd said earlier at the Elysian. They were hard working, eager to learn, and they hung out with him most afternoons at the pool. Mark was okay too, but he disliked his bullying ways, and resented him for causing all this. He dropped his eyes before replying to his cousin.

"It's all my fault then. As field team leader I should've been paying more attention. If I had, I could've packed the tools away on the back of the Landy a little earlier when I noticed something wasn't right. Instead, I just made it worse. Mark could have died because of me and now I've caused all of them to lose their jobs!" Rod hung his head miserably.

"Yes Rod, it's a hard lesson for you too. But, look, nothing happened and it was all okay in the end, and I'm sure you'll do it better next time. Sometimes there's just nothing you can do, but as a leader you have to be mindful of everything, even matters unrelated to the job you're doing."

"Can't we give them another chance, René? I'll watch everything more closely from now on, I promise." Rod made one last appeal to his cousin.

"Look Rod, don't worry yourself about it. I have to lay them off next week anyway. I told them the work was only temporary when I hired them, so they knew that. You've just about finished cutting and pegging the grid—well ahead of schedule, I might add—and now we're going to start collecting the magnetic data, pinning down the depth and angle of the ore lode so that we can get it positioned just right on the map. You'll be doing that job, and you'll only need one assistant helping so you can focus on recording the readings in the notebook. I didn't think it fair to pick just one of the three boys, so I promised that job to another young bloke looking for work; Pete Hayricks is the lad's name. Keen as mustard he was, so I reckon he'll do."

René started to pack up his things lying on the dining room table. "So, you see," he concluded, "I'm not punishing Dan or Mark for the incident by sacking them. They've worked really hard so I'd have kept them if I could. It's just a coincidence, but they've all got to go now anyway."

"Yes, I understand," Rod capitulated. Coincidence it might be, he reflected, but he was sure the boys wouldn't see it that way. Everyone knows jobs don't grow on trees around here. What was he going to tell Dan and Rick?

"Goodnight René, I'll see you in the morning."

CHAPTER 11. BETH, PETE'S SISTER

THE NEXT WEEK Rod started working with Pete, a broad-shouldered ox of a bloke, round faced with an easy-going smile, and always ready with a helping hand. They were tasked with recording the Earth's magnetic field along the grid lines, slashed and pegged by Rod's team during the past few weeks. Pete wore the instrument for the job, a proton precession magnetometer, in a chest harness, its clips straining tight around his bulky torso. He carried a tall aluminium pole, with a sensor head atop. He'd been stripped of his belt and anything else magnetic that would affect the readings. They read a number from the instrument's illuminated screen every ten metres, which Rod recorded in his field notebook along with the Texta-lettered grid coordinates from the side of each marker peg; each reading taking about 10 seconds.

Rod enjoyed the new work. He loved how the instrument sensed what was going on below the ground surface, watching the magnetic readings rise and fall as they passed over the ore body. He imagined what lay below; a deeply-buried treasure chest chock-a-block with heavy golden- and silver-coloured minerals and crystals. Chipping at the rocks with his geological hammer he'd find traces of the lode—rusty iron-rich cubes known as 'devil's dice' and greenish black copper stains along the cracks. Some evenings he would help René plot up the traverse lines and predict the best spots to drill exploration holes into the ore body.

After work they'd drop Pete off at his parents' house in town. He liked to chat a while with them before heading to his own home.

OUTBACK SUMMER

"BETH"

One afternoon, as they pulled up in front of their quaint weatherboard house with the pointy green roof, Rod noticed a girl in the front yard, immediately recognising her aqua-blue bikini.

"Hey, it's Beth, one of the girls from the pool," he told René as Pete climbed out of the Land Rover. "She must be Pete's sister? You wouldn't know it to look at them; they're chalk and cheese."

She wore huge rubber gumboots, her body and hair wet from the sprinkler she pulled about on the lawn by its hose. Rod laughed at the unusual scene—oversize black boots contrasting against her lithe tanned body.

"Hey Beth." She looked up as Rod called from the passenger window. "Are y' going to the pool this arvo?" He asked.

"G'day Rod," Beth said. "Yeah, just getting ready to leave. Pete mentioned his new job, but I didn't know you two were working together." Smiling, she came up to the window, studying the gear on their work ute, sunlight sparking from the water droplets budding on the tips of her lank hair.

"And what about you Pete?" Rod asked. "Wanna to come along with us today?"

"Nah! I wouldn't be caught dead hanging around with my sister," Pete winked at her. "I'm gonna stay home for a quiet drink with the oldies. Thanks all the same, mate." He turned, heading towards the front door of his parent's house.

"Yeah, it's a really big town, isn't it?" Rod laughed. "What about this weekend, Beth?" he continued. "You going to the pool?"

"Probably, but I don't know for sure," Beth replied. "A few of my friends are coming around to watch Countdown on TV. You can come join us if you want? See what new bands Molly Meldrum's got lined up this week."

"Yeah, that'd be great thanks Beth." Rod had no idea of what Countdown was all about, but who cares; it was an invite to spend time with Beth and her friends, and he really enjoyed hanging around with them.

"What time's it on, Beth?" he asked just before René pulled away.

"We're meeting here around six, so see you here then, ay?"

Rod had been waiting for Sunday afternoon all weekend, so after finishing the chores, he headed round to Beth's house early, arriving before the others. Her mum and dad, relaxing on the front porch in the afternoon shade, ushered him into their living room. A wood-veneer TV set stood against one wall, enjoying pride of place at the room's focal point, with a big comfy couch along the opposite wall.

"Beth… Rod's here,' her mother called. "Maybe ask him to help with your homework seeing as he goes to university." Turning towards Rod, she said, almost apologetically." It's all a bit beyond us nowadays I'm afraid."

Beth was sitting at the kitchen table on the opposite side of a curtained archway separating the two rooms, head bent forward in earnest concentration, her blonde brown hair tied back in a ponytail, exposing the graceful arch of her neckline. She was writing in an exercise book, her maths textbook open beside her and a set of logarithmic tables beside that. He took in the scene momentarily before speaking.

"G'day Beth."

"I just don't get these log tables!" She looked up at him, exasperated. "Why'd y' have to go through all of this, Rod, when y' can do it in five seconds on the calculator? But the teachers won't allow calculators and say you've gotta do it this way!"

"I really don't know, Beth," Rod replied coming around beside her, studying her books arranged on the well-worn Laminex-topped table. "The logarithmic tables have been around for a long time before calculators were invented. They're a clever, quick way of multiplying or dividing huge numbers. I guess they're paying homage to that historic fact. But I suppose they don't tell y' all that at school?"

Sitting in the chair beside Beth, Rod took a page of scrap paper and wrote down three large numbers. "Think about how long it would take to multiply these three together by hand, and now look at this." He went through the process of using the tables to convert the numbers to powers of ten, adding the three of them together, and, using anti-logs, converted the total back to a normal number, explaining each step to her in detail. "And 'hey presto' Beth, look there's the answer." He smiled at her. "Don't you think that's neat?"

"I guess I hadn't looked at it that way before. Thanks Rod." She smiled back at him, their eyes locking briefly. "Do you want to show me one more time how it's done before my friends get here?"

Despite the heat of the summer's afternoon seeping in through the curtained windows, Donna, Trish and Beth sat pressed together in a line along the couch facing the TV set. They were wearing their swimmers and shorts, their towels damp from the pool. Rod was squeezed in there too, between Beth and Donna, skin to sticky skin, closer than he would normally sit with a girl.

"I can't believe Bourke's only got the ABC. "We've got four TV channels in Sydney."

"Tell us what the other ones are like, Rod?" Donna piped up.

"Shhh Donna, not now!" Trish countered. "I can't hear what Molly's saying about this week's greatest hit."

Not until later did Rod realise he was participating in an iconic Australian tradition as Molly Meldrum, unmistakable in his signature white Akubra hat, brought the music of Australia's favourite bands into the living rooms of the nation's outback. The film clips entranced him; the hypnotic beat of the music and catchy lyrics, especially with the girls beside him swaying to their rhythm. He figured he could easily get used to spending his Sundays like this.

"Who's coming to mum and dad's wedding anniversary? They're having a party next Saturday night?" Beth announced right after Countdown finished. "They said Pete and I could ask some of our own friends along. You'll come, won't you Rod?"

"Sure, I'd love to," Rod replied, studying her pretty face. He couldn't believe Beth had asked him to come, just like that. Did that mean she liked him—perhaps just a little bit? Beth really was prettiest of the pool girls, and the blokes all thought so too. Hoping it was true; a warm feeling began spreading within him as imagined the possibility. But then he stopped himself, trying to shut down his overactive imagination, to come to his senses, worrying, too, that his face could begin to colour were he not careful. It's probably just because he was working with Pete nowadays, he reasoned, that's why she's asked.

The following Saturday, he was there. The party was quiet, mostly older friends of the family sitting out in the back yard with a smaller huddle of Pete's mates off to one side—nobody he knew other than Pete. The laminex kitchen table was out on the lawn, a glass bowl of fruit punch at centre, surrounded by an assortment of sandwiches, party pies, lamingtons and ANZAC bikkies. Rod mingled with the adults awhile, answering the usual questions asked of a newcomer to the town, then a bit with Pete's group, before drifting inside the house where Beth and her friends were sitting in the lounge room playing music and chatting idly about the latest town gossip. Rod relaxed into the scene, chatting, laughing and recognizing some of the songs he'd heard on Countdown while hanging out with the girls the previous Sunday. He found it strange how all the blokes gathered in one place with their beers and the girls in another, wondering why they didn't mix. Not wanting to transgress some social norm by spending too much time with the girls, he circulated around the party and, before he knew it, the evening had flashed past.

Later, as the party wound down, Rod went about thanking his hosts and prepared to take his leave. He met Beth around the side of the house. It was darker there, away from the party lights illuminating the front and back yards.

"Thanks for inviting me, Beth. I had a really great time." He stood facing her.

"Thanks for coming, and thanks again for your help with my maths homework the other night, I've got it now." Beth moved toward him. She was very close and, despite the heat of the night, he could feel the warmth of her skin through her clothes. Her upturned face was very near to his. Time's passage had slowed to a crawl, seconds ticking by like hours as the darkness enshrouded them.

For Rod, this was one of those 'movie moments' when the two stars, drawn together in the heat of the moment, are meant to kiss. It felt so right. Beth's face was gorgeous; even close up it was flawless, and to top that, she was so considerate, welcoming, and thoughtful. Rod could sense the intensity building, feel her warm breath on his cheek, the authenticity of her feelings for him, their strength matching his own.

"You're different from anybody else I've ever met," she whispered, "although I've never met anyone from outside of Bourke before."

Rod knew if she moved ever so slightly closer to him, they would kiss. He was burning to do that, but, in that same second, she hesitated and spoke instead.

"Rod, you're gonna have to leave Bourke an' go back to Sydney at the end of summer, right?"

She was far more pragmatic than Rod. She'd hit him with the very thought he'd pushed farthest from his mind; the horrible thought he was refusing to accept. He loved Bourke, his new friends and his work, and never wanted to leave the place. He knew his seemingly endless summer would eventually draw to a close and he would be duty-bound to return to Sydney, to the family home, to his university studies.

"Yeah, I guess I will have to, Beth." He forced himself to say it, slowly; painfully.

"I have a boyfriend, y' know Rod, his name's Steve. He left school and he's out working on the stations," Beth opened up. "We don't get on too well; we fight all the time, breaking up then getting back together again," she said quietly, her face still very close. "He wants me out there with him."

"You can't Beth. You've gotta only do what makes you happy. You're way too smart. You've gotta stay in school." Rod said it with conviction, looking deep into her eyes, searching for the smallest sign that he was getting through to her. "You really mean a lot to me, Beth, even if I have to be five hundred miles away in Sydney. And I really want to know that you're happy and not settling for second best, and doing things y' really don't want to do."

Beth's face lit up a little as she lifted it, moving slightly closer, leaning forward a fraction. Rod imagined that their lips touched, ever so lightly, just for a moment; or was he just dreaming of love, dreaming of a life with Beth that was not meant to be his[11]. He was lost for words.

"Rod, you will write to me from Sydney, won't you?" Beth finally asked. Their bodies moved apart again as somebody brushed past them in the dark driveway. The spell entwining them had been broken, its magic was fading.

"I promise I will, Beth."

CHAPTER 12. CARLA

R OD AWOKE EARLY, heading out into the cool of the outback morn just as the rising sun's red glow lit the eastern skies. He'd been waiting all week for Sunday. Within minutes he was where he wanted to be. He had a choice of three or four run-down tin houses which, softened by the morning light and a blanket of dew, looked invitingly homely. In one, a kitchen light was on, shining yellow through a small, wood frame window at the end of the house. Blue smoke curled gently from the stone chimney telling of a morning's routine already underway.

Still unsure, Rod decided to wait by the Land Rover until he either caught sight of the Chief or somebody else he could ask about where Chief lived. It wasn't long before his presence in the street attracted the attention of the person working in the kitchen window. Rod heard a bolt slide open and a stout, dark-skinned lady peered cautiously around the half-open front door.

Rod spoke first. "Er… Excuse me. Sorry to trouble you, but I'm looking for Chief. Does he live around here?" He walked towards the chicken wire fence surrounding the house.

The lady, wearing a white apron, came out to the wooden front gate, looking at him. "You're the young geologist bloke ain't you?" Her work wizened face softened. She dried her hands on the front of her apron. "Chief's talked a lot about you."

"Yes, I'm Rod Conway from Sydney, he smiled, shaking her hand. "Chief said he wants to show me the river country out past North Bourke. It's my day off so I thought I'd come round and see if he wanted to go this morning."

"I'm sorry Rod, Chief's still asleep."

"That's okay; I'll wait in the car then."

The woman leant over the gate, closer to Rod, speaking softly now. "He's not a well man, y' know."

"I'm sorry to hear that," Rod replied softly, having also moved over a little toward the fence to catch what she was saying. She spoke in little more than a whisper, barely audible. He wasn't quite sure what to make of her words. "Chief looked okay the other night. I'll come back next Sunday then, an' in any case I'll see him during the week and organise something then." He straightened, ready to turn and leave. "Tell him I called and I hope he's feeling better soon."

"He's tired and sick, Rod," the lady continued quietly, eyes downcast. She seemed embarrassed by what she was telling him. "He does the odd job around the place but most of the time he's never out o' bed much before supper, y' know. Then Eddie will come by and take 'im down to the Carriers'. That's his whole life, y' know; him and his mates at the Carriers'. He's got nothing else left."

Rod was silent, a sad and sorry picture of the old man forming in his mind; his dream, his image of the Chief, now an illusion, smashed like a broken beer glass.

"Look Rod," the lady continued. Don't tell Chief y' came 'round here lookin' for 'im. Real 'shamed he'd be if he found out y' knew about how he really lived. He's only got the past t' hang onto, his stories, y' know, an' if he didn't have that he'd probably die."

"Yeah," Rod's head hung a little low. He stood there for a moment, scuffing the ground with the toe of his shoe. "No, I promise I won't say a word. He'll never know I was here," he said sadly as he turned and walked away. The man he thought he knew had just died.

"You'll still go see him at the Carriers', won't you?"

Rod pulled himself into the cabin of the Landy, struggling beneath the sodden blanket smothering his spirit. Chief, Eddie, Sammy and the few others he'd gotten to know, were all waiting for something—a hope or dream that might take lifetimes to come—waiting to be rescued by their River God and taken back to good times past —talking about it every night at the Carriers' Arms Hotel, talking their lives away. Rod knew now all their talk was pointless, that their all dreams amounted to nothing but vague morning mist before the rising reality of the coming day.

Rod drove the Land Rover back home, eastwards into the warmth of the rising sun. Somehow, the rays of golden morning light bathing the inside of the cab seemed to wash away his emptiness.

The hands on Rod's clock were frozen forever in the present moment. Chief's sad old river could do as it damn well pleased—perhaps rising in rebellion some other day, a day in the far distant future. For now, it could just lie quietly in its levee, patiently in wait.

"I think I'll head down to the pool later this morning," he decided out loud. "Do a bit of diving, hang out with the gang, chat with the girls…"

It had dawned upon him, the Bourke he loved was alive, vibrant and present, not just a nostalgic dream from a time long past or a bright hopeful future not yet come, but something real to be experienced each and every day. Images of today's town and its people, his friends, and the relaxing rhythm of his life flooded his mind, bright and cheerful like the morning sun. As far as Rod was concerned, it could go on forever and ever—day after day of tough physical yakka, hard as you can possibly go, followed by afternoons of pure bliss at one or another favourite place, and after that, perhaps even a yarn or two to round out the evening: Yes, of course he'd still go see Chief.

That evening on his nightly walk, Rod made sure to stop by the Carriers Arms. Despite the rawness of this morning's revelation, the old lady's words burnt true, he felt a need to support the Chief with his friendship. He pushed through the main door for a quick yarn, but Chief wasn't there at his usual table, and neither were Eddie and Sammy.

The place was darkened and crowded with a younger scene—some kind of noisy disco night—so little wonder they hadn't shown up. Rod turned and was about to leave when two girls by the door spotted him. The elder, a little overweight with short curly hair, moved purposefully towards him, while her friend, slim with ebony black hair cascading into the small of her back, tried to restrain her. In the darkness, he recognised her now; she was the girl on the bike

"What r'y' doing in here, handsome? Are y' lookin' for good time?" The large girl had pulled away and stood in front of Rod, blocking his exit. "We'll show him a thing or two, won't we Carla?" She narrowed her eyes, studying Rod's face, interrogating him. "You're not from around here, are ya? What's y'r name and where're ya from then?"

"I'm Rod, and I'm from Sydney." He looked away then down at his shoes, not really sure how to deal with the situation. He noted that she was slurring her words. It was definitely time for him to leave. He'd wanted an opportunity to speak to the other girl, but not in here, not like this.

The younger girl looked embarrassed. "C'mon Elsie, that's enough. Leave him alone. Go and get Johnny, he must be really tired. We've gotta go home now." She looked back towards Rod, her pretty face framed by long glossy dark hair. "I'm sorry about Elsie; she's not normally like that."

Carla seemed very young, Rod thought, perhaps even too young to be at a pub, and she was holding a full glass of red wine. Inexplicably, the significance of a timeless classical image—innocence versus temptation—wrenched his gut—that unrecorded moment of loss everyone faces just once in a lifetime. In a bold move Rod reached out and took the wine glass out of her hand, firmly but gently. It was an instinctive action, automatic, he couldn't even explain to himself.

"Heyyy!... Do you want to try some?" Carla looked surprised.

Rod upended the contents of the glass in the shiny metal trough drain running along the bottom of the bar. He felt way out of line, but was on his way out of the place and had nothing to lose. After this morning, alcohol sickened him now.

"Hey, you're wasting it! My sister Elsie just paid for that."

Rod's bold move surprised even himself; he was lost for words. "No…No, sorry, er..its…er, alright. Sorry."

Rod muttered as he looked down at his feet, not knowing what to say. Waves of disappointment surged into his mind, flooding it with sad images, as recalled what the old lady said about the Chief. He pictured the threesome sitting around their table lamenting over a past that had been—clandestinely plotting the River God's second coming, desperately hoping for it. They'd normally be here at the Carriers' right now. Rod hadn't been smart enough to get it at first. When would they ever have time to do the things they talked about if they spent it all doing nothing? Pathetic images of Freddie the Failure came back too; unrelated yet linked.

He lifted his head and looked directly into Carla's dark-brown eyes—still wide with surprise.

"You don't have to do this, y' know." As hard as it was for him to do, Rod maintained full eye contact with her. "They've got no right at all to give this stuff to you, nobody's got that right. I refuse to drink it now, if anybody ever offers me some." Somehow his words had managed to come out smoothly, clearly, as he had intended.

Carla met Rod's gaze shyly. She was listening, but she didn't say anything, so Rod dared continue. He knew he didn't have much time left, maybe just a few seconds more, at best. He could see Elsie making her way back through the tables. She was carrying her handbag and a baby wrapped in a blanket

"You shouldn't be wasting your time here. There are so many other better things to do—to study, to learn. You're young, beautiful," Rod could feel the colour rising in his cheeks as he dared use that word; but why not use it, it didn't matter anymore, she was about to go and he'd probably never see her again. "And you've got your whole life ahead of you, y' know—a life full of interest and adventure. There's a whole world out there waiting for you, Carla. Whatever you do, don't waste it away in here." He pleaded.

"C'mon Carla, let's get home." Elsie started for the door. "See ya next time Rod from Sydney." She turned and winked at him.

Carla stayed silent, she looked down at the floor, her pretty face hidden now by a curtain of glossy black hair. "Yeah, I gotta go now." He knew that in the next second, she'd turn and walk away but, for the moment, she just stood there.

"Hey, why don't you come down to the swimming pool in the arvo? I've got a whole group of nice friends there. You can meet them all," Rod blurted on the spur of the moment—nothing to lose for trying.

"They'd never accept me." Carla answered softly, resignedly, still looking down at her shoes.

"Yes, they would," Rod replied, puzzled by her reply, glossing over it enthusiastically. I'd be there to introduce you. Y' can sit on the grass and the water's so refreshing." Barely milliseconds remained between them now.

"Why don't you give it a go?" Rod finished.

She glanced up at him, their eyes locking briefly. "I gotta go now." A fleeting smile lightened her face as she turned and left.

CHAPTER 13. THE SWIMMING LESSON

ONE OR TWO afternoons later, Rod could barely believe it when he spotted Carla sitting alone, over by the shallow end of the pool. As casually as he could manage, he got up from his towel spread out on the grass by the diving boards, and walked over to say hello. Carla was wearing cut-off jeans and a white t-shirt, sitting on the pool's edge, her feet dangling in the water. She smiled at him as he sat down beside her.

"Hello Carla, glad you could make it," Rod opened casually. He couldn't help but notice the mellow honey-brown colour of her arms, legs and face; glowing richly—more golden in the full afternoon sunlight—than he remembered from under the dim lighting of the Carriers' Arms .

"Er… That's a really nice tan, y' got there." Rod wished he could've thought of something more normal to say to her than that. He felt a bit silly. "Donna'd kill for a tan like that, y' know," he finished weakly.

"I'm like that all over." Carla replied, smiling at him, confident.

Rod imagined the smooth gold colour of her skin continuing evenly under the hem of her shorts, under her t-shirt, all over. Did she sunbake in the nude? He could feel the colour rising in his cheeks. He hated how that always happened to him.

"Er…that's good, Carla," he stammered, wondering how he could ever think of a non-embarrassing answer to a statement like that.

"Scientists say that it's better like that for not getting cancer. People with pale skin shouldn't even be out in the sun with their funny red tan lines and freckles." Rod felt like he was babbling incoherently. He stood up quickly and jumped in the water to cool his burning face. Relaxing under the water and holding his breath, Rod turned around and came up alongside the edge of the pool. In desperate need of something better to do or say, he grabbed Carla's ankle and started gently pulling. "Hey, are y' coming in then, or not?"

Carla lifted her other foot out of the water so that the sole of it was right in front of his face. "I'm tanned all over, except for the bottoms of my feet. See!" she said laughing at him, a hint of teasing in her voice. Perhaps she sensed his discomfort.

"Er…I guess the sun doesn't get under there very much," Rod replied. He ducked his head below the surface again. The pool water felt refreshing on his burning face. Resurfacing, he pulled on her foot again, sliding her gently towards the edge of the pool, then stopped.

"Do y' wanna come in? C'mon go get your swimmers on."

"I don't have any." Carla kicked a spray of water at Rod, laughing again.

"Don't have swimmers?" Rod asked incredulously. "Everybody's got swimmers."

"I don't, I've never had any." She answered proudly.

Rod wondered if he was ever going to get his foot out of his mouth. Right now, it was stuck so far down his throat that it was choking him. How could it be that that she'd never had swimmers?

"Come on in, in your shorts and t-shirt then?" He tried again. "They'll dry quick enough in this heat. The water's great, y' know."

"No, the pool people don't like that. Clothes aren't allowed in, and I can't swim anyway," Carla said, a hint of resignation in her voice.

Rod couldn't imagine that anyone living in Australia couldn't swim. "I could teach you," he blurted out enthusiastically. "It's easy! Couldn't you try get some swimmers?" Rod climbed out of the pool and sat beside her, dripping on the tiled edge.

"Swimming lessons! I dunno," she hesitated. "I might just have to take you up on that offer next time," she smiled.

"Anyway, do you want to come an' meet my friends now? They're all sitting on their towels over by the deep end. Come over and watch us do some diving?" He asked. "It'll be fun!"

"Er... No, not now, thanks Rod, another day perhaps." She glanced away, as if wanting Rod to drop the subject before looking back at his face. "I'm happy just sitting over here for now. Perhaps we can talk some more before I have to go to the shops. My sister Elsie's coming by to pick me up in a moment."

Rod was feeling elated with the way his afternoon went at the pool[12]. That evening over dinner, he was busting to tell René all about Carla.

"Well then, tell me all about her and how you met?" René opened broadly encouraging Rod to take the floor.

"She's the girl I wave to most days on the way to the shops and today we finally got to talking," Rod explained, leaving out the bit about the Carriers' Arms. "Carla's her name and now I'm gonna see her every day at the pool and teach her how to swim. Can you imagine, René, she says she doesn't even have a pair of bathers and has to go find some."

René sat back, gazing into the distance, seemingly delighted with his young cousin's stories—perhaps remembering his own youthful experiences, but as he didn't elaborate, Rod didn't quite think it proper to ask.

"She doesn't talk about herself, so I don't know much about her yet. She's so sweet and funny and laughs a lot at everything I say. I reckon it must be my city accent, although she hasn't started calling me mister professor head yet," Rod's conversation wandered about aimlessly. "She says I'm different to her other friends and make her forget about everything else going on in her life. I haven't asked her about those other things yet because I don't want her to think I'm getting too personal or anything like that," Rod babbled on as René took it all in.

A few afternoons later, Carla returned to the pool. Waving at Rod as she came in through the turnstiles, she walked over to the shallow end.

"Y' must've got yourself some swimmers ay? Rod called, coming from the diving boards over towards where she was laying out her towel on the grass.

"You bet. Take a look." She peeled off her shorts and t-shirt and stood there in a pretty-looking, low-backed white one-piece which, Rod couldn't help but notice, had seen better days.

"Hey that's pretty cool. It really sets off your tan," he complimented her.

She smiled in reply, lowering herself into the water and they stood together in the shallow end of the pool. Rod began with the basics and some water survival skills.

"Look Carla, the most important thing I'll show you is how to float on both your stomach and back—that way you can never drown... First, try taking your feet off the bottom. Hold your breath and lie face down in the water," he gently instructed. "I'll hold you up till you get used to it." Rod placed his fingertips very lightly against her stomach. Her muscles were tense and hard beneath her skin; she was obviously nervous.

"You'll have to completely relax, Carla. Feel the water around you. Imagine it sliding all over you; two hydrogen gas atoms and one oxygen combined into something amazing; its molecules wetting you, welcoming you, lifting you up and floating you. Water is such an amazing, beautiful, natural thing." He concluded, daydreaming about how his adjectives were intended for Carla, as much as they were for the water. Rod continued to talk, smoothly and soothingly to her using the water metaphor, his fingertips still supporting her firm, flat stomach, but he forced himself not to focus on that.

"Water's almost got the exact same density as us because we are over eighty percent water. You've gotta relax completely and become one with it, Carla. You are water and the water is you. You and I and it are all one."

Rod could instantly feel his words resonating with Carla. Her stomach relaxed, she lifted gently off his fingertips and began to float.

"Yesss... Hey, you're a natural, Carla!" he cried out enthusiastically. "When you feel like it, lift your head out of the water while pushing your arms apart, and take a deep breath. Then put your face down in the water again."

Rod watched her with admiration. "You're a fast learner."

She's real fast, he thought, and in the days that followed he found Carla to be a quick study as she stayed some afternoons for a longer or a shorter time, depending on what else she had to do that day.

***

Later that evening, Rod showed up at a party Paddy told him about. It was in somebody's back yard near the pool. A fairyland of party lights illuminated the scene; music played and people he didn't know milled about in groups or grooved to the throb of Deep Purple's heavy metal beat[13].

A steel barrel sat perched in a half 44-gallon drum full of chunky ice to keep it cool; coiled hoses fed in carbon dioxide gas from cylinders topped with brass valves and pressure gauges, while another thick hose led from the barrel to a macho chrome handpiece.

OUTBACK SUMMER

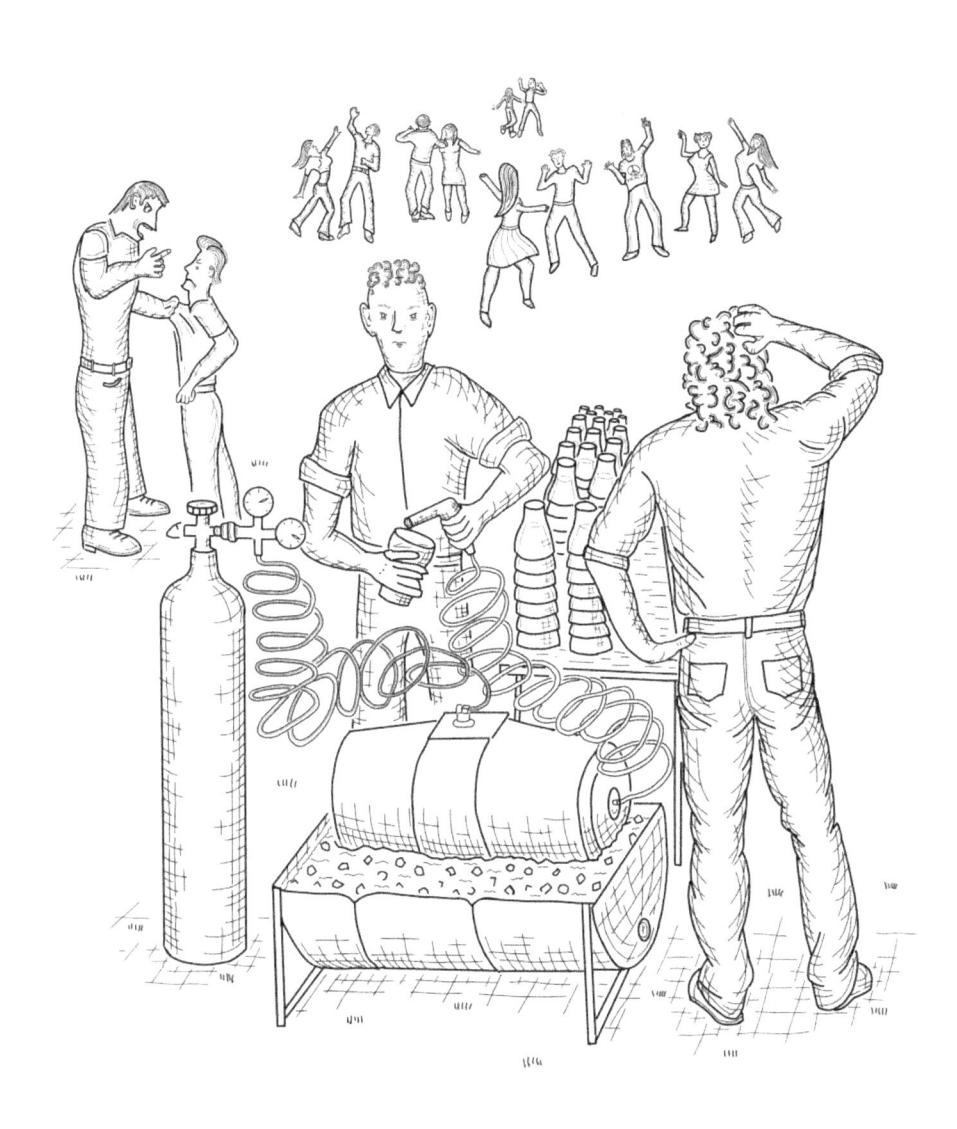

"THE PARTY"

Robert Coenraads
2024

Despite the warmth of the summers' evening, the contraption gleamed with condensation, its tubes and pipes covered with a misty frosting of ice like some kind of wondrous science experiment. Rod approached with curiosity.

"G'day, I'm Bruce." A red-haired bloke in stubbies and a t-shirt spotted him. He was grabbing empty glasses from stacks on a plastic tray, deftly filling them from the handpiece, and handing them out to thirsty passers-by.

"G'day Bruce, I'm Rod. That's an interesting -looking setup you've got here. Must be the keg Paddy was boasting about to everyone."

"Yeah mate, I reckon this little beauty will keep us going for the whole night, no worries. Schooner mate?" He held out the glass he'd just filled.

"A little later thanks mate—keep up the good work." Rod wondered if that strange apparatus could be converted to make drinks other than just beer. He turned, heading off to see if he could find Paddy or anybody else he knew.

He found a garden tap against the house right where he knew it would be. Turning it on, he let it flow for a few seconds to chase out any red-back spiders whose home it may have been. Bending down he quenched his thirst with a massive slug of water. Funny how there's never anything other than bloody beer at these parties.

Suddenly, amidst a hell of a din, there was Paddy. He was squared off against a big brick of a bloke, facing him with fists clenched in rage. It was clear that within moments the incident was going to turn into a nasty punch up, a real blue.

Moving like lightning, Rod came up behind Paddy, circling his arms around his torso until he could grab his own wrists in front. Rod locked him in—his bear hug pinning Paddy's arms to his side. For a few moments Paddy, lean and strong, struggled fiercely to break the grip, but was no match for Rod's powerful arms, toned by weeks of brush cutting.

"What's the matter, mate? Start a fight and then don't finish it." The human brick was shouting down at Paddy. "You're just a wanker mate! C'mon then, I'll have ya on." He watched the two of them struggling for a moment, a look of surprise on his face. "Stone the flamin' crows," he snorted, then turned and left.

Paddy shouted angrily, trying to break Rod's grip. "Fair go mate, now he's callin' me a flaming wanker. No one calls me a wanker and gets away with it! Let me go Rod or I'll job you too."

"C'mon leave it alone Paddy. Look it'll just ruin your night anyway. C'mon mate, forget it. By tomorrow, that big galah's never even gonna remember, mate." Rod spoke quickly, only loosening his grip slowly when he was sure that Paddy had calmed down enough, not to turn around and hit him. "Here ya go mate, here's your glass."

Bloody drongos!" Paddy was calming down, but Rod noted other emotions emerging now, forcing their way through his shield of defiance and anger.

"Yeah, too right, ay?" Rod added, encouraging Paddy to elaborate.

"Fightin's the way of life around here mate. You'll never stop it. Sometimes you win, sometimes y' loose, that's just the way it is around here. If we don't fight now, we're gonna do it at the next party anyhow. Everybody ends up fixin' their problems by fightin'.

"Did ya know that if someone owes you a favour, you can nominate them to fight for you? Stupidest thing I ever saw was Bald Pig havin' a punch up with his own brother, Little Pig down at the bridge. Goin' at it hammer and tongs they were too." Paddy paused for effect. "Each of 'em had been seconded to fight by someone else. Can't even remember who it was now or what it was about; only how stupid it was to see those two dumb brothers fightin' each other an' everybody else standing round cheering them on. They couldn't've stopped even if they wanted to."

"Why do ya bother, Paddy? You don't have to do all that drinking and fighting thing y' know. Can't you just stop!" Rod implored, searching for solutions. "Why can't you put some other stuff in those keg things anyway?" Rod tried, already suspecting it wouldn't have a hope in hell's chance of working.

"Nah mate," Paddy replied, discounting Rod's strange suggestion. "Drinkin's the way of life around here. There's nothing better for people to do. You know y'rself there's practically more pubs than people in this town. If y' didn't have any beer at your party no one'd come to it. You'd be the laughing stock of the town."

Paddy was becoming deep and philosophic. He clearly understood the hard practicalities of life and the system he was part of. "If y' keep puttin' rounds of beer in front of people, they'll just keep drinkin' 'em until they fall off their stool. Last one down's the winner for the night, proud that he can hold more beer than his mates." Paddy spat contemptuously. "Luckily the pubs have to close at ten otherwise nobody'd ever get home for a sleep in the whole week. There's no rules here mate, this party'll go all night, or until the keg runs dry. Then people'll rest up all day Sunday.

"Stupid town! I gotta say I hate it here. Stupid people. Nothin' to do and nothin' to see." Paddy appeared completely calm now but he was still simmering inside, resentful, deeply wounded beneath his defiant facade.

"Don't say that Paddy," Rod replied. He understood what Paddy was telling him, but also believed that there had to be a way forward. He continued with conviction. "Just think of all your friends at the pool. Bourke's a great little place, sunny weather, friendly people, pretty girls, and it's no more than five minutes to anywhere y' want to go to around town. I really like it here."

Paddy paused to think about what Rod was saying for a moment.

"Look mate, you're not stupid by a long shot, but you haven't lived in town long enough. You're not seeing the full picture. It's a small town and you can't do a thing without everyone talkin' about it. Everybody knows everybody's business. The only jobs are at the meatworks murdering bloody cows or cooking y'self to death all day out in the cotton fields. It's back breakin' work, and y' never know what's gonna happen day to day'. Y' just have to keep fronting up every morning and see if they'll pick y' out of the line-up. If not y' just go home, sit around all day waiting, an' then go try again next morning—one boss, another boss, old boss, new boss, it's all the same thing[14]."

Rod thought about how much he was enjoying his own job; hard work, outdoors in the sun, making him strong and fit. "They can't be the only jobs around, Paddy? What about out on the stations, or what about the shops in town?"

"Nah mate, I reckon my life ain't been that rosy compared to yours. I never finished high school. Sometimes I wish I had've though. I'd feel a little 'shamed going back now," Paddy said, opening up to Rod, becoming more reflective. "Can you imagine it… me sittin' down there with all the girls…in a uniform," he laughed.

"Look Paddy, go see them at the school." Rod was sure, by the way Paddy was talking, that he had the brains to do anything he wanted. "You wouldn't have to sit in class with everybody else or wear a uniform. You could do your subjects by correspondence, and when you'd finished y' could go to uni and study whatever you wanted there. It's completely free nowadays. Y' don't have to pay a cent y' know." Rod thought a moment longer about the practicalities of all of that, before concluding enthusiastically—ninety percent sure that his parents wouldn't mind. "Y' can come an' stay at our place in Sydney while you're going to the uni there."

"Thanks mate," was Paddy's only response to Rod's offer. He seemed pensive, lost for words; the normal negative objections and counter points were not there. "Do ya reckon I could really do it?" For a brief moment an inner light seemed to shine in his eyes.

"Sure, you could do it, mate," Rod encouraged, imagining he'd just caught a glimpse in Paddy of the possibility of a bigger, brighter future, a range of opportunities far beyond what he'd ever imagined. He pictured Paddy's fledgling dreams, like a door opening briefly to the world, allowing sunlight to flood into a small corner of his mind, awakening it—even momentarily.

"Thanks mate," Paddy repeated. "I'll have a bit of a think about it and let you know."

"Anytime mate," Rod replied, hoping he'd been able to kick his foot far enough into the gap, before the door creaked slowly closed, overpowered by self-doubt and the humdrum of daily life. "Anytime you want, mate."

CHAPTER 14. THE KILLING ROOM CHALLENGE

OUT IN THE BACKYARD of their tidy weatherboard home on the southern edge of the town, Dan was talking with his older brother Brad while their mother prepared dinner. For once Ricky wasn't there; he'd gone out of town for a few days, helping his dad with the fences on their sheep property. Dan stared down despondently at the can of Tooheys on the wooden table in front of him. He was bored; he'd been out of work for about a week now and was having little luck finding anything else to do.

"Don't worry about it, mate," Brad told him. "Soon as the holidays are over you can go back to school and finish off y'r last year. I'll talk to the boss—see if he can find a place, so as you can start with me soon as you're done. It'd be a good one, full time, good pay."

Brad had always been Dan's role model; he'd been first to finish high school, first to go to the pub with dad, first to get a good job—and he had one of the best in town. He had a motorbike, brand new it was, and to top it off, he hung out with a good-looking sheila too. Since their father left, he'd always been there helping Dan through the hard times[15].

Brad was glad when Dan got the job with the mining company, though he didn't trust that out-of-towner Conway bloke Dan kept talking about. He'd met him when Paddy brought him round to the Oxford. Bloody Paddy! What in the hell was he thinking, bringing him into their group?

"Look Dan, I'm fed up with y' tellin' me all about this bloody Rod Conman and how good everyone thinks he is. He doesn't belong here, mate. He'll be gone when the project ends, an' you'll probably never see him again. Remember mate, he dobbed you and Mark in to the boss the other day, and straight after that they laid all of you off—Ricky too.

"Yeah, and now I heard they hired Pete Hayricks," Dan added. "I dunno, but I reckon Conway might've organised that to get in good with his sister, Beth. He's been talkin' to her a lot at the pool lately."

"Bloody hell!!! The girls are like desert flowers after the rains, mate. He'll get in there, rooting around, like the filthy feral pig from the city he is—root 'em all up with his bloody snout and scatter 'em about, lookin' for the prettiest. Sowin' his bloody wild oats, they say. He'll piss off back to the city in a couple of months, then next season a new bloke'll come along and do the same thing—steal yer flowers or leave 'em here broken and holdin' the baby. Nah, I don't think too much of your Conman mate, I've seen it all before. That kind of bloke just spells really big trouble," Brad concluded. "Have y' asked him yet if he wants to come out and see the killin' room?"

"Yeah, I did ask him, Brad, but he said he wasn't interested—said he'd rather just hang out at the pool. He reckons he's got everything he needs there."

"Thought so! Bloody wanker! He's too gutless to go. Y' can tell him that, Dan, or maybe I'll just find him myself and tell him straight. Hang out at the bloody pool! And mark my words; he'll end up pinching Beth or another one of your girls too. I might have to set some of my mates onto him; they'll punch him up real good."

Rod could put his finger right on moment he started noticing the changes happening around the pool. He reckoned they must've started the day René laid the boys off about a week ago. He tried to explain what René told him; how it had nothing to do with the trouble between Dan and Mark, nothing to do with him; how it had always been planned that way.

Dan and Ricky had become more distant. Even his mate, Paddy seemed somehow colder, more aloof. Rod found it much easier talking with the girls these days, they hadn't changed—in fact, since the party, he'd been getting on with them better than ever. Things weren't quite right with the blokes though, and he knew he'd have to talk to them about it—but before he had the chance, one afternoon at the pool just before closing, Dan confronted him.

"Brad says you're too gutless to go to the killing room! Is that right, mate?" Dan's tone had changed; it was more like Paddy's. He was challenging him now too—spokesman for his brother, Brad.

"Look, I told y', mate, that I wasn't interested. What would I wanna go see Brad there for anyway?"

Apart from that evening at the Oxford, he'd had never met or spoken to Brad, just seen him once or twice riding around town on his bike, yet Rod knew he had an enemy now. For some inexplicable reason Brad was out there, on the hunt, and would stop at nothing to bring him down in his tracks.

"Brad, Paddy an' their mates have to go there every day," Dan replied. "Brad says he's going to take me there soon as I finish high school, an' get me a really good job. I'm not going to say no! Either you think you're too good for us or you're a bloody coward!"

Dan's unexpected insult cut deeply, to the core of Rod's very being, and at that moment he knew he'd have to face up to Brad and his mates in the killing room. It made him sick to the stomach, but there was no other way. It was either that or be branded a coward in front of whole town.

"Your talkin' rubbish mate, there's nothing to it, and if you're gonna make such a big deal out of it, I guess I'm just gonna have to go there and prove it."

Rod was there at the appointed time, just before 3:00pm afternoon smoko, outside the side door of the run-down complex of corrugated iron buildings. He felt sick in the pit of his stomach, and had been feeling that way all week, at the thought of what horrors he'd have to face within those rusty tin-sheet walls, and now that hour had finally arrived. His thoughts drifted to the tranquillity of the pool, where he'd normally be at this hour, when a shaved head peered out of the side door. It was Bald Pig, the elder of the two brothers.

"Brad's waitin' for y' upstairs. He didn't think y'd have the guts t' show yourself here." He turned around and disappeared inside.

Rod followed Bald Pig through the spartan complex. Inside he could hear the whirr of electric motors and the clanking of metal conveyor belts. Rows of stainless-steel benches lined the shiny concrete ground floor, upon which hair-netted, white-aproned workers moved around like ants packing various body parts into boxes for dispatch and distribution to regional butcheries.

OUTBACK SUMMER

"MEATWORKS"

Robert Coenraads
2024

On the second level, raw red corpses, crudely dangling from meat hooks, clanked slowly down a production line running the length of the floor; the metallic stench of blood was overpowering. Workers, wielding thin steely knives, skilfully sliced body parts from the carcases as they moved by, systematically stripping each one back to a bare backbone, placing the offcuts on another conveyor that ran down to the lower level. The workers looked up at them as they passed, staring briefly at Rod

"C'mon, this way," Bald Pig announced as they climbed one last short metal staircase. "The killin' room's right at the head of the line."

Shafts of bright afternoon sunlight from the outside world angled in through rows of small windows set high in the corrugated sheet walls, casting shiny squares on the hosed-down floor. The killing room stank of sweat, urine and faeces, and of palpable fear. The cattle knew that it was the end of the line for them.

The last beast came up the long ramp from the yards below and was pinned in place, its head held firmly in the metal press, the whites of its eyes flashing as it looked about wildly, somehow sensing what about to happen. Brad quickly moved the hydraulic gun into place, positioning it against the beast's head, before pulling the trigger. The animal collapsed lifelessly onto the ground. Another worker moved in quickly, forcing the point of a meat hook between the two bones of the leg, just above the hock, and the big round carcass was hauled up on to the line.

Paddy was there too, wearing his hair net and white apron, same as the others. He ran his razor-sharp knife along the midline of the beast in a swift hari-kari movement, slicing open the stomach and spilling the guts into a stainless-steel container. The speed and clinical efficiency of the process made Rod feel sick to the stomach; he repressed a momentary urge to vomit.

Just then, a whistle sounded signalling smoko break and the clanking belts ground to a halt plunging the place into an eerie silence. Rod looked over into the bin, surprised at just how little blood there was in there, just organs, a slippery mixture of crimsons, reds, pinks, marrons, and purples. He recognized them all from text books, knew what each of their function was, or what it had been just moments before, as they now lay in a useless jumbled pile in the waste bin. He watched now as Paddy leant over, his gloved hand reaching into the bin. He picked up a glistening transparent orb about the size of a small soccer ball that stood out in sharp contrast, floating on a sea of different shades of red. Rod watched mesmerized as Paddy plucked up the orb which came away easily.

"Here Conway," he called. "Catch!"

Rod's hand moved instinctively into place, intercepting the sphere. He had somehow expected it to be hard and glassy, but instead it was warm and rubbery. He just stood there, staring down at it in his hand, a stretched translucent skin bag covered by a fine spidery white network.

"It's the bladder, mate," Paddy called, laughing.

A waterspout, a thin stream of hot urine spurted from a small round hole in the bladder where it had torn away from the urethra. It was all over his hands now and running down his trouser leg. The others were all laughing too.

"Bloody hell, Paddy!" Rod hurled the bladder hard, back at him. "You bastard."

Paddy stepped back deftly as the bladder exploded against the side of the waste bin, much to the amusement of the others.

"Brad'll show you the gun now, mate," Paddy replied, changing the subject; his words slow and deliberate, their tone serious. The mood in the room suddenly turned darker, claustrophobic.

"Yeah, Brad, show him how it works," another worker murmured ominously while the others, now that the production line had stopped, gathered in for a closer look, all in their bloodstained white aprons. The killing room was silent with anticipation as Rod moved toward the opening where the ramp from holding pens came into the building.

"The bolt goes in right here," Brad said stabbing a bloodied finger against Rod's forehead. "It smashes through the skull straight into their brain an' they drop to the ground on the spot, stone dead. I've seen 'em turn mad though, if it don't go right; kickin' and bucken', knockin' everything over."

With the skill of a thousand kills behind him, Brad had the gun in Rod's face, the bolt pressing hard against his forehead.

"I never miss though, mate," he whispered in Rod's ear.

"Go on, Brad, pull the trigger," Somebody in the audience called, perhaps Paddy. Rod couldn't make out who it was, his vision blocked by the wide metal frame of the headpiece. Out of the corner of one eye he could see Brad's finger poised over the firing button.

"Pull it... Pull it... Pull it," the others began to chant, their voices nearly drowned out by the roar of blood pumping through his ears. He felt his knees weaken, buckling slightly, but they managed to hold.

Rod didn't pull back. He knew Brad wouldn't pull the trigger, but this device, designed by human scientists in white lab coats in their spotless city laboratory, designed to do its job cheaply and efficiently, terminating the lives of thousands of sentient creatures, sickened him. Here it was now, being used for a game of Russian roulette in a bloodied, gritty room in a meatworks in the middle of the Australian outback; a place those scientists couldn't even picture in their wildest imaginings; and now it was hard up against his own head.

"Pull it… Pull it… Pull it," the background chant continued for what seemed like hours to Rod.

Brad, judging the timing perfectly, whipped the gun back from Rod's forehead while at the same time firing it. Rod watched the stainless-steel bolt shoot out momentarily, in front of his eyes and etched forever in his memory, before it slid back automatically into the firing chamber.

His heart still pounding, it took Rod a few moments longer to realize his ordeal was over; he started breathing again.

"Y' didn't get this one t' wet himself, mate," one of the workers said, turning away disappointed. Bored with the game now, the others disappeared to enjoy the remaining few moments of their smoko, leaving Rod alone in the room with Brad. He knew it was time for him to go too.

Rod was silent for a long while, finally forcing words to come, pointless as they were, totally meaningless words. "Thanks for showing me round the place," he murmured, barely making eye contact. "It's a job I could never do," he capitulated for want of something better to say, relieved he was about to leave that dingy hell-hole of a place, never to darken its doors again; his job lay in the bright sunshine under clear blue skies.

"I'd say that would be about right, mate," Brad replied. Then he continued, almost philosophically, opening a window, just a tiny crack, into himself. "It takes a lot of gettin' used to, to work in here. Maybe you never do, but it's the only place around. My job's the most important one in the place. Someone's gotta do it, and I know that by doing it right it's gonna be quick and painless for the beasts."

The whistle blew signalling the end of afternoon smoko break, closing the moment.

"Well piss off then," Brad growled, closing the window. "There's men's work to be done around here."

Later that evening, Rod's mind was still in turmoil over the powerful events of the killing room. Sitting at the table with René, he tried to crystallize his thoughts into words.

"I could never kill one of those animals myself," he admitted to his cousin. "I'm just a bloody coward and a hypocrite, you know. I love my meat so much that all the vegetables and other stuff around the plate are just trimming you need to get through to get at the good bit."

"Well, you've seen what most others never will, Rod. I don't know if I'd ever be able to skip eating meat either," René added in support.

"But it sickened me to see all of these animals dying on the production line in there just so as I can sit here and enjoy myself."

"Look Rod, these beasts enjoy a good life until they have to face the abattoirs. Maybe they can sense when their time's up, but it's as fast and painless as it can be. If nobody wanted to eat meat, those animals wouldn't even be born and bred."

Later, in the quiet of his room, he realised René was probably right—but it had taken Brad to show him just how wide the gap was between his belly and brain; irreconcilably wide. The day had wounded him deeply. Maybe it was all part of the give and take of life out here, walking the knife-edge line between bully and victim, nevertheless he felt isolated and betrayed. He'd handled the teasing and bullying—that had hurt—but he was disappointed his mate Paddy had turned on him again—that probably hurt him more than anything else. He felt angry too.

"The bastards, they can all go and get stuffed."

CHAPTER 15. ROD MUST CHOOSE

"COME ON CARLA, why don't you come over and talk to the girls?" Rod asked his usual question during one of their lessons. He'd tried the same line, or a variant of it, most afternoons but now was beginning to worry if something might be wrong. She always had an excuse. "You never wanna come over to say hello," he pushed, perhaps a little petulantly, that afternoon. He'd been spending a lot less time with them since he'd started giving Carla lessons.

"It's not that I don't like them or anything like that, it's just we don't hang out together. That's just the way it is," she explained.

"Why's that?" Rod pushed.

"It beats me how a clever bloke like you, doesn't seem to know anything about how things work around here," Carla responded enigmatically. "But then again, I've never been out of Bourke, so maybe things are different in the big smoke."

Rod could see Donna and Beth sitting in their usual spot on the grass by the diving boards. They were watching him. He waved at them. He'd felt a bit of tension growing between him and the girls ever since they'd seen him with Carla—or perhaps it had something to do with his fall out with Dan and Rick, he couldn't be sure. He felt a little awkward for not spending as much time with them these days, nervous as to how they might react.

"I'll just go pop over and for a quick hello." Rod decided to take the opportunity, leaving Carla to finish her practice laps across the shallow end of the pool. He grabbed his towel and walked over to the diving boards.

"Rod," Donna piped up first, "What are y' doing hanging out with her for instead of us?" She and her friends are sluts, y' know." She wrinkled her nose in disgust.

"No, she isn't Donna. Carla's normal, just like you and me. She's just a bit shy though," Rod said glossing over Donna's comments. He wished he'd pushed Carla harder to hang out with his friends earlier, figuring this wouldn't be happening if he had. He was confused as to why she'd come out of the blue with such a nasty judgement about Carla. He'd never seen Donna behave like that.

Rod continued enthusiastically, masking his doubts. "Look, how's about I bring her over right now? I'll just go and get some chips and we'll sit on our towels and you can get to know her. You'll see she's okay. I'll do it right now." Rod had made up his mind, and made to get up and go. "Don't go away; I'll only be five minutes…"

"You're a psychopath, Rod," Donna replied, using the group's big word of the week.

"Thanks so much for the compliment, Donna," Rod replied sarcastically.

And Carla's got a much nicer tan than you have anyway, he added in his head, wisely restraining the thought from taking voice. It wouldn't be the best thing to say to Donna right now.

Beth remained silent, eyes downcast, idly tracing the pattern on her beach towel with her big toe. It was obvious her loyalty between friends was compromised. Since the night of the party, they'd developed a pretty good understanding of one another. Rod had a feeling that if she weren't already hanging out with Steve, they could've really gone for one another. She was fair and honest, and he admired her for that. She must be able to appreciate what he was trying to do, but Rod could tell from her body language that she agreed with Donna. She sighed and looked up at him.

"Look, Rod, it's not that we don't want to, but we really can't talk with that mob. If our parents found out, they wouldn't even let us out of the house anymore, y' know," Beth tried to explain.

"How could they tell you things like that…?" Rod asked, lost for more words.

"I'm sorry but that's just the way it is…"

It was Rod's turn to look down at his feet, sad and confused, wondering what in the hell was going on? He was facing a wall, a completely solid yet invisible barrier running right across the manicured lawn of the Bourke Memorial Pool complex on that hot sunny afternoon, dividing it completely in two. For him the wall was non-existent but for the others, his friends, it was real—real and impenetrable as the one dividing Germany—the one made of concrete, barbed wire and steel mesh. Carla wasn't going to try to talk to them, try to become accepted by them, as much as Donna and Beth would never speak to her. As Beth had just put it, 'that's the way it is around here.'

"I don't get it Beth. Can't you even manage to shout out a friendly 'hello' from a distance as you come walking by?" Rod concluded as he turned and left, feeling quite disappointed, almost angry, by the conversation."

Ricky ran to catch up with him as he headed back towards the shallow end.

"I reckon Donna's just jealous, mate. I overheard some of the girls sayin' that she's got the hots for you, y' know."

"Well, that's news to me, Rick, but she's being a real pain about it all today, y' know mate."

"Yeah, right," Ricky laughed, "…freckled bitch! But, ya gotta remember, Carla's not one of us, mate. Y' can't just hang round with her. She's different, y' know."

"Look, Rick, it's like a Christmas present. Who cares about the wrapping paper? Y' don't ever bother about that, do y' mate? It's what's inside that counts."

"Yeah, I gotta admit it to ya mate, that Carla is a real good looker, but you're only gonna wind up in a whole heap o' trouble. Her mob ain't gonna like it either when they find out you're hanging around with her. You're gonna have to watch your back from now on, mate!"

"I'm just teachin' her how to swim, Rick. Nothin' serious. Nobody's ever taught her before, if you can believe that."

"Yeah right, tell us another one mate!" Ricky laughed before heading back over to the group.

"I think Carla might be Aboriginal," Rod finally stated after spending most of the evening in silence. His outburst interrupted René's train of thought, who sat with his nose buried in the pages of the *Western Herald*. The Aboriginal word stuck in Rod's throat. He was worried, wondering how René would react. It seemed worse to be an Aborigine than a Greek, Itie or even a Jew. Rod braced himself for what René might say.

"Oh," René said, coming out of his trance, then remained silent a moment longer contemplating what Rod had just told him. "Do you think that matters?"

"No, not really," Rod replied, feeling strangely defensive towards René's interrogation. "But do you think I should ask her about it?"

"I'm not sure, Rod. Is it the kind of thing you need to ask somebody? Everybody in town probably knows already. It depends on how important the question is to you. Would it change the way you feel about her?"

"I don't think so. I don't think it's important, but it's interesting—I'm curious, that's all."

"And what happens if you go asking her and she isn't?"

"I'm already really sure she is. None of the gang will have anything to do with her, and she won't talk with them either."

"Well, sounds likely then, but I wouldn't go mentioning all this to your mum or dad… at least not straight away."

"Why not René? Do you think it matters?" Rod replied, pushing René to answer the very same question.

"No," René replied, "It's completely irrelevant."

"If it's irrelevant," Rod asked, "then why shouldn't I mention it to them?"

"Well," René thought a moment, "because it's completely irrelevant and so why go mentioning something irrelevant to somebody who might think it's relevant? I'm not saying your mum or dad would think it matters, but why risk worrying them when they haven't even met the girl."

"Yeah…. I suppose…"

"Have you told Carla that you're only in Bourke for the summer?" René asked.

"Er…" it was Rod's turn to fall silent. He shuddered at the thought wondering if he could ever do it. "Well… I guess I haven't quite said anything just yet…"

"Don't you think it's only fair that you do?" René added.

René had just flipped Rod's world on its head by bringing up the painful fact that he'd have to leave Bourke.

"I suppose I'll have to break that news to her pretty soon then."

It was 9:30 pm Saturday night. Rod, and what seemed like half the town, were on the outskirts of town, on the Mitchell Highway where the long straight stretch started. Paddy, Dan, Ricky and Mark were there plus a few other familiar faces in the crowd. There was an element of dangerous anticipation as to what was about to happen next. He looked into the crowd searching for Beth and her brother Pete, but couldn't see them.

Rod and Brad were sitting astride their respective Kawasaki's, one in each of the highway's two lanes, facing southeast into the darkness, with their engines roaring.

Rod really didn't want to be where he was right now! Hadn't he already just faced Brad in the killing room? He wondered how he'd managed to get himself into another challenge. Perhaps because he'd told Paddy and the others that he'd rebuilt his bike from the ground up, how he'd ported the cylinders to produce a narrower, stronger power band, and how it was the meanest, fastest, most dangerous bike around? Word must've gotten around town like it always does. He didn't think he was bragging too much—that was the furthest thing from his mind… Or was it? Anyway, he never intended it to sound like a challenge. Brad and his mates had taken it as a challenge though—perhaps this city boy coming into town and hanging out with all the Bourke girls at the pool needed to be put in his place. Perhaps, Brad decided, he should be the one to do it.

Rod felt the weight of the whole town on him, unified against him, hoping he would lose—be taken down a peg or two.

There were two pig-spotters positioned closer in towards town, keeping a watchful eye out for any uniformed interference in the night's activities. Everybody else was gathered about 500 meters down the highway at the finish line. Master of ceremonies, Paddy O'Sullivan stood between Brad and Rod on the centreline of the highway, an old pair of checker shorts in his hand which he raised solemnly above his head.

Brad's bike had a bigger engine than Rod's, a 4-cylinder 650cc four stroke, and he'd just bought it brand new. He was the clear odds-on favourite with his mates and there was obviously a lot riding on this win for him. Rod could tell Brad was cocky and sure he'd thrash his opponent hands-down in the race—certain he'd beat the city slicker. A huge crowd of supporters stood around him.

OUTBACK SUMMER

"THE RACE"

Robert Coenraads
2024

Rod sat alone with his thoughts. He knew that his bike was capable of the standing quarter-mile in 12.9 seconds, perhaps even better with the port job on the motor. All he had to do was keep enough rubber on the tar, and watch that his machine didn't get the death wobbles and throw him all over the road. He screwed both his bike's steering dampers to their stiffest setting. His hands were sweating in his gloves as he waited– his muscles tense.

Paddy's arm dropped and the two bikes roared away head-to-head in a blaze of smoking rubber. Rod pulled ahead rapidly, feeling the motor's vicious power band cut in. He leant forward over the fuel tank, tucked in behind the faring, right hand on the throttle, left foot and left hand working in unison as he shifted upward through the gears, rapidly gaining more and more ground by the second.

Time seemed to stand still as Rod's thoughts crystallized, sharpening into focus momentarily despite the adrenaline and endorphins pumping through his veins.

If I win this it'll only make things worse, he realised, his hand easing off the throttle involuntarily, allowing Brad's bike to close in from behind and draw alongside. To let him pass or not to pass, that was the key question see-sawing in Rod's mind, clouding his response.

Do I take the loss now, hang my head in shame? Maybe then everyone will leave me alone?' Rod wondered. Isn't that what he wanted—a hassle free life? Brad's front wheel slowly nudged ahead. He could see it out of the corner of his eye.

Testosterone kicked in clouding his thoughts[16]. "Hell No!!!" He flicked open the throttle, his bike screaming down the highway, gaining ground, pulling ahead slowly.

Rod crossed the finish line with a bike-length's lead—shooting onwards down the highway into the black void of the Mitchell, blood pounding in his head. Rod was elated with the win. He pulled the bike around, dropped a few gears and, standing on the foot pegs, lifted the front wheel high into air for a victory run back up the highway past the excited crowd.

Pete's broad smiling face appeared in the crowd gathered by the finish line. He was the first over and full of congratulations.

"Great ride Conway. Nice wheelie!" Pete's big bear paw of a hand slapped hard on the back of his leathers, "That sure is a great bike y' got there mate. You're gonna have to tell us again what you did to her to make her go so fast. I mean Brad's new bike's got an extra 150cc over you and still y' beat him hands down."

"Yeah, thanks mate. We'll go over it Monday at work." Rod knew he'd done nothing special. Nobody seemed to recognise the fact that any two-stroke motor in a lighter bike is easily capable of out accelerating a larger sized four-stroke engine in a safer, heavier machine. He'd keep that fact to himself for the time being he—he was the hero that night and feeling great; he was on top of the world.

That is, until he came back past Brad, beside his bike on the edge of the highway, sitting on the ground—most of his mates had already gone but a small, fiercely-defensive group huddled around him. Rod overheard the tail end of the conversation with one of his mates before they turned and caught sight of him.

"It cost me a lot of time and hard work to buy that bike but I don't think she's real good, mate. I reckon I'll have to do a bit of work on her motor, perhaps some new pipes as well?"

He looked up at Rod, a mixture of savagery and despondence in his face,

"What in the hell are you staring at Conway," he shouted, angry and frustrated. "Why don't you piss off back to Sydney!"

That was the last thing that Rod had wanted to come out of this whole crazy evening; the magic and fun of it ebbing away, disappearing in an instant as the reality bit home and leaving him with a sick feeling in the pit of his stomach. He was an outcast from the group, his only friends Pete and maybe Beth.

He knew what he should be saying to Brad, if he could only bridge the yawning chasm between them.

Look mate. It's you who's really got the better of the two bikes. She's brand new and reliable compared to my old machine. I wouldn't do a thing to her because she's fine as is. My bike's only faster because she's lighter and she's been worked, but she's an old two stroke. She handles shockingly, and any hot day, I've literally got to ride with my hand over the clutch ready to pull her in in case the engine seizes and throws me onto the road. I reckon that's what happened to the last guy, before I got hold of her as a wreck. He's probably dead!

But the chasm was far too wide for that, and everything Rod did just seemed to worsen it. Brad lost the race, and that was the fact of the matter, and the only thing everybody would be talking about around town tomorrow. It would always come back around, time and time again, to the win—the speed and bravado of the night.

Paddy was there close by, Ricky and Dan too, but they hadn't come over to congratulate him—obviously torn between their loyalty to their kinsman

Brad and their friendship with him, an outsider. They turned and started walking away. Bastards, they can all go and get stuffed, Rod thought, standing all alone now. Especially Paddy—he's the one responsible for all this!

He scanned the crowd for Pete or Beth but couldn't see them or anyone else he knew now. They were all turning away.

"Piss off mate," was the only comment he heard.

Rod avoided meeting the gang at the pool the following day. In the afternoon he headed straight over to the shallow end to meet Carla. She didn't say anything about last night and he wasn't going to be the one spreading the gossip.

"Er…just a quick question Carla." Rod was nervous before even before finishing the question. Should he just leave it there? He could easily make up something else. Her answer was of no importance to him, but the concept somehow excited him, making her even more exotic and beautiful in his eyes.

"Are you… Aboriginal? I mean…," he paused, "that's if you don't mind telling me."

Carla looked at him strangely, and smiled. "Of course I am silly. Didn't you know that? Can't you see it?"

"Well, no… not exactly," he held out his arm, laying it alongside her leg. "See, we're the same, there's hardly any difference. I'm a little browner and you're more honey-coloured.

"You're so funny Rod," she laughed. "Do you want to compare the colour under our bathers?"

Oh no, not again, Rod mouthed silently. He reddened, remembering the last time she brought that up. An image of her, gloriously golden brown in her all-over-tanned nakedness, crossed his mind briefly. He'd trespassed into dangerous ground again, trying desperately not to trigger his face.

"I'm sorry, Rod," she must have sensed his discomfort. "But look at my face, my eyes and my hair. You can see it, can't you?"

"I can't see anything. You just look beautiful to me," he dared say it. "I thought, perhaps you might be Greek or Italian or something like that."

"What do they look like? I've never seen any of them around here."

"Well, I don't really know. They have dark hair, brown eyes and olive skin, like my friend Harry. I dunno, I thought you might have been one of them."

"Aren't there any Aborigines out where you live?"

"Well, I didn't think so, but I really don't know. I thought they looked different. You know…er… I mean really black."

"Full bloods are…"

"Do you mind being an Aborigine?" Rod ventured to ask, thinking about the near-fatal argument he'd witnessed between Dan and Mark.

"It has its disadvantages sometimes. Does it matter to you?"

"I think it sounds exotic," he answered, remembering René's words, "but my cousin René says it's irrelevant."

"Your cousin René sounds very smart. He's not from here either, is he?"

Later that afternoon Beth detoured by the shallow end of the pool on her way towards the turnstile, her towel draped around her bronzed shoulders. Rod watched her approach, wondering what she would say. She knelt down on the tiled edge of the pool where he was instructing Carla to keep her legs straight when kicking.

"Hey guys, how's the swimming lesson coming along?" She shouted above all the noise of the splashing.

Carla looked up at her, wiping the water from her eyes, smiling at Beth. "Rod's a really good teacher, y' know."

"I know. He's helped me out a lot with my maths homework too," Beth replied smiling back at her. "I'm off home now, so I'll see you guys tomorrow arvo. Keep up the good work."

As Beth stood up to leave, Carla returned to her swimming, plunging confidently under the water.

"Thanks for stopping by to say hello, Beth. I really appreciate it, and I think Carla did too," Rod said quietly.

"You're right, Rod, she's nice."

CHAPTER 16. CARLA'S BROTHER, JOEY

ONE AFTERNOON, on his way home from the pool, Rod took a detour. It was still early, only about five, and René's turn to cook tea, so he had some spare time. He rode through the town centre, then west along Oxley Street curious to explore the town's 'other side'. Although there was a lot of heat left in the day, the temperature was falling and the breeze of the ride felt pleasant. He idled up and down a few of the side streets.

Rod wanted to see west Bourke; he'd only been there twice before; once when he went to the tip with René, and again when he went looking for Chief. He hadn't gotten around to asking Carla about where she lived yet, somehow, he'd hesitated; but maybe her house was around here somewhere. Surely not one of these run-down houses; he couldn't picture it, the stark contrast between a priceless artwork housed in a dilapidated gallery of decay and neglect. He came upon a small local park. It was dry, dusty and treeless, with its brown grass worn to bare grey dirt in patches. A bunch of kids were playing cricket with an old tennis ball, using a rolled newspaper for a bat. They stopped their game and stared as Rod rode past.

"Hey mister, nice lookin' bike y' got there." One of them standing closest to the street shouted, waving his arms enthusiastically.

Rod slowed to a stop, lifting up the visor of his full-face helmet. "What are you guys doing?"

"We're betting on who's goin' to win the World Test Series."

Rod hadn't expected such an enthusiastic response and within a few seconds they had all come running over to him, surrounding his bike, a sea of faces, all of them talking at once.

"What type of bike is that? What's your name? Where're from? Do y' want to come and play cricket?"

"It's a Kawasaki 500. I'm Rod from Sydney and, no thanks, I won't stay today. I've gotta go," he finished, and then, after thinking about it for a bit, he continued. "I'll tell you what; I'll take each of you for a turn around the park on the bike. How'd you like that?"

Whoops of joy rose in unison at that suggestion. Talking over the top of one other, they told him their names which Rod promptly forgot amid the excited babble of their conversation. They wore grey shorts and blue button-up short-sleeved cotton shirts, regulation primary school uniform, and close up he could see they were grimy with grey dust, each and every one.

"Take it in turns. Use the foot pegs to climb on behind me and watch out for the exhaust pipes, they're very hot," Rod cautioned. He took the first boy for a slow ride in first gear around the perimeter of the park amid a chorus of shouts, with most of the others running alongside trying to keep up. Well, there goes the rest of my afternoon, Rod thought, but what the heck.

"How come I've never seen any of you guys down at the pool?" Rod asked while they milled, choosing who was going next.

"We go swimmin' in the river." One of the boys spoke for the group.

"Ya don't have to pay t' go swimmin' there," another added.

"Do y' want to come down with us one day? A third boy added hopefully.

"Where do you go?" Rod replied, taking care not to commit himself.

"Anywhere along it is okay," another replied. "But the best place is out at North Bourke boat ramp, next to the bridge. We go out there on weekends."

One of the boys who'd been quietly watching Rod, piped up. "Hey, are you the bloke who's been teachin' my sister to swim at the pool?

"Carla?" Rod studied the little boy's face; whose name he thought might have been Joey. "Yeah, that's right, I've been teachin' her." He noticed from what he could see beneath the layer of dried sweat, dust and grime, he was the same rich golden colour as Carla. "Doesn't she go down to the river with you lot?"

"Mum never let 'er go," Joey replied. "Ever since our cousin drowned ages ago when Carla was little. The river was up that weekend and flowing real fast. My auntie lost sight of her for a moment, and then she was gone. The police came and looked for a long time, but they never found her." Joey paused, his face briefly sad, then continued enthusiastically. "Mum can't stop me though. I've been sneakin' down to the river without her knowin' all this time and I'm a real good swimmer." He finished proudly.

"And so's Carla now!" Rod replied. "Do you wanna come down to the pool one day and race her?"

A broad smile stretched across Joey's face, his white teeth contrasting his grimy skin. "Bet you I can still beat her," he stated defiantly, and then added hopefully. "Do y' think y' could lend me the sixty cents to get in?"

Rod continued doubling the kids in slow circles around the park with the rag-tag group running alongside getting smaller and smaller as the turns went on. By the time he'd finished, the sun was low and red on the horizon, and he knew it was nearly dinner time.

"I've gotta go now," Rod finally found the opportunity to announce, readying himself to leave.

"Can't ya please stay a bit longer?" One of them pleaded.

"Some of us are going to hang round a bit, maybe head over to the main street an' see what's happenin' down there. Why don't y' come with us?" Another boy piped up.

"Sorry, there's a heap of important things I got to do tonight." Rod tried to cut their pleading short, kick starting his bike, making to leave, even feeling guilty as if he were spoiling their fun by going.

"Wish I had something important to do," a smaller girl stated matter-of-factly to no one in particular, almost philosophically.

"Can't ya come back tomorrow arvo, Rod?" Another of them shouted as he rode away. "We're gonna be here or down at the river."

Later, over dinner, Rod told René how he'd ventured into the western side of town, "just for a quick look"; all about how he'd "ended up spending hours there with a big group of kids", he'd run into. After finishing, he was surprised, even shocked, by René's response.

"They're a bunch of trouble makers, those kids, coming into the main street, roaming around after dark. You don't want to be hanging around with them too much, Rod."

Rod didn't think that they were like that at all. They were really nice kids, every single one of them, polite and respectful, perhaps a bit bored, perhaps needing something constructive to do. Unable to find the words to explain his feelings, he remained silent as René continued.

"I was having a drink with Ed down at the RSL the other afternoon and he was telling me about the problems the shop owners down the main street are having with broken windows nowadays."

"Broken windows?" Rod echoed, encouraging René to add more detail. "What's happening?"

"The little buggers are throwing stones at their shop fronts for a joke, smashing the glass and running away. It's a game for them. Ed's had to replace two windows in the past six months, and they're not cheap, y' know. The police can't do anything about it either because they're under age. If they catch them, all they can do is to take them back home and have a word with their parents, but they're back out there again the next day doing the same thing."

Rod remained silent, wondering if they could be the same group of kids. Surely not, he concluded, but then again, Bourke wasn't such a big town, so how could he be so sure, they all had to know one another. Then there'd be the pressure too, pressure to be part of the group, to conform; he remembered what had happened to him at the meatworks. Still unsure what to say, he asked René another question.

"What are they going to do about it then?" Rod remembered how hard they'd tried to get him to stay, how they'd practically begged him to come back the next day. "They really need to find something for those kids to do,"

"It's difficult, Rod," René replied. "They're thinking of putting up shutters, Ed was saying, metal screens they can roll down at night and roll up again in the morning. Otherwise, the only other thing to do is round up all those bloody kids and put them in a home where they can be looked after properly."

Saddened by the finality of René's words, Rod never mentioned the street kids again. It was another of those intractable situations, another wide gulf that no amount of discussion could bridge. He could see he had René worried, firstly about the Carriers' Arms, then Carla, and now all this about him hanging around with street kids, and if he made René anxious enough, he might even call Rod's parents. No, Rod realised, it would be better if he left the matter completely alone. He'd already made up his mind he would go find those kids again—he just wouldn't make such a big deal of it with René.

A few afternoons later, Rod took Joey up on his offer to go see what it was like swimming in the river. They had to be there, Rod noted, as he passed the empty park on the way. He left the bitumen and rode along the top of the dusty levee scanning the eucalypt-crowned banks and brown waters of the Darling. Alerted by joyous whoops and shouts echoing among the red gums, it didn't take him long to spot the kids splashing about in the dappled afternoon light as it filtered through the drooping eucalypt branches. Sunlight danced on the rippled surface of the river—the scene before him a delicate play in brown, gold and olive tones in contrast to the vibrant grass-green and aqua hues of the open-skyed pool environment he was used to. The dusty bank below him plunged steeply into the opaque waters of the river as they swirled around fallen limbs and tree roots sticking out at grotesque angles and telling of what snags lurked dangerously below. Rod could imagine Joey's mother not being keen on the idea of her kids swimming here, worrying about the ever-present risk of another tragedy. It was a far cry from the safe and organised pool environment. He dismounted, pulling his bike onto its centre-stand.

"Hey Rod! Down here! Come on in," they shouted out as soon as they spotted him. "We didn't think you were gonna make it."

There were about six of them he recognised from the other day in the park. They were all wearing their same grey school shorts, wet now; their blue shirts, shoes and socks thrown together in a heap higher on the dusty bank.

Rod laid his clothes and towel on the seat of his motorcycle and climbed gingerly down the bank. Approaching the water's edge, it became slippery, muddied by much activity. The afternoon sun shone strongly on his back and the cooling river water wrapped around his legs, sparkling in the sunshine.

"Watch out," Joey cautioned. "There's a big snag under the water over where you're standing."

"It's safe once ya know where everything is," another boy added, observing Rod's slow deliberate movements.

Rod inched across and lowered himself into the brown waters, his feet sinking into the soft mud.

OUTBACK SUMMER

"RIVER SWING"

Robert Coenraads
2024

He felt around cautiously, fingers outstretched for the snag until he could feel the smooth form of a massive trunk just below the surface. He steadied himself, climbing onto it.

"There's nothin' more out further," Joey called.

Rod plunged into the river, its cool brown waters embracing him as he swam with slow powerful stokes towards the middle. Bobbing to the surface, now alone out there, he watched the distant banks lazily drift by, the perfume of wet silt and eucalypt evoking a timeless sense of oneness with nature he'd never felt at the pool. He remembered the Chief's stories about the river country—channel ways charged with water and life-giving greenery; their delicate dendritic networks stretching like winding serpents across a thousand miles of endless desert—living highways interconnecting every corner of the continent for those who understood the secrets of how to travel them. The thrill of an ever-present element of danger, heightened his senses too, reminding him of the Murray River at Albury, where his parents stopped for a break on their annual pilgrimage to family in Melbourne. They'd certainly never let him swim in the river when he was younger, apart from paddling his feet on its silty edges, their tales of strong currents and submerged dangers still vivid in his mind. Returning to the present, he swam towards the bank to socialize with the others

A thick rope with a few knots in the end hung from one of the high overhanging branches, with each of the kids taking turns to swing out over the river—releasing their grip at the perfect moment and performing various acrobatic feats on the way down. It was clear they practiced here a lot.

"Do you come here often?" Rod asked, waiting his turn with the rest of them.

"Almost every day in summer," came back the obvious answer.

"And what do you do when it gets dark," Rod decided to probe a little, remembering René's comments, hoping to prove his cousin wrong. "I suppose you go home and have tea then?"

"Nah, we go hang around the main street with the older kids for a bit of fun. You can come along with us if you like."

"But everything's already closed now. It sounds pretty boring to me."

"I reckon it is boring," the smallest girl in the group admitted—the philosopher he remembered from last time. "But there's nothing else to do around here."

"Why don't you get a little job then, perhaps for a few hours each day after school? Earn some pocket money?"

"There aren't any jobs like that around here. Believe me, I've been lookin' everywhere and I know!" Joey answered for the group.

"Yeah, and even if there were any jobs, nobody would trust us to do 'em anyway," the little girl added.

After the noisy mob dispersed, Rod sat on the levee a while longer in the late afternoon quiet watching the sun sink amongst the red gums on the far bank, their shadows slowly lengthening across the river. Joey decided to stop a while too, sitting down beside him.

"Carla's the clever one, y' know," Joey started back on their earlier conversation as Rod listened idly. "She doesn't work for nobody. She's got her own business going on the side in her spare time. She's nearly as smart as me, I reckon," he added, his eyes glistening cheekily.

"What's that?" Rod asked, the mention of Carla stirring his interest.

"She collects refunds! She pedals everywhere around town, hunting for empties—Rice's cordials mainly, and lots of other bottles too. She stacks 'em in her carry basket, real careful so they don't smash. An' when she gets enough she'll ride to the shops and cash 'em in."

"Nice one!" Rod whistled.

"She gets real mad though, if I nick 'em from her and get down to the shop before she does," he added cheekily.

Rod, suddenly remembering, reached into the pocket of his jeans.

"I've brought the sixty cents for you, Joey," he said, placing a neat stack of coins into his outstretched palm.

"Thanks Rod."

"So you'll come to the pool tomorrow arvo then?"

"Yeah, maybe," Joey flashed a mischievous smile. "I guess, unless I spend it on a bag of lollies first."

CHAPTER 17. THE COUPON

ROD LAY COMFORTABLY on the pool lawns under a shady tree, its leaves jigsaw silhouettes against the brilliance of the ever-cloudless azure vault. He idly watched Carla pull her tight jeans shorts over her wet swimsuit and stretch her arms gracefully skyward. Arching like a ballerina, her t-shirt slipped naturally over her lithe body like a glove. The world's cares and worries lay a million miles distant.

"See ya later Rod," she smiled, bending over to gather her towel which was spread out next to his. Just as she turned to leave, Rod remembered what he had wanted to say.

"Hey Carla, hang on a sec." He sat up, searching around, and pressed three 20 cent coins into her damp hand. "Could you give these to Joey? He was supposed to come down to the pool this arvo. He wants to race you... And he reckons he'll win too!" Rod said smiling. "Do you think you're up to it?"

"Him, beat me? No way! Carla's lips parted in a broad smile. "He said he'd seen y' at the river the yesterday."

"Yeah, it was great fun. I already did give him 60 cents but I figured, when he didn't show up today, the cheeky bugger spent it all at the lolly shop."

Carla stuffed the coins into her shorts' pocket, starting towards the pool turnstile where her bike waited, propped against the pool fence.

"And tell him not to waste it on lollies this time!" Rod called after her. He watched her hesitate a moment, turn around, and start walking back towards him.

OUTBACK SUMMER

"CARLA"

Robert Coenraads
2024

"Thanks for the money, Rod…" She paused, uncertain for the right words. "It's a little hard for us sometimes, y' know, Mum and us, our family…"

Rod remained silent, not exactly sure he wanted to hear what might come next, but he waited for Carla to continue. He lay down again on his towel, idly watching the wetness from her swimsuit seep into the fabric of her jean cut-offs; her shoulder straps showing as damp lines along her white t-shirt.

"Dad's drunk all the time," her words tumbled forth. "We never see him 'cause he's either at the pub or shut up in his room sleeping, so mum's gotta work and look after the family all by herself. And on top of that, now there's the grandkids to look after too."

"Your mum sounds like a real saint[17]."

"I help her a lot with the little 'uns now." Carla smiled briefly, a flash of pride, before again turning serious. "I really hate his guts sometimes, y' know, when I think about what he's done to our family; what he's been puttin' mum through." She looked up at Rod's face occasionally, checking his interest, but mostly down at her feet, her head lowered.

Rod winced. He really didn't want to hear about any more differences between him and Carla. He couldn't imagine anything worse than a pig of a father like that, a real pathetic brute. Why couldn't everybody just be the same? Thoughts of his own family rose, mingling with her words; his own dad always ready to help, always around for him, for as long as he could ever recall, a powerful, solid, reassuring presence in his life. He felt sorry for Carla, really sorry that she could never experience that joy of a caring, loving father, instead of the deep brooding resentment she felt for the parasitic demon lurking in her home. Rod never wanted for anything in life; everything he needed was always there. All his parents ever asked of him was to do well at his studies.

Rod waited for Carla to continue, but she didn't. She sat looking at the ground, head lowered, eyes downcast. He wondered if she felt ashamed of all she had just told him, ashamed of her family. Maybe they didn't have much money?

"I'm really sorry to hear that…," Rod muttered lamely. He was at a complete loss for words, floundering out of his depth. How could he cheer her up? Perhaps she just needed someone to listen to her?

"Hey Carla… How about we share a bag of hot chips, if you've got the time? We can eat 'em here in the shade and talk some more?"

"Yeah, thanks Rod." She looked up, a brief smile lightening her face. "That'd be great."

After Rod returned with the chips, and sat down beside her on the grass, Carla continued on the same theme, revealing more of her story; the flood gates of the dam now wrenched wide, her words gushed in torrents. There were tears too.

"Mum's hardly got anything in the house for all the kids 'cause of Dad's drinking; that's where all the money goes, any money he can get his hands on… That's just how it is… We'd be starving if it weren't for the coupons, y' know, they're the only reason we've got any food in the house at all."

"Coupons?" Rod repeated the word, wondering what they were. He dared not ask any further, not wishing to appear any stupider than he sometimes felt in front of her; not wanting to put his foot in his mouth again. Sometimes he just didn't get this town at all, the way it seemed to work. It must be pretty hard for Carla to tell him all this stuff, he thought; all of her family's problems. Rod couldn't do much, couldn't offer any advice; there was really nothing much he could say, apart from listen to what she had to say, caringly, sympathetically, tears welling in his own eyes at the thought of what Carla must be going through. Those food coupons must be some kind of charity thing, he thought. Perhaps René might know something about them.

"I've never seen one of them before, Carla? What do they look like?" he ventured for want of something better to say.

Carla pulled a crumpled piece of blue paper out of her damp shorts' pocket. "I've got one right here. I was going to stop by Permewans on the way home and pick up some things for mum." Smoothing it flat, she handed it to Rod.

"Redeemable for ten dollar's value" Rod read out loud. What a strange concept he thought, like some kind of licence for printing money. Why would they do that? He reached into his own pocket and pulled out a ten dollar note, comparing it to the strange counterfeit. "I've also gotta go to the supermarket and get some things for dinner, so I'll give the voucher a try," he said idly as he handed the ten-dollar note to Carla.

"Same difference," she smiled, eyeing him curiously.

"If you're going there now, maybe, I might just see y' there too," Rod finished.

"See ya then, maybe."

Rod's gaze followed Carla as she headed towards the turnstiles. He'd make sure of it though, he decided, no maybes about it.

A few minutes later Rod angle-parked his bike in the main street outside of Permewans. He found Carla alone in the dried foods aisle of the near-empty store, engrossed in the task of scooping out rice, peas and beans from the powdery sacks open on the shop floor. She smiled warmly, looking far more cheerful now, greeting him as he approached.

"And what are you planning for this evening's dinner?" she began drawing him into conversation, seemingly eager to chat about lighter things.

"Lately I've been calling mum for recipes and other tips. I need to cook something different for poor René. I reckon he must be getting sick of lamb's fry, boiled spuds and peas! Although, sometimes I swap carrots for peas for a change," Rod laughed, entertaining Carla with his ramblings. "I made him meatloaf the other night, which he liked. Mum taught me how to put hard-boiled eggs into the mince, plus chopped onions, mushrooms, carrots and peas for variety, and even stale bread to soak up all the fat from the mince. It's the cheapskate's way to save on meat, y' know, but it does create an interesting taste and texture."

"What's your favourite dish?" Rod asked before going on to explore what ingredients she preferred, how she prepared them; hanging on every word of her replies. He found their conversation strange—even exciting. He'd never had conversations about food with a girl before and, somehow, it seemed rather intimate and personal—perhaps like discussing the seductive qualities of lingerie, aftershave or perfume; probably things that married people talk about, when they spend their whole lives together, Rod dreamed briefly, before pushing the concept from his mind, hoping that his cheeks wouldn't colour up. He hated how that could happen to him whenever he started thinking about it.

A short while later Carla stood ahead of him at the checkout. He was daydreaming, his mind pleasantly distracted, still idling over the fun that he'd just had, doing something that he normally found a bit of a chore. Snippets of conversation between Carla and the cashier wafted lazily by.

"How's y'r mum and the rest of the kids, Carla?"

"We're all fine thanks, Mr Symonds. And yourself and Mrs Symonds?" He heard Carla answer, her words filtering through his mind, triggering lines of random thought. It's funny how you can get to know nearly everybody in a town this size. He liked how that happened, Henry Lawson's words ringing true, 'Bourke is mateship country'. Often people would stop and talk to him too, ask him where he was from or what he was doing. Then he'd add them to his own growing list of folks he could wave at, or nod to when he was out and about the town. There were way too many people in the big city for anything like that to ever happen. Rod liked that about Bourke, the country, but it did mean you could never expect to do anything in a hurry. He reckoned that it was a fair exchange though; about the same amount of time lost in friendly conversation as all of the time lost in the big city travelling about from place to place in traffic and congestion.

"Here, take this other bag as well, Carla. Mrs Symonds put aside an extra bottle of milk and loaf of bread for your mum. Please give her our regards, won't you love?"

"Thanks Mr Symonds. Will do, I'll tell mum that. See you later." She headed out the door, a grocery bag tucked under each arm.

Rod's mind was still distracted as he came through the checkout. If he was quick, he could catch up with Carla again out front, as she packed the shopping into the basket of her bike. He handed over a bunch of notes to the cashier.

"Hey mate... Where'd y' get this from?"

Rod's mind suddenly snapped back to the present. Mr Symonds' tone had turned challenging and confrontational. What was he talking about anyway? Rod looked up and saw he was holding the coupon up to the light, close his glasses, studying it. Mr Symonds turned back toward him, his eyes focusing hard on him, boring into him. "Well???"

"Er... I..." Rod was at a loss for words. "I gave somebody ten dollars for it," he stammered, grateful that Carla was out of hearing range.

"Y' don't give nobody any money for these, mate! They're here for a purpose. Who'd y' get it off?"

"Er..." Rod didn't know what to say. He felt pretty foolish, but he knew one thing for sure that he wasn't going to dob in Carla. What was this all about anyway he wondered. "Er... I'm not sure... I dunno who it was? Can't I use it?"

"Very well then, mate." The cashier spoke in a measured tone, quietly, but obviously very angry with Rod. "You keep hold of your own money in future. I'm accepting it this time, but if I ever see you in here again with another one of these, I'm going to take it off of you, y' hear, and report you to the police?"

Rod felt hot and bothered, red with embarrassment, as he took his shopping bags and walked out of the supermarket onto the footpath; the breeze cooling his face and ears. Carla was waiting, astride her bike, ready to leave. He hoped she wouldn't notice his discomposure as he readied himself with a smile to say goodbye.

"What's the big deal about these money coupons, René? Have you ever heard of them?" As they sat at the dining room table enjoying their regular nightly conversations over dinner, he told René about what happened in the supermarket that afternoon.

"Coupons!" René stretched back in his chair before continuing. "They're food vouchers. Each one has a certain redeemable value. The government hands them out to the unemployed, Aborigines mostly, so that they can exchange them for food in the supermarket."

"What's the point, why not just give them the money? And why'd the bloke in the supermarket get so worked up about me having one?" Rod was still perplexed over the whole incident.

"Food vouchers can't be traded for anything else but food, and that means no booze or cigarettes. When Ed Symonds caught you with it, he wouldn't have known how many more you might've bought—perhaps cheating some desperate drunk out of them for five bucks apiece—then he'd figure there'd be some poor family out there short of money, whose kids are going hungry this week."

"How can you give somebody coupons, René? That's like telling them that they're totally incompetent. You're saying to them that they're not capable of being given real money."

"Look Rod, it is a bit degrading I guess, but what else can you do, if they're going to keep on spending all their money on grog down at the pub? And don't think that it's just the blacks that have that problem; there are a lot of white families in trouble with the drink as well," René explained.

"Can't the pub just stop serving people and send them home when they get drunk?" Rod was interested now, animated, exploring the theme from different angles.

"They sometimes try, Rod, and sometimes they don't. People get angry when they're drunk and, besides, that's how the pubs make their living. It's not an easy situation to solve. Anyway, if they can't get their grog in the pub, they'll just go buy it down at the bottle-o. Most of them do that anyway, it's cheaper than the pub, so they can buy more. There's no easy solution."

OUTBACK SUMMER

"ED SYMMONDS" Robert Coenraads 2024

Rod thoughts turned again to Carla, his heart swelling with indignation as to what she had to go through each day, just doing simple things like shopping for the family.

"But it's not fair for Carla," he blurted out. "She's the one that's gotta use those things every day!"

"No one's going to be blaming Carla. Nobody can pick and choose what family they're born into, Rod. Ed Symonds—everyone else around town—knows it's not her fault. Carla's family's problems are all to do with her father, nothing to do with her. Being an Aboriginal kid, she'd be so used to it anyway; that's just the way it is around here Rod. Carla wouldn't notice the difference half the time if she pulled a ten-dollar bank note or a ten-dollar coupon out of her pocket to pay for the food and neither would Ed Symonds," René concluded philosophically, then softly added an afterthought. "Her father would spot the note though—in the blink of an eye."

An Aboriginal kid! René's description of Carla using those words knifed raw zigzags through Rod's brain, slicing it free from its basal medulla—the sturdy pedestal upon which complacently sat his cherished concept that everybody should be the same, equal no matter what. Aboriginality sounded so derogatory the way René put it, even though Rod figured he didn't mean it that way. So what about being an Aborigine? Why did everybody always make such a big deal about the Aboriginal thing around here? Paddy's parents were Irish, his own were Dutch, nobody ever bothered to talk about that. What's the big difference anyway? He'd admired her deep golden skin down at the pool, so strikingly perfect he could barely take his eyes off her, but his own deeply-tanned skin, apart from his backside, wasn't all that much lighter. Why should her life be so difficult while his was so easy? It wasn't fair.

CHAPTER 18. THE ELYSIAN

THERE WAS always a big crowd at the Elysian Café of a hot afternoon, always one or two groups, lounging out front of its fly strap screen under the shade of the ample awning, scanning the main street for any interesting goings-on, or inside, sitting around the Laminex tables and Art Deco booths, gossiping over a hot bag of chips and a milkshake. Rod liked it in there too, usually wanting not to buy anything in particular, but just for a short social visit or a quick chat with one or another of their gang, usually in that spare few minutes between leaving the pool and returning home for dinner on the nights that René cooked. It was only three minutes' walk from the house and there was always someone he knew, either coming or going.

Paddy was never there, of course, because the place was somehow beneath his social status. Being older, he went to the pub with workmates instead. Rod had experienced that. He knew how it all worked now; it was just that he still couldn't figure out why it had to be like that. Given the choice between the Oxford and the Elysian, he'd choose the Elysian any day.

Carla would never go either. He knew that too now; he'd even asked her a few times before he figured out how the town's social norms worked, so he never tried again after that. All that rubbish about being part of a one or another group too; he'd made up his mind that he was above all that. He was feeling extra cocky that afternoon. He was the one bloke in town who was going to do whatever he liked, wherever he liked, and with whomsoever he liked!

That afternoon, he spotted Carla on the opposite side of the street. She was on her pushbike in front of the Post Office Hotel, surrounded by a group of about six young blokes standing on the footpath outside the saloon doors. Rod couldn't quite make out what was going on from his vantage point behind the shopfront glass of the Elysian, but in an instant, he'd made up his mind—he'd go over there right away, introduce himself, and say hello to her group of friends.

He cut across Oxley Street diagonally, quickly coming up under the awning of the Post Office Hotel.

"Hi Carla, How're you doing?" He started casually. "I saw you from the Elysian and thought I'd come over and say g'day."

"Er…Hello…" Carla mumbled weakly, almost inaudibly, looking down at the ground.

Rod looked around at the others, their eyes all on him, to a man. In an instant he understood, knowing he'd just made the biggest mistake of his life. He could feel it, but there was no turning back. He turned red instantly.

"Er… Hello… I'm Rod from Sydney…"

Silence….

Carla was still looking down at the ground, avoiding eye contact with anyone. He could sense the wordless tension. Then, to make matters even worse, Brad emerged from the Post Office hotel and joined the others, glaring in silent disbelief at the presence of Rod in their midst.

Finally, one of them spoke.

"We've had a gutful of this joke? Who do y' think she is, mate? —A slut for any new whitey that comes into town?"

"No… no, it's not like that… We're friends, that's all," he protested weakly. "I'm teaching her how to swim…" Damn! Why was he so bloody slow? He should have figured that out all along. Ricky had even told him so. Carla was theirs; she'd grown up with them, and she belonged to them. He knew any attempt at stupid, idle, small talk would be useless, so strong was their contempt for him, the outsider threatening their property, stealing what rightfully belonged to them. More silence followed.

Then another spoke,

"I think you'd better just piss off then, mate!"

A stubby bottle dropped to the ground, smashing on the pavement. He noticed Carla flinch.

'Well, what 'r' y' waitin' for? Rack off then!" A third added.

"Er… Yeah!" Rod felt himself shrinking down to the size of a bug about to be squashed under their shoes.

"Piss off, and stay the hell away from Carla if ya know what's good for you. I'll bloody-well kill ya if I hear otherwise," Brad finished.

OUTBACK SUMMER

"BUG EYE VIEW"

Robert Coenraads
2024

Rod backed away, bowing to their numbers, looking down at his feet, embarrassed and shocked by the whole incident. Red faced, he turned away without a further word, and headed home.

Damn it, they were right. He thought about it as he crossed Central Park in the golden afternoon light. Who in the hell did he think he was anyway? Was he trying to win her heart for the sake of winning it? Just for fun and challenge? Trying to win the heart of their most prized trophy; to steal the most precious gem in their crown? He knew it was true. He couldn't deny his feelings for her, and that he would defy anybody who stood in his way. But what was he planning to do with her confidence and trust—and any nascent feelings she might have for him? What would he do? Cast her aside broken and sad, her honour lost, when he had to inevitably leave his precious Bourke at the end of his seemingly-endless summer? What an idiot! Who knows how much trouble he'd just caused for Carla? He'd probably wrecked her life. She obviously hated his guts now anyway; he hated his own guts; and he knew for sure she'd never come back to the pool again.

Carla still sat astride her bike, head down. Out of the corner of her eye she watched Rod disappear. She felt shamed and desperately wanted to leave too. She knew it wasn't finished yet.

"What a bloody nerve to try it on with you—right in front of all of us. Can you believe the stupidity of that?" one of Brad's mates started. "Now we're gonna have to find him and bash him up. He won't stand a chance."

"I've warned you about talkin' to out-of-towners?" Brad began softly, trying to engage eye contact with Carla. "Y' know they're nothing but bad news—here one minute gone the next."

"You've gotta listen to what Brad tells ya Carla[18]," another mate added.

"We're family, Carla, and we gotta stick together. We're the only ones who really care." Brad crooned softly before his voice hardened. "That Conway's a creep. Dan tells me he's a real smooth operator. He'll try and crack on to every sheila he meets. So far, they've all been smart enough to reject him and now he's worked his way down the list to you. How'd he talk you into wasting your money going to the bloody pool?"

Carla sat lost for words, waiting for Brad to go on.

"Well…" cut in one of his mates. "Brad's askin' ya."

"It's just for swimmin' lessons…" Carla answered weakly.

"Swimming lessons!" Brad retorted. "Why don't you ever come down to the river with me? I can show you how to do all that down at the river."

"You know I'm not allowed…"

"Mummy's little girl's not allowed," another of Brad's mates echoed mockingly.

"Conway's a bloody clever one y' know," a third began. "Now the filthy bastard's got the perfect excuse to finger ya off under water every day. Like a rat up a bloody drain pipe."

"Just shut yer trap, ya dirty-minded bastard," Brad cut him off, turning back towards Carla, apologetic now. "Let's just forget all this happened. I'm going in to buy a round for my mates. Do you wanna hang around for a bit and have a drink?"

"I'm sorry Brad, I gotta go now. Mr Symonds' closing up soon an' he's waiting for me to pick up the shopping."

"Why so quiet tonight, Rod?" René asked as they ate dinner in silence.

"Dunno, just really tired tonight I guess," Rod managed, deflated like a week-old party balloon. He'd just done such a stupid thing. Perhaps his whole friendship with Carla was stupid; he couldn't even bring himself to say anything about it to René. He'd just say the same thing as Paddy, Donna, Rick or anyone else for that matter—you just don't try to do things like that around here—it's not the way things are done. It just won't work—it never has and it never will!

"I think I'll go do the dishes and have an early night."

Later, a quiet knock sounded on the front door. Rod was at the sink, his hands in the suds, so René stood up from the table to answer.

"Rod, its Carla," he called, returning to his paperwork.

Rod came through the flyscreen door onto the porch, his eyes adjusting to the moonless night. Carla stood out in the dark away from the door, her face hidden in a world of shadows and streetlamp silhouettes, her bike leaning against the side of the house.

"I'm so sorry…" Facing each other, they both began in unison, and then paused.

"Rod, I'm so sorry about what happened today…" Carla went first, her head down.

"No, Carla," he interrupted her, "I'm the one who's sorry. It was so dumb of me to come over there, to disturb you and your friends…"

"They're not really my friends, Rod," she answered, interrupting him. "But they're part of my gang, my mob, y' know. You've gotta understand about that, Rod. I can't just do as I like. There's a heap of unwritten rules that you can't read, being an outsider. You grow up with them here, so nobody ever has to explain them to you. They just are! Everybody living here, your friends, my friends, everyone knows about them."

Rod had no answer to that. He wanted to say, just forget about the rules—free yourself from them, just do whatever you like—but he was beginning to comprehend now—he'd learnt the power they wielded. He remained silent.

"You just can't come up to me in front of all of them and say hello. It doesn't work that way." Tears began to stream down her cheeks now as she spoke about the unspoken rules, as she explained them in words to an outsider for the very first time in her life.

"They're really not all that bad, those blokes, but they've got it in for you, Rod, because you've been so nice to me. They resent me because I betrayed them by talking to you, but they hate you because you're different; you're an out-of-towner. It's worse now that you've crossed them. I'm so sorry, Rod" Carla started sobbing quietly. "Promise me you'll be careful going anywhere around town[19]."

Rod broke down, looking at her pretty tear-streamed face, feeling her anguish, aware of the shame and ridicule she'd have to suffer around town, all because of him. More than he could bear, it was his turn to weep quietly now. Her face said it all for him—lowered in shame, it spoke the whole terrible story—a thousand words in its pained expression. Only now he fully realised the effort she'd been putting in all these weeks just to be at the pool, just being here right now. Turning away, he hid his face, wakening fully to the pain he'd put her through.

"So, I won't be able to see you any more…? I've ruined your life" He blurted. He looked away feeling hot tears streaming down his cheeks, trying to hide them. "I guess that means you can't come to the pool then?" His own beautiful world collapsing too, now that he'd completely destroyed hers.

"Please Rod, I don't want to talk about this anymore," Carla concluded, not really sure how anything at all would turn out now. She'd crossed an invisible line into uncharted territory, into a dark place where she'd never been before, and with absolutely no idea of where that would lead her next.

She was scared, nothing was certain any more, yet, somehow, through the mists of darkness, she sensed a light ahead, a dim hope—a sense of freedom from having chosen to take that first bold step across the line regardless of the consequences. She looked up at his face.

"No more talk about the ifs, buts and maybes of tomorrow, it's all about today—right now."

Later that evening, Rod thought about the promise he'd made to Carla—never to speak about it with her again. He went to bed hoping that if he did just that, and buried his head back in the sand, perhaps his life and everything else might just carry on as normal.

CHAPTER 19. ROD PLUMBS ROCK BOTTOM

IT DIDN'T TAKE LONG for news of the incident in front of the Post Office Hotel to get around to Paddy.

"Geez mate, she's Brad's sheila. Didn't ya know he's hot on her? It's one thing talking to her here at the pool, but in the main street? Geez mate, that was dumb! Brad's on the lookout to bloody-well kill ya now, and when the rest of the town finds out there's gonna be even more trouble, and that ain't gonna take too long 'cause Bourke's a small place. I've told ya that[20]."

Paddy had come straight over to meet him as soon he came in through the pool turnstiles. He could see the rest of the gang sitting on their towels over by the diving boards; their eyes were all upon him, boring into him, obviously curious to know what Paddy was saying

Rod hung his head in shame; sensing the whole of Bourke staring at him. Now everybody would know what he'd done. He couldn't think of a reply, so Paddy continued.

"It's just not the way things are done around here. You've gotta give it up mate, for your own good."

"But… I…haven't done anything," Rod managed to stammer. "I've been teachin' her how to swim. We're just friends, that's all."

"Your friends are the ones sitting over there where they sit every day, mate! Do y' think they're happy about all of this?" Paddy paused to let the question sink in then softened his tone. "I wouldn't be telling you all this if you weren't a good mate, y' know."

Rod sat on his towel forlornly at the edge of the group. Dan and Ricky weren't there. The girls weren't saying much to each other and barely two words to him. Donna looked visibly upset.

Carla didn't show up at the pool that afternoon either; perhaps the reality of the situation he'd triggered yesterday made it difficult for her. Maybe she'd realised the whole friendship was a bad idea? A thousand other possibilities flashed through his mind. Despite the hot sunny skies and cool water, Rod sank into an abyss of his own making. The afternoon seemed to drag on for ever, until finally he made up his mind to leave.

"See you later, Rod," Beth managed a fleeting smile, a momentary understanding glance, which he returned briefly. He knew she understood how he felt, but there was nothing she or anybody else could do about it—the town's rules were about as rigid as commandments chiselled into slabs of stone.

Later, to make matters worse, as Rod pushed through the turnstiles, he saw Brad on his bike by the gravelled road edge, a group of younger admirers hanging around the machine. Brad was talking to them, while his eyes focused intently on the pool entrance. Was he lying in wait? Rod speculated on the likely possibility, moving quickly away from the gates as discreetly as he could, his head bowed to avoid eye contact. He jogged along the footpath towards home, his senses heightened as to what was happening behind; his worst fears confirmed at the sound of Brad thrusting down hard on his kick-starter, his bike's motor roaring into life.

Rod didn't look back, sensing he was being followed slowly at a distance through the menacing burble of Brad's machine. The rumble increased in pitch to the whine of an angry hornet as the bike flew by, zooming ahead to the end of the block. Brad chucked a U-turn in another shower of gravel then accelerated fast toward him. Protected by the gutter and a row of trees, Rod dissimulated, nonchalantly looking away as the bike passed.

"Go bloody home! You're not welcome in Bourke," angry Doppler-shifted words rose above the roar of the speeding bike, then further insults he couldn't make out as the bike distanced, something about Carla. Chancing a quick backward glance, Rod saw Brad race as far as the pool and throw another U-turn in the gravel to the delight of the onlookers. Then the burble of the engine told him Brad was stalking behind again, lurking longer this time, before a repeat of the angry joust.

"Piss off home, Conman…," sounded among other taunts. Several more aggressive charges and intimidating tirades followed.

Brad stopped the charges as Rod reached the corner of busier Richard Street, dropping back the distance of about a block or two.

What was Brad up to? Pursuing him—trying to figure out where he lived? He'd never mentioned it to anyone, so obviously that was the reason.

Rounding the corner, Rod seized the precious moments he was out of Brad's sight. He sprinted along Richard Street then, instead heading straight homeward, he dodged behind some trees, angled across Daley Street, and cut into the anonymity of Central Park where he quickly hid behind a tree, straining to hear above the din of his heart pounding in his ears, hoping Brad would have no idea where he went.

Having thrown his stalker off the track with his deft move, Rod walked along one of the diagonal paths, heading home the long way, unawares that further trouble lay in store.

Dan and Ricky were at the other end of Central Park walking towards him. He hadn't said much to them since the bike race, and after what had just happened, wasn't in the mood to talk to them now. They hadn't seen him yet, so he veered off the path, and, finding a suitable tree, began to climb it. He'd always enjoyed climbing trees, he reflected, pulling himself easily through the branches, but about halfway up he realised it was yet another stupid thing to do. Who did he think he was fooling?

Next minute Dan and Ricky stood at the base of the tree looking up.

"What do you think you're doing up there?" Ricky called. They picked up handfuls of bean-shaped seed pods lying on the ground, hurling them angrily at him.

"Come down out of that bloody tree, y' cowardly bastard," Dan demanded.

"I'll come down all right," rising anger beginning to replace his feelings of foolishness. "And I'm going to bash you both!"

"Yeah! You try it then," Ricky countered.

"You're a bastard Conway," Dan shouted. "Why'd y' have to go tell René about the fight between me and Mark?"

"Yeah," Ricky echoed, "Why'd y' have to tell him?"

"It was only harmless fun and now we lost our jobs because of you," Dan continued angrily.

"Harmless fun? That's bullshit mate! You came within inches of chopping Mark's bloody head off, mate. The work ran out anyway—René told you that already. Nothin' to do with me."

"Piss off mate. If the work ran out why'd y' hire Pete then? To get in good with Beth, I reckon it was," Dan spat angrily.

"Haven't y' even heard about her boyfriend Steve?"

"Yeah, we know about Steve."

"Well get lost then! Mates don't pinch other mates' girlfriends, even if they don't know the bloke."

OUTBACK SUMMER

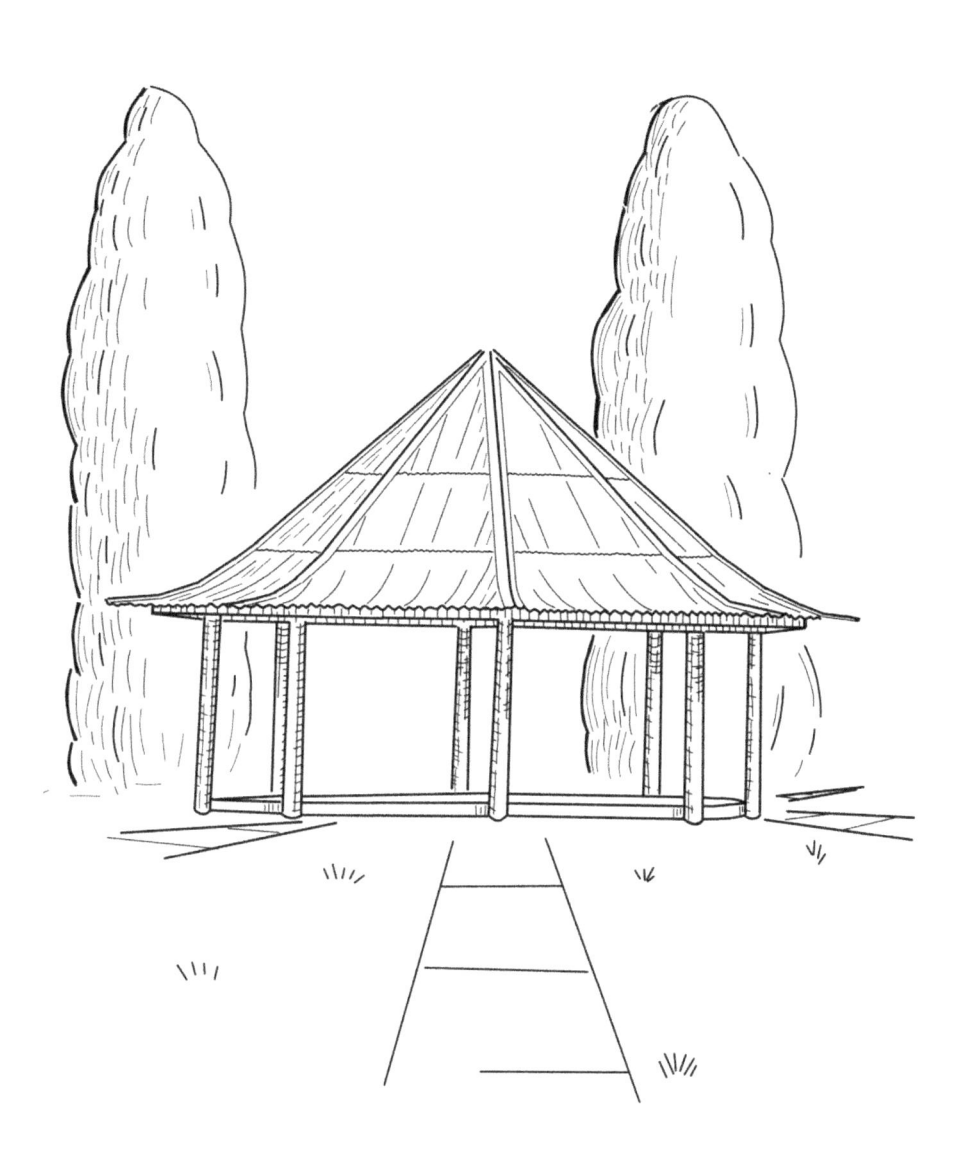

"THE ROTUNDA CENTRAL PARK"

Robert Coenraads
2025

"Yeah, and why didn't y' tell us about her party then?" Rick added. "You're trying to pinch all our bloody sheilas, aren't ya mate? It looks like y' want 'em all for yourself."

"It was René who hired Pete," Rod shouted, the branches shaking angrily, as he began climbing down. "And as for the party, I'm not the one to do the inviting. I got invited because I was helping Beth with her maths. Why didn't you do that?"

"Tell us another one mate!"

"Look mate," Rod continued, "I'm not interested in none of your bloody sheilas. Y' can go and ask Beth. Nobody at all from the gang…" He began before realising he didn't want to go there for quids.

"Who's that then?" Dan demanded, picking up on it immediately.

"None of your business!" Rod replied, feeling foolish then, angry. "Nobody you'd even give the slightest damn about anyway."

"Try us then, mate."

"Nah, I think I'll leave it just there."

"I reckon its gotta be Carla, then," Dan insisted. "I heard what happened outside the Post Office Hotel yesterday arvo. What do ya reckon Ricky?"

"For sure mate," Ricky agreed. "He's been hanging around with her at the pool a lot lately, and the other day he said he was gonna unwrap her like a bloody Christmas present! Donna wasn't real happy to hear that either."

"My brother's gonna kill you if you're trying for his sheila, mate," Dan menaced. "So, I reckon y'd better just leave 'em all alone and piss off back to Sydney."

"You piss off, you bastards. I'll do as I please," Rod retorted.

"Not around here ya won't mate!"

"You bastards," Rod swore angrily, as he rode the trunk down like a fire pole. He dropped through the lowermost branches, landing on the ground at the foot of the tree. "That's it then; I've completely lost it with you guys."

By the time Rod touched down, Dan and Ricky had moved back about twenty feet, standing one on either side of the tree, obviously figuring he couldn't go after both of them at once.

"You're the one who nearly chopped off Mark's head, not me, and René already said you didn't get sacked for that. You've done the job and you've done it well, and it's over now. And René said he'd write you a reference letter about it if you wanted, so piss off, both of you inventing bastards."

Dan and Ricky half-heartedly threw a few more seedpods at Rod's feet, symbolic offerings of their disgust. They walked in a wide circle around him before coming together and continuing on their way through the park, leaving Rod to lick his wounds, realising he wasn't as deeply wounded by the name calling as he thought he would be. He had no friends left in Bourke, probably not even Carla, now that the gossip had spread around the town. Dejected and miserable, Rod headed home. He didn't even talk about it with René because he'd probably say the same thing as everyone else. Maybe René had already heard about it anyway.

The whole town seemed against his unholy alliance with Carla. Even when he walked down the main street or into Permewans for groceries, he felt everyone staring. He couldn't shake the feeling; even Mr Symonds, when he thought Rod wasn't looking, seemed to stare at him strangely, almost pityingly. Was he just imagining it or, perhaps, did they all think he was a dead-man walking toward his own funeral.

Resolutely, he put the afternoon's events out of his mind; vowing to return to the pool tomorrow anyway, just in case Carla showed up. And as for the group, he'd stand up to them if he had to, for what he believed in and for what was right. He knew he could count on Beth's support at least.

Over the next few days Rod reached a cautious ceasefire with the town. Somehow, he'd managed to steer clear of Brad and his gang, and stay alive, maintaining his daily routine as best he could. He said nothing to René—no point in worrying him too. He even took his customary evening walk, though decidedly ill at ease, flinching at every sound[10], taking more than-the-usual odd backward glance and keeping to the shadows cast by the street lamps.

He swam at the pool, while Paddy, Dan, Rick and the girls begrudgingly accepted the situation, allowing him to lurk in silence at the fringes of their group in some form of uneasy truce. Maybe Beth had something to do with it or perhaps they respected the fact he hadn't run like a bunny from Brad's threats. Carla never showed up and Rod resigned himself to the fact that she probably never would. Best thing he could do for her, when the time came, would be to leave town without further word or backward glance.

Then as hope, like the sun-bleached colours of his beach towel, had all but faded away, his salvation, an apparition in black t-shirt and faded jean cut-offs, materialised from his once-carefree past. A wave and a smile, and they were, again, sitting close in their special place on the tile edge of the pool's shallow end; a magical moment of sheer elation lifting Rod's spirit to eternity and beyond.

"Hey, what are you doing here Carla? What about Brad's gang?"

"I think it'll all be okay, Rod. There are places around town they never go, and the pool's one of them. You be careful going home though," she added, her tone indicating concern for Rod's safety rather than her own reputation. "Cause they're still on the lookout for you."

"But Dan's here, and he'll go home and say you were…"

"I don't care! Please just leave it now, Rod, I don't wanna talk about it anymore. I'm gonna forget it ever happened."

The idea of him and Carla being the odd couple about town still troubled him deeply. She was the one who'd have to live in the place long after he'd gone—and the words 'whitey's slut' still rang in his ears. She'd be the one left living with that reputation long after he'd gone.

The home truth he'd avoided all summer caught him off guard, slamming him hard in the pit of the stomach—his inevitable departure from Bourke as the curtains of autumn finally fell and the icy fingers of winter tore out his heart, cruelly squeezing its life blood into a sacrificial chalice. What would happen to Carla then? What would her family think when word reached them? Carla hadn't said much about parents, only that her father was a drunken bum, so he wouldn't likely give a damn about anything anyway. Rod couldn't fathom the sheer evil of the monster lurking in her house—the beast she had to go back and face up to each and every day. How could such hellish creature have created a sensitive and beautiful angel? He didn't want to go anywhere, he wanted to stay in Bourke and protect his lovely maiden—to be her white knight in shining armour, but he was compelled to return to the path laid out before him, to his studies in Sydney. He owed it to his own parents who had devoted their entire lives to his.

Oppressive feelings of loss of control overcame him; of being trapped on a treadmill, on a trajectory he didn't want to follow toward a destiny not of his choosing. The sodden blanket smothered him, only this time he couldn't fight it off. He'd promised Carla he wouldn't speak of the 'ifs, buts and maybes' of an unknown future, but think only of the present moment—and in that promise they both fully believed.

Rod could only live day by day now, knowing his outback summer was slowly passing and its inevitable end would soon be in sight. He'd never prayed before but now vowed to worship each precious day as it came, one by one, giving thanks for its beautiful sameness and simplicity, for the routine he so loved—in the morning, working his special land to uncover its mysterious mineral treasures hidden deep within, then, in the afternoon, his euphoria climaxing as he came together with Carla poolside, where they would swim or lie talking on the grass. She was an expert now, a natural, and he was proud of his part in her achievement—her grace, skill and speed improving to the point where, with little more practice, he reckoned, she'd be even better at it than him.

CHAPTER 20. NIGHT IN WONDERLAND

ROD SENSED something special about Carla, a growing feeling he couldn't quite put his finger on. She never made a big deal over anything, rarely showed off about she what knew, but he was sure she was clever. There were still thousands of questions he wanted to ask.

"How are you doing at school Carla?" He asked her one afternoon as they lazed around on the grass by the pool edge in the late afternoon sun, resting between swim practice sessions.

"Okay, I guess. The stuff's easy, really easy, but, I mean, why do I really want to know about finding the roots of quadratics, graphing parabolas or solving simultaneous equations? I end up sitting there bored most of the time. How am I ever goin' to use that stuff? It's not gonna solve the solutions of my own life?"

Perhaps wise might be a better word, he reflected. She seemed to have a depth and breadth of knowledge of all sorts, wise to the world in so many ways. He never thought about stuff being applicable to his own life or about his future, he was only clever at science and geology, and that's why he did it. What problems did he have to solve?

"You're dead right, Carla. I know what you mean," Rod laughed, awakening to the fact that everybody in Australia must've been taught about simultaneous equations at some time or another during their school career, graduated, then gone off and never used them again.

"No one ever bothers to talk about them at parties, do they?" he joked. Only him and Carla, he thought, talking about them now, having their own private party! He felt a ridiculous urge to solve an equation with her, right there at the pool—giving into the impulse, just for fun.

"Hey smarty-pants, here's one for you," Rod said, counting back on his fingers, rehearsing the question in his mind; he knew she was in fifth form, which meant she must be seventeen. "How old am I, if 14 years ago I was twice your age? Go on then; solve for x."

Carla laughed. "That's way too easy to bother solving. You're 20!" She teased. "I can do it straight away in my head."

"How did you do manage that one so quickly?" Rod was caught by surprise.

"All right then, I'll do the long way, just for you, slow coach!" she teased. Let 'x' be your age now. At the age of $x-14$ you were twice my age, which, as 17 minus 14 equals 3, means you were 6. So, x minus 14 equals 6, and so that makes you 20, right?"

"Heyyy, brilliant!" Rod exclaimed, even more amazed. "But I'm a bit old, don't you reckon?" he asked, feeling suddenly self-conscious. He was used to being a teenager, hearing the word twenty still sounded strange. He'd never mentioned his age to anyone else. "Three years difference is a lot, isn't it?"

"No silly," she quipped, laughing at him. "When I'm one hundred, you'll only be 103, a difference of just three percent."

"Well, what about the other stuff then? History? Geography? Aren't you enjoying them?"

"Nah, they're even worse!" she retorted. "I'm fed-up hearing about Captain James Cook's arrival in Australia in 1770, his heroic landing at Botany Bay, the hoisting of the flag ceremony; and the beginning of a brand-new British Colony. I don't even get to school every second day, and still I must've heard that same story at least once or twice a year for the past eleven years. It does begin to wear a little thin after a while y' know," she complained. "Like it's been burned into the back of my brain. But they never talk about what it was like beforehand—that's what I really wanna know about."

Again, Rod pictured that arrival; fleeting fragments of historic sketches and artworks melding together, his mind conjuring up a colourful scene of white-skinned men in blue and red uniforms, longboats, kangaroos, with dark-skinned men standing around with spears and boomerangs; then Phillip's First Fleet eighteen years later, with old Sydney town springing up, rough farms hewn out of the bush, convicts in chains, drunken soldiers and wooden barrels full of rum.

"My parents' countrymen were here over a century and a half beforehand, my mum told me; Willem Janszoon visited in 1606, but nobody bothers to remember off-by-heart when that was."

"I'd never heard about him before," Carla replied.

"Yeah, that's because 1770 is stuck in everyone's brain. That and 1788 are the only dates we're taught about," he quipped. "I reckon I got it branded on my skin around here somewhere." He rolled over on the grass, craning his neck, to look for it on his back.

"Hey, Carla, I think I've just found it—right under here!" He rolled over onto his back, inscribing with his fingernail gently on Carla's side, close to her armpit, calling the numbers out as he did so…1…7…7…0."

"Heyyy…cut it out, silly," She laughed. "That tickles!"

"Why don't you go to school every day though Carla?" Rod asked, returning to the theme. "It's not that bad, is it? I mean some of the classes are interesting, aren't they? And lunchtimes with all your friends must be fun?"

"It's not that I wanna wag school, Rod," Carla replied becoming more serious. "Sometimes my sister Elsie's gotta be somewhere and there's no one to look after little Johnny, or Mum asks me to do something for her, or if Dad's sick I have t' stay home and look after him. It's sorta just one small thing after another, really. Most of my friends don't go anymore anyway."

Rod was silent a while. He hadn't expected to hear something like that, and a smart reply to serve up in return eluded him. All he had to do was pick up his cut lunch that his mother prepared for him, nicely wrapped in its brown paper bag, each and every day without fail, and walk out his front door. His parents had organized their whole lives around his own and his brother's upbringing and education. That's just what parents do for their children, don't they? Rod wanted to share that thought, holding back only as he remembered it wouldn't be in keeping with Carla's own experience, and likely be hurtful.

"So, y'must be doing fairly okay in your exams then?" Rod searched a little further

"The tests, yeah, they're too easy," she replied, "so there's no point. I usually hand them back blank."

"Blank! Why…" Rod was horrified. The thought of throwing a test was completely alien. He was intent now on probing more deeply into the psyche of Carla.

"Who wants the attention? Everybody turns 'em in blank and I don't wanna stand out from the rest of the gang. I once did a test auntie Maisy gave me. She sat me down and said, 'Carla, love, you've gotta do this one for me. Do the best you can.' So I did—it wasn't hard—and she took it away with her, and I haven't heard anything since."

It must be hard for Carla to even find time out to come to the pool each afternoon let alone pay the 60 cents entry fee, Rod reflected, remembering what Joey had said about her 'own business going on the side' to earn that money.

Her resourcefulness impressed Rod; he'd never struggled for anything. Why did life have to be like that for some and not for others? It was so unfair—Carla's life held her in some kind of prison. Pondering those thoughts, a new truth began to crystallize in the mists of his mind. He'd recognised it before, talked about it with Beth and Paddy, but now it was becoming clearer, crystal clear. Suddenly words sprang forth, unrestrained, from his mind, out through his mouth, unexpectedly.

"Knowledge is the key to the world, y' know, Carla, a skeleton key capable of unlocking any door in life you may, one day, care to enter, doors leading to anywhere, any magical place you want to go. Or perhaps think of knowledge as a powerful bulldozer under your control, its massive blade capable of smashing though any barrier, any obstacle in life, that might be blocking the highway to your goals and dreams…" Rod slowed to a pause, stopping for a moment. Did he really presume to blurt all of that stuff out at Carla? He looked down at his feet, a little embarrassed.

"Yeah, that's right," he muttered, still looking down, and then up again at Carla's face, into her eyes.

"Nice poetry, Rod." Carla was looking at him a little strangely. She didn't say anything else, but seemed to be interested, still listening, so he continued, choosing different words.

"School's really important, Carla, especially this last year. You've gotta try and go all the time and study real hard so you do well in your Higher School Certificate exams. It's not a competition, but more like your ticket to the future! And university's free, y' know Carla; you don't have to pay a cent. If you do well, they'll even pay y' a scholarship to go anywhere in the world, to study anything you want!"

Carla remained silent. Rod took a guess at what she was thinking, figuring she'd probably never thought about school as he did, nor the opportunities it could open up for her. How could she contemplate a rosy career when she was so busy surviving each day in hell? Finding nothing useful to lift her out of her humdrum existence, she'd obviously taken what knowledge she could as it came along and left the rest drift by. Obviously, she was no show-off and never felt the urge to compete with her friends in exams, but to master concepts as alien as simultaneous equations without trying meant she was absolutely brilliant.

"Think about it, Carla. Your life's in your own hands, nobody else's," he concluded philosophically. "You can study your way out of anything, y' know."

"Yeah, you sound like my auntie Maisy, she tells me all that same stuff too. She lives in Townsville, but she made me promise her to see the school year out and turn up for my final exams. So, I was gonna do that for her, and now I'll do it for you too," she smiled.

"How come life has to be so hard for some?" Rod commented to René later that same day, as they were finishing dinner,

"Why so?" René looked up.

"I'm just thinking about Carla, she's got so many problems and other responsibilities and the family's so poor. Her parents don't even have the 60 cents to give her for the pool. She has to earn it herself. It's not fair."

"Well, you did tell me about the father, which would have a great deal to do with it."

"Yeah, Carla hates him, and I reckon that he should be put in jail!"

René looked up at his cousin seeming to remember something. He pulled a folded envelope from his wallet.

"I won some tickets in a chook raffle at the Oxley Club—they're for a show at Wonderland. Would you like to go tomorrow night? You still haven't seen a show there yet. I think they're playing The Pink Panther this week?

"Hey…thanks René, that could be great fun!" Rod exclaimed enthusiastically, imagining what lay within the tall grey corrugated iron fence near the corner of Oxley and Sturt streets. He'd never been to a picture theatre without a roof before.

"I've got three tickets, so why don't you ask Carla if she'd like to come along?" René continued. "I'll bet she doesn't get the chance to go to the pictures all that often."

"Great idea, René. I'll ask her tomorrow at the pool,'" Rod reflected on that possibility. There'd certainly be no harm in trying, but he was pretty sure that her answer would have to be 'no'.

OUTBACK SUMMER

"WONDERLAND THEATRE"

Robert Coenraads
2024

At the appointed time, the tall iron gates rolled back, allowing the massing crowds to swell into the grassed space within. A gaily-lit ticket booth stood inside, to the right of the gate, now swamped by a sea of patrons eager to see the latest releases out of Hollywood, which somehow, sooner or later, always found their way to the farthest and remotest corners of the world. Above the ticket box rose a two-storey tower; the projectionist juggling his precious cargo of two metal film canisters, made his way up a narrow flight of steps ascending ladder-like to a small door in the side of the projection room. A broad screen framed in white lattice and backed by a row of poplars stood at the far end of the field of awaiting deck chairs. Tall white picket fences and manicured hedges enclosed the magic of Wonderland from all the cares and worries of the town beyond[21].

Rod and Carla took their places in one of the back rows of canvas cloth deck chairs, reclined at the perfect angle to view the screen, or to gaze upwards at the open vault of the now-darkening heavens. Some of the brightest stars had already started to appear.

"I can't believe how nice it is in here. There should be more of these open-air theatres around the place," Rod said as they settled in, laying back against the canvas. "Here take some of this." He handed her a spray can of mosquito repellent. "René said we might like to put some on just in case."

"Thanks Rod… Yeah, I've only been here a couple of times, but each time I've really loved it… See those rows of metal benches down the front," Carla pointed, "that's where the little kids sit because the tickets are cheaper. That way they've got more money left over for lollies. And the owners really like it too," she laughed, "because they can keep an eye on them so they can't get up to any mischief. I wouldn't recommend it though, 'cause they're not real comfortable, 'specially after sitting on them for a few hours."

"Bourke's a funny place, Carla." They laughed together at the thought of all those little kids eating their lollies and wriggling about on their sore bums. "But y' know what, I really love it here."

"And, speaking of lollies," he smiled over at her as she lay back on the canvas, breathing in the night air. "What will it be—popcorn, Maltesers, ice cream?"

OUTBACK SUMMER

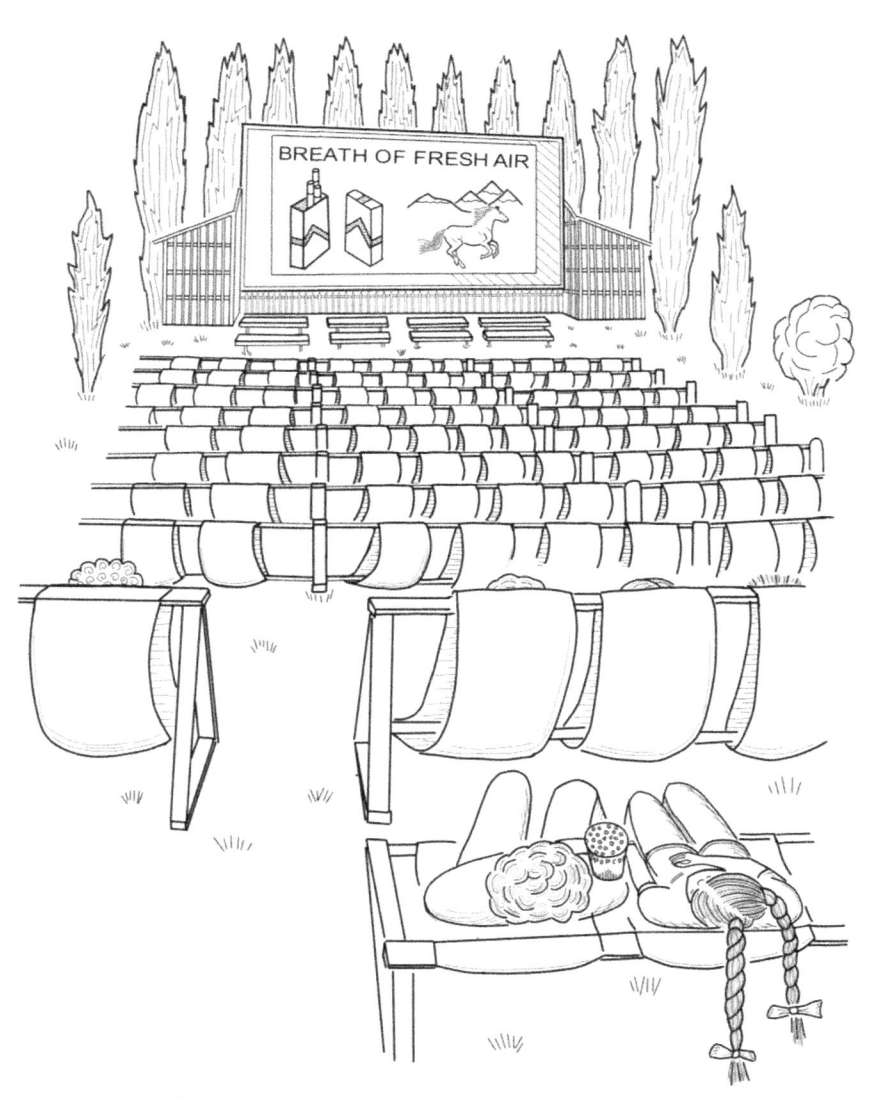

"NIGHT IN
WONDERLAND"

Robert Coenraads
2025

It was a magical evening Rod wished could last for ever, lying there in the evening freshness, the projector beam cutting a bright swathe through the night sky above their heads, watching the ridiculous antics of Inspector Jacques Clouseau as he solved the crime, Carla beside him, feeling the warmth of her shoulder, her arm, next to his[22].

Carla looked across at Rod from time to time, studying his silhouette in the darkness; he was different, a proper gentleman, someone she could really trust. He was different from the boys in the gang she hung out with as a kid. She didn't feel so comfortable around them anymore. Somehow things had seemed to change now that she'd grown up, like she wasn't the same person as before. Nowadays, sometimes, out of the corner of her eye, she'd catch the older boys looking at her in a funny way. Then they'd go all dark and moody, showing off and smashing things—and they were always trying to get her off by herself somewhere. Hanging out with the gang wasn't light and fun anymore.

She'd nearly told Rod that she couldn't make it tonight. Embarrassed by where she lived, she'd talked him out of picking her up at home. And then she had to make double sure they wouldn't run into any of the mob in the main street—they'd be likely to bash him up if they caught him with her—and she'd never be able to stop them. That's why she told him to meet her just inside the entrance to the Wonderland—she knew her mob never went in there. Her life was way more complicated than he'd ever realize.

She noticed Rod's arm, his hand lying next to hers on the deck chair, knowing instinctively he'd never presume to take it; never do anything to make her feel awkward or uncomfortable. She toyed with the idea of taking his hand, thinking about it, losing focus on the film now and again. She was really beginning to like Rod a lot, so just maybe, she might do that next time, perhaps! Then, on an impulse, she reached over and touched his hand lightly with her fingers, holding it just for a moment, before letting go again. Leaning over, towards him, she whispered.

"Thank you for bringing me here tonight, Rod. I'm really having a great time, y' know."

Rod looked back at her, smiling. "Me too Carla, I really am!

CHAPTER 21. POLYGONUM BILLABONG

A FEW afternoons later, Rod and Carla found themselves about three or four kilometres out of town, along an area of the Darling River flats known as Polygonum Swamp. She'd asked him to double her out there on his bike. She wanted to show him something important to her, something magical, 'to share a special place', she'd said. He relaxed in the late afternoon sunlight, realising how free he felt out there, away from the inquisitive, prying eyes of the townsfolk.

They'd followed a small dusty track just out of North Bourke he'd never noticed before, leading away from the main road, stopping and parking the bike where it ended in a small grassy clearing. Ancient gnarled and twisted River Red Gums stood beside a broad body of still water, a billabong, an ancient meander cut off from the main flow of the Darling River. A luxuriant swathe of grassy reeds grew along its edges. Late afternoon sunlight filtered invitingly through the trees, and the swamp was alive with all manner of diving and wading birds, noisily hunting and fishing.

"It's part of an endless cycle," Carla spoke quietly, almost reverently. "The water comes with the rains and with it comes life, then the water goes away and life goes into hiding again. The seasonal floods keep the River Gums healthy and it's been like that for ever. The story comes through our dreamtime. It's like our link to the country. Our connection to the land is as old as time itself, a link forged strong by time itself. The two hundred years since your people have been here is so short."

Rod found Carla's words beautiful, poetic and mystical; he'd never heard her speak like that before. But the implication of a difference between them—words like 'your people' or 'my people', 'your past' or 'my past'—

made him sad. These evoked a sense of separation of him from her, and he only cared about the here and now, the present day and the present moment. Nothing else mattered for him but the journey forward into the unknown, the mystery of discovery—and that grand adventure could be shared with anyone willing to take it. Now was not the time or place for that discussion, nor did he have the right words to express his feelings to Carla.

Carla continued speaking, drawing thoughts and memories from a time long past, things she'd heard about, learnt from her parents, her aunts, uncles and cousins. Things she felt deeply in her heart and knew to be true.

"The river's like a giant snake connecting one place to another; place to place, people to people, people to animals, people to land, land to sky and everything to spirit." She studied Rod's face carefully as she spoke. "Biame's his name, y' know," she spoke it quietly, respectfully. "I want you to hear it. He's God of the land, God of the Kurnu-Baakandji-Ngemba, God of me. He's everywhere."

"That's beautiful. It's something you should be really proud of, Carla," Rod said turning towards her smiling. "You should be shouting that name out at the top of your voice." He paused a moment, his thoughts reluctantly returning to Sydney; a life a world away, but a life to which he would soon have to return. But how much does it really mean nowadays in this world of things?" Rod added resignedly.

"Things? What do y' mean by things, Rod?"

"Y'know, things. Everybody's got their own things. They own them, like clothes, cars, boats and houses," Rod explained. "In Sydney all they think about is getting money to buy more and more things. They buy the land, cut it up into squares with fences. You can't walk anywhere anymore, only drive on roads, disconnected from the land, inside a box of glass and steel with a blaring radio. You can't sleep on the ground and watch the stars anymore, only sleep on a bed in a house. People even go inside a church to pray to God. It's like the spirit of the land's all been chopped up into tiny little wriggling pieces."

"Maybe in the city it's like that, even in town, but out here it's different. The land means a lot to me, Rod."

"Yeah, I know that, and I know it means a lot to other people too—like Mick and Chief. And even I can feel it too when I'm working out here."

Carla stood and gazed out over the billabong. "When you told me how you felt about water at the swimming pool, I thought you might have the connection, Rod, I knew it. Out here you can really feel it. It's strong, really strong. Here we can share without speaking." She took his hand, instructing him. "Close your eyes, Rod, clear your thoughts and concentrate. Feel what I am feeling."

Rod relaxed, enjoying the feel of her hand in his. He cast his mind back, imagining the scene. It was as if he were in a trance, or a dream, the edges of it surreal, blurry as Carla's memories flowed in. She stood beside him leading him, her body ochre-painted; they were no longer in the present. Hand in hand, minds united as one—their blood coursing through joined veins. Was he dreaming, he wondered as he let it all wash over him. They watched the first people going about their daily routine in an unshackled land; back in time, generation after generation, two hundred times before the two hundred years ago when Western civilization first laid footprint upon this continent. The land unchanged in its seasonal rhythm, when Carla's people first arrived across the exposed stepping stones though Asia and Indonesia to become first custodians of the land. Then she stopped, wordlessly letting the power of the land take over, leading Rod deeper in time to the world of his studies. An indescribable power surged deep within his very being as together they stepped back, tens of thousands of millennia, to the time of the Great Australian Inland Sea teeming with ancient life; plesiosaurs hunting its warm shallow waters, its ancient shores flanked by unfamiliar coniferous forest. Then even further they travelled, to the time of formation of the rocks he was drilling at Doradilla mine site—giant volcanoes strewn across the landscape erupting lava and ash laden with gold, copper and other metals—the very birth of the land itself. He'd fleetingly sensed it before, but now he could feel the strength of the connection through every part of his being, a direct link to the very forces that created the Earth itself. He felt them call his name, inviting him to understand something more real and intense than all of the science that he had ever studied. He was being offered a gift—a glimpse of the great spirit, the force responsible for the law stating that energy will condense into matter, and that matter will eventually organise itself into living cells—culminating in intelligent life capable of self-realization and, ultimately, recognition of the existence of this very same creative force—an unbreakable bond with the greatest of all forces within their very being. He'd never imagined anything like it before.

"This secret is for everyone to discover," Rod whispered awakening from the dream, "no matter who they are or where they're from."

"The first people know this," Carla replied. "It's around us all the time, everywhere, sometimes weaker sometimes stronger. All you have to do is look—clear away all of the things out of your life, and look. The same spirit that is within us is within everything; the sun, stars, water and earth. My people have always been especially aware of it because of our long connection with the land."

"Your love is strong and your motives pure; I can fulfil your quest for understanding," a new and powerful voice began to reverberate in the afternoon heat, emerging from nowhere, yet everywhere at once, within and without—somehow from the billabong—the river. "I can grant you an answer to your most primordial question."

Rod and Carla looked at one another and instantly they knew the question. Gazing into each other's eyes, hands clasped and fingers interlocking, Carla spoke.

"We want to know you?"

Suddenly they felt themselves being lifted up and stretched. Rod and Carla, ying and yang, boy and girl, black and white, country and city, opposites intertwined into one body, fingers and toes growing longer and thinner, and reaching far into every corner of the grand expanse of eastern Australia—northwards far into Queensland, eastwards into the Great Dividing Range and Snowy Mountains and out into the Western Desert. Their trunk powerful and strong, coursing ever southward down to the Murray Mouth and out into the Great Southern Ocean. They could feel the rhythms and songs of thousands of generations; past, present and future, dependent on their life-giving water. Rod felt the laughter and shouts of the children swinging and diving into the river at their favourite swimming holes, as he had experienced only weeks earlier—their joy merging with his.

They felt themselves pulsing with the seasons and the decades and the centuries—shrinking in the dry and swelling with the rains, some years more and some less, surging over the floodplains, filling the marshes, swamps and billabongs, sustaining the wildlife and flooding the roots of the mighty river gums.

"You can feel me within you," the voice said, "and my love for the country and its people. You can feel my desire to nourish my land and my people. I am powerful enough for all, but yet I need your help."

But they could not comprehend. "What could we possibly do for you?" Carla asked.

"In time you will discover that answer for yourselves when the opportunity comes. For now, I need you to feel my pain. Experience what I feel."

Suddenly, they felt a sharp pinprick like a cannula needle being thrust deep into their side—a tube filling with their blood, draining their life-giving fluids—a cut through the riverbank, a pump and a canal, channelling life-giving water over the parched lands, turning desert to green wherever it touched. They could feel the power of their life-giving essence nourishing acres and acres of cotton. Then another stab to the side, and another to the leg and to the arm—acres and acres of vibrant green cotton and other crops growing around them. Moaning with mixed pain and pleasure, they could feel the full extent of their desire spreading everywhere around them through each new canal—acre after acre of lush fruits, vegetables and other crops—a field here and a field there—their ecstasy growing with each.

Slowly the pinpricks began to intensify over their entire body, thousands of needles and thousands of draining tubes, each one of them insignificant on its own, yet together completely overpowering. They began to feel dizzy and their mouth and throat felt dry and parched. Their power was fading—their main trunk was drying out. The Murray Mouth was already dry—withering away, and they could no longer spread their life-giving water over the plains to satisfy all.

"You are now one with me. Do not lose focus of your one main goal and desire," the voice cautioned, beginning to fade, and suddenly they were back on the bank of Polygonum Billabong.

"The Chief's got to see this place, Carla." Rod exclaimed. "He's always said he'd take me out here and now I really want to share it with him. I'm going back to the Carriers' Arms to get him right now. I'll get the Landy and we'll go pick him up. C'mon Carla." He walked over towards his bike, continuing to expound enthusiastically. "You're really gonna like him." He was anxious to leave now, driven by the urgency of his idea.

"I know how much you admire Chief," Carla started, then paused a moment, her eyes downcast. "So, I never told you this before," she took his hand again, grasping it tightly, her voice subdued. "But… y' gotta know the truth now…. Chief's my father… I'm sorry Rod; I didn't want to tell you that, but there's no other way."

Rod was stunned, completely lost for words while he took in all what Carla was saying; his mind yanked roughly, like an electrical cord from its socket, disconnecting from the spiritual power of the billabong, as negative energy flowed in its place. He reflected on that vile, repugnant image he'd formed in his mind of Carla's negligent bastard of a father from all she'd told him, and now in contrast to that, all he knew about the Chief, his wonderfully gentle, kind and wise friend and mentor; a father figure to whom he felt such a close bond, like they had known one another their entire lives. It couldn't be possible that they were one and the same. How could the noble Chief not be capable of being a real father to someone as special as Carla; nor care for a real family? Rod had no reply for Carla. He remembered when he'd tried to visit Chief's house—Carla's home, recalling what the old lady—Carla's mum—had told him about the Chief. Perhaps it was all starting to make sense now.

"I never wanted to spoil your feelings for him or ruin your dreams to share his world. I've wished my whole life he'd become the person you thought he was."

Rod sensed Carla understood the conflict going on in his mind; he knew she didn't want him to build his hopes too high about Chief, only to see them dismally smashed.

"I'm so sorry Rod," she continued speaking. "Dad knows this place, he talks about it all the time, and that's how come I know about it too. I've ridden out here a lot of times t' see it for myself, to learn about it and make my own connection, but he's never been here—for as long as I can remember anyway. He talks a lot, but he really doesn't do anything." Her words came out all in a jumble, a mix of love, sadness and disappointment. "I dunno if you'll get him t' come out here tonight, Rod."

Rod could picture a different man now, obviously aware of his connection, but somehow bound and shackled to the routine of his life; a life slowly fading away to nothing, telling empty stories within the pub's cell-like walls.

"C'mon Carla, maybe we've got to at least try," Rod replied, pushing aside the overpowering negativity. "Please come with me and help try convince him right now?"

The Chief looked up, his weary bloodshot eyes full of surprise, when both his daughter and Rod came in through the doors of the Carriers' Arms together. He'd settled in for another quiet evening with Eddie and Sammy, but looked anxious now, his eyes moving from one to the other for answers; clearly worried that something bad might have happened. He put down his drink resignedly and waited for them to come over to the table.

"Chief," Rod spoke first, excitedly, coming straight to the point. "You've gotta come with us right now. We want to show you something. It won't take long. I've got the Land Rover and I promise we'll bring you straight back here afterwards." He spoke quickly, trying not to give the Chief too much time to think about things, to start objecting or finding excuses not to go.

"But where? What's going on? Is… is everything OK at home?" Chief stammered, looking around at Eddie and Sammy questioningly, then back at his daughter.

"Everything's alright Dad, Rod just wants to bring you out to Polygonum Swamp," she started softly. "We both do, Dad, and you've gotta come now." Carla spoke in a measured tone, still quietly, but with deep, strong feeling and conviction; and with an authority normally reserved for parents speaking to their offspring, not the other way round. Rod had certainly never spoken to his own father like that before.

"Rod and I have just been out there this afternoon. We want to show you some important stuff we found. It's really strong out there right now, that's why you've gotta come, Dad!" It was an appeal straight from the heart, from daughter to father.

Eddie and Sammy had been listening with interest as the story unfolded—anything out of the usual at the Carriers' was always of interest.

"Why don't y' go with 'em, Chief?" Eddie started.

"Yeah, you're always talkin' about that place, so y' might as well go. We'll still be here holdin' the fort for when y' get back," Sammy finished.

The Chief shrank a little in his seat, looking quickly at each of them, realising he was now the centre of attention of the entire pub; being put on the spot. Everyone's face was turned towards him.

"Righto then," the Chief sighed resignedly, clearly knowing they wouldn't let the matter rest until he agreed. "Let's go then." He stood up to leave.

It was nearly dark by the time they got back to the billabong; a thin bright orange line still glowed through the trees on the western horizon in an azure sky. As they got out of the Land Rover, Rod noticed that the evening chorus of insects and frogs had already begun.

Chief was very quiet, a resigned look on his face. He began to walk slowly towards a semi-circle of Red Gums on the edge of the water. Rod made to follow him, but Carla took his hand, stopping him. They could both sense something, a different feeling from before, something telling them that Chief was meant to go there, and he was meant to go alone. His white shirt disappeared from sight behind the trees in the dusk light.

They waited together by the vehicle for what seemed like an hour, as the sky slowly turned deeper violet and finally black. They didn't speak, each experiencing a range of emotions as the time passed; peace and belonging, oneness with the place, feelings of majesty and grandeur like standing in the middle of a massive gothic cathedral, and then later, even anxiety, concern for the Chief, growing as the minutes wore on.

Finally, the Chief returned, shuffling slowly out of the circle of trees. He looked scared now, his face a ghostly pale.

"What happened in there," Rod struggled for words in that wordless place, then waited beside Carla for Chief to reply. They waited in silence until finally he did.

"They told me that soon it would be my turn to join them, to be with them. Then they would show me everything. Then I would see everything."

It took Rod a few moments to register what Chief was telling them. He remained silent waiting for the Chief to continue. It seemed easier not to speak.

"They told me that I've been wastin' my life away, said that I haven't been doing a very good job of looking after my family." He paused a while to remember, to collect his thoughts before continuing; he looked drained, completely exhausted as if he had just fought a huge emotional battle. "Taking care of them that depend on you is y'r most important task in life. They were gonna give me a bit more time to set things straight before I join them. Otherwise, it might've been tonight. I reckon I knew it all along, or I should've known it anyway, for a long time—just needed someone or something to put it right in my head. I'll be proud to join them when I finally get it right."

Rod was shocked. Wordlessly he looked across at Carla who ran to her father, flinging her arms around his neck, hugging him, tears flowing as she cried, "Dad, please, I don't want you to go, not now, not ever. I love you."

"Don't worry about that Carla, love, I'm not goin' anywhere for the time being."

CHAPTER 22. FAREWELL TO BOURKE

EVERYTHING STARTED to happen very quickly after that afternoon at Polygonum Billabong. Rod would have liked a lot more time to think, to take everything in. He wanted to tell Carla about his feelings for her—to understand them. He needed to find out what she thought of him. What he could do about it all, but change was in the air, everywhere. Midnight was fast approaching and his Cinderella dream world was crumbling away. The day Rod dreaded most of all had crept up slowly upon him, like a stealthy tiger slinking up from behind ready to pounce, ready to tear his very being to shreds. One day he was alive and the next he would be dead; and that day was tomorrow.

He sat on the grass waiting for Carla in their usual spot under the shady tree, the calming azure of both pool and sky today doing little to still his tortured thoughts as they boiled in a sea of turbulent emotions.

He watched her come in through the turnstiles, her familiar gait, instinctively heading over to where they always sat. Same as ever, but not for ever now—there was no hiding from it any more—today would be their last. He hated goodbyes. Waves of adrenaline-induced panic surged through his body as he imagined how their conversation might go. His feelings for her were so strong his whole body ached, and he was just coming to terms with that now, the very moment he was destined to go.

She approached him, smiling.

"Hiya Rod. How're y' doing?" She dropped beside him onto the towel.

"Great! And you?" Holding his thoughts in check, he let their small talk do the talking, relaxing for the last time into the familiarity of the sunny poolside afternoon, drinking in her aura. 'I can't leave,' he breathed; his resolve growing. I'm not gonna go and that's it! I'll toss in everything just to be with Carla. He readied himself to disclose his true feelings and plans.

"Carla…"

But Carla, took the lead, breaking her news to him first—a strange look of exhilaration yet sadness and resignation mixed in her face. Rod sensed big changes in the air for her too.

"I'm sorry Rod, I can only stop by a few moments this arvo, and then I've gotta go meet Auntie Maisy down the main street. She's waiting for me but I told her I had to come see you first. It's all happening for me today, right now!"

Puzzled, Rod waited for Carla to continue.

"Yesterday my aunt drove up from the coast to come and collect me. None of us knew, but… now I'm gonna go live with her, and finish my final year of school in Townsville. I've already said good bye to mum and dad." She paused, searching Rod's face before continuing; excitement now dominating the sadness. "Auntie says I'll have a room, all to myself—my very own room with my own desk, and a chair and a lamp. She says it'll be a place where I can concentrate and study for my finals."

Rod immediately knew what that meant. He'd felt it before with Suzie. Their trajectories were changing, diverging. New doors were opening, old ones closing. The words he'd planned seemed hollow and empty now, even selfish. He again felt powerless, crushed beneath the cruel hand of fate, but recognised she'd been presented with an opportunity she could never refuse; Carla had important things to do with her life now. His viewpoint suddenly flipped.

"That's amazing news, Carla! The best news I've heard around here with all that's been happening. We've both got to go now, both got to leave Bourke." He placed his hands on her shoulders. "What your aunt's doing for you now really makes my day… No, it really makes my whole life!" He kissed her gently on the cheek preparing to reveal the whole truth about his feelings. "Carla, you're such a special person to me." He looked deeply into her eyes. "Polygonum was a really precious time together for me—for us. I mean… I reckon we're soul mates now… don't y' think?"

Carla went silent, contemplative. Her look had Rod worried for a second; he didn't want this moment, their last together for who knows how long, perhaps forever, to be a sad one. Nor did he want to stand as an obstacle in the path of her opportunity. She smiled, gazing deeply into the blueness of his eyes, studying their detail carefully, committing them to her memory.

"You've got eyes as beautiful as my outback sky, Rod, and I'm gonna miss that sky, those clear, understanding eyes, when I'm away, down on the coast... I mean, y' know ...I knew you couldn't stay in Bourke for ever." She paused for a few seconds. "I love you, Rod."

Rod gazed at Carla's beautiful face, her eyes deep transparent pools, gateways into her spiritual soul[23]. "And your eyes, dark as the desert night, against the gold of your beautiful skin; gold as the setting sun casting its rays upon the desert sand; gold as the precious metals lying undiscovered beneath," Rod breathed. "I love you too, Carla, I'll always love you and I'm going to wait for you, for as long as it takes."

The heavens and the stars invisible beyond the blue vault spun, weaving a silken cocoon around them, sealing them into their own sacred place on that otherwise crowded, noisy pool lawn. Their shared spirit rose from the serpentine river, from the earth beneath them, pushing through the grass, twining its meandering loops around Rod and Carla, around their legs. Rod could feel its raw power, surging upwards, majestically drawing their bodies closer, its coils tightening, until their lips touched, gently, tenderly, for a beautiful moment; a moment when all time stood perfectly still.

"I'm sorry, I've really gotta go now, Rod," Carla said finally pulling away.

Desperate to spend a few more precious moments together, to say goodbye again, Rod and Carla met in the main street, on the footpath outside the Elysian Cafe, speaking in quick sentences. With only a few minutes to spare, their last words were to be few, but came directly from their hearts.

They locked in a farewell embrace oblivious to the passers-by, their lips touching again briefly, time again standing still, momentarily, before the spell was broken by the slam of a shop's flyscreen door. A well-dressed middle-aged lady, Carla's aunt, hurried out of the Elysian Café carrying a bunch of delicious-smelling white paper bags.

"Supplies for the road," Aunt Maisy said cheerfully, unlocking her polished teal-glow blue Ford Falcon angle-parked in front of the milk bar. She caught sight of Rod standing next to Carla

"Hello, you must be Rod, I've heard a lot about you," she smiled, her intelligent eyes studying him for a moment before returning to her niece. "Hop in the car now love, I want to make a bit of headway today so we won't be caught on the road after dark." She turned back to Rod, "Hooroo, and have a safe trip down to Sydney tomorrow, won't you, dear?"

They were down to their very last few precious moments together now as Aunt Maisy organised the food bags into a cardboard box on the back seat.

"FAREWELL"

"You're really gonna love the coast, Carla, and the beaches. The deep azure ocean against the light turquoise sky, stretching along a perfect horizon; flatter than you've ever seen, flatter than the desert plains against the desert sky; it'll be nothing like you've ever imagined before, Carla," Rod said poetically, walking with her to the passenger door, trying to evoke a few last beautiful images in her mind.

"Thanks to your swimming lessons I'll be really able to enjoy the sea now, Rod." She kissed him one more time, gently, beautifully, before slipping into the car, sitting on the bench seat next to her aunt, winding down the window and fastening her seatbelt. "Goodbye Rod, I'm really sorry I've gotta go just now."

'Carla…"

As he watched them drive off along Oxley Street, her hand waving from the window, Rod wished that he could be there with her when she saw the ocean for the first time. He daydreamt of Carla standing on the golden sand, her dark hair blowing in the sea breeze, the warm sun caressing her honey-coloured skin, as she faced the open Pacific. She'd never been on a beach before. He wondered idly which one it would be, where she would go with her aunt, before lurching from his daydream. Suddenly, with all that had happened in those last days and his refusal to accept that his time in Bourke was ending; he realized he'd forgotten to ask her Aunt Maisy where in Townsville they were going, those mundane and trivial details of life, and now Carla and her aunt were memories, heading east to the coast, and next it was his turn to fade. Tomorrow at first light he'd be heading southeast down the Mitchell, on the road back to Sydney, back to his life at the university. That was his fate, and his fate was sealed.

Despite all this, somehow, Rod felt quietly confident, his body still tingling from their last embrace. Somehow all the technicalities didn't seem to matter anymore, as he knew how deeply their spirits were intertwined. He and Carla were soul mates, now and forever, bound together beyond the physical limitations of time or place. Rod relaxed knowing that wherever she went, he would always be able find her again.

ROBERT R. COENRAADS

"SYDNEY HARBOUR"

Robert Coenraads
2025

CHAPTER 23. SECOND SUMMER

THE BOUNDLESS Australian outback was part of Rod Conway now, intimately fused with his very being. Its heat and passion coursed through the veins of his body. Even deep within the shady concrete walls of Sydney's urban canyons, the desert sun seemed able to reach out to him; the red iron-stained soil of the Outback and the iron of his own blood were somehow mingled; able to communicate, one with each other. Whenever he thought about it, which was often enough, he thought of Carla too. His passion for the land and his passion for Carla had intensified, blurring into one burning singularity. She and her people were the human incarnation of Country—each unable to exist without the other. And he was now part of that too—part of an eternal triangle. He'd learnt how to connect with the land, and in every waking moment, and in his dreams, he passionately yearned for it.

Rod had to set aside that passion now for the sake of his studies—a passion that was beyond words. He couldn't explain it to his parents or his university friends, they wouldn't understand—maybe Banjo Paterson could, were he still alive. It took a long while to settle into old routines.

Rod thrived in his final year of undergraduate university study, relishing the experience as his breadth of geological knowledge grew exponentially. He topped his courses with A-levels and was offered an Honours scholarship at Macquarie, yet during all that time, what he yearned most was summer's return and the chance to head out west, out along the Mitchell Highway into the outback. He worked harder on that project than anything else, addressing reams, entire forests, of application letters for summer vacation work to mineral companies exploring the district, desperately awaiting a reply.

"The swimming pool was crawling with pretty girls. I'd head there after work every afternoon. I'd lounge around on the grass with them, and then we'd go hang out in the café or the open-air picture theatre...," he'd brag to his ever-present circle of mates, always eager for detail—something larger than life, he figured, suitable for their basest requests, something they could connect with.

"Tell me more, tell us more... Did you get very far[24]?

"Sure did mate… Soon as the exams are done, I've gotta get straight back out to Bourke. Carla's waiting for me there, y' know."

But now nearly a whole year on, Rod was no longer so confident about finding Carla. He worried about their spiritual bond, their impassioned promises, and his link with her and the land. Had all been, perhaps, a figment of his wishful imagination, a dream, that night at Polygonum billabong? He'd buried his head in the sand, ignored the unavoidable reality of his departure, flatly refused to accept the fact until the very day it finally happened, and since then life in Bourke had moved onwards without him as it inevitably does: René had gone, transferred into the western Tasmanian wilderness to supervise a tin exploration project: Beth had corresponded with him a few times, so he knew Pete had married and left home, and that the rest of the family was moving to Dubbo: And he'd even sent a letter, on the off chance, to Chief, care of the Carriers' Arms, in which he asked about Carla, but never received a reply.

Pushed for detail by his mates now, Rod's confidence floundered on rocky shoals. "She's either got to be somewhere up the coast or back in Bourke," he admitted to the eager circle in exasperation, "You know, I could've bloody kicked myself for not going straight back to the Carriers Arms one last time to get Carla's address off of the Chief."

As Christmas drew near, Rod was ecstatic when, finally, one of his countless applications came through, two vacancies for geophysical field hands—one for him and a spare job for a mate—exploring his beloved Darling River country to the west of Bourke. He chose his classmate, Michael, a sensitive, highly motivated sort of a bloke, to be companion for the summer.

Rod had become closer with Michael that year, perhaps being the only one able to understand his passion for the outback, and his growing sense of loss. Michael's mother had lived awhile in northern Australia, a slightly-built, single mum fighting zealously alongside the Gurindji People for their land rights, while Michael spent his childhood playing in the desert sands with the Gurindji kids.

That summer they were tasked with exploring the flat expanses of river country between the Paka Tank-Tilpa and Louth roads. The closest town was Louth, a tiny dusty spot on the map, marking a pub and a handful of plank houses at a road junction and river crossing. The field team's job was straightforward; follow up on prospective gold targets generated by the aerial magnetic surveys; cut lines through the scrub and lay out grids; run ground magnetic surveys and draw geologic maps, all with the aim of finding the best places to drill for minerals. It was the same work Rod loved, knew like the back of his hand. They were based in the old Eldorado Homestead, an abandoned wooden house on the banks of the Darling River, rented by the Company as a field camp. There was even an old grave on the property. Local rumour had it an old river captain spent his last days there, and his spirit now haunted the place.

In all there were six in camp; Greg, the experienced team field leader, Trevor the geophysicist, Bruce the lead field hand and cook, and the new season's fieldies, George, Rod and Michael. Unfortunately, the university new-chums didn't get off to the best start with the seasoned team. On their very first night, Michael's girlfriend Loretta showed up at camp well after lights out. And making matters worse, she brought Gladys and Louise with her, two local girls she'd met in the North Bourke pub where she'd planned to spend the night before heading to Sydney. Everyone was sound asleep when they came in, banging nosily through the fly screen door, the pencil beam of their torch probing about in the darkness.

"Yoo hoo… boys, anyone home in there?" Loretta called.

They were blind drunk, laughing and giggling, still in fancy dress, masks and glitter from the party.

"The bastards threw us out into the street," Gladys slurred. "Can y' bloody well believe it? I'll give 'em bloody noise!"

"We've got nowhere else to go Michael…. Michael, where are you Michael," Loretta shrieked inconsolably.

"Hey shoosh you lot," Michael whispered, waking in horror. Rod could hear from his tone that he wasn't too impressed with the situation. "Whatever you do, don't wake the others."

"Don't you shoosh us, Michael," Loretta chided, stumbling over to where he lay in his camp stretcher.

"Why don't y' grab that spare bed on the far end of the verandah," Rod advised gently, trying not to stir things up. "Keep the noise down though.

Michael an' I gotta get some rest 'cause we got our big first day tomorrow," he suggested, hoping nobody would come anywhere near his bed. Rod couldn't picture a worse start to the job, knowing how stories can grow gigantically out of all proportion.

'Have ya heard about the things those blokes get up to in their field camp?' Rod imagined what people would say. Word would spread out of the camp and race through a small town like Bourke, like a fire in a haystack. Others were stirring now.

"Why don't you jump into bed with Trevor? He's the ranga chain-sawing in the back room," George added, now also wide awake and obviously finding the whole situation quite comical. "I don't think his eczema is contagious," he added.

"Gawd strewth, I could really go for Trevor," Rod heard Louise reply, "with a flaming meat axe t' put him outta his bloody misery."

"Michael, why don't you ever tell me you love me," Loretta whined, blubbering softly. "Michael…"

"Shhhh… Go to sleep."

Next morning the team rose at the crack of dawn. Not a word was said about the incidents of last night. Greg issued his instructions for the day as they ate a quiet breakfast around the small kitchen table. They packed lunches and loaded the field gear into the four-wheel drive, checking fuel, oil and water. Before leaving, Rod ventured a glance at the bed down the end of the verandah, catching sight of an image etched into his memory to this very day—three large girls crammed into the tiny camp stretcher, packed head to toe like oversized sardines in a small tin. He was glad they were dead to the world, and looked as if they would remain so for at least the next few hours. The rest of the team, too, couldn't have helped but notice the pile of snoring bodies in the corner, but still no-one said a thing.

It was clear open country and good going so they laid a good portion of their first grid that morning. Later, at about lunchtime, as they sat under a shady tree eating their sandwiches, the team leader Greg, in his softly spoken, gentle way, came up and took Michael aside for a quiet talk. Rod watched them walk a little bit away from the rest of the group. Michael stood there, head lowered and eyes downcast. He knew what was coming.

OUTBACK SUMMER

"PARTY GIRLS"

Robert Coenraads
2025

"Look, I'm sorry Michael, but, y' know, this is a working camp," Rod overheard. We can't have your girlfriend and her friends staying in the house. Can you imagine what would happen if we did? Unfortunately, those are the rules mate, so they'll have to go home today I'm afraid."

"Yeah, yeah…I'm sorry…," a deeply ashamed and reddened Michael muttered inaudibly.

In the following weeks, the unsettling events of their first night slowly faded away into a comfortable routine of daily work. Rod found life simpler, quieter and less eventful than his previous summer in Bourke township. It had been a wet year; the river and billabongs were full and wildlife was in abundance on the floodplains. There were galahs and cockatoos, emus goannas, kangaroos, mobs of wild pigs, and fish were plentiful. The field team relaxed in the Darling's cooling waters on lazy hot afternoons after work, fired up the trustworthy old Lister generator as evening's darkness approached, and cooked up simple Australian fare—meat, potatoes and veggies on the old-fashioned wood-fired stove. Later, after the thump of the Lister died away, they'd tell yarns before drifting off to sleep, or lay in bed on the broad flyscreened verandah of the old wooden homestead in the night-time stillness gazing up at the countless stars of the Milky Way on their nightly trajectory across the coal black heavens.

Deep in his heart, a burning desire overcame Rod, especially in those quiet moments at night or in the late afternoon sun. He'd not forgotten last summer—it was the reason he was here. He still had to find Carla. But between him and Bourke lay the extensive station lands of Toorale, Gunderbooka and Yanda, He may as well have been a thousand miles distant.

OUTBACK SUMMER

"MICHAEL LEU"

Robert Coenraads
2024

"ROD CONWAY"

CHAPTER 24. BOURKE STILL OUT OF REACH

"DO YOU get into Bourke much?" Rod asked Greg one afternoon by the river, trying to sound casual. "I was based there last summer, y' know." Rod knew the town lay tantalizingly close—less than an hour's drive away—and somehow, he needed to get there.

"Not all that often, mate," Greg replied. "Bruce goes in once a week to pick up supplies and mail while we're out working. And then we got BP Bertie bringing in our fuel drums, so we're completely self-sufficient out here."

"Wouldn't we have been better off living in town," Rod probed, "where you can easily get everything you need?"

"There's less distractions out here and it saves us the daily drive in and out. Eldorado's a dry camp and there's less trouble with the men that way. The Company learnt that trick the hard way!"

"Once in a while of a Saturday or Sunday we'll go in perhaps," Trevor added, "for the races, or if something special is happening at the pub." He seemed to sense Rod's frustration—perhaps a frustration that they all felt, of being completely isolated in the bush for the entire summer.

Rod's hopes were dashed—his prize may have well lay a thousand miles distant. Later, Rod released his pent-up disappointment, penning a letter to his father, saying amongst other news;

'I made a big mistake hitching a ride with Michael... Loretta took the car back to Sydney and we've got no way of getting around... I'm sorry for the bother, but could you please take my bike to Chatswood freight platform and rail it to Bourke? I'd really appreciate it, Dad. I can pick it up and ride back to Sydney at the end of summer. Love to everyone back home, Rod.'

Like always, Rod threw himself one-hundred-percent into his work. But as he mapped the countryside beneath the intense outback sun his thoughts invariably turned to Carla. He couldn't get her out of his mind, the Bee Gees' running through his head, over and over again, making him drunk on their song's powerful riff.

"Where is the girl I loved…All along[25]?"

With nobody around for kilometres, he shouted those words at the top of his lungs, suffering in their desperate pathos, switching between reality and the dream world which he inhabited for hours on end, punctuated only by the rhythmic monotony of the task at hand. The painful truth was dawning upon him that he may never see Carla again.

"Has she really gone from my life for ever?" He lamented, imagining her thriving under her aunt's influence in a new school with a new group of friends.

Afternoons, his thoughts oscillated between Carla and the cool aqua expanse of Bourke pool stretching like a mirage before him and, sometimes too, he wondered about his old mates from the gang, as the Bee Gees riff ran on.

"Where is the light… that would play… in my streets[25]?

And where are the friends… I could meet…I could meet[25]?"

Occasionally, of a Saturday, Greg packed the exploration team into the four-wheel drive for a night on the town. "A bit of a break from the daily routine," he said. Rod was always the designated driver, volunteered for the job, being the only one who didn't drink. But those visits only made him feel more miserable than if he'd never gone—being always late by the time they got there, and the pool always closed.

"We're not gonna risk our lives by going into that place!" was Greg's response to Rod's urgings that they try the Carriers' Arms. Despite Rod's assurances that all would be okay, Greg chose the more friendly-looking Post Office, or perhaps the Royal. Rod was hostage to the routine, utterly powerless to alter his course as the river of life dragged him along in its current. He knew the feeling well.

On one occasion only, they left for town earlier than usual. That day Rod convinced the others to swing past the Bourke Memorial Pool. He'd take a quick dip before walking to the Post Office Hotel. Michael decided to join him. Greg dropped them off and, resisting once more the offer of a swim, headed off for a Saturday evening of drinking.

After pushing through the turnstiles, Rod paused a moment, mesmerized, nostalgic; the pool's waters sparkling in the afternoon sunlight, the air full with the smell of salty chips, wafts of chlorine and the sounds of gaiety and laughter. Ecstatic with anticipation, like at a long-awaited reunion with an old familiar friend, he'd finally made it home again. Rod led off in front of Michael, striding quickly across the lawn; everything exactly how he remembered—but something was definitely wrong.

"Hey Rod, long time no see." Roscoe, the swimming pool attendant, recognised him. "I didn't think I'd see you back here. It's been over a year, hasn't it?"

"Yeah, it's been about that, mate." Rod knew that Beth had gone to Dubbo, Carla was in Townsville of course, but where was everybody else. The complex was abuzz with activity; groups with their towels, lying on the lawn, under his tree, others waiting their turn for the diving boards—favourite niches he knew so well—but only now everyone was new. There was not a face he could recognise.

"I don't understand it Roscoe," he said to the attendant who was still nearby, uncoiling a sprinkler hose ready for the evening's watering. "I can't see anyone I know."

"New year, new bunch of kids—it's always the same," he replied philosophically. "Y' might find one or two though."

"C'mon mate," Michael's voice cut in. "Let's have our swim and get back to the others at the pub."

"Hey Rod," a familiar voice piped up.

"Hello." Rod looked around, recognising the glasses if nothing else. "How are you going Donna?"

"I'm just fine! I'm married now and we'll be starting a family soon," she smiled glowingly.

"Hey, that's fantastic news, Donna. I'm really happy for you. Do I know the lucky bloke?"

"Yeah, sure you do! It's Ricky. We'll have to get together one of these days, but I won't hold you up from your swim right now," she said, heading for the turnstile. "I've gotta get home and start cooking tea."

"She's a bit of a porker mate," Michael said after waiting for Donna to move out of polite earshot. I thought you said they'd all be good lookers?"

"Well, they were last year," Rod replied, standing there watching her leave. "I can't believe it. She was talking about having a kid…," he added, still half in shock, half jumping to her defence. Had all the others changed that much as well, he wondered.

"C'mon then, let's get a move on," Michael said, sensing Rod's disappointment. "That's life, don't worry about it mate."

Accepting his situation, Rod began to relax, hypnotised by life's daily rhythm. He felt very much at home in the bush as he worked those long hot summer days, mostly by himself and at one with the landscape, its rocky red hills and flat black-soil plains. Images of ancient forests, raging torrents of water, angry volcanoes spewing lavas laden with precious metals, and strange creatures from a bygone era, rose like ghostly images before his eyes as he studied and interpreted the now bone-dry and dusty outcrops in the parched land, as he connected again and again, each time more powerfully than before, with the living essence of the river country. What the rest of the world saw as a flat, dry and changeless landscape, stained crimson, red and yellow by iron ochres, Rod visualised as a dynamic ongoing continuum of which his whole life—the scene around him—represented but a mere split second. Lost in the mists of time in his own four-dimensional world, Rod found he could look forward in time too—into a future too vast to imagine. Hundreds of millions of generations from now, the Australian continent, pushing relentlessly northward, would close the Coral Sea and ram into greater Asia—and the Great Australian desert floor would, once again, buckle and twist upwards into an imposing wall of Himalayan giants. Earth's volcanic juices would once more squeeze into the crushed and folded rocks forming brand-new deposits of gold and mineral riches—which people, of that age, would probably neither want nor care about—assuming the human race still existed and walked the face of the earth millions of years from now.

Rod was awestruck, focused on his work, imagining life, past, present and future, in his cherished river country, during his wholesome daily routine. Sometimes he'd cross paths with Michael and the others engrossed in their own tasks.

"Hey Rod, did you see the old Yanda homestead down by the river?" Michael broke into Rod's dream world as he was closing his mapping traverse loop around one of their aeromagnetic exploration targets. If there was anything interesting to find, it was always Michael who found it, collecting all sorts of stuff. His bedroom at home in Sydney was a museum of antiquities—guns, spears, tribal masks, books, stamps and other *objets d'art* he'd either found, or bought in one or another of Sydney's second-hand shops.

"Yeah mate, nothin' left there now other than an old chimney stack and a bit of rusty iron from the stove." Rod replied. "I was thinkin' about the family that must've lived there—probably about a hundred years ago now, I'd reckon."

"I found some purple glass scattered around the place," Michael continued, pulling a broken piece from his pocket, handing it to Rod, "and some other bits along the river bank. I reckon they threw their old bottles and rubbish in the river. Do ya wanna go swimming there this arvo and see what we can find?"

Rod glanced at his watch; it was already half past three and stinking hot. "Yeah, sure Michael, what a great idea. I reckon nothing could beat a swim right now. I'll be done with my traverse in ten minutes."

That afternoon they pulled a treasure trove from the murky muds of the Darling –countless whiskeys, beer, wines and spirits—and domestic items too—cobalt blue medicine and poison bottles, ink bottles, ornate Rosella tomato sauces, preserves and pickle jars, flasks of Eno's health salts, and cordial bottles—antique porcelain ones made for Rice's bottling plant in Bourke. They even found torpedo bottles and sea-green lemonades—the ones with a marble and O-ring seal.

Old Charlie Bowman, stockman from Toorale Station, later told them why marble-tops were so rare.

"Life was real tough back then. As kids we had to invent our own games and make our own toys. We were always smashin' the end off of them bottles to get the marble out."

They spent the whole afternoon, and plenty more after that, trawling the Darling near the old homestead, duck diving into its brown waters—gingerly probing their fingers into the ooze of the pitch-black river bottom, feeling for the tell-tale smooth curve of a bottle, then shooting back up to the surface, gasping for breath, to take a look at their prize.

Rod was pleased with his haul, a teapot, a broken porcelain doll's head, but enviously recalls the day when Michael found the rarest prize—a small, delicate, rose-coloured bottle with raised letters, embossed on the glass.

"Maaate, check this one out," he shouted gleefully waving the bottle about in the air. It's a Lily the Pink's Medicinal Compound'. They even wrote a song about it." He began an ebullient chant; "Lily the Pink, the pink, the pink … saviour of the human raaaace…[26]"

"Lydia E. Pinkham's magical elixir– a cure for all ailments," old Charlie later explained. "Boxes of it, along with hundreds of other tonics and ointments, came out from America by ship. It was popular in the mother country and the colonies at the time. I dunno if any of 'em really worked, but I'm still here, so it didn't do me too much harm either!"

They discovered ancient camp sites too as they wandered the river country, especially around the base of Mt Talowla (or Withawitha Iaana, but we never knew its original name back then); stone fireplace rings, nardoo grinding stones, polished axe heads, and pressure-flaked chert spear tips and cutters, all exposed for only brief windows of time from beneath the shifting wind-blown desert sands.

Although Talowla's outcrops rose no more than some twenty five metres above plains level, the low barren mesa had a certain impalpable mystical or spiritual feel about it.

"This place is so weird," Rod said, moving the magnetic sensor head by a few metres and pressing the instrument's button another time. "I can never get a consistent reading. Every time I traverse the top, the mag field numbers are all over the place, different from the plains on either side. Something really strange is happening up here."

"I reckon Talowla was an important place; a stopping point for ancient travellers crossing the Darling on their way north or south. A local landmark written into their song lines," Michael surmised. "I've come across bones too, and a skull, so I reckon they're definitely human."

OUTBACK SUMMER

"DIVING FOR BOTTLES"

Robert Coenraads 2024

"Don't you go muckin' around with any of them cursed bloody dead-feller bones," Charlie warned when he heard. "If y' know what's good for yer."

"I reckon they quarried chert from the ridge rocks here too—for their knives and spears," Michael added. "And their big flat grinders weigh a ton, so they must've hidden them here, ready for when they came back. I wonder how long they camped each time?"

"Some of them might even be Chief's," Rod mused, remembering the stories about his stashes of stone tools and equipment he kept hidden about the place, ready for when he'd go bush. "But I reckon these ones are probably way older." Rod sorely missed calling in at the Carriers' whenever he felt like it, to hear Chief's stories.

One afternoon Michael returned to the homestead, pulling out of his bag the weirdest stone object anyone had ever seen.

"I'll trade you for it Michael," the lead geophysicist, Trevor, exclaimed immediately upon spying it, barely able to contain himself. "Will you take that autographed copy of Milton B. Dobrin's book you've been wanting?"

"Hey, wait a minute, I own that book," Rod retorted.

"Well, how much do you want for the book then?" Trevor countered, turning to Rod. "I'll buy it off you?" he demanded cockily.

"Well, I reckon my book might be worth a lot of money too," Rod joined, feigning indignation. He knew Michael well enough to realize he was leading Trevor on.

"I dunno if I want to sell it," Michael considered indecisively? "I'll bet the anthropologists will pay me a lot of money for it, y' know."

The item in question was an unmistakable stone penis—conical shaped with a flat base, it stood upright about fifteen centimetres tall with an inscribed circumferential ring close to its domed end and a short slit across the top.

"I don't think it would be worth that much," Trevor bargained, "but what will you take for it anyway, Michael?"

"I reckon it might be a very rare artefact," George countered, objecting to Trevor's attempts to devalue it. "I've never seen or heard of anything like it before.

"It must've had deep cultural and ceremonial significance," Rod mused, picking it up from the table, studying it carefully.

"Yes, it was part of the… 'penis cult'," Michael expounded, "a significant underground movement, passed down from culture to culture, and one which still exists to this very day. Even at Macquarie University, males still worship daily in a small temple with individual cubicles, the walls of which are adorned with all manner of penis images." He paused for effect in front of his dumbfounded audience. "And then in the evening the same students gather in another place of great ceremony where special substances are imbibed allowing participants to reach extraordinary heights of spiritual self-awareness. Sometimes even ganga is smoked in peace-pipes beneath the auspices of the Student Union banner…"

"Those are our society's problems, Michael," Rod cut in. "I reckon indigenous cultures were far purer than that—much better than ours' in the way they…"

"Cut the Arcadian crap! All that bull about the noble savage is just a myth mate. We're all humans and we're all the same!" Michael spat before turning to Trevor. "Nah, forget about it mate. I reckon I'll just hang onto it for the time being."

"Huh?" George exclaimed as Trevor walked away in disgust. "What was that all about?"

"Look, make what you will of it, but I reckon some bored kid picked up that fortuitously-shaped rock all those years ago," Michael explained, "and spent about an hour carving it while hanging around Mt Talowla waiting around for something to happen—maybe nothing more to it than that. The anthropologists will never be able to tell you either."

"Oh," exclaimed Rod, disconsolately knocked down a few pegs from his moral high horse, "I'd have preferred a more spiritual explanation than that…"

"Yeah, sorry about that Rod—but I'm afraid there was never such a place as Utopia. The first time man picked up a rock he realised—this will do nicely to hit my enemy over the head with! Then people learnt to pressure-flake chert and next thing they've made spears and they're throwing them at one another. Later came copper, bronze, gunpowder and iron, forged into guns and bullets—blood and guts and gore followed on a massive scale as inventions became bigger and better weapons of conquest, and society rose against society. Finally came the atomic bomb, vaporizing whole cities of innocent women and children…"

"Hey, that's so gross. I'm not sure I really needed all that detail, Michael," Rod laughed, trying to make light of his disgust. He was losing focus. He desperately wanted to find Carla. There had to be more to the human race than just cruel survival-of-the-fittest evolution. He needed to rekindle that spiritual connection— that special bond he felt with her—but was that just a lost dream now? —a small flame trying to rise within him only to be extinguished by life's harsh reality? It had been over a year now. The truth was she'd moved on and he'd never find her again.

"There's no limit to what one human will do to another," Michael continued. "No matter who it is they'll come up with some reason or another to justify it. Hitler was the very worst, and he was one of my dad's own people."

"I'd hoped that people could be better than that—that I could somehow make a difference," Rod struggled dejectedly with the argument.

"Humans are disgusting, Rod," Michael concluded philosophically. "But it's up to you whether you're gonna be disgusting or not. You reach the crossroads, mate, and you know your options—left, right or straight ahead. The choice is yours—no one can make it for you."

CHAPTER 25. TOORALE HOMESTEAD

DAY AFTER DAY the team of explorers worked the river country on the both sides of the Darling. Progressing from property to property, they moved steadily eastwards towards Bourke. In the next few days, they would enter Toorale Station land.

Rod remembered the name Toorale having heard it from Mick Tallon, the drover's cook whom he'd met the previous summer in Bourke. So, when they stopped by the rambling old homestead one morning, en-route to work, he wasn't too surprised to run into his old mate.

Mick was cleaning up after breakfast, a tall stack of dirty pots and pans cradled in his wiry arms, as he shouldered open the fly-screen kitchen door, bumping into them on the back porch.

"G'day mate! Long-time no see." Mick's face creased into a broad smile.

Placing the dishes in the trough, he greeted them with work-roughened hands as Rod explained the program planned for the property and where they were based.

"Eldorado Homestead! That's just over the other side of Mount Talowla—about forty kilometres as the crow flies—so that makes us next door neighbours for sure," Mick began, and before long had them all feeling real welcome with his country hospitality—a steaming mug of tea on the kitchen table in front of each of them.

"What's say ya stop in for a freshly cooked lamb's fry and onion sanger for tea on yer way back through? You'll be able to meet the rest of the boys them?"

"That's an offer; too good to refuse, Mick," Rod replied for the others from the driver's door as they set off to locate their first survey site of the day.

And so began their regular visits whenever they passed by Toorale of an afternoon and, more often than not, lured by the promise of tall tales and true. Rod, Michael and George would stay long into the evening, joining the drovers and stockmen for supper around the big kitchen table. There was Clancy 'of the overflow' MacIntosh, leader of the team; Ian, the master whip cracker; Aspro, the harmless dope, and Charlie Bowman, 90 years old and the oldest of the stockmen.

Charlie had his own single-room shack a hundred metres distant from the main homestead and sometimes they'd drop by and see him there. He would always be attending to something or another around the property, perhaps a poddy calf or lamb, the runt of the litter, he'd saved from abandonment by its mother. Rod loved feeding these tiny helpless creatures with formula in a baby bottle, watching them, as the days wore on, growing stronger, more independent, but never forgetting the warmth and kindness of the human hand that had saved their lives. And Charlie was that kind of person who could also spin a great yarn. Charlie was retired nowadays, but he'd certainly experienced plenty of history, and entertained them nightly, never short of a tale of his youth in the district's early days.

"The place was built in 1896 by Bourke's big sheep boss, Sam McCaughey, for his favourite niece Louisa," Charlie explained, "a big family with lots of kids. I remember 'cause I was already eight back then. They had garden beds full of veggies and trees chock-a-block with fruit. Back then the workers lived with their families on the outstations, with a live-in governess to teach all the kids. They'd be big parties on Saturday nights, piano playing and dancing in the grand ball room with its marble fireplaces and stained-glass roof. It was big enough to hold 'em all.

"The shearers' quarters were full back then too," Charlie went on, "and the shed by the river bustled with activity—46 stands an' the first in Australia with electric lights—as the gun shearers worked non-stop all day to out-compete one another. The biggest fleece tally meant the biggest pay packet. At the end of the season the silly buggers threw it all away down at the pub in town. Then they'd all come back broke, to a man, and start all over again next year. There was no talkin' any sense into 'em. That's just how life was.

"That was back then, and the big families have all since moved on," Charlie finished philosophically. "Probably all ghosts now, except me."

As Charlie spoke, Rod imagined life at Toorale during those heady years around the turn of the century, saddened that, these days, the piano in the old ballroom stood dusty and silent. Toorale lay in sad disrepair; floral wall paper peeling away like old skin, plaster walls crumbling in places from their skeletal frame, verandah sagging miserably, its once-abundant gardens parched and uncared for. Only the two palms remained, standing majestically tall on either side of the homestead's ornate front entrance.

"Why don't they fix up Toorale, Mick?" Rod asked. "She's been a good house all right, but now she's really falling apart."

"The pastoral company was lookin' into doing 'er up at one stage," Mick replied slowly, recalling rumours that he'd heard about town. "But she was already too far gone. They reckon termites had got into her walls and it was gonna cost too much. They were talking about taking out the marble fireplaces, but I reckon they've forgotten all about her now."

One afternoon Rod walked into the kitchen after work as Mick announced they'd hired a new jackeroo.

"He's a real smart young bloke and a hard worker too. Come meet him Rod,"

"G'day…" Rod started, casually extending his arm in the direction of a silhouette seated at the table as his eyes adjusted to the kitchen's darkened interior.

"His name's Brad."

Then, in disbelief, as recognition dawned, he dropped his hand knowing the-one-and-the-same Brad from Bourke would never take it!

Brad never said a word, simply staring at him in the way he remembered from that evening in the Oxford, as Mick's voice droned in the background. Rod figured he must be thinking the very same thing—What in the hell is he doing here? Rod recalled their last meeting outside the Post Office Hotel that day along with his mates, the ones from Carla's gang. He could see the dislike simmering, boiling over, in his silent stare. No point in saying anything to him, Rod thought, and, least of all, asking anything about Carla. Rod turned away, pushing through the flyscreen door onto the verandah. Brad followed.

"Carla's gone y' know. She never came back," he spat. "It's always the bloody same. Only the mongrel dogs and the no-hopers stay in town, 'cause they're the ones that can't get out. The bloody out-o'-towners, like you, piss off with the rest."

"Nothin' t' do with me, mate," Rod answered, realising that any further explanation would be useless.

"Yeah, well you'd better always be lookin' over y'r shoulders in the bush, 'cause y' don't wanna be getting in my way around here, mate."

Again, that afternoon, like the summer before, they faced off. Between them lay an insurmountable gulf of background and prejudice, the same as the invisible wall between Carla and the girls he'd experienced at the pool, only this time he was stuck on one side of it and Brad was on the other.

He was probably a fairly nice bloke otherwise, Rod reflected later. Carla said how as kids the gang hunted in the bush for emu eggs. They'd use a pointed stone to chip a hole in each end and blow out the egg's innards with their mouths—a sometimes-disgusting process if it was already rotten from sitting out in the sun! Next, they'd carve into the shell's different coloured layers, delicately scraping them away to create beautiful scenes. Why couldn't we talk about interesting things like that and forget the tension, hatred and jealousy? It was all about Carla, and she was gone from both of their lives, probably for ever; a clever kid with a big future on a new bright and shining path.

Anyway, who gives a damn, Rod concluded, giving up on the thought. It'd never work. Anyway, I won't be bumping into Brad again.

It's funny how things in life can turn out though. Whilst exploring Toorale, they camped at the homestead a few days to avoid the 80 km drive to and from Eldorado each day, and, as coincidence had it, Brad was assigned to drop Rod off at the survey area each day, as the vehicle was needed elsewhere.

Apart from curt directions, they barely spoke. Brad would return to collect Rod at a pre-arranged place and time each afternoon. If he finished early, Rod would pass the time exploring around the pick-up site which, one afternoon, happened to be near the fireplace rings on the eastern slopes of Mt Talowla.

Brad inched forward, driving the Land rover in a wide circle until the passenger door came alongside Rod who was engrossed in laying out a selection of different artefacts beside his day pack.

"If you're gonna take those stones out of here then I'm not takin' you anywhere." Brad's voice cut into his thoughts.

Life in the outback could be a darn sight tougher than a city boy might expect. Out here, beneath the simplicity of its harsh blue skies and sun-drenched desert, its complex undercurrents, social norms and customs needed to be obeyed to the letter, if one were to survive for long. For some reason, that afternoon, Rod missed the clues and chose to argue as he gathered the pieces into his bag.

"You gotta leave 'em here," Brad insisted.

"What's the use of a bunch of old dead-fella stones going to be to anyone if we leave 'em here?" Rod could feel the weight of the stones in his bag—he had a number of pressure-flaked chert spearheads and a ground quartzite axe head, one of the best he'd ever seen. He was a collector; it went against the grain to leave behind anything he'd found. He knew, in the shifting sands on the flanks of Mt Talowla, they could easily disappear in a windstorm overnight, and might stay buried for decades. More than anything he really wanted to keep them—especially the axe head.

"Just leave 'em alone," Brad repeated emphatically. "It's stealing from the dead. Can ya go to the cemetery and pinch a bunch of the headstones just because you like the looks of 'em? Hurry up and empty them out. It's getting dark and I'm going."

It was the most words he'd ever heard Brad string together, yet still Rod persisted.

"Don't be bloody silly. It's not stealing; headstones are different, these are just old stone tools." He went for the passenger door of the ute, but could see by the look on Brad's face that he was upset, visibly restraining his anger. Rod paused, trying to think of something else.

"Well, you can spend all bloody night with the ancestral spirits if ya wanna think about it much longer!" Brad cut in. "Then we'll see how you feel about it in the morning."

"Damn'" Rod swore. He figured he'd have to leave the stones behind to appease Brad. He hesitated, looking around for some landmark. Maybe next to something he could recognise, perhaps a clump of distinctive bushes. He'd just have to come back and get them some other time.

"Hey!!" Rod spun around only to see Brad taking off towards the homestead in the Land Rover.

"Bastard! Come back!" his voice echoed in the emptiness, trailing away as the ute disappeared in a dusty trail. He realised it was futile. "Bastard," he swore under his breath, repeating the word every few seconds, as if it might somehow drive away his anger.

The sun dropped quickly below the bulk of Talowla, the low mesa's icy shadows stretching quickly across the plains engulfing him in the onset of darkness as he walked homewards. The temperature drop was sudden, making Rod angrier still, the day's heat draining almost instantaneously into the cloudless desert evening.

"Damn," he swore again, starting to shiver as night's darkness came quickly "I didn't count on needing a jumper. I'd better keep a bloody move on."

As Rod walked, some lights appeared in the distance, and the roar of a motor. He recognised it—Aspro's ute—he must be out with the boys. Although, in the darkness, Rod could make out nothing more than headlights—four of them; two smaller yellow dots on the outside, and two larger, brighter spotlights in the middle—their strong rays scanning the total darkness, bouncing about as the ute sped over the rough landscape. Rod turned to face them, waving his arms and shouting. He'd get a lift. He knew Aspro and his mates were out kangaroo hunting—collecting a bounty from the pet food industry—but it meant more to them than that, it was their nightly sport—far more entertaining than the telly. The vehicle was set up for hunting, every cent of its owner's wages pumped into 'roo bars, gantries, pullies, winches and armouries full of guns and steely knives; a meatworks on wheels.

Rod heard energetic whoops and loud music as the vehicle approached; its roof-mounted searchlight sweeping over him briefly. Then, suddenly, two whistling retorts shattered the stillness—way too close for comfort.

"Bloody idiots," Rod shouted, shutting his eyes and diving for cover—angrier at himself for his own stupidity. "Dumb bastards!" he swore. They'd caught sight of his retinas reflecting in the darkness—twin tell-tale iridescent spots—and shot without even checking first. How many cows and sheep end up in their bounty as collateral damage, he wondered in the split second as he hit the earth, rolling under a bush as the ute slew past showering him in dust and sand. A moment later, he stood up watching the red of their tail lights shrink into the distance, as they left him behind—again in darkness.

"Bloody Larrikins," he repeated angrily into the emptiness.

He could wait for moonrise, still several hours away, but instead chose the saviour of many a night traveller—the brilliant half-dome of stars vaulting above. Mt Talowla lay immediately west, its outline only visible by the dark shape it cut out from the luminous heavens.

The Southern Cross sat nested in a basket of minor stars, in a sky so bright with pinpricks he could barely make out the constellation. But there it was, shining like a familiar friend, the distinctive blackness of the Coal Sack along its longer edge and two unmistakable pointers heralding its presence. It would have been beautiful if he were in the mood to enjoy it, but he could orient himself in the blackness now. The Cross and pointers showed him south, so he turned and headed north towards the road. Keeping Talowla on his left, he should eventually reach its safety and from there follow the road north-eastwards to Toorale homestead. With that plan in place, he began to feel a little better, even proud of his navigational skills— the soft thudding of his feet on the dry desert sand being the only sound breaking the night's dead stillness.

"Geographically misplaced," Rod muttered towards the look of surprise on the sea of upturned faces seated around the kitchen table. He saw Brad there too, working away on an emu egg, quietly in the background. His anger spent on the walk, he wasn't going to start a war of words and accusations; it was close to 10:30pm and all Rod wanted to do was go to bed.

"We just got back from hunting and Charlie said ya never showed up back at camp. We was just about to send out a search party for ya, mate," Aspro jeered, mocking Rod's incompetence, while Mick consoled. "I've saved ya some tea, mate. It's in the oven."

"Sorry for troubling you all," Rod added, eyes downcast, but offering nothing further by way of explanation. He felt like an idiot for nearly getting killed over a bunch of old stones, and Brad was probably right—just like the bones of their creators—they weren't even his to take. He was left pondering the strangeness of that powerful urge driving him to find, collect and possess things?

CHAPTER 26. THE RESCUE

ONE EVENING, heading home late from Toorale, a violent electrical storm centred itself on Mt Talowla, Brad and Rod saw it looming on the horizon as they drove westwards towards Eldorado, becoming increasingly ominous as they approached; its staccato shafts firing into the hilltop every few seconds, lighting the inside of the cab and their faces in stark whiteness—and the road they were taking headed for the middle of the tempest, straight over the top of the hill. Michael and George had crossed earlier that evening and were already at Eldorado. Play it safe, or give it a go, the choice was Rod's. He'd never seen a storm the likes of it before.

Finally, after waiting as long as he could, Rod spoke. "I think you'd better turn her around, mate."

"You aint got the guts, have ya mate? You sure ya don't wanna go for it, or are ya too spineless?" Brad jeered, testing Rod's resolve. "I reckon the spirits are out to get ya."

"Just do it, will you mate. There's no need for any heroics tonight," Rod insisted, feeling a little cowardly for not daring to try.

"Wisest decision y' ever made t' turn back, I reckon," Charlie told them later, when they arrived back at Toorale looking a little sheepish. "Y' never muck around with things like that, y' know."

The storm worsened, the rain and wind lashing the homestead in fury. As the weather became wilder and turned cold, old Charlie began to tell stories about furious storms past.

"Like you blokes, I remember one time when we turned back at Talowla. We were on it when the first bolt struck, and then they were all around us like an electric cage. We chucked a U-ey on the road then and there and sped back down as fast as we could. We were so lucky to get out of that one. I've seen it a couple of times in my life—that hill's like a lightning magnet."

Rod's decision meant they would need to spend the rest of the night at Toorale, and it meant they were there when Charlie took a call from the station owner on the other side of the Warrego. He hung up the phone, a worried look on his face.

"Mrs Fenwick left town a while back but hasn't made it home yet. She must've been trapped somewhere along the way by the rising Warrego."

Charlie was way too old; Mick, Aspro and Ian were stranded in town, so that meant Brad and Rod would be the ones to go out looking for her.

"Throw a few sheets of roofing tin on the back on the way out," old Charlie called as they left. "Ya just never know if yer going to need 'em."

Rod remembered the roofing tin trick he'd heard about in one of Charlie's stories, He tied the sheets of corrugated iron sheets onto the back of the vehicle to stop them flapping about in the wind, and, drenched to the skin by the downpour, climbed into the passenger seat of the cab.

Brad captained the vehicle like a ship in a tempest; the wipers beat uselessly against the rain squalls and the headlight beams seemed to be sucked into the blackness before they even hit the ground. Having fenced the track over the past few weeks, he seemed to know every foot of it like the back of his hand.

"I can just make out the fence on our right," Brad shouted over the drumming on the roof. "It'll take us straight down to the river."

After reaching the flooding Warrego, they spotted a vehicle by the far bank. It was trapped on one of the small islands formed by the many branches of the river. Mrs Fenwick was caught by the rising floodwaters. From that island, she could go neither forward nor back.

A faint torch beam waving about in the darkness meant she was okay and had spotted their oncoming headlights. They stopped about 40 metres back where the track dipped into the flowing river and Rod got out, checking the crossing, wading in a few steps. The ground was soft and sandy, while the swirling waters felt patchy, warm and cold—a sure sign that the river was rising fast.

"I don't like it one bit," Rod called. "The bottom's soft and if we get stuck in the middle we'll be washed downstream as she rises for sure."

"If we don't take the chance now, we'll miss our opportunity. That island is likely to go under before the night's out," Brad shouted back.

"If you take it real slow then, I can feed Charlie's tin sheets under the tyres and you won't sink into the sand. Once you're off the sheets I'll carry 'em back round to the front."

Brad engaged four-wheel-drive low-range and eased the Landy steadily forward, as Rod walked alongside. He felt the current pushing him hard against the side of the vehicle and was comforted knowing the tray was heavy with gear and rock samples pushing down on the rear wheels, providing traction.

"I hope we've got enough weight on board," he prayed aloud as they passed through the deepest section of the crossing. The water swirled around his thighs making it difficult to stand up, let alone steady the corrugated sheets as Brad inched the vehicle forward.

It was close, too close for comfort, but the wheels held firm as they rose onto the far bank.

"Thanks…" Drenched and shivering, Mrs Fenwick was lost for many words. "Thanks for coming boys."

It barely took moments to get Mrs Fenwick and her gear on board, before the challenge of re-crossing the rising torrent. They moved quickly, wordlessly, synchronized like clockwork. There was nothing they could do about her ute, just leave it there, windows open, parked up against the fence.

Back at Toorale, Charlie was ready with dry towels and mugs of steaming sugary tea.

"I really owe you one for coming out to get me, boys," Mrs Fenwick said, giving each of them a hug.

"Nothing much to do with me," Rod spoke in place of Brad's silence. "I was just along for the ride. Brad did the driving and he knew where you'd likely be."

***

For the next few days exploration came to a complete halt as the roads were impassable. Rod stayed stranded at Toorale longer than he anticipated, spending his time assisting with the clean-up.

After the floodwaters eased, Mrs Fenwick's daughter dropped by the homestead with a big tin of home-made blueberry cupcakes to share around with her mother's rescuers. Brad and Rod returned with her to the island, now just a slight hump in the flat landscape, to search for the ute. Her job was to get it running again, if it weren't a complete write-off.

The muddy ute sat pushed hard up against the fence, debris piled against its doors and the ground eroded away on its lee side; the scene telling all just how lucky they'd been. The river had completely topped the island that night and everybody could see it plain as day.

"I reckon we did a pretty good job there, mate," Brad spoke softly to Rod. "She'd 've been as good as gone," glancing at Mrs Fenwick's daughter as he referred to her mother's near demise, "y' know, if we hadn't got to her in time."

"Yeah, you're not wrong," Rod replied, then, lightening the tone, he spoke louder so all could hear. "I reckon you must be a pretty good fencer though. Look at the way it held the ute. I reckon she'd be over on her roof somewhere miles down the creek if it weren't for your fence, mate—and there's not a bend in your posts either," Rod laughed.

Pretty in her tight R.M. Williams jeans and check shirt, Mrs Fenwick's daughter reminded Rod much of the driller's daughter, Suzie. Skilled in bush mechanics, she worked to drain the tank, fuel lines and sump—methodical and confident in her actions. Rod admired the kind of girl a life in the outback seemed to breed.

Brad assisted her, their body language demonstrating they made an able and competent team. Together they pulled out the floor mats, dried the air filter and checked the electrics. There appeared to be little damage other than a number of gashes along the side of the vehicle caused by the barbed wire fence.

"They're the ute's badge of courage!" Mrs Fenwick's daughter exclaimed running her fingers along the deep cuts to the paintwork. "Everybody'll ask about them, so we're never gonna forget what we owe you guys."

After clearing away the branches and other debris from around the ute, there was little left for Rod to do and he became pensive, his thoughts turning to Carla. How would he ever find her again? Brad was right, she was gone, and what he'd said was probably true—once girls leave, they never come back. His life's path seemed to wind aimlessly in the spaces between everyone else's trajectories as if intersections were being deliberately thwarted. Frustrated and bored, he slumped down on the edge of the track. The sun beat mercilessly down on his back but he lacked even the motivation to move himself into the nearby shade. The Bourke he once knew had changed so much, and when this field season was over, he'd probably just end up going home. Mrs Fenwick's daughter was real pretty; he should be trying to help her more too. What was her name again? If he had to take a guess, she's probably studying agriculture at uni and back home over summer break helping her parents on the farm. His mind drifted back to the day he was Suzie's hero, as a near-identical scenario now played out before his very eyes. He wasn't feeling so good, melting even more miserably under the intense noonday sun—a little sick inside, he felt like vomiting. Perhaps it was the fact he hadn't bothered to drink much water today.

Listlessly, Rod grabbed a handful of soft desert sand from the track edge and let its silky red iron-oxide-coated quartz grains slide through the gaps between his fingers. It had been blowing around the desert for perhaps millennia and, now, in his hands, its effortless fluidity, pouring like sand through an hourglass, somehow relaxed him. At the same moment, near his foot, he saw three ants, oblivious to his presence, dragging a leaf many times their size towards their nest. It all reminded him of his own transience—a sentient being connected to this timeless land, with his own not-insignificant role in the greater scheme of things. Then slowly, inexplicably from nowhere, a new feeling of warmth spread through his being, a feeling of magnanimity and kindness towards his fellows. He and Brad had been arch foes for over a year, yet, in the past few days, things had changed and now he found himself wishing Brad happiness, and the same with Mrs Fenwick's daughter, another person with a whole life story to tell; a story he hadn't even bothered to get to know.

He moved into the nearby shade and sat watching them as they replaced the sump oil, refilled the fuel tank and primed the carburettor. And when the engine finally roared into life, they whooped in unison, slapping hands and laughing as collaborators in a major achievement.

"Thanks for all your help, boys," Mrs Fenwick's daughter said smiling, her pretty face grimy with grease and sweat, as she tossed the tools in the back, preparing to drive her prize home. "I'll be back around later to collect the cake tin," she said, "and I hope I'll run into you then," addressing the latter comment particularly towards Brad.

The normally-dark Brad was ebullient, smiling, watching her as she tore away toward home. She tested the vehicle's horn, steering and brakes as she went, resulting in a series of enthusiastic doughnuts in the still-soft soil. Rod sensed an opportunity and took a chance.

"Congratulations on a job well done, Brad," he said formally, at the same time extending his hand tentatively. Brad took it and they stood that day in the middle of the track under the clear outback skies, shaking hands for the first time.

"By the way, Brad, if you don't mind. I've seen the way you carve those emu eggs. Do y' reckon I could watch how you do it…?"

OUTBACK SUMMER

"CHARLIE BOWMAN
SPIRIT OF TOORALE"

Robert Coenraads
2025

For a brief while from then on Rod enjoyed Brad's company more than he could have possibly imagined. Maybe it was for a few weeks, but after that Brad didn't stay long at Toorale. The Fenwick's offered him a permanent job on their property as station manager saying they needed a strong local lad with a good head on his shoulders to assist Mr Fenwick who wasn't getting any younger. After that, life took its natural course as it always seems to do, and in good time another generation was born to work the land and reap its bounty and riches.

"From disaster sprang good. There were stock losses of course, and much work to be done, but it was divine providence, I reckon," Charlie would always say when finishing that particular story. "The storm that nearly drowned Mrs Fenwick was the very same one that stopped her only rescuers from going home early, y' know." He'd then fall silent a moment and conclude, "if any one single thing had gone wrong that night, or they'd waited a few minutes longer, none of them would have made it back alive! The moral of the story is things change quickly in life, for better or for worse, so make sure you enjoy whatever you are doing now, because it will inevitably change."

Unfortunately, old Charlie died not too many years after that, aged nearly a hundred—his repertoire of stories forever lost into the mists of history, never again to be told—but not really, as most, including the story in which he and Brad starred, remained alive in the hearts and minds of all those who experienced them.

'May Charlie's spirit live on forever at Toorale!' Rod prayed quietly at his passing years later.

CHAPTER 27. CHIEF STANDS TALL

BUT, AS ALWAYS, that year's summer eventually came to an end and once again, it was time for Rod to farewell the river country, to pack up his belongings and saddle up his trusty bike he'd hidden under a dusty tarpaulin out in the shed, and ride back to Sydney.

On their last morning, the three field hands said their goodbyes to the team and prepared to go their separate ways back to the city. Rod was ecstatic, because it meant he could now stop a while in Bourke—he was his own master once more, free to do as he pleased. He spun the crank handle of the black Bakelite telephone sitting on the small table on Eldorado's verandah.

"Operator, could you please put me through to 2K Paka Tank?"

"Connecting you now…. Go ahead please."

"Hello Mick, is that you? Just checking if you're in as I'll be coming through in about an hour. I wanna drop in and say goodbye to you and the boys. I'll leave you my address in Sydney so y' can come and visit one day."

He'd thought about it a lot, what he was going to do. After he saw all of them at Toorale, he'd go straight to the Bourke Memorial Pool for a swim and find out from Donna what all the others were doing nowadays. Later he'd go to the Carriers' Arms and see if he could find Chief who'd be able to tell him about Carla. After all of that, he'd probably book a room in the Royal, perhaps stay a few nights as he was in no great hurry to get back to Sydney.

The Central Australian was nearly empty when Rod arrived at about two in the afternoon, and he picked Dan immediately, sitting on a stool at the bar, right where he expected. "What're y' doing here, Dan?"

"Nothin' much mate." His eyes stared vacantly ahead, fixed on the rows of bottles on the shelf behind the bar, barely registering Rod's presence, as his arm automatically lifted the schooner to his lips for a sip of beer. "I'm just waiting for some work to come along."

"I went to the pool lookin' for y' all, but no one I knew was there. I met Donna in the street; she looked a lot bigger than I remember, and she was pushing a baby pram. Then I went round to your mum's, and she said you'd be here."

Dan took a while to reply and Rod could sense that the conversation wasn't going to go anywhere fast. It seemed like he'd aged an eternity in the space of just one year; his face pale and lined; his youthful vigour and excitement for life drained away completely.

"Nah mate, nobody goes there anymore. The pool's just for the kids. Ricky might be round a little later this arvo after he finishes work, if y' want to stick around, Rod. The Central's our meeting place nowadays."

"How's Brad doing now?" Rod asked. "I saw him a while back, before he left Toorale."

"He's still workin' outa town on the Fenwick's station mate. He's hot on the sheila out there, and says they're gonna get married later on when he gets some more money together for a honeymoon."

"Hey, do y' remember the day when y' nearly cut Mark's head off with a slash hook?" Rod asked, changing the subject, trying to draw a bit more enthusiasm from Dan.

"Yeah mate." Dan's lips curled briefly into the slightest of smiles. "He deserved it too the bastard. He's an ambo now at the station down the road." Dan took another sip of beer.

"What about Paddy? Y' heard anything about him?"

"He went off to Coonamble a while back lookin' for work."

"Coonamble?" Rod asked. "What's happening there?"

"Not much mate—just a bunch of old blackfellers wandering about the place doing nothing. A bit of fruit picking I think." Dan fell silent and automatically took another sip from his schooner. His tongue swept the froth from his upper lip. "They say he's dead, mate."

"Dead!" Rod echoed. "What? Paddy?" He was lost for more words. Despite the oppressive heat of the summer afternoon, a sudden tremor shook his body chilling him to the bone.

"Yeah, they say he started a fight at a party. There was a real big punch up and he got king hit square in the head. He was dead by the time the cops got there…"

Rod couldn't hear Dan any more, his lips moving soundlessly; all of his senses had suddenly switched off, fused like a burnt-out light bulb. Paddy was dead, gone for ever; his short promising life ended in a moment of blind stupidity, in a stupid, bloody useless fight. That was the final straw! Rod thought at least Paddy would've found a way out of all this. What in the hell was happening around here?

Rod felt the walls of the Central Australian closing in around him, folding over him, smothering him. What he'd hoped wouldn't happen to his mates this time round had happened. He'd tried to warn them. The very society they'd all been born into, and briefly enjoyed the opportunities of youth and vitality to change, was now moulding them back into its own—its long elastic tentacles wrapping around them, conforming them into the great Australian stereotype, this generation, his generation, just as it had done for generations before. Rod felt sick to the stomach, like he was about to throw up. He knew he had to get out of there fast, out of that stale pub, out into the fresh air. There was nothing more to say to Dan, or any of the others for that matter. There was nothing left but a whole lot of talking all about nothing—a whole lot of hot air, broken promises and smashed dreams.

"I'll see y' again later, Dan. Say hello to the others for me, would y' mate." He shot out of the door into the broad daylight, out under the changeless blue vault of a cloudless outback sky.

Rod gunned his bike over to the Carriers' Arms, drowning in a growing sense of desperation, worried about what he'd find there—or not. Pushing in through the doors, Chief's normal chair, table, stood empty. Perhaps he was a little early in the afternoon, he hoped, as he raced over to the barman, not really recognising him either.

"Where's Chief? Have you seen Chief?" he asked.

"Chief," the barman thought for a moment, frustratingly taking his time. Rod felt the urge to shake his miserable frame, to hurry him along, but remained silent.

"The Chief… Ahhh… Yes. He doesn't come here anymore." Another long silence. "I haven't seen him for a while now. His mates don't come so much either nowadays," he concluded delivering Rod the final body blow.

"Thank you," Rod barely managed to mumble. Turning, leaving, all was lost. Everything he'd loved had gone; the town was just a shell—a collection of old buildings. He realized he'd never loved the town. It was the town's people, the people he'd gotten to know, but all that had changed too. There was nothing left for him here.

Completely empty now, emotionally drained, Rod realised his beloved Bourke had moved on without him, its familiar patterns and rhythms he cherished so dearly were changed, gone for ever, and the next generation had taken their place. Even though the town looked exactly the same, its parks and buildings unchanged, he was no longer part of it, just like Lawson's Bourke, old Charlie Bowman's Bourke and the Bourke of countless others before him.

Rod headed out of town, along the highway towards the North Bourke Bridge; he needed to see the River Country one last time, right now, before he left it behind him, possibly for ever. He'd head straight home. There was no point in staying over in Bourke now.

As he swept around the approaches to the lift bridge, he noticed a mob of kids playing in the river shallows by the boat ramp, an elderly white-haired man, sitting higher up the bank under a shady gum, was watching over them. Rod had a sudden hunch; braking hard and flicking down through the gears, he spun his bike sharply around, turning onto the well-worn dirt access track. By the time he reached the boat ramp the kids were waving and cheering, starting to come out of the water towards him.

"Joey spoke first, "G'day Rod, we heard your bike coming. Do ya wanna come in for a swim in the river with us?"

"Chief's set up a swing for us, from the Red Gum over on the far side," a smaller girl added."

"Chief!!!" Rod exclaimed, a sense of relief sweeping over him. He looked at their smiling white teeth and brown skin glistening in the golden sunlight as they gathered, dripping wet, around his bike. Apart from their muddy feet padding around in the dusty soil, they were a lot cleaner than he remembered from last time, and maybe an inch or two taller.

"Yes…Yeah, you bet I will!" Rod replied enthusiastically, smiling broadly, relieved that not everything he knew had changed. "I gotta try the Chief's new swing, don't I?" Rod looked up and waved at the white-haired man sitting high on the bank. He looked somehow younger, prouder.

"Why don't you come up here and sit for a while, son." He called from his vantage point. "Once you've had the chance to cool off a bit with the kids."

OUTBACK SUMMER

"NORTH BOURKE BRIDGE"

Robert Coenraads 2024

Rod smiled and saluted the Chief before quickly stripping down to his bathers and plunging into the cool waters of the Darling. He caught up with Joey who was racing towards the other side, determined to get to the swing first.

"What about y'r sister Carla? Where's she?" He asked Joey casually enough, although it was the one question he'd desperately wanted to ask for a year now, and for most of this last summer as well; it was the question he had almost lost all hope of asking.

"She's been at university up at Townsville this year. She's been living up there with Auntie Maisy," Joey replied, satisfied that Rod wasn't going to try and overtake him before he got to the far bank.

"University? I thought she was finishing high school?"

"I'm gonna go there too when I'm old enough," Joey said in between strokes. "Auntie Maisy's already told me I could."

"Well good for you! As long as you're doing okay at your school work?" Rod replied, probing if Joey realized the importance of that connection. "In that case you can do anything you like."

"Okay? I'm doing better than okay—I'm doin' real good at school." He replied proudly. "I come first in class in most of my tests!"

Rod chuckled. "Yeah, looks like you're a clever kid. I guess it must run in the family then?"

"Yeah, I guess so," Joey replied, thoughtful for a brief moment, as he scrambled up the far bank and grabbed the rope hanging vertically from the thick branch of the river gum. "But I'm much smarter than Carla," he called out, sailing through the air, high above Rod's head. He let go of the rope at the end of its swing, arching over into a graceful dive. A few seconds later his head bobbed up out of the brown water. "I can't wait to tell her y' came back to Bourke."

Rod sat on the bank next to Chief watching the kids play in the water below, the gentle breeze refreshingly cool on his wet body. He had many questions he was burning to ask, but sat quietly, respectfully, waiting. Presently the Chief spoke.

"I spend a lot of time with the young ones these days, watchin' over them, letting them explore around the place. Sometimes they ask me about life in the olden days and I teach 'em things; 'bout the way we used to fish, trap and hunt. Next week I'm taking 'em all up to Bree, t' look at our old stone fish traps. The Bowling Club's gonna lend us their minibus for the day." He paused, thoughtfully stroking his white beard. "These kids're what Australia's future is all about y' know."

"And how's Carla doing?" Rod asked. "Joey said she's at Townsville? Y' must be proud of her, Chief?"

"Yeah, real proud I am." The Chief's face brightened, smiling. "She's my shining star, Rod." He looked at Rod and his face became serious again. "I'll never be able t' thank you and her enough for what y' done in bringin' me out to Polygonum Swamp that evening. A real wakeup call it was. My spirit's alive and free again. It was never about the river being trapped by the white man's levee. It was all about my own spirit, old and tired, trapped within the thick stone walls of the Carriers' Arms all those years. It would have been broken and busted, and I would've died last year if Carla and you hadn't come along, Rod. I'm tryin' t' help Eddie, Sammy an' the others now, but it ain't easy."

Rod smiled graciously and remained respectfully silent for a few moments to be sure the Chief had finished his story.

"So, what's Carla studying?" Rod asked, focusing Chief's attention back onto his daughter.

She's already started Environmental Science and Land Management at James Cook University, up in Queensland. She got a scholarship and they didn't even make her finish school. I might take the whole family up there next Christmas holidays, to see how she's doin'. Maisy says she's been missin' us all."

"That's great news Chief... At James Cook University ay?" Rod repeated the name softly, smiling quietly to himself, remembering last year's conversation with Carla at the pool, restraining his laughter as the memories of it flowed back. He knew the irony of that name wouldn't have gone past Carla. It looked like the spirit of the good Captain would be around to haunt her for a few more years yet!

"I hear it's a good school, Chief," he focused his mind back on the conversation, turning to face the proud old man. "And y' know what? She's studying the subject of tomorrow's Australia."

"Say Rod, why don't y' stick around Bourke for a few days. Y' can come round home to tea with us all tonight?" Chief asked. "The family would really like that... I'd like that."

"Sure, I'd love to Chief."

And Carla's coming back with Maisy over Easter to spend her holidays here. Y' can come back then if you like and the two of you can catch up."

"Carla…" Rod's heart skipped a beat. "Thanks Chief."

In the early morning cool, Rod eased his bike around the s-bend across the railway line on his way out of Bourke, taking his last look at the familiar scene—the town water tank, the cotton fields, the looming buildings of the abattoir complex. His feelings were a mixture of sadness and hope; sadness over what had happened to his friends in the space of a year; of what seemed to happen year after year, generation after generation, in an entrenched cycle of hopelessness; and hope for the one bright spark, Carla, a beacon of expectation on the horizon, the pride of her father and her family. He'd be back this Easter for sure.

Rod smiled, turned ahead, and gunned his bike forward along the ruler-straight Mitchell Highway heading southeast to Sydney.

CHAPTER 28. DAY OUT WITH CARLA

IT WAS a perfectly-formed, stone axe, rounded on one side tapering forward to a sharp ground edge on the other, with a distinct groove where a handle could be tied. It was one of the best he'd seen at Talowla.

"Hey, check this out Carla, isn't it a beautiful piece of workmanship?" Rod said, pointing to the stone implement lying on the red dirt. "Hours of work. I can't understand why anyone would have left that?" He looked at it longingly, waiting for some kind of a comment from Carla, but she said nothing. "I guess nobody's going to be using it again now?"

"I reckon groups travelled here from Mt Oxley via the river and then took off north using Mt Talowla as a stopping point," she reflected finally. "Why cart all that heavy stuff around when you can have a permanent stash of tools at each campsite, knowing they'll always be there, like faithful friends waiting to greet you at day's end—ready to chop, grind, clean and cook. They'd serve generation after generation that way, barely moving metres from where they were first made. See that fireplace ring, waiting patiently still, but now it's only gonna be for the spirits of times past that come by, following their long-lost song lines."

Rod shuddered at the talk of spirits, remembering how real they were that night at Polygonum. He had no inclination to get on their wrong side.

"I suppose we shouldn't really touch them, ay?" But, emboldened by the mid-day sun, he bent down to examine the glazed white quartzite axe. He recognized it as the one he had in his bag that afternoon with Brad, thankful for the insights gained through that experience. He wouldn't be making a fool of himself twice; that story would have to forever remain his own little secret. "We've got leave it right where it is, ay Carla?" Rod concluded, hoping his tone sounded respectful enough.

"Yeah, that's right Rod, it's part of history now. A song line would be broken if the tool were moved. It's part of a story—the more we look, the more we can read—turn the pages of time. All the answers lie here for us and future generations, and this axe is one tiny piece of the jigsaw."

"Hey, how's James Cook been treating you?" Rod changed direction. "You're really different now—a uni student and all. You're not the quiet shy girl anymore, the one that showed up at the pool for a swimming lesson."

"I am woman hear me roar[27], Rod!" Carla replied confidently. "And there's an indigenous groundswell happening on campus, a lot of activist groups, so the likes of Captain Cook better keep well out of our way!"

"Way to go, Carla! What's say we spend a bit of time travelling around once you're done with all your studies? I'll be done with my Honours by then…"

"Or maybe I'll even beat you to it if they keep accelerating me," she smiled assuredly at him.

"Well…whenever we're both done then, we can explore Australia's furthest hidden corners where no one else goes, getting to know the country folk along the way—just like the ones you're going to meet today."

Returning to the bike, they left Talowla, riding along the dusty road towards Toorale where Rod had organised to meet Mick, Clan and the boys for lunch. He was looking forward to presenting Carla to them, eager to talk over plans for their future travels together.

Rod pulled up behind the homestead, parking near the open kitchen door where the welcoming aroma of eggs, chops and bacon mixed with wood smoke lingered in the air.

"Nothing like that to build the appetite when you're hungry," Rod inhaled deeply, smiling at Carla.

Mick stood at his usual place by the back door.

"Long time, no see, Rod," he said pushing the flyscreen door open and thrusting his hand forward welcomingly at the same time. "Come right on in." His work-roughened paw firmly engulfed Rod's outstretched hand.

"Yeah, long-time Mick."

"G'day, you must be Carla?" He turned to toward her, studying her face. "Rod's told us a lot about you."

"Hello Mick." She extended her hand and he took it more gently. "Nice to meet you."

OUTBACK SUMMER

"MT TALOWLA"

Robert Coenraads
2025

"Back in Bourke on holidays from Townsville, ay?" He asked, turning into the kitchen, "Come on inside and make y'rselves at home. The boys will be in from mustering any moment. Why don't you show Carla round the place while I put the finishing touches on lunch?"

"How's old Charlie going, Mick?" Rod asked.

"Same as ever; way too many bloody dogs. He'll be out in a moment too. He won't miss the smell of lunch."

Rod and Carla left the kitchen and walked through a dark corridor into the old ballroom.

"What a grand old room. Can you imagine this place in its heyday, Carla?" Rod asked, hoping she could picture what he could, beyond its present miserable and gloomy state; crumbling walls, stained glass ceiling mostly smashed away, with the floor space in the old room now dominated by the bulky cube of an industrial freezer unit. Rod walked over to the piano tinkling a few out-of-tune keys. "Perhaps with an old rag and a bottle of teak oil I could have this old girl looking like a million dollars."

"Shall we dance," Rod turned to face Carla, bowing deeply.

"The honour is all mine, sir," she replied gracefully outstretching her arm.

Angry shouts cut into their daydream as the smell of burning chops wafted in from the kitchen.

"Christ Mick, you've burnt the bloody chops again!," Aspro's rude voice echoed from another room.

"Calm down mate," Clancy's voice soothed. "Y' know the kitchen's no place for Mick."

"Well you've got two choices," Mick retorted testily, "y' can either eat 'em or or y' can bloody well wear 'em."

At lunch, they all sat around the ample wooden table, tall tales and yarns weaving around like the plates and bowls shuttling back and forth; their conversation knitting them together, strengthening friendships in a social ritual that has been around since humans began sharing food with one another.

"So, Rod says you two might go do a bit of travellin' around the country?" Old Charlie was in fine form that day too. "Nothin' beats travelling. I'm told I was born December 1888, and I up and left home at fifteen. I put a saddle on m' horse, packed a swag and a little tucker, and said, 'I'm goin', and I've never been back since. I seen my fair share when I was young and it was hard yakka back then, y' know, the land was a lot wilder, but we've managed to tame it a bit since then.

OUTBACK SUMMER

"TOORALE BALLROOM"

Robert Coenraads
2024

It'll be easier for you and Carla these days, but still you gotta put some money together for the trip."

"There's a couple of great projects you should go see, I reckon," Clan took his turn. "Take the Ord River Project, one of our country's great success stories, opening up the savage north to irrigation—huge tracts of otherwise useless savannah. You'll see acres of cotton fields stretching from horizon to horizon. Let me tell you about some of the other great dams too—now take the Snowies…"

"Yeah, The Snowies, what a grand project that was; cheap, clean power and abundant water for a parched nation, the country's population swelling with immigrant workers, the largest wave since the gold rush days heading to the work camps in this land of milk and honey…"

Rod always enjoyed the stories; his dad was one of those that walked in after the war when Australia threw open its doors. But today, with Carla here, he felt uneasy with that kind of talk. He glanced at her face, trying to gauge how she was taking to their 'pioneer' frame of mind—and winced a little every time old Charlie's talk came back around to taming the barren wasteland that was Australia, breaking in the young nation like a high-spirited brumby, harnessing its raw potential.

Rod figured she'd be thinking about the land, from her own people's perspective; a country already peopled and being used in so many different ways, of which the first settlers were completely unawares. The colonists didn't care or were too busy to notice, occupied with their own struggle for survival—initially facing starvation on the barren sandstone soils of the Sydney basin. He'd learnt about that struggle in his geology classes. An Amazon-sized river, several hundreds of million years old, coursed over that land once, the likes of which the country has never seen since. It dumped billions of tonnes of infertile white-quartz sand onto a massive delta that stretched from Newcastle to Wollongong and back over the Blue Mountains. The First Australians not only knew how to live there, but they'd thrived for tens of thousands of years—up until precisely 18th January 1788 when the immigrant ships arrived. Rod was keenly aware of all this now and how the indigenous peoples suffered.

What Rod felt for the first time, in Carla's barely perceptible reactions to the stockmen's stories, was how strong and deep those feelings ran for her. Her people had been displaced; their skills, customs and lore, carefully honed over the millennia, lost forever in a single generation over the course of a few short decades, as these new men overran the land.

Aspro and Ian weighed in with their stories too, stories of cattle stations bigger than European nations, with heads running in the hundreds of thousands; places where the stockmen exchanged their horses for helicopters to muster over such vast areas.

With full stomachs, and with final hearty well wishes for their studies and future travels done, Old Charlie bade everyone farewell; the stockmen off to their afternoon's labour, and Mick to ready his kitchen for this evening's tea. It was time for Rod and Carla to leave.

"She's a real lovely girl, Rod." Mick gave him a quiet fatherly pat on the shoulder as they walked out the kitchen door. "She's a one in a million y' know. You look after her!"

"Thanks Mick, I know," he replied proudly. "I'll take real good care of her."

Afterwards, alone by the motorcycle, Carla was quiet and introspective. Rod guessed the problem but wasn't going to try to mend the facts with a band aid, glossing over what he'd just witnessed. He knew Carla understood full well these fine upstanding people of the land meant no harm, especially not to her—but harm they had inadvertently done.

"I'm really sorry about all their stories, Carla. I know how you must feel about it, because I can feel it too now, just from what I've learnt in the short time we've known one another. They don't get it. They don't have the education to get it."

"A year at uni now and I'm only beginning to scratch the surface on the damage that some of those major projects are doing to the land, or have the potential to do to the land in the long term—environmental damage on a scale I never imagined possible." Carla had changed tack slightly. "Most people understand nothing about the history of anything that came before them, and only see the land as a resource to be used—how it can best serve their needs in the present moment."

"But they've gone through the Australian school system, Carla, you know what it's like," defending their point of view, realising it was little different to his own of a short while back. "So little is taught about those who were here before and how they managed the land; I learnt nothing and I'm sure it was worse decades ago. These old men, they'd be lucky if they finished primary school back then."

"We learnt about the big projects in school, sure, but it's nothing like the full story I'm getting at university—but how many people go to uni? I only hope some of it filters back into the classroom."

"Carla, they're not the places we want to see on our trip, I promise you," Rod repeated with conviction. "Sure, we'll pass by them to get to other places, but we'll go further, really remote."

I brought this along for you to take a look at," Carla said pulling a crumpled foolscap sheet from her pocket. "It's one of my essays on first settlement."

"Not bloody Captain Cook again?" Rod smiled at her, taking the sheet of paper and starting to read.

"Yeah, same story, I'm afraid, only this time I've written it from an indigenous viewpoint."

Rod began, reading it aloud.

"The British swarmed the new colony, like ants into every nook and cranny. Within months they were along every stretch of coastline, into every bay and rivulet, everywhere where waterways would allow them entry, like swarms of pesky flies on a mid-summer's day worrying at the corners of our eyes, nostrils and mouths. Planting disease and infection wherever they planted the British flag—18th January 1788 Kurnell, 26th January 1788 Port Jackson, March 1788 Broken Bay; April 1788 Hawkesbury...

"Hey, you're a pretty evocative writer Carla; great use of simile and metaphor," Rod smiled, pausing to look up at her face before continuing.

"By June 1789, smallpox, believed deliberately released, rampaged through our Indigenous population, leaving bodies littering the shores of Port Jackson. Captain Phillip documented innumerable indigenous people dying from the disease that barely affected the colonial immigrants. As many as ninety percent perished in the Sydney region amid cries that extinction was inevitable. Survivors fled inland, tragically spreading the disease they sought to escape, while the explorers followed closely on their heels; 1802 Port Phillip Bay, Victoria; 1803 Derwent River, Tasmania; 1823 Brisbane River, Queensland...

"I've never heard it put this way before," Rod exclaimed.

"Before long Explorers penetrated deep inland along the river systems—those vital lifelines into our country's very heart. Lists of those heroes' names and accomplishments slide easily from every Australian school student's lips—Lawson, Blaxland and Wentworth—Blue Mountains crossing in 1813; Evans—Lachlan River in 1815;

Mitchell—Darling River in 1835; Bourke and Wills—Gulf of Carpentaria in 1860-61.

"*Rum was there in quantity from the very beginning. It quickly became 'black man's poison', a tradeable commodity undermining the fabric of the new colony but absolutely destroying any Indigenous Australian culture chancing to cross its path.*

"*Estimates put it that by 1830 at least, 50% of Australia's indigenous population had perished…Then came the massacres…*

"I can't go on, it's too depressing," Rod said, handing back the sheets. "No wonder they didn't want to teach that awful stuff to the school kids!"

"Don't you see Rod, these hard Toorale men are the last wave of that colonial surge that swept the country. The invasion that started 200 years ago is still going on today."

"You can't hate them for that, Carla? They probably don't think of it in that way; if they even think of it at all!"

"I don't hate anyone, Rod. It's just a fact; but their attitudes make me feel uncomfortable nowadays. Like my people don't matter anymore—just another culture lost in the advancing wave of European civilization sweeping the globe.

He desperately wanted to focus on what honest hardworking people those men were with their well-intentioned counsel, in the hope that Carla might forgive their myopic viewpoint, but that would be pointless because Carla already knew that—she'd lived a whole lifetime in Bourke alongside them knowing that fact deep in her heart. It was just the way of her world. Only now she also understood it academically

"Maybe it's even hard for you to look at their faces and not feel the way you do, let alone hear the stories of these new men of the land," Rod said after thinking about it for a minute, his eyes downcast, "… Even including me, perhaps? I'm a new man of the land, a geologist, and my parents came to this country as immigrants from Europe on a ship…" He paused.

"But where's my culture Carla? All this has made me realise I'm a cultureless phoney, deceitfully arrogant, just like the rest. I've refused to be ethnically fingerprinted. My parents are Dutch, but there's no way I'd ever walk around in clogs, baggy blue trousers with a red scarf and a funny looking hat. Once my mother told me I could have been called Rodericus van der Cornhuijizenweg, but they changed my name to Rod Conway and spoke to me in English so that I'd fit in, and I'm bloody glad they did too. René's parents didn't do that—they kept the surname Schellekens and everybody called him René instead of Robert, so the name stuck. He doesn't seem to mind though," Rod rambled to a halt.

Rod had avoided his usual modus operandi where, with a little give and little take, everyone ends up happy, because nobody really cares anyway. Carla was so important to him, and he knew the give was all one way and always would be. She and her people always took the hurt and punishment, be it incidental or intentional, and had done so for the past 200 years—because in that short time, after tens of thousands of years of existence in partnership with the land, they'd become a voiceless minority in their own country, buried beneath wave after wave of immigration under the cries of 'grow or perish' from a never-ending succession of white prime ministers. He felt for her so deeply and was painfully aware, for the first time in his life, of the enormity of the gulf separating them—him, the colonialist, on one side and Carla, the original Australian, on the other. His gaze remained on his shoes. He couldn't even bring himself to look at her now. He was broken to the point of being suicidal, ready to commit hari-kari in her honour.

"But I don't care about culture, and never have. I've adapted as I've needed, to be able to dominate and conquer my environment. I'm just one in the line of succession of conquerors, and you're going to always end up hating me for that. I don't think that I think in the same way as you."

Rod's world began to collapse around him as he went on. Maybe those artefacts are better off out here where they've lain for thousands of years under the outback sun—but did he really believe that? Why couldn't he think like her? His mind wasn't on the same high-plane as hers, he lacked the respect, but he would sacrifice anything for her, including himself.

"I lied to you before about that axe," he confessed. "I wanted to take it for myself. I had it in my bag once last year and I was ready to steal it. It was Brad who showed me how wrong that would be. But I probably would've taken it again, when I found it today… if you weren't around. I'm a collector, Carla. Wouldn't these things be better off in a museum where scientists can study them? That's what anthropology and archaeology is all about, isn't it?"

Rod sank lower, eyes downcast, realising where his line of argument was taking him. He wasn't good enough for Carla now she'd found herself. She'd come so far; confident, self-assured, and powerful, her interests had changed, developed. She was more spiritual. What did he still have to offer her anymore?

OUTBACK SUMMER

"INVASION DAY"

2024
Robert Coenraads

"Don't you understand Carla," the words seemed to come from nowhere, "I'm not good enough for you anymore. You've grown beyond me, just as you've moved on from your town, your school and your mates." It was the last thing he wanted to admit, but now was the time for honesty. "You'd be much better off going your own way with your new activist friends from campus[28]. C'mon I'd better take you back home now."

Rod could see the severity of his words had wounded her, but he knew he was right, and had been naïve to think otherwise.

"So, what if you did take the axe, Rod?" Carla asked, ignoring his conclusion. "It would have become part of your story, and it would have resolved itself and ended up back here eventually. We're still a living culture with ties to a rich deep past. Trying to pack all that into a museum display case kinda disconnects it from reality. The person who left that axe here could have never imagined, even in their wildest dreams that forty thousand years later it would be bringing two people together from completely different backgrounds."

"Or cleaving them apart!"

"It's not like that, silly billy," Carla cupped her hands around his face, finally causing him to look up into her eyes. She kissed him gently. "People are people and we all share this Earth together—beneath our thin skin of race and nationality we're all the same. Don't you remember, you told me that at the pool once, a long while back?"

Rod looked at her, unable to answer.

"Don't you see, that axe is already part of our song line," she continued. "It's yours and mine now. We could keep it for ninety years and bring it back the day before we died. It would be silent witness to our life story too, along with the hundreds of lives it has witnessed before ours. It really doesn't matter where it is—in your bag, somewhere in your home, a museum, or lying here on the ground at Talowla. It's safer out here because we'll always know where it is, whenever we come back to this special place… I'm not interested in anyone else, Rod. I haven't stopped thinking about you all term… And I want to spend my life with you..."

"You never did read the conclusion of my essay," she continued, handing him back the crumpled sheet. "I used your words in there."

"Since when do the victors in battle ever acknowledge the losers? Especially if they don't even realize they've been in a battle and won, or even that there are losers. The winners reply, "what battle, what victors, what losers?" And the losers, who have lost so utterly and completely, they're not even acknowledged as being losers, to the point that they

themselves don't even realise what they have lost. They're devalued to the point of personae non gratae in a Terra Nullius—nobodies in a no-man's land, simply existing day-to-day in a cycle of hopeless misery and despair. If you dwell on it, it might not make you feel so good, so perhaps it's better to put in the effort to resolve it and then move on…

People are people and we all share this Earth together—beneath our thin skin of race and nationality we're all the same."

"So, let's move on then," Carla interrupted, "you and I, together into a future we make for ourselves."

"You're right…" Rod replied, still overwhelmed yet so proud of the powerful woman Carla had become.

"C'mon Rod, let's go to the river for that swim you promised? I reckon it'll wash away all our cares and worries."

CHAPTER 29. A NEW BEGINNING

A FEW TENS of kilometres west from Talowla, they turned onto a deserted station track and headed towards the low ribbon of trees marking the line of the Darling. Rod parked his bike by the house gates of the Eldorado homestead.

"I really loved spending the summer in this place, y' know," he told Carla, pointing out the deserted wooden homestead with its flywire-enclosed verandah, its solitary bush dunny and the dilapidated generator shed, its walls blackened with soot from the antique Lister engine. "I've spent the whole summer wishing you could see it, but the place is ancient history now. I wonder if anyone will ever live here again."

They walked on towards the steep banks of the Darling passing through a lonely clearing amongst the red gums.

"Look, there's Henrietta Leggatt's grave—responsible for many a scary story, let me tell you! The locals won't come anywhere near the place," Rod recalled nostalgically, examining the illegible wooden cross rotted away at the base and now listing severely to one side. "I guess it'll decay into history along with everyone's memories of it."

"Could you hold the cross upright while I stack a few rocks around it?"

"What stories then?" Carla asked as he worked.

"They told us she was murdered by a rogue riverboat captain whose ghost still haunts the district. Michael would raise the hairs on the back of our necks, saying he could sense his evil spirit lurking about the place. I never believed him of course," Rod laughed. "But one night Michael insisted his menacing presence was stronger than ever, just I was heading out into the pitch dark to visit the dunny. Well, just as I finished there came an eerie wailing and awful clattering on the tin walls. I flew out the door so fast you wouldn't believe it, running towards the homestead and hitching up my trousers as I went, only to be greeted at the back door by Michael's joking face."

"I wish I could've seen the look on your face!"

"BP Bertie used to deliver our fuel. He was so beefy, legend had it he could singlehandedly carry a full 44-gallon drum… one on each shoulder actually…" Rod told her as they walked towards the river. "And over there on the far bank, that's where I caught the baby pig. Bruce was fattening it up in the pig pen, but I let it go before it became dinner," Rod continued idly recounting snippets of interesting yarns collected over a long glorious summer.

"It's such a pity to see the place like this. I'd really like to do it up though. Wouldn't you like live right here by the river Carla?"

"Look at the place, Rod, it's decaying back to the earth from where it came. You could spend a dozen lifetimes fixing up what others have left behind, trying to slow the march of time, but you'll never stop it. Don't you reckon it's best to let nature take its course, healing the scars? Look, green shoots are sprouting everywhere now the pressure is off. We can live anywhere we like Rod, it doesn't matter. Home is wherever we can be together."

"I could fix up the place no problems. It wouldn't take too long! Or I'll build you a brand new one. I reckon it'd be fun to live on the Darling."

"You are a real pioneer, aren't you Rod? But you've gotta relax and look at it differently. Sure, perhaps after we're done with uni and travel, we can live anywhere it suits."

"What a shame I didn't think to bring my cozzie," Rod said taking in the vista; the Darling's tranquil brown waters swirling invitingly in dappled shade beneath overhanging rivergum boughs.

"Silly Billy! I'm wearing mine under my clothes," Carla laughed. "But then…" she ventured a moment later, "there's no one around here but us, is there?"

"So perhaps we should skinny dip?" Rod added cheekily. "I'm not gonna do it alone though y' know."

"If you're game, I'll do it too then… Promise you'll shut your eyes?"

"Yeah, I promise," Rod agreed, solemnly resisting the urge to peek, imagining what he would miss—pure gold from head to toe.

Carla moved away a discreet distance, hidden behind a fallen trunk, slid out of her clothes at and slipped quickly into the opaque waters of the Darling.

Rod faced away from the river, unbuttoning his shirt and dropping his jeans and undies on the dusty bank. Glancing over his shoulder, suddenly self-conscious about the full-moon of his exposed white backside, he saw Carla drifting slowly down current, about mid-river, looking back at him.

"Hey cheat! You shut your eyes," he yelled, crouching and dropping into the river's cooling embrace.

"I never promised anything," she called back cheekily, laughing.

He swam with the current swiftly towards her as she skilfully avoided his attempts to duck her under.

Later, they lay together, hand in hand, on a picnic rug by the river's edge in the afternoon's warm dappled sunlight.

"I enjoyed swimming here every afternoon after work," Rod reminisced, drinking in the familiar surrounds of the Eldorado Homestead. "All summer, I waited to show you this place."

"It's a long time since I've been in the river, y' know, with mum being dead against it."

"Yeah, I know all about that, Joey told me," Rod replied, sparing Carla the need to dwell on the unfortunate circumstances of her mother's decision.

"I was so worried I was never going to see you again," he confessed. "I had no idea how I'd ever go about finding you and even began to lose hope. I always had this feeling we'd be guided together. But when everything had changed so much, I couldn't find your dad or anybody else I knew…"

"It was a test you would only pass if your feelings for me were deep and strong enough. Otherwise, the magic would've faded and we would have continued on our separate paths. But you passed Rod!" She lifted his hand, kissing it. "None of that other stuff we were talking about before matters. Nothing else is important—not what's happened in the past—not what one of our dumb ancestor's done to another ancestor we never even knew. Who gives a damn about all of that?"

Y' know," Rod said as they lay staring at the sky, "you're right, this is our special day, our moment in history, just the two of us. We're right here now, same life, same education, same opportunity to do whatever we like with it. No one's telling us what to do anymore. We're in charge, responsible for our own future. You're so right; we dump the baggage and move forward."

Rod's thoughts had clarified and his confidence grown over the past year and a half, even in the last hours. Alongside Carla, he felt comfortable in her love and in control of his course through life, captain of his own destiny as his ship sailed forth from safe harbour. He was truly free now.

"You know, I might just have to head up to Townsville this year. I've heard they've got a pretty good postgraduate program in geology up there."

"I'd really like that, Rod."

"We'll finish uni soon, free to do what we want, and that means being together."

"It was glorious spending summer here, and, now, sharing the Darling with you." Rod leant over her neck and shoulders, savouring the cool droplets of river water on her skin with his lips. He put his arms around her waist, drawing her close as she sat up. Carla came readily to him and they embraced, gazing over the serene river. Something unbelievably powerful was rising deep within them, drawing them together, toward one another and toward the river[29].

As they gazed over the Darling, its serpentine coils began to crystallize; its waters, firming and becoming solid. The river's shimmering surface seemed to quicken into a glistening eel-skin; it's surface no longer flat, rising towards the middle and withdrawing from the banks, exposing their feet which had been resting in its coolness. Bright flashes pulsed across its surface and deep within its translucent crystalline body, rippling like static electricity. Unable to comprehend what he was seeing, even being here with Carla too good to be true, he shook himself to ensure he wasn't dreaming. Perhaps he was fantasizing? Rod slid his hands over Carla's shoulders and back, feeling her solidness. He squeezed her tight around the waist drawing her body yet closer to his as she moaned in pleasure. She felt firm and real, alive and warm, yet, surrounding them, the stately, solid River Red Gums seemed to sway in a surreal rhythm despite the stillness of that sunny summer's afternoon.

"I can't believe what I'm seeing. It's like the river itself is becoming alive."

She squeezed him in return, confirming her reality.

"It's always been alive though most can't see it that way; a giant living entity flowing since the beginning of olden times, from headwater to mouth, unifying the entire eastern half of Australia. You remember what happened last year at Polygonum?"

"Yeah, it's like a dream I'll never forget. But can you actually see what I'm seeing now, Carla?"

"Yes, I see it, and feel it in my being Rod. It's just for you and me this time. The lights illuminate the paths of those who came before and, in turn, our own. The river is showing us it is really alive; a vital piece in the jigsaw of the planet's living green cloak. It's part of the same complex web of life to which we belong. We're not separate or apart from this land, we are one with it. We sleep when it sleeps and wake when it wakes with the dawn sunlight and morning chorus. We hunt, gather and eat from its bounteous green robes. We are its extremities, its fingers. We dig into its rich earth to plant crops, and you dig even deeper to extract its golden riches which we also need in our lives. You remember the river asked for our help last year, and I've been working on that at uni!"

"I believe you, beyond question of a doubt. I know it to be true and I'm going to do everything I can too," Rod exclaimed. "I need no further proof."

Goal accomplished the river slowly subsided resuming its daily disguise, its guardian Red Gums resuming their duty as silent sentinels marking its endless course. The river waters rose at the bank, liquid once more, lapping over their toes.

"We are one, Rod, the continents and the oceans, the animals and plants that live on and within, and you and I. We are all one."

Rod and Carla took each other in their deepest-yet embrace; their damp skin tingling as they came together, bodied intertwined, savouring the ecstasy of the moment, the acceptance of their oneness; Rod acknowledging the triviality of their differences and their unity with the universe; oneness with each other, now and for all eternity.

Rod lay back drinking in the sky completely at peace with the world, "You know, I'm kind of starting to take all of this magic for granted. It feels so natural."

Carla lay across his chest, her face close to his, studying the sky's blueness reflected in his eyes. He felt the warmth of her body as her skin pressed against his.

"It feels so familiar, like it was always meant to be."

"We're closer than ever now Rod. Can you feel it?"

"How could have I ever doubted it Carla. We are together, and nothing will ever break us apart."

"Link your soul with mine now Rod. I want to share some things for which there are no words, only images."

OUTBACK SUMMER

"ELDORADO"
"RIVER OF GOLDEN LIGHTS"

Robert Coenraads
2025

He took her body tightly and they kissed again. Electric energy crackled and buzzed around them, as he felt himself deep inside her head, and her presence within his very being. Fuzzy images appeared, slowly sharpening. He saw a child riding her bike around the streets of Bourke, her basket filled with bottles. He saw her mother and Chief, and recognised their little house, smoke curling from its chimney, many touching scenes, then baby Joey playing in the garden. At the same time, he could sense her emotions. It was indescribable, beyond words.

"Take me inside Rod, show me something," she whispered into his ear, caressing it with her lips, biting it gently.

He could feel her there and gave little resistance, opening completely to her. He felt her leafing through his childhood like the pages of a book. She kissed him gently around his neck, her damp hair sweeping over him, caressing his chest. He moaned with pleasure as he gave himself up to her, fully and unreservedly.

"It's so beautiful, Rod; so much family love. I can see now why you're the way you are."

"And yours looks so good too, especially now your father's back in your lives," he mused brushing tenderly through her pages. "Joey's got a big future and same for your sister's boy, especially having you as his aunt."

"Give me something more, Rod. What are you thinking about us now?"

Suddenly a magnificent panorama unfurled about them; vistas of Australian deserts, mountain ranges, wild rivers, and tropical forests stretching as far as the eye could see. Scenes from Earth's far corners poured out of his very being; books of images otherwise needing libraries of words to describe[30]. Carla was drawing it from him; but he couldn't figure it. Was it actual reality or some future potential? How could they possibly see where they, yet, hadn't been?

"Can you see it all too Carla?" He mouthed, his words clumsy and inadequate.

"Is that where you want to take me?" he heard her whisper, and then the flicking pages began to slow, with one image crystallising above the rest—the broad serpentine coils of the Darling River wending across the Western Plains; at first the entire basin, the scene then sharpening, focusing into the bank where they lay. The Eldorado homestead sat high on its edge, its gardens lush with fruit trees, flower beds and crops; smoke curling from the chimney of the gaily painted cottage, the smell of a roast in its wood-fire oven.

"I offer you this, Carla, my love. Will you take it?"

"Come inside, Rod, come deeper, beyond even the images, and feel my answer, my passion. Share it with me."

"Take me there, Carla," He pressed her lips against hers, kissing her again, as he entered the deepest recesses of her being, an indescribable furnace of pure emotion. He could feel her raw passion like slashes of primary pigment across a bare primed canvass—magenta, red and crimson, rich, thickly applied and textured with a pallet knife, light glistening from oil-paint globs and streaks, speckled with star-points of yellow—tinges of her tenderness. The firmament towered over him as his being slid onto its seething wet surface; slippery and messy, uncontrolled wild passion, absolutely liberated from the iron grasp of a normally-dominant right hemisphere.

"Can you understand how I feel now?" She gasped, exhausted by her revelation, sweat beading on her forehead.

"I can," he whispered, also totally spent by the experience

"Let me take you somewhere even more special now my love."

They interlocked fingers, looking into each other's eyes and then even deeper within. The landscape, the trees, the river swept past them in a blur, as if they were fast forwarding through some kind of movie…

Then, they saw themselves walking down towards the river—laughing, smiling, hand in hand, two fine, strong, young girls following behind. Adept and agile, the girls leapt into the river, swimming powerfully to the middle, bobbing to the surface, their wet hair and bronzed faces glistening in the golden sunlight.

"Mum, Dad, catch us if you can," the girls shouted tauntingly before turning to escape, pulling away fast as they could, their parents diving into the river after them in hot pursuit[31].

Rod was mesmerised by the scene, his heart melting.

"It's our potential, our destiny, if we choose that path. It's our future life together, Rod. For me the choice is natural, easy and beautiful, and I have already willingly made it. Pledge to make it yours too and we'll walk hand in hand from here into eternity. Take me now if you so desire, my Darling. My love is the greatest gift I can ever offer you."

CHAPTER 30. FUTURE TOGETHER

A UNIVERSE OF BRIGHT PIN PRICKS lay above them in timeless rotation around the south celestial pole as they lay under a blanket outside their tent, at the foot of Mt Talowla. The last embers of their cooking fire glowed umber in the ancient ring of stone, dwarfed by the Milky Way's column of smoke majestically rising from the horizon and cutting a bright swathe across the infinite depths of the heavens.

They'd dined on damper and billy tea earlier. It was long past sunset (as reckoned by the celestial clock marking passage of the nocturnal hours) and all was quiet in the night's absolute stillness, except for the murmur of two voices laying plans for their future exploring the vast ancient continent that lay beneath them, the world beyond, and a universe beyond that.

OUTBACK SUMMER

Our future begins this second!

Confucius says, *"We have two lives,*

and the second begins when we realize we only have one."

EPILOGUE

COUNTLESS FEET have walked Baaka (Darling River) country since pre-historic times; those Arcadian times when the First Nations peoples walked alone. The settlers, traders, agriculturists and pastoralists then came, building homesteads and establishing extensive landholdings. Bourke grew from a tiny frontier fort at the outer edge of the newly-Europeanised world into hub of a thriving river, rail and road network.

Later arrived the mineral explorers stalking the desert plains with instruments and drills in search of buried mineral wealth—gold copper and other metals—until finally the cycle turned full circle, the land now returning to the care of its Traditional Custodians and the curative forces of nature.

The Baaka with its billabongs, river red gums, swimming holes and swings, and the North Bourke lift-bridge, long-time gateway to the outback beyond, hold a special place in the hearts of many; special memories as reflected in the words of Meredith McGowan's 'Bourke Song'[32] and Colin Buchanan's 'North Bourke Bridge[33]'.

They sing of a community where the townsfolk stand together to face any adversity under the bond of mateship, be it the drought of ninety-one and ninety-two, the worst in recorded history—the Bourke of Lawson—or perhaps the floods of 1950s, when, together, the townsfolk built the levees right around the whole town. The raw power of this starkly beautiful but dangerous land has long been the subject of artists, poets and dreamers.

Rod Conway built his dream career travelling the world in search of ores and precious gemstones, all built on those humble foundations of several summers' field work on the Darling Floodplain. Since then, he has toiled in the world's poorest countries, in rough mining camps; open pit and underground[34]. Yet despite such a full life, the characters and places of his first assignment retain a special place in his memory.

Bourke township of the new millennium is a different place to the one of this novel. Most of the pubs have long since closed and gone out of business, their empty shells awaiting re-invention; rebirth into new roles for the future. The meatworks too has shut down, its rusty tin buildings deteriorating in the elements, and its killing room silent.

Gone too is the hard societal edge and lack of opportunity felt so keenly by the intelligent and sensitive Paddy, and the soul-destroying racism which Carla endured on a daily basis, so subtle, yet pervasive and unquestioned that it was simply accepted as the norm. Apologies have since been made at Federal Government level, community awareness continues to grow and Indigenous Australians have representatives in Parliament. For the rest, life's traditions and steady routine continue on now much the same as it did back then.

Today, the explorers and pastoralists have moved farther afield too, after the River Country between Bourke and Louth was gazetted as Toorale State Conservation Area (54,385 ha) in 2010. Nowadays people commune with the river; they come to feel the power of the timeless land in which once-great homesteads have become the museum pieces—relics of a bygone era—preserved from decaying into oblivion. The old crumbling Toorale homestead, once centre of a pioneering empire and home to the likes of Charlie Bowman, Clan MacIntosh and Mick Tallon, has undergone restoration under the auspices of the National Parks and Wildlife in partnership with the Kurnu-Baakandji Traditional Owners. It will now serve as a heritage visitor's information centre for coming generations.

While old Charlie, Clan and Mick now rest beneath the dry river sands of the town cemetery, Bourke's current generation of friendly welcoming residents proudly maintain the towns tidy garden parks and public facilities, and still enjoy a traditional Morrall's meat pie lunch washed down with a Rice's cordial—Australia's finest. All of the town's 'gateway-to-the-outback' country appeal that so charmed Rod Conway, continues to charm a steady stream of visitors to this day.

Today, a forward-thinking shire council, backed by modern educational, health, police and community services, offer sensitive and knowledgeable solutions to the social issues faced by the community. Programs run by Desert Pea Media at Bourke High School empower students to express their deep love for town and country in today's beat and rhythm, their songs full of can-do positivism[35,36].

OUTBACK SUMMER

"MORRALL'S PIES &
RICE'S CORDIALS –
AUSTRALIA'S FINEST"

Robert Coenraads
2025

253

Tourism is today's regional growth industry as Bourke's townspeople recognise they have an interesting product to offer, one that has lain untapped all this time, previously discovered and written about from time to time, only by the chance visitor who happened to stray into the town; visitors like Henry Lawson, A.B. 'Banjo' Paterson, Will Ogilvie, and Rod Conway, who felt keenly the beauty and allure of its stark desert landscape cut by the narrow green swathe of the River Country. A landscape long cherished by its indigenous inhabitants.

A river boat, modelled on the historic paddle steamer 'Jandra' plies the waters of the Darling River near North Bourke, re-creating the heydays of river transport for visitors from the big cities. A modern Back o' Bourke Information and Exhibition Centre brings the colourful indigenous and pioneering history of the region to life. The colourful history of the town and its inhabitants feature in periodic celebrations such as the 'Festival of a Thousand Stories.'

The situation with the Baaka continues on shaky ground with complete dry-outs and mass fish deaths all too common, and all exacerbated by climate change. Nowadays, the Murray-Darling Basin Authority manages the river system on a national scale, with some water allotment buy-backs from the agriculturalists returning vital, life-giving flow into the parched and dying system. Unfortunately, there is still way too much demand on this limited and precious resource. Yet there is some hope. The need for periodic flooding of the river plains has been recognised and, in limited areas, riverine habitat of old is being reintroduced, thereby revitalizing these highways of life.

On the banks of the Baaka, Eldorado Homestead patiently awaits restoration and the return of Rod and Carla from their life's adventures[37].

Gaia

The Spirit of the Land

The Spirit of the Land lies just beyond the realm of the visible,
but it is there nevertheless, subtly hidden just behind the everyday.
"Why can I sense it so strongly, its heat and passion coursing through my veins?
Even deep within shady city canyons, the desert sun seems to reach me;
the red iron-stained soil of the Outback and the iron of my own blood
are somehow co-mingled; able to communicate, one with each other."
"Because you belong to Me!"
Those who are born, live or work on the Land
seem to possess an extra ability—
although for most, that innate ability lies dormant and must be rekindled.

Those who are called upon by Gaia must rise to serve.

PLAY LIST

1. 'Radar Love', Golden Earring, 1973.
2. 'Living and Working on the Land', James Blundell, James Reyne, 1992.
3. 'Crimson and Clover', Tommy James & The Shondells, 1969.
4. 'Sugar Sugar', The Archies, 1968.
5. 'Living Next Door to Alice', New World, 1972.
6. 'Our House', Crosby, Stills, Nash & Young. 1970.
7. 'Don't Stop', Fleetwood Mac, 1977.
8. 'I Can See Clearly Now', Johnny Nash, 1972.
9. 'The Ballad of Henry Lawson', Slim Dusty, Songs from Down Under, 1976.
10. 'For What It's Worth (Stop, Hey What's That Sound)', Buffalo Springfield, 1966.
11. 'Love is Blue', Marty Robbins, 1968.
12. 'Hooked on a Feeling', Billy Joe Thomas, BJ Thomas Greatest Hits, 1968.
13. 'Smoke on the Water', Deep Purple, 1972.
14. 'Won't Get Fooled Again', The Who, 1971.
15. 'He Ain't Heavy, He's My Brother', The Hollies, 1969.
16. 'Bat out of Hell', Meatloaf, 1977.
17. 'Lady Madonna', The Beatles, 1968.
18. 'You Don't Own Me', Lesley Gore, 1963.
19. 'Bad Moon Rising', Creedence Clearwater Revival, 1969.

20. 'I heard it through the Grapevine', Creedence Clearwater Revival, 1970.

21. 'Summer of 69', Bryan Adams, 1985.

22. 'Saturday Night at the Movies', The Drifters, 1964.

23. 'Brown Eyed Girl', Van Morrison, 1967.

24. 'Summer Nights', John Travolta & Olivia Newton-John—Grease, 1978.

25. 'Spicks and Specks', Bee Gees, 1966.

26. 'Lily the Pink', The Scaffold, 1968.

27. 'I am Woman', Helen Reddy, 1972.

28. 'Go Your Own Way', Fleetwood Mac, 1976.

29. 'Softly Whispering I Love You', David & Jonathan, 1967.

30. 'Orinoco Flow (Sail Away)', Enya, 1988.

31. 'Teach Your Children', Crosby, Stills, Nash & Young, 1970.

32. 'Bourke Song', Meredith McGowan, 2015.

33. 'North Bourke Bridge', Colin Buchanan 2006.

34. 'Working Man (The Miner's Song)' Rita McNeil, performance David Alexander, 2015.

35. 'Rewrite Your Story', B-Town Warriors, DesertPeaMedia, Dec 11, 2017.

36. 'People of the Red Sunset', B-Town Warriors, DesertPeaMedia, Sep 19, 2016.

37. 'I'll Find My Way Home', Jon and Vangelis, The Masters of Chant Chapter IV, 1981.

GLOSSARY

Australian Slang, Idiomatic Expressions and other Iconic Terms used in Outback Summer.

Aborigine: An indigenous person, hence Australian Aborigine, an original inhabitant of Australia. Previously shortened to Abo, but this usage has fallen out of favour and is considered derogatory because of its negative historical connotations. Nowadays, the term Indigenous Australian or Traditional Custodian is preferred and these words are capitalised.

Aboriginal: Adjective, hence Aboriginal Elder, Aboriginal site. The term is always capitalised.

Ambo: Ambulance. This Australian word shortening refers to ambulances or the paramedics who drive them.

ANZAC bikkies: Rolled oat biscuits or cookies originally sold at fairs to raise funds for the ANZAC (Australian and New Zealand Army Corps) war effort.

Arvo: Australian colloquial shortening of the word afternoon.

Aussie or Ozzie: Slang for a person from Australia and pronounced Ozzey.

Ay: Word placed at the end of a sentence to indicate that a question has been asked, or that agreement is being sought and a response is required.

Baaka or Barka: The Barkindji people's name for the Darling River. The river was renamed in 1928 by explorers Charles Sturt and Hamilton Hume after the Governor of New South Wales, Sir Ralph Darling.

Baakandji or Barkindji: The Traditional Custodians of the Baaka who lived along the Murray near the Junction with the Darling River, north along the Darling including the region around Bourke.

Baiame: (or Biame, Baayami, Baayama or Byamee) in Australian traditional mythology was the creator god and Sky Father in the dreaming of several language groups of Indigenous Australians of south-east Australia.

Big Smoke: Australian slang term, often used by people from rural areas, referring to a large city, especially Sydney or Melbourne.

Billabong: Traditional Australian term for a for a body of still water formed when a meander loop of a river channel becomes cut off and isolated from the main channel.

Billy: A lightweight metal pot with a wire handle used for boiling water, making tea or cooking. It is an Australian symbol of a bush life.

Bloke: Australian slang term for a man.

Bottle'o: Short for bottle shop in Australian slang, a shop where alcoholic drinks can be purchased by the bottle or in bulk boxes, generally for a lower price than at the hotel.

Bowman, Charles 1888-1995: Great Australian stockman and storyteller who lived and worked in the Bourke district. Charlie lived on Toorale Station for the latter part of his life and is buried in the Bourke Cemetery.

Brumby: A free-roaming feral horse in Australia descended from domestic horses introduced in the late 1870s.

B.S.: Short for bullshit-- stupid or untrue talk or writing; nonsense often deliberately intended to deceive or entertain.

Blue: Australian slang for brawl, fight, dispute or row (It was a real big blue. a really big fight) in use since the 1940s. Blue is also a common nickname for anyone with red hair.

Bugger: An impolite word for an annoying person way. The term cheeky bugger, is used in a playful or friendly way, for someone who is slightly rude or disrespectful.

Chain sawing: Rhyming slang for loud snoring

Chook: A chicken or other domestic fowl.

Chook raffle: A lottery usually held in a club or hotel in which one of the prizes was traditionally a chicken.

Clobber: Clothes and other belongings—or also to hit someone.

Cocky: Slang for over-confident or even arrogant, comes from the Old English word for male bird referring to the brash strutting stance of the cock or rooster

Cook, Captain James, 1728-1779: Famous English mariner and explorer arrived in Botany Bay, Australia on the ship *Endeavour* on 29 April 1770. He planted the British flag and claimed Terra Nullius for the Crown.

Countdown: A weekly Australian music television program broadcast by the ABC (Australian Broadcasting Corporation) from 1974 until 1987 hosted by record producer and music journalist Ian "Molly" Meldrum.

Cozzies: Also known as bathers or swimmers- an Australian shortening of the terms bathing costume or swimsuit.

Crack on: To attempt to flirt with somebody.

Crikey: Australian expression of surprise – 'by crikey she's pretty'; thought to originate as a euphemism for the blasphemous exclamation, 'Christ'.

Cyclone fence: Chain link wire fencing developed in Christchurch in 1903, by James Ower, becoming New Zealand's oldest farm fencing brand with an outstanding international reputation for quality.

Damper: A mix of flour, water and salt baked in the ashes of a wood fire to make a simple bush bread.

Dob in: Inform upon or incriminate someone to an employer or other authority. Betraying the ethic of standing by one's mates means that many Australians take a dim view of dobbing.

Dobrin, Milton B. 1915-1918: Canadian-born American geophysicist, academic and author of renowned textbook *Introduction to Geophysical Prospecting*. McGraw Hill Inc 1952, 1960, 1976.

Double: Carry a pillion passenger on a motorbike.

Drongo: Australian slang for slow-witted or stupid person: a fool. This insult stretches back to the name of the racehorse Drongo, who ran in the early 1920s but never managed to win a race.

Dry Camp: A camp in which alcohol is not permitted.

Dry Out: Slang expression for becoming sober.

Dunno: Australian pronunciation of 'I don't know'.

Dunny: Toilet, traditionally a non-flushing pan toilet located in an outhouse away from the main house.

Elder: Someone who has gained recognition as a custodian of knowledge and lore, and who has permission to disclose knowledge and beliefs. The word 'Elder' should be written with a capital letter as a mark of respect.

Elysian Café: Café in Oxley St, Bourke, originally owned by Sam and Petroula Agiakatsikas. 'Elysian' refers to the mythological paradise of the ancient Greek Gods; a place of ideal happiness. Purchased by the Yang family in 1998 but now closed.

Esky: An ice box developed in 1884 by Francis Malley and sold under the trade mark Esky® in Sydney. In 1952 Malley's launched the first Esky portable cooler. Today the term 'esky' is used colloquially in Australia to refer to any type of cooler.

Fag: Cigarette, derived from the British word 'faggot' for a bunch of sticks tied together for use as fuel or lit as a torch.

Fair Dinkum: It's the real thing, the truth or genuine deal. This slang term dates back to the 1850s gold rush. Din Kum means 'true gold' in Cantonese. Chinese gold rush miners responded to the question: "Are you finding a fair amount of gold?" with the answer "Fair Dinkum".

Fair go: Slang term meaning 'be reasonable or fair about something, stems from an ingrained social belief founded in Australia's colonial past that all of people should be treated equally and with fairness.

Fibro: Australian shortening for fibrous cement sheeting—a cheap, grey-coloured building material, popular in Australia and New Zealand during the post war building boom. Asbestos fibres, found to be carcinogenic, were replaced by cellulose fibres during the mid-1980s.

Fieldies: Australian slang shortening for field hands or field workers—the singular is fieldie.

Flaming: A very fiery argument in which people shout at each other: We had a flaming row over a sheila last night.

Fly strap screen: A curtain door made of overlapping, coloured or clear, strips of PVC vinyl acting as a barrier against insects, dust and temperature change.

Footpath: Australian usage for sidewalk or pavement.

Fruit punch: A refreshing drink served at Australian functions made from fruit juice and lemon squash, or lemonade, with mixed diced fruits. Alcohol is often added, deliberately, or clandestinely, to liven up the party.

Galah: The Australian pink and grey cockatoo. Also, Australian slang for a fool or idiot. This term dates from the 1930s and is based on the perceived stupidity of a galah.

Gawd strewth or 'strewth: An Australian exclamation of astonishment or dismay which derives from God struth a contraction the older British expression God's truth.

G'day: Typical Australian greeting, short for 'good day' and used at any time of the day or night.

Gonna: or 'gunna': Common Australian pronunciation for 'going to'. For example, 'Are you going to go to the party,' sounds like 'Are y' gonna go t' the party' and is fairly unintelligible when heard by most foreign visitors for the first time.

Grog: Australian colloquial usage for any intoxicating beverage dating back to 1740s England.

Gurindji: Indigenous Australian group living in the Northern Territory known for the 1966 Gurindji Strike, led by Vincent Lingiari. Granted freehold title to their tribal land on Wave Hill Cattle Station by Prime Minister Whitlam in 1975, the Gurindji paved the way for other land rights victories in Australia.

Gunned: Accelerated very fast—he gunned his bike hard along the highway.

Gun shearers: Highly experienced and lightning-fast sheep shearers. Shearers are paid by the number of sheep shorn per day.

Gutful: More than enough (I've had a gutful of this – I've had enough).

Guts: Courage or internal fortitude 'the guts' to do something, or 'hate someone's guts' to 'dislike or despise someone very much'.

Henrietta Leggatt: A note in the Supplement to the Cobar Herald Saturday Dec 2, 1899 reads: 'Drowned at Louth. News has been received in town to the effect that Mrs Leggatt, wife of Mr George Leggatt, of Eldorado station, Louth, was accidentally drowned whilst bathing in the Darling on Thursday. The body has been recovered.'

Higher School Certificate: A certificate awarded to students finishing their final year of education at New South Wales secondary schools. This certificate allows students with grades above a certain cutoff to enter university.

Hills Hoist: A height-adjustable rotary clothes line manufactured in Australia by Lance Hill since 1945, based on Gilbert Toyne's 1925 patent with enclosed crown wheel-and-pinion winding mechanism. So convenient, popular and virtually indestructible (unless a gum tree branch drops on it), Hills Hoists were found in almost every Australian back yard.

Hoon: Stupid or uncultivated person, lout or hooligan; also a fast or reckless driver. Also used as a verb for example, they were 'hooning' about in their car.

Hooroo: Goodbye.

Hung a right/left: Australian slang for, 'made a right (or left) hand turn'.

Jackaroo or Jackeroo: A male gaining experience in working with cattle or horses on a pastoral property. The term has been in use since at least the middle of the 19th century. The female equivalent is Jillaroo

Job: Punch (I'll job you – I will punch you); also, any kind of task (I've got a job for you)

Jumper: Australian term for a woollen sweater or pullover.

Kelpie: A medium sized Australian sheep dog bred for mustering and droving of livestock with little or no command guidance. Kelpies are bred for their working ability rather than appearance.

King Hit: An Australian term for an unfair knockout punch, or cowardly attack. The term was popularised during the First World War.

Knowledge is like a skeleton key capable of unlocking every door in life: A core piece of Australian philosophy crystallized by Rod Conway during one special afternoon at the pool with Carla.

Lamb's fry: Fried lamb's liver and onions with gravy; a traditional English dish popular in Australia.

Laminex: A decorative laminate used on chairs, tables and benches, and the name of the iconic Australian company, Laminex, founded by Bob Sykes in 1934 in a garden shed in Melbourne.

Lamington: Iconic Australian soft yellow sponge cake, typically in blocks coated with chocolate icing and grated coconut. sometimes with a layer of cream at centre. Named after Lord Lamington, Governor of Queensland from 1896 to 1901.

Landy: Short for Land Rover, the most popular four-wheel drive vehicle in Australian during the 1970s. The aluminium-bodied vehicle was developed by Maurice Wilkes in 1947, founder of the Rover Company.

Larrikin: Boisterous young person; uncivilized, loud, rowdy, but generally good-hearted person.

Lister: Engine produced by R. A. Lister and Company for driving electric generators or irrigation pumps. With a reputation for longevity and reliability, the engine was exported widely to Commonwealth countries.

Log Tables; Abbreviation for logarithmic tables, an essential mathematical 'trick' used by everyone in pre-hand-calculator days for multiplying or dividing long strings of unwieldy numbers. The example Rod works for Beth at her kitchen table demonstrates how to multiply three large numbers by converting them to powers of 10 which can be added.

Lollies (plural), Lolly (singular): A sweet, originally made from hard boiled and flavoured sugar, but generally referring to all sweets in Australia, with the exception of chocolate.

Longneck or tallie: A 750ml tall brown coloured glass bottle of beer with a long tapering neck.

Maltesers: Chocolate coated balls of malted honeycomb developed by Mars, Incorporated in the UK in 1937 and since sold in Europe, Australia, New Zealand, Canada, United States and Middle East.

Mate: A good friend, 'a good mate' in Australian usage; often used to address anybody in general, or someone whose name is not known, 'excuse me mate'; or even used aggressively between enemies, 'I'm warning you, mate'.

Mateship: The strong bond of friendship that exists between good mates.

Meatworks: Local name for the Bourke abattoirs located southeast of town on the Mitchell Highway. It was built by the Tancred Brothers in 1938 and closed permanently in 1997.

Milk Bar: A neighbourhood corner shop or café where people can buy milk, newspapers, fish and chips, hamburgers, milkshakes, soft drinks or lollies. Formerly social gathering places for local youth before being replaced by fast food franchises and shopping malls.

Morrall's Bakery: Iconic Bourke Bakery on Mitchell Street famous for its pies, pastries and freshly baked bread; a family business in operation for over 110 years popular with locals and tourists alike. Its award-winning gourmet pies include Steak Dianne, Steak and Kidney, Minted Lamb, Chicken and Vegetables

Mongrel: A dog or other animal of random or unknown parentage as opposed to a pedigreed pure breed animal, so also used in Australia as a term of insult for uncouth, untrustworthy or degenerate individuals.

Mulga: Australian acacia tree or shrub with greyish foliage, or an area of dense scrub or bush dominated by mulgas. Its brown and yellow timber was traditionally used for boomerangs and digging sticks.

Nardoo: Indigenous Australian term for a flat stone used as a grinding implement to make flour from native grass seeds.

Ngemba or Ngiyampaa: One of the original Indigenous Australian groups living in western New South Wales.

Nick off: Somewhat rude term for telling someone to away, you're not wanted here, or 'get lost'. Synonymous with rack off or piss off.

Nobby's Nuts: Popular Australian brand of salted beer nuts founded by Max "Nobby" Noblet in the 1950s. He began his nut business, using his nickname as the brand and devised the memorable slogan "Nibble Nobby's Nuts".

North Bourke Bridge: Opened on May 4, 1883, this bridge over the Darling River was designed by J. H. Daniels with a central liftable section to allow the passage of paddle steamers beneath. A Bourke icon, this bridge served as 'gateway to the outback' until it was bypassed in 1997.

Outback: Dry country of inland Australia, west of the Great Dividing Range. Anywhere far away from the capital cities.

Permewans: A station supplies chain that began in Geelong, Victoria in 1854 and grew to 48 stores in the principal towns of the Murray, Murrumbidgee and Darling rivers.

Pig-spotters: Pig is slang for police and spotters are lookouts strategically placed to warn of the unwanted arrival of the police at an illegal event or gathering.

Piss off: Go away, you're not wanted here, or go get yourself lost, Synonymous with nick off or rack off.

Polygonum: The name of a swampy billabong near North Bourke named for a genus which includes grassy, herbaceous plants or aquatic plants in ponds.

Porker: Short for 'Porky Pig', rude Australian slang for someone who is overweight.

Preggers: Australian shortening for pregnant.

Rack off: Go away, you're not wanted here, or go get yourself lost, Synonymous with nick off or piss off.

Randall, Silvia Faith (birth name Carmichael) 1910-1998. Together with her husband Arthur James Randall, Mrs Randall ran "The Wonderland Open Air Garden" from 1927 until the end of summer 1984 when it was closed due to the rising popularity of television.

Ranga: Short for orangutang—derogatory slang for any red-haired person.

Reckon: Slang for a good educated guess—for example; I reckon we'll be there in five (I think we will arrive in 5 minutes).

Rice's Back O' Bourke Cordials: A lemonade factory bought by local entrepreneur John Rice in 1997 and now run by his great grandsons, Daniel and Sam Rice. Today Back o' Bourke Cordials boasts 10 flavours including Splashe Cola, Creaming Soda, Lemonade, Mint Freeze, Lemon Soda Squash, Pineapple, Club Nectar, Orange Raspberry and Mandarin.

Righto: All right, OK then.

Roo: Short for kangaroo. Roo bars are steel bars mounted on vehicles to protect against impacts with kangaroos which are commonplace on country roads between dawn and dusk.

R.S.L: Returned Services League of Australia—a network of organisations formed after the First World War to support veterans and their families.

Ryan, Ronald, 1925-1967: The last person to be legally hanged in Australia on 3 February 1967 for the killing of a prison officer during an escape attempt. Massive public outcry led to the end of executions in Australia.

R.M. Williams: An iconic Australian company recognised worldwide for creating a uniquely Australian style of bush wear, clothing and footwear. Its founder R.M. Williams AO 1908-2003 was an Australian bushman and entrepreneur who rose from a swagman to a millionaire.

Sanger: Shortening of the word sandwich.

Schooner: A 425 ml (15 imp fl oz) glass of beer, or three-quarters of an imperial pint pre-metrification. It is the most common size in New South Wales, Queensland and the Northern Territory.

Shed: Short for shearing shed, a purpose-built warehouse and processing plant for shearing sheep, classifying and bailing wool. Toorale Station's shed on the Darling River was the largest in Australia with 46 stands. Wool bales were shipped from Toorale to market by paddle steamer.

Sheila or shelah: A girl or woman. This word first appeared in Australian English in 1832 coming from came from the Irish name Síle. It has fallen out of common usage these days.

Shout: To buy a round of drinks for all your friends at the pub. Typically every member of the group takes a turn at 'shouting a round'.

Silly Billy: A childish rhyming name for a person acting foolishly or nonsensically, derived from the name of a type of clown common at fairs in England during the 19th century.

Smoko: Short mid-morning and mid-afternoon break in the day's work, originally to allow time for workers to smoke tobacco.

Snowies: Short for Snowy Mountains Hydro-Electric Scheme—a large hydroelectricity and irrigation complex in the Snowy Mountains (Snowies) of southeastern Australia built between 1949 and 1972.

Spud: Australian and New Zealand slang for a potato—from the Middle English word 'spudde' for a short, stout tool for digging up potatoes.

Station: Landholding used for producing livestock, predominantly cattle or sheep, that extensive grazing land up to thousands of square kilometres in area. The owner of a station is called a pastoralist or a grazier.

Stand: An area of the shearing shed with a series of overhead belt-driven mechanical shears (previously hand clippers) for the shearer to remove the sheep's fleece.

Steel caps: Short for steel capped protective boots in Australian usage; designed to protect the toes in a work environment where heavy objects are being moved about.

Stone the crows or 'stone the flamin' crows': An Australian exclamation of surprise or incredulity. Thought to have originated in the 1910s when stones were thrown at crows to prevent them plundering crops.

Stubby: or stubbie: A small typically brown-glass bottle holding 330ml of beer designed for one person and often held in an insulating foam stubbie cooler to keep the bottle's contents cold.

Stubbies: Brand name for mens' work shorts made in Australia and New Zealand produced by The Workwear Group introduced in 1972. Since then, the Stubbies workwear range has expanded to include both men and women.

Swag: Light bedding roll, generally designed for being carried around from place to place, hence a swagman or transient labourer who travelled by foot from farm to farm carrying a swag.

Swimmers: Australian shortening of the term swimming suit or swimsuit.

Tea: The main evening meal is often referred to as 'tea,' a tradition stemming from British influence.

Telly: Short for television set or TV

Texta: A felt-tip pen, often coloured and usually wide-tipped for use by children. Originates from Texta, a registered trademark of the Australian stationery company Jasco Pty Ltd

Tinnie: A can of beer typically 375ml. In 1958, tinnies were introduced in Australian and in 1968 the ring pull was developed which avoided the need for a can opener. Ring pulls created a litter problem which was only solved with the pop-top that arrived in the mid-1970s

Tip: 'The tip', an Australian abbreviation for rubbish tip or garbage dump.

Too right: An enthusiastic Australian exclamation meaning 'I fully agree'.

Tucker: Food in general, or lunch. Tucker may be taken to work in a tucker bag or tucker box or Esky

U-ey: Shortened speech for U-turn. For example-We chucked a U-ey' means 'we made a U-turn'.

Uni: Australian colloquial shortening of the word, university.

Ute: Short for utility, an open backed pick-up truck.

Wag: To miss school or play truant; for example, "She wagged school yesterday".

Wanker: A general insult of English origin in common usage in Commonwealth nations, including Australia, New Zealand and Ireland meaning someone who wanks (masturbates).

Western Herald: The Western Herald is Bourke's locally-owned and independent newspaper proudly serving the community since October 1, 1887, covering news, sport and other events in Bourke and surrounding districts of Barringun, Brewarrina, Byrock, Enngonia, Fords Bridge, Hungerford, Louth and Wanaaring and Lightning Ridge.

Wheelie: Australian shortening for "wheel stand", an action in which a motorcycle is ridden with its front wheel lifted in the air.

Whitlam, Gough: 1916-2014. Australia's 21st Prime Minister from 5 December 1972 to 11 November 1975 becoming the longest-serving federal leader of the Australian Labor Party.

Woop woop: Out in the middle of nowhere, away from the capital cities in the outback.

Write-off: A thing that no longer has any value; a totally hopeless individual or drunk person.

Yakka: Hard or heavy physical work. The word, which first appeared in the 1840s, derives from the word yaga, meaning work in Yagara, an Indigenous language in Australia.

Yarn: Australian colloquial term for a story often told in pubs or around camp fires. (He spun a good yarn' or he told a good story). Yarns may contain some element of truth, but are mostly heavily embellished, and becoming even more so over time.

Yobbo: Australian slang for a loud mouthed or stupid uncultivated person.

In Memory of:

Charles William (Charlie) Bowman
25 September (8 December?) 1888, Mungindi – 2 May 1995, Bourke

Clan Wallace McIntosh
1914 – 22 Aug 1981, Brewarrina
Plot: Ang V, 12; Memorial ID 191895588

Robert René Schellekens
4 September 1944, Queanbeyan – 14 February 2012, Perth

Raymond George Michael (Mick) Tallon
25 March 1934, Greenacre, Sydney – 13 October 2017, Bourke

And the countless members of the Kurnu, Baakandji and the Ngemba First Nation groups—Traditional Custodians of that Country
.

Printed in Dunstable, United Kingdom

Dr Robert R. Coenraads is an artist, explorer and educator who travels the world in search of treasures such as exotic minerals, gemstones and unique cultural experiences which form the basis for his writing.

As President of FreeSchools World Literacy Australia, Dr Coenraads believes strongly in the value of education in today's society. Education betters the quality of life of individuals, lifting families, villages and entire countries out of poverty. It gives meaning, hope and purpose to those fortunate enough to receive it, bringing harmony between the diverse peoples of our planet.

Outback Summer is a spirited coming-of-age romance set in a picturesque country town on the Darling River. It seems like there are gorgeous girls everywhere in this town and Rod Conway has his heart set on getting to know one of them better. But the girl of his dreams seems to elude him. And the town is divided, its unwritten rules and social norms catching out-of towner Rod off guard, until even his friends turn against him, and, to make matters worse, he is hunted by a mysterious "Dark Rider" clad in black leathers and helmet, in love with the same girl.

Outback Summer is set amongst the mesas and desert plains of Australia's sparsely populated red interior—the hot, dry, rugged Country of Traditional Custodians, stockmen, miners and poets, where mateship is key to survival. Oases are few, but the shade-dappled reaches of the Darling River (Baaka) meandering lazily over its floodplain provide respite in an otherwise tough outback environment.

Rod's bond with Country deepens as he learns more from Chief, but will he win the heart of the girl of his dreams as the vast cultural gulf separating them becomes increasingly apparent and their lives are wrenched apart on opposite trajectories.

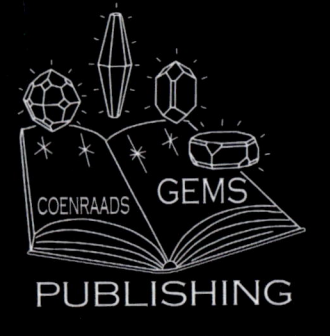

COENRAADS GEMS PUBLISHING

ISBN 978-1-923330-00-9